RAGING AT
THE STARS

What Reviewers Say About Lesley Davis's Work

"*Playing Passion's Game* is a delightful read with lots of twists, turns, and good laughs. Davis has provided a varied and interesting supportive cast. Those who enjoy computer games will recognize some familiar scenes, and those new to the topic get to learn about a whole new world."—*Just About Write*

"*Pale Wings Protecting* is a provocative paranormal mystery; it's an otherworldly thriller couched inside a tale of budding romance. The novel contains an absorbing narrative, full of thrilling revelations, that skillfully leads the reader into the uncanny dimensions of the supernatural."—*Lambda Literary*

"[*Dark Wings Descending*] is an intriguing story that presents a vision of life after death many will find challenging. It also gives the reader some wonderful sex scenes, humor, and a great read!"—*Reviewer RLynne*

"[*Pale Wings Protecting*] was just a delicious delight with so many levels of intrigue on the case level and the personal level. Plus, the celestial and diabolical beings were incredibly intriguing. ...I was riveted from beginning to end and I certainly will look forward to additional books by Lesley Davis. By all means, give this story a total once-over!"—*Rainbow Book Reviews*

Visit us at www.boldstrokesbooks.com

By the Author

Truth Behind the Mask

Playing Passion's Game

Dark Wings Descending

Pale Wings Protecting

Playing In Shadow

Starstruck

Raging At the Stars

RAGING AT THE STARS

by
Lesley Davis

2017

ISBN 13: 978-1-62639-720-0

This Trade Paperback Original Is Published By
Bold Strokes Books, Inc.
P.O. Box 249
Valley Falls, NY 12185

First Edition: January 2017

Credits
Editor: Cindy Cresap
Production Design: Susan Ramundo
Cover Design By Sheri (graphicartist2020@hotmail.com)

Acknowledgments

Thanks always to Radclyffe for more reasons than I could ever express.

Enormous thanks to Cindy Cresap for making the editing experience a positive finale to the writing process. Your patience is unceasing, which is fortunate because my use of British-isms is not going to stop any time soon!

Thank you to Sandy Lowe for always answering my "I have a question" emails and to all the people at Bold Strokes whose hard work gets these books out there.

Thank you, thank you, thank you, Sheri, for the most eye-catching, spectacular, blockbuster of a film-like cover I could ever have dreamed of for this story. I'm totally spellbound by it and I can't thank you enough. It's truly out of this world!

Thanks always to my awesome friends and readers who support me in my writing and make me want to keep telling stories for them:

Jane Morrison and Jacky Morrison Hart

Annie Ellis (It's here at last! Go read it!!) and Julia Lowndes

Pam Goodwin and Gina Paroline

Kim Palmer-Bell

Cheryl Hunter and Anne Hunter

Kerry Pfadenhauer

To all my readers out there, a huge thank you for your boundless enthusiasm for my works. Keep reading please! There's still more to come!

And always, thank you so much Cindy Pfannenstiel, for being the best sounding board when I have a crazy idea or two and want your opinion while trying not to give too much of the plot away! Thanks for always being supportive and for cheering me on. I appreciate it all and you so very much. XX

Author's Note: This is a work of fiction and poetic license has been liberally used. However, should *any* of what is written here be found to be true I will take my "I told you so" sweets/candy in the form of copious bags of Maltesers please!

Dedication

To Pam Goodwin

Thank you for "Driving Miss Davis," figuratively speaking,
across America in assistance for this story.
Your help was invaluable to me. You, my friend,
are truly every shade of awesome. xx

Chapter One

The night sky above Groom Lake, Nevada, was the clearest Emory Hawkes had ever seen. It was a pitch-black night that made the stars appear to shine twice as bright. A diamond studded vista that stretched as far as her eyes could see. Emory marveled at it as she drank deeply from her Coke can. She drained it dry and crushed it in her hand. The noise was loud in the stillness of the night. Emory was tempted to toss the can as far as she could to see if she could set off the remote sensors she knew were planted far and wide for miles around the perimeter of Area 51. She'd driven past the endless signs warning her to stay away from the area many times. Now, she was parked and looking out on the military base. She was far enough away not to draw attention to herself from the guards driving around the perimeter. Emory had been here before; she knew how close was close enough and how long she had before they'd come and chase her off.

She took a slow walk back to her Volkswagen Bus. She settled herself in the driver's seat and opened up her laptop to return to the sites she'd been perusing earlier. Emory was reaching for a large bag of Lay's chips when her phone rang. She picked it up and groaned when she saw the caller ID. She toyed with not answering but knew her brother wouldn't stop until he reached her.

"Hey, Bradley. What's up?"

"Emory, where are you?"

"On vacation, soaking up the sun, catching some rays by the sea," she lied.

"Then you must be inside your hotel room, little sister, because I don't hear any sounds of waves crashing against any particular shore."

Emory tugged her keyboard closer and pressed to open a new tab.

"So, unless you're going to try to fool me with that video of the sounds of the sea you've got saved on YouTube…"

Emory cursed softly and closed the site down. "I wouldn't do that. You're too sharp for your own good, Brad."

"You did it the last time you were trying to convince me you were vacationing in some rain forest when, in fact, you were hanging around a military base looking for flying saucers."

Emory huffed. "The conspiracy theories you constantly mock me for have a weird way of becoming acknowledged. Truths and lies are eventually revealed. Just like the Warren Commission being a total whitewash of what happened in Dallas. And the whole moon landing being a giant setup on a sound stage somewhere in Hollywood. Five key words for you on space travel, Bradley: *the Van Allen Radiation Belt*. But, for all the things I would stake my disbelieving life on, you know I believe that any UFO sightings are instead top secret military craft using a technology we have no frame of reference for. So, like I tell you every time we have this conversation, I do *not* believe in aliens. There is no such thing as little green men from outer space."

"So you *are* up at Area 51 again? Goddammit, Emory! You're supposed to be playing by the rules right now."

"I may or may not be vacationing some ninety odd miles or so away from Las Vegas. I'm just taking in the sights, enjoying the nightlife." She looked out at the sky again.

"You'd better be staying away from the perimeter. I am not coming out there again to bail you out of prison like I had to last year when you were caught trespassing on private property."

"I paid you back every dime so quit holding that against me." *I'm never going to hear the last of that adventure. Next time I'm calling an ex. If they'll even answer.*

"You were knowingly trespassing on federal land."

"It was night time. You can't see any borders when it's dark as fuck out here."

"Well, try to employ night vision this time and stay out of trouble if that's possible for you. I thought you'd like to know I'm meeting with your boss and his bosses next week. Here's hoping I can smooth out the mess you got them into by trying to spill military secrets on that so-called news site you work for."

It galled Emory to do it, but she managed to get a "Thank you" to pass her lips. Her brother was the bane of her existence, but he was her go-to man when she needed bailing out...again. This time had been due to her posting a leaked document she had received from a very reliable source. Unfortunately, the source in question had been forced into hiding while Emory and the online news site she worked for were under investigation. Emory stood by what she'd posted, but it looked like it was the last straw for her boss. So she was on a forced vacation while the investigation was underway.

"God knows why you think there's a secret military hiding in plain sight among the *real* military. It would be so much easier and you'd be considered less of a nutball if you actually believed in aliens, Emory. Raging against the government and the military, secret or otherwise, isn't going to get you anywhere. They're untouchable."

"And raging at the stars would make more sense to you? I'm not looking up at the night sky in fear of something out there sending saucer shaped ships to invade us and mutilate our cows. That strikes a little too close to home in my view. It's something humans would do for some bizarre reason."

"You subscribe to all these conspiracies, though. Isn't believing in aliens top of that crazy ass list you live by?"

Emory smiled without humor at his attempt to be funny but instead was putting her down, as usual. He never listened to her, never took her seriously. She'd had to suffer him going through college to become a highfalutin lawyer, but the minute she mentioned what she was passionate about she was ridiculed and scolded like a child. "Fuck you, Bradley. One day you'll have your eyes opened to the worldwide conspiracy I've been warning you about for years."

"Yeah, well until that little miracle happens how about you come visit your family instead of hanging out in alien territory like a loser? Your nieces want to see you for reasons I'll never understand. And I'd rather tell them you're alien hunting than you're watching the base in case some high-tech plane gets rolled out of the hangar there. Like that's big news to report. They *are* an airbase after all."

"You'd rather tell them I'm waiting to get abducted by aliens," she grumbled.

"To be perfectly honest, yes. They've watched *V*. You're a hero in their eyes, right up there with Elizabeth Mitchell. And her character at least knew aliens existed."

"Goddammit, Brad! There's no such fucking thing as aliens. How many times do I have to say it?"

"It's all a conspiracy, right?"

"Right. Misinformation to keep the population in fear." Emory was getting annoyed with his winding her up; it was his typical big brother move. She popped open the door of her van and stepped outside. It took a lot to resist slamming the door to relieve some of the tension she could feel boiling through her. The silence of the night pressed in on her. "Tell the girls I'll come see them soon."

"Before or after you try to breach the fence again to find proof of something that doesn't exist? Because I'm busting my gut here to keep you from serving jail time for what you posted, and yet, there you are, right back in the lion's den searching for more clues. I can't keep representing you when you keep doing stupid things that land you into trouble."

"I have to go, Bradley. You're pissing me off, and you know I'm prone to do *stupid things* when you piss me off. And, sadly, you're the only lawyer I have on speed dial to bail me out before our sainted mother hears about it." She leaned against the side of her van. "I've got to go. I've got aliens to chase, apparently."

"God only knows what you would do if you really saw one," he said.

"I'd expose it for the lie it is."

Bradley laughed. "Keep looking to the skies, little sis."

"Keep burying your head in the sand, big bro." She ended the call with a sigh. She was certain she was somehow adopted because there had never been two siblings who were such polar opposites as she was to him. He didn't have an ounce of imagination and believed the law to be absolute. Emory had a more "fluid" notion when it came to finding out the truth.

She raised her head, looking to the night sky to give her some sense of calm after he'd succeeded in riling her up. She blinked as she stared above her.

The stars had *disappeared.*

Emory couldn't tear her gaze away from the vast blackness above. There were literally no stars visible for as far as her eyes could see. There wasn't cloud cover, and the stars hadn't winked out of existence. She'd only just looked up and they had been there. The air around her started to vibrate, and Emory could feel a rhythmic pulse tickling across her skin. She rubbed at her bare arms. Her black T-shirt had been plenty warm enough in the night air, but now her skin felt as if it were being touched by a live wire. It was very disconcerting.

She scrambled back into her van's front seat and yanked her laptop toward her. She furiously tapped out a message to a friend.

Chicken Little says look up at the sky.

A reply wasn't long in coming. *What are you seeing?*

A whole heap of nothing.

Switch to audio and visual please.

Emory found her earpiece and popped it into her ear. It was a wireless piece that received its audio via Bluetooth. The built-in microphone allowed two-way conversation. She just had to carry her phone so that the Bluetooth radio frequencies could mesh. She snatched up a pair of heavy framed glasses that housed a hidden camera. Finally, she grabbed her phone and slipped it in her pocket. Spy Tech 101.

"Wired for sound and visual, Dink. I'm setting the bigger camera on top of the van so you can get a panoramic view." Balancing on the doorframe, Emory made sure the heavy-duty suction cup clamped to the roof of the van as she quickly fixed the video camera in place. Once that was sorted, she grabbed her night vision binoculars.

"All systems are working. I can both see and hear loud and clear. So, my friend, what's got you all excitable over there in Nevada?" Dink's voice was clear as a bell in Emory's ear.

Emory was glad to hear his voice. "Are you aware of any military exercises in the 51st area tonight?"

"No, all quiet on base according to the radar and sensors I'm monitoring. What's up?"

Emory made a face at his choice of words. "Nothing. That's the problem. The stars have just disappeared above me."

"Disappeared?"

"Winked out, blacked out, totally disappeared like someone switched them all off." Emory got out of her van and looked up again. The hairs on her arms began to rise, and she could hear a faint humming noise above her. "And now there's humming."

"Emory, get the fuck out of there now!"

All above the Area 51 base, the stars were missing and the electrical charge in the air made Emory feel like there was a storm brewing.

Unfortunately, Mother Nature had no hand in what was coming.

❖

The humming noise began to make Emory's ears ache. She cupped her hands over her ears to try to ease it. The noise didn't abate. It vibrated through to her very bones. She could feel her body shuddering as the pain manifested inside her.

Then it stopped.

Then the lights came on.

Emory was blinded by the brilliance that lit up the entire area. It was as if the sun had fallen to Earth and exploded onto the base. Fighting against both the disconcerting hum and the blinding light, Emory stumbled back to her van. The whole area was lit up like the Fourth of July. Emory fell against the side of her van with a jarring thud and tried to shield herself there. She moaned with relief as the torturous brightness was extinguished as quickly as it had appeared.

"Emory?"

Dink's voice was loud in her ear.

"I don't think this is a test," Emory said, trying desperately to see what was happening. As her eyes grew accustomed to the dark again, she finally saw what was above her. She couldn't believe what she was seeing. In the night sky, there appeared to be a fleet of triangular aircraft. From the size of them, she calculated they were at least three lengths of a football field each. A multicolored light was situated at each of the three points of the ship's shape. They flashed out a rhythmic pulse that was almost hypnotic. The lone light in the center was a pure white beam. It was obviously those beams that had flooded the area with light. Only one remained now, directed toward the ground. Emory tried to count how many ships she could see. She was guessing two, maybe three, hidden in the darkness.

"Dink, multiple black triangles, all over my goddamn head!"

"I can see them, but they aren't showing up on any radar. The Area 51's camera system that I hacked is, however, giving me an amazing view. But I still want you to get out of there. Who knows what is going to happen, and you're slap bang in the middle of it!"

"I can't move now. What if they see me?" Emory clung to the side of her van as if hoping to blend into its black painted panels. "Besides, this is what I've been waiting for all these years. This is it, Dink. Something is going to happen and I'm here to witness it. I'll finally get my validation, and I can tell my brother to kiss my ass." She watched as the ships above began to shift. "God, it's like watching a load of sharks in the water circling blood." She tried to see if she could spot any identifying marks on the ships, but they were so black they blended into the night and it was only the lights that gave away their outline. "Dink, what do you think? Is it the Russians maybe? Or some other superpower that's been hiding this kind of high-powered tech from prying eyes?"

Before Dink could answer her, the first explosion hit and blew Emory flat on her back. Debris flew wildly into the air, and it was only when the dust settled that Emory could see that a large crater had been left in the middle of the air base.

"Holy shit!" She watched with a dawning horror as small saucer-shaped objects flew out from the belly of the bigger ships. They just appeared as if they'd been cloaked from view. All of them took aim on the vast area below. Whatever weaponry they were equipped with cut through the ground with ease and laid waste to any buildings in the way. The iconic hangars were blown to smithereens, and the earth was scorched beneath them. Electricity sparked and fires began to blaze as pieces of the buildings were scattered all over the runways. The buildings were reduced to little more than kindling in seconds as the saucers flew with alarming speed all over the base. They annihilated everything in their path. Within seconds, the area was obliterated, all the buildings erased, and the ground was nothing more than a mass of huge craters. The runways and the airplanes that had been on it were disintegrated to dust.

Emory didn't know what to do. She was rooted to the spot watching the silver saucers take aim at Area 51 and wipe it off the face of the earth. The saucers were able to move at incredible speeds and maneuvered with abilities Emory knew no known craft had the capability of employing. It was terrifying. It was also fascinating, and Emory couldn't tear her eyes away. It was like watching a real life *Star Wars* battle, or something equally heavy on special effects that one of her favorite films had created. But this was *real*. Emory didn't believe what her eyes were showing her, but she couldn't stop watching. It was all she could have hoped to see as an observer. It was every science fiction film come to life. But this was reality and totally devastating.

"Dink, tell me you can see all this?"

"I can see it, but I can't honestly believe it. And *I'm* a believer!" He sounded as awestruck as Emory felt.

"It's military though, right? Terrorists wouldn't have this much tech at hand to be able to build what we're seeing here."

"Can you see any kind of insignia on the crafts?"

Emory squinted up at the saucers. They moved faster than her brain could comprehend. "These things don't keep still long enough for me to read a license plate." She ducked as three saucers appeared out of nowhere and flew over her head. "And they don't make much noise in flight either. They epitomize silent but deadly. It's the triangular ships that are making the noise that sets the hairs on my arms tingling."

"You're not safe there."

"Thank you, Captain Obvious," Emory muttered. "I can't exactly start my engine while they are bombing the bejeezus out of the base below." Something caught her eye, and she saw a thin light appear out of nowhere, deep from within one of the craters. She trained her binoculars on that point. "Dink, I told you there was hidden stuff underneath this base. I'm seeing a beam of light coming out of a crater. None of these ships have landed. It's got to be the 51st staff in there." She focused the binoculars in further. Thankful again that she had parked in an area that gave her an excellent view down onto the base, Emory watched as people started scrambling over the crater's edge.

"I can see people evacuating. They're coming directly out of the crater so there has to be something down there." She tried to pinpoint where on the base the fissure was coming from. "I think they're where there used to be an office building above ground." Wherever it was, the debris of the attack wasn't stopping the people from trying to escape. They filed out in an endless stream. Emory silently urged them on, watching as they stumbled across the ruined runways, heading in every direction.

"Incoming," Dink said, and Emory watched as two saucers broke off from the rest of the group and headed straight for the survivors.

"No!"

Emory could do little more but watch as the saucers emitted a thin beam of light directly into the people's path. They stood paralyzed by it until one by one they started to rise off the ground. They were suspended in the air as if held on strings wielded by a master puppeteer. Then, without warning, they were sucked up into the saucer and the light extinguished.

Oh my God. Emory gaped. *I did not just see that.* The binoculars fell from her eyes and landed heavily against her chest. She felt her blood run cold, terror striking her heart and rendering her immobile.

"I don't think that's the military, Emory." Dink's voice was unusually quiet in Emory's ear.

She stared up at the saucer that had taken the people. It spun in the air like an old vinyl disc on a turntable, smooth and slick, playing out its own deadly tune.

"But I don't believe in this," Emory whispered, watching as the saucer shot up into the air at an alarming speed. It disappeared as quickly as it had appeared. Here, then gone. Just like the people it had taken aboard.

"I don't think you have a choice. It's too late, Emory. *They're here.*"

CHAPTER TWO

Emory lost count of how long she crouched against her van, watching what was playing out below her. Her cheek was cold against the metal as she hunkered down trying to keep as small as possible to avoid detection. She had a front row seat to the destruction of Area 51 by Unidentified Flying Objects.

"It's all over the news," Dink said in her ear. "Some stupid TV station sent up a helicopter to film where you are. Live at eleven. But they didn't get that far. Those of us glued to our TV screens got to witness it being blown out of the sky by a saucer. Everyone on board was screaming until a blue beam hit them, and then the crew on the ground filmed their colleagues' helicopter plummet like a stone. Not exactly the exclusive they were hoping for."

"Are these craft only here?"

"No. According to my sources on the Dark Side of the Internet, there are large black craft being spotted all around the world."

"Worldwide?" Emory couldn't fathom what she was hearing. "What's our military saying about this?"

"There was a brief statement saying that this isn't them and they are preparing for war."

"Distract and deny," Emory muttered, all too aware of the ploys certain agencies took to keep the general public in the dark.

"Emory, I don't think this is them either."

"So it's what? Flying saucers from outer space who just happened upon Area 51 and decided to test their weapons?"

"There's obviously something down there because whoever it is doesn't want it left on view."

Emory heard a noise. She looked over her shoulder. "I'm seeing fighter planes."

A multitude of air force craft shot over her head, the noise was deafening in contrast to the black craft humming. The sound of missiles being launched from the planes tore through the air.

"You really need to get out of there," Dink said.

Emory was too busy watching the night sky alight with open fire as the jets chased after the saucers and fired every weapon they had available at them. The flashes from the arsenal launched against the saucers exploded like fireworks against the darkness.

"I want to see where that light is coming from in the crater, Dink. I can still see it shining from here. They obviously didn't close whatever it is. It might lead me to answer the question of what lies hidden underneath Area 51."

"There's the rumor there are forty levels dug deep into the ground. That crater you're eyeing looks fucking huge. I can't begin to imagine the damage that's been done to whatever is left down there."

"I'd be missing out on a golden opportunity if I didn't go look. I'm all for scrabbling for clues in the rubble and getting down in that crater to check it out. The fact there's a light shining out of the earth has to mean something is still intact there. I'm going to see."

"These crazy bastards are all trying to blow up the base from above your head, and you want to go down into the pit that they're so determined to blow up? Are you insane?"

Emory considered that. "I'd like to think of myself as stubborn. I want to prove my point. I believe this is our technology being used for some kind of," she searched for an answer, "I don't know, false flag operation, maybe?"

"You're thinking whoever is flying those crafts is bombing because they have some hidden agenda? For what end?"

"I don't know, Dink," Emory said. "Maybe it's an excuse to start a war with whoever is the villain of the month this time. Since when does the end matter? We'll never understand why governments do what they do. You know as well as I do there are hidden agendas to everything that goes on." She watched as the saucers and the jets moved away from the area. "The planes are shifting the saucers off target. This might be my only chance. I'm taking it."

"You're going to get yourself killed."

"I'm going to be saucer fodder anyway if they keep leveling the area. So while the jets are chasing them like X-wings chasing after Star Destroyers, with the same devastating results, I'm going in."

"You did not just equate all this to *Star Wars*."

"Dink, if there really are UFOs from another world here attacking us, then I'm going to want to see how close George Lucas's creatures were to whatever *you* think is invading us. You know I believe in his aliens more than I do the ones you subscribe to." She cautiously moved from her position. "That crater is calling to me."

"You're going toward the light even if I tell you not to, aren't you?"

"I'm your eyes and legs out here. I have the chance to get closer to a place we've both been desperate to explore. I have that chance to get closer, and you're going to be with me every step of the way." She scrambled to her feet and pulled herself into her van. She flung her binoculars onto the passenger seat and reached for her keys. Emory left the headlights off and knew the fracas above would mask the sound of her engine roaring to life. She figured the patrolling guards had long since disappeared in the chaos. She released the brake and drove until she was well into the restricted area. It took more time than she wanted, but the distance she'd had to view from was miles away. She cursed the fact the base hadn't let her just sit outside its main gates. Deliberately, when finally within range, she aimed for the last perimeter fence. "Knock, knock," Emory muttered and rammed through the paneling and barbed wire with great satisfaction. With the state the airbase was now in, shattered fencing was likely to rank low on the list of Area 51's problems.

Emory drove toward the light marking Area 51. It cast a glow over the huge gaping wound that was now in the earth. She parked her van as close as she could, but rubble littered the runway and she finally had to stop to tackle the rest on foot.

Emory tapped the side of her glasses. "Still eyes wide, Dink?"

"Everything is working fine. Just don't forget your ID card, Agent."

Emory grinned as she slipped the forged document into a wallet and then into her jeans pocket. Dink had mocked her up a very credible, and more importantly, passable ID. She'd only used it once before. She had gained entry onto another air force base where Dink believed they were working on a new space shuttle. Emory hadn't gotten much further once she was found wandering down a restricted corridor that even her credentials had no sway over. It had proved that the ID wasn't questioned, and she had been able to walk out without any hindrance.

"I'm not exactly dressed to be an agent tonight, Dink. I'm more dressed down for an hour or two of watching spy planes take off like I expected. I hadn't intended to witness flying saucers tearing up the air base."

"It's my guess no one is going to be left in the underground base. *If* it even exists."

Emory laughed. "Oh, you so know it exists. Those people came from somewhere. We both know there's something going on underground here as well as above." Emory zipped up her hoodie and hoped that the black jeans and black boots she wore did enough to make her look suitably *Men in Black*. She gathered her hair off her shoulders and fastened it into a loose ponytail. She could hear her brother's voice asking why "someone like her" would still keep her hair reasonably long when she favored men's style of clothing. His comment of "shouldn't you be sporting a shaved head" only made her dislike him even more. Since when couldn't a lesbian wear her hair longer than an inch and still carry off that more masculine side of herself? She wondered if he was worried about her. After all, he knew she was up here. She reached for her phone and dialed his cell. It just rang out.

"Dink? Any particular reason as to why I still have cell service when we have spaceships invading?"

"Maybe the rumors are true and they use our energy to power their ships," he said. "Might go a long way to explain why so many are seen hovering over nuclear power plants."

Emory tried again, but there was still no reply. She left a message on Bradley's answering machine and then got out of her van. She locked it automatically.

"I really don't think aliens are going to try to commandeer your old Bus," Dink said dryly.

"Just playing it safe. You can't trust anyone these days."

"Only you would worry about your van being stolen while you're on a military base that has just been blown to kingdom come by little green men."

"Color me cautious. And shouldn't the correct term be grays, not green?" She patted farewell to her van and made her way carefully across the mounds of rubble. She got her bearings then ambled off in another direction.

"Hey, where are you off to? The crater is back the other way."

"I want to see where those beams hit the ground. There might be evidence or something they left behind I can get for you to analyze." She ran to the spot where she had seen the saucer's beams touch down. Curiously, the earth wasn't marked, neither was the fencing nearby, but she noticed something dangling from a broken fence rail. The lanyard swung gently, causing its prize to twirl in the night air. Emory plucked it free and held it in her hand so that Dink could see it properly.

"Oooh, a swipe card," Dink said. "Nice find. What's the name on there?"

"Jessica Sanders. She must be one of the base's military population." She looked up at the sky. "Or was." She pocketed the card. She hoped it would be of some use. Satisfied with her find, Emory headed back toward the crater. What she found there shocked her.

"Dink, I don't know what kind of laser weaponry they're using, but it's powerful." She looked around cautiously before flipping her flashlight on. Its narrow beam shone over the mound she was climbing up. It appeared to be made up of the pulverized remnants from an office because she could just make out what was left of a telephone. The scorched remains of a filing cabinet smoked and smoldered beneath her feet.

There were other remains that caused her to pause. "Dink, there are people here too."

"Anyone alive?"

Cautiously, Emory looked closer. "No. They never stood a chance." The crater wall was littered with tiny body parts; no one had survived whatever had hit them.

"If you can get inside, do it. I've got a live stream from over Las Vegas. Emory, they're laying waste to it."

Emory stopped in her tracks. "My family?"

"Who knows? The bright lights and the Strip are in tatters. I can't see if they're aiming for the residential areas yet."

Emory considered rushing back to her van and driving out to see if her brother and his family were safe. Torn with indecision, she kept climbing but fished her cell phone out of her pocket and tried his number again. It still rang out.

"There's nothing you can do. It's miles out from here. Maybe they'll be lucky."

Emory could tell by his tone even he didn't believe his own words. "How bad does it look, Dink?"

"Bad enough."

Emory put her phone away and picked up her pace. She had to put everything out of her mind to get the job done she was here to do. She scrambled over everything that littered her way to get to where the light shone out like a beacon. Twisted metal and concrete were visible, and Emory could see they were no match for whatever power the saucers had. She picked her way through it gingerly, slipping on the loose dirt and rubble. She finally crested the top of the crater and looked down into it.

"Oh my God," Dink breathed, clearly seeing what Emory was seeing. There was an underground labyrinth uncovered in the blast. The force of the explosion had blown some of the building to pieces, but there were structures still intact below.

"I'm seeing a stairwell under that pile of debris. It's got to lead somewhere."

"Are you ready to go down the rabbit hole, Alice?"

"Flying saucers above my head and a staircase that might lead me to answers I could only dream of. Or it could fall to pieces with my weight on it and drop me to certain doom or bury me under tons of debris. Choices, choices." She took a step over the lip of the crater. "Alice, out." She slid and slipped her way down the huge crater's side. She scrambled to slow her decent, but the rubble under her feet was loose. She cut her hands on the rocks and concrete as she tried not to fall headfirst into the gaping crevice. She could see now where the light was coming from. The crater had cut a perfect hollow into the ground and exposed a concrete wall and stairs that ran along it and down into whatever lay beneath. "Damn good thing I'm not claustrophobic," she muttered, a little unnerved by how exposed the stairwell appeared to be and how much damage it had sustained.

"I doubt if the elevators will still be running in there after the show the saucers put on. So it's either the stairs or you get the hell out of there."

"Whose stupid idea was this again?" Emory reached the exposed wall and stared down into the stairwell. It seemed never ending.

"That would be yours, my friend."

"Damn it. Be sure to remind me, if I get out of here alive, what an asshole I am."

"Duly noted. Can you see if there are any levels marked as you go down? It might be interesting to see if the rumors were right."

"Forty levels?" Emory slowly put a foot on a metal stair and pressed to make sure it would hold her weight. "I'm screwed if I have to climb down forty fucking levels to find something. I'll be here all night." Once the steps felt sturdier under her feet, Emory began to climb down a little faster. She was hindered by chunks of debris blocking the way, and she either managed to push them aside or had to climb over them. Dust clung to the air and made breathing difficult. Coughing at the cloying air, Emory was aware that the angle she was traveling down was changing. Finally, below her, she could see a doorway that had been buckled by the blast.

"Let's see what's behind door number one, shall we?" Dink said as Emory pressed her shoulder against the ruined metal. The metal screeched as it was forced open.

Emory blew out a breath. "Saves me worrying I was going to need my swipe card to get in here. The security has to be tougher the lower I go, right?"

"I'd imagine so."

"Time to see what secrets Area 51 has been hiding from us."

Chapter Three

The hallway Emory stepped into was still half lit. Most of the ceiling had come down on one side, effectively cutting off the rooms that were on the right. Emory managed to pick her way across the floor toward a door on the left and stepped inside. She found a room decked out with computers and desks. "What is this? Area 51's call center?" Emory snorted. "Hi, this is Dreamland Surveys and we'd like a moment of your time to ask you if you're buying the cover-ups we keep perpetrating in the name of national security."

She heard Dink chuckle in her ear as she skirted around the rows of desks. She didn't see anything of any interest in the nondescript office. She did, however, spot another door so she headed toward it. She was relieved when it opened with just a little force. "Ooh, pay dirt." She had found another office, but this one was still up and running. The computer screens had been left on, and the servers were flashing. "Wow, blasted from above but the electricity is still working down here. Curiouser and curiouser..."

"Emory..."

"Before you dare to ask, I am *not* lugging a computer out with me."

"Think you can find a hard drive or two then?"

"I'm not exactly carrying the tools of the trade to dismantle a government computer for you."

"I need to build up your spy gear. I'll get you a tool belt."

Emory huffed. "You're already in my ear and using my eyes. Outfitting me with a utility belt like Batman is going to make me stand out even more." She wandered through the room and came to idle by a large desk. She warred with herself, but the need to know won out. "How much trouble do you think my brother would have to bail me out of if I appropriated a laptop left behind in the mass evacuation?" She picked it up, turning it over to check it out. "According to the desk plate it belongs to someone with a rank."

"Grab it and bag it. If nothing else you can plead you took it so no one else could find it. Before you do that, get me hooked up so I can get inside."

Emory took a USB stick off her keyring and quickly inserted it into the laptop. With directions being issued in her ear, Emory had Dink walking her through the installation of a remote access bot so that he could take over the laptop and plunder it from afar.

Once he was in, Emory hunted around the desk and spied its bag. "We're taking it for safekeeping, right? National security and all that shit?" She shoved the laptop in the bag and slung it over her shoulders.

"You're stopping it from falling into enemy hands."

"Which, according to you, are small and gray and probably only sporting three fingers." Emory hunted in the desk to see if she could find anything else. "And what are we exactly? Do we count as enemy in the government's and military's eyes? I'm in here masquerading as a CIA agent when in reality I'm just a concerned citizen who thinks nothing of exposing national security secrets on the Internet for the world to see."

"Yes, but you're revealing the truth behind the secrets they are trying so hard to hide from the general public."

"I'm also a conspiracy theorist who sees signs and symbols in everything. With a major leaning more toward the truth in spy tech than the out of this world explanations you believe in."

"And if what you've already seen outside proves you wrong?"

"Then I owe you a beer." Emory rolled her eyes at his muffled cough to press her for more. "And three large Butterfinger candy bars."

"I'm eagerly awaiting you paying up. I haven't had chocolate for a month."

Emory opened up another drawer and riffled through it. "Damn it, Dink. You have to get out more."

"You know as well as I do that I'm perfectly happy in my bunker monitoring the planet out of the way of prying eyes and cyber spies."

"Then get someone to deliver your groceries. Man cannot live on ramen alone."

"Ooh, you can bring me some of that too when you have to eat your words." Dink sounded smug.

"Unless you are seeing more on those streams than you're telling me, you have no proof of what or who is piloting those ships. They could be remote controlled for all we know."

"Even now you're *still* going to argue with me?" His laughter sounded in her ear.

"I don't deny there are UFOs, but we haven't seen who is piloting them. You know and I know that remote drones have been in use for years now. Maybe this is the next step up."

"Well, let's hope for your sake if it is aliens that they look like the traditional grays everyone says they've seen. If they resemble spiders you'll be completely useless to me."

Emory slammed a desk drawer. "Shut the fuck up," she grumbled. She hated being goaded about her greatest fear. She could hear Dink snickering and ground her teeth in annoyance.

"You're so…hey, wait. Go back there." Dink directed Emory to a cubicle. "There. Look through those files."

"Do I really have time to read someone's team building notes while all hell is breaking loose outside?" She flipped through the files quickly, ready to discard the mundane.

"You don't need to know what is going on outside while you are in Aladdin's cave. Just stuff them in your bag. *I'll* read them later."

Emory did as she was told and continued working her way around the room looking for anything she could take. She stuffed more files into the laptop case. *I've already stolen a laptop, what's a few assorted files and folders to add to the list?* She was headed toward the door at the far end. "I want to check out the next room then see if I can venture any farther down to see what lies beneath." She had the key card in her hand ready to swipe the machine and was reaching for the door handle when she heard the door unlocking from the other side. She jumped back as the handle began turning before she touched it. She barely stifled the "Shit!" that escaped her lips and quickly looked around for somewhere to hide.

"Go! Go!" Dink hissed in her ear, and Emory scrambled to quickly press herself between two servers and ducked out of sight. She could feel herself shaking as the door opened slowly. It stopped halfway. Emory tried to make herself as small as possible. She held her breath and strained her ears trying to hear if the person at the door was going to come in or leave. She fervently hoped it was the latter.

Please don't be an alien. Do not let me be killed by something I've never believed in. That would so suck as my final epitaph.

❖

Captain Sofia Martinez kept her gun drawn as she cautiously took a step inside the office. She couldn't see anything but the endless rows of cubicles all left empty after the evacuation. She silently took another step forward, ready to face the intruder she'd seen.

She'd been passing by the surveillance office on her security sweep to make sure every floor had been evacuated when she had spotted something on one of the screens. She'd watched as a woman walked around the desks, looking like she was hunting for something. Sofia had studied her. Whoever it was she didn't hold herself like a soldier. She was all in black, but there was something off with her bearing. Sofia switched cameras so she could look more closely. The woman looked to be around Sofia's own height of five foot five. This Sofia could tell from judging her height against the partitions she was skirting around. She had blond hair, parted to frame her face. Sofia guessed her hair was usually shoulder length, but at the moment it was messily escaping a makeshift ponytail. She was attractive, Sofia noted distractedly, taking in the woman's slightly rounded face and the prominent dimples in her cheeks. She had a slender build with a distinctly tomboyish air, one of Sofia's personal weaknesses. But this woman, as intriguing as she seemed, was wandering around in a restricted area.

"What are you looking for?" Sofia had spoken out loud, her suspicion rising the more she watched. She unholstered her weapon. "Let's go see why you didn't leave when everyone else did."

Sofia had been ordered to remain behind by the base's superior officer, Lieutenant Colonel Colin Jones. On hearing the blaring of sirens going off and feeling the floors shudder beneath her feet, Sofia hadn't been happy to be left behind with only a vague idea what they were being evacuated for. Instead she had to coordinate the escape of the senior staff through to the tunnels where they boarded underground trains. These would take them to undisclosed areas miles away from Area 51. Other staff were sent out on another train heading to the basement of a high-rise office complex in the nearest city. She had no idea what had happened to those who had been caught in the explosions she'd been told had smashed through the higher floors. She'd learned in the course of her career not to ask many questions. Too much knowledge was a dangerous thing. She did her job and left others to do theirs. No knowledge meant no culpability and nothing to hide when asked. It was safer that way.

Now she edged farther into the room, purposely stepping away from the door. It wouldn't pay her to get hit by it if the other woman was behind it and used it to disarm Sofia. She was met by silence. She took the safety off her gun and spoke out.

"I know you're in here. I've been watching you on a monitor so step out where I can see you and keep your hands raised." She waited, her eyes running over the office for signs of movement. "You have a choice. Surrender to me and tell me what you're doing here or I leave you in here and whatever is above us can come down and find you." Sofia let that sink in a little. "I can promise you, I'm the lesser of the two evils today."

She heard a noise a few desks up and turned her gun toward it.

"I'm unarmed."

Sofia watched as the woman finally struggled out into view. Keeping her gun trained on her, Sofia scrutinized her. The woman's blue eyes were fixed on her and on the gun in her hands. Sofia sensed no fear though. She was surprised when a smile broke out across the woman's face. It gave her a rakish air.

"Hi. I was here for a meeting when it was seemingly gate-crashed by the flying saucers above."

Sofia felt herself go cold. *The saucers have been seen?*

The woman was still grinning disarmingly at Sofia. "Best excuse I've ever had for canceling a meeting. Sadly, no one thought to brief me on where I should go in the event of an evacuation so I got left behind in the panic. I had no idea who to follow, got turned around, and was left wandering the halls." She shrugged but kept her hands raised.

"Show me your credentials."

Slowly, the woman lowered her arm and reached for her wallet. She tossed it onto the desk by where Sofia stood.

"Agent Ellen Mays?" Sofia couldn't see anything fraudulent about the CIA ID and motioned for Emory to lower her arms and take her wallet back.

"Yes, ma'am."

"It's Captain," Sofia corrected her. She'd worked hard for her rank; she expected the recognition of it.

"You look too young to be a captain," Emory said with a flirty air. Sofia stared stonily at her.

"So I've heard from countless old men of higher rank who've never moved out from behind a desk."

"I meant no disrespect."

"Who were you here to see?" Sofia caught the hesitation flash ever so briefly across Emory's face.

"I couldn't tell you."

"You don't remember?" Sofia's suspicions were on alert.

"No, it's just that I wasn't told. I was given orders to be here and told someone would see me. It was all very cloak-and-dagger. More than usual, to be honest."

Sofia thumbed the safety back on her gun and holstered it. "You'll find everything is shrouded in mystery here. It's standard procedure." She looked Emory up and down. "You're not exactly dressed like a CIA agent."

Emory tugged at her hoodie with an embarrassed air. "I was told it was Dress Down Friday."

Sofia stared at her. She wasn't quite sure if she was being blatantly lied to or just being teased. She didn't do either very well. Sighing, she gestured for Emory to follow her. "Let me escort you back outside. I'm sure someone will reschedule for you."

Emory laughed. "Seriously? With all that going on out there? I think a meeting is going to be the last thing on anyone's agenda."

"Then let me get you to safety at least." Sofia gestured for Emory to leave the room and waited to follow her. Once outside the door,

Sofia ran into the back of Emory who had stopped dead in the middle of the corridor for some reason. Sofia was so close she could feel Emory's hair brush against her cheek. Close up, the pale hair was a rich honey color and held in place by a leather tie.

"Why have you stopped?" Sofia asked, annoyed with Emory and herself for being so distracted.

"We need to get out of here right now." Emory took hold of Sofia's hand and pulled her behind her as she ran back through the room they had just left.

"That's what we were doing." Sofia tried to get her hand free to no avail.

"More saucers are on their way and they're bringing the bigger ships with them. This place is probably going to be targeted again, and I don't intend to be caught in here while they blow Area 51 through to the other side of the planet." Emory tugged harder on Sofia's hand and nearly pulled her over. "So shift your ass, Captain, and let's get out of here."

Surprised by Emory's change from formal to more urgent, Sofia let herself be led back through the offices.

"How do you know they're coming back?" she asked as they burst through the door and the cooler night air hit Sofia, shocking her. Sofia got her first chance to see what had happened so many floors above where she had been. "Oh my God." She stuttered to a halt, but Emory tugged at her roughly.

"You don't have time to stop and stare. Big Brother is watching out for us, Captain." She drew Sofia's attention to the earpiece hidden inside her right ear. "And he says to get the hell out of here because the fighter jets your military are sending up against the saucers are proving no match. The saucers are trying to get back to where we are. And I want out of here *now*."

Sofia climbed up the broken staircase and clambered out into the crater. She followed closely on Emory's heels, picking over the rubble and trying not to think about what or *who* she could be clambering over. She'd seen combat; she recognized the terrain that was underfoot. The sound of a furiously fought battle was clearly heard in the distance.

"Oh my God," she whispered, desperately trying to hold back a sob as she saw the devastation wrought as she climbed higher. She scrambled up the crater's sides, her boots slipping out from under her numerous times. She was grateful that each time she fell, Emory was reaching for her and pulling her along. Only when she crested the crater's rim did she stop to fully take in the scene. She tried to see any familiar landmark. There was nothing left anywhere, not even the runways. She followed after Emory who surprised her by how fit she was as they ran the whole way at a breakneck speed. The wrecked earth of the base gave way to scrubby brush and greenery as they ran into the surrounding desert and Sofia finally caught sight of what Emory was directing her toward. A VW Bus was the only thing not touched in the whole vicinity. It was hard to see, as it was predominantly black with only a few white accents. Sofia couldn't help frowning. Since when did CIA agents drive vintage Buses?

"You're not really CIA," she said when she reached Emory's side as she hurried to unlock the vehicle. Emory gave her a look and grabbed Sofia by the collar to fling her inside the van.

"Believe me, Captain, tonight that is the least of your problems."

CHAPTER FOUR

Emory gunned the engine and spun the van around as fast as she could to head back out to find a main road. The ride was anything but smooth as the van bounced and crashed over the debris that covered the field.

"So I'm going to survive an airborne attack and instead die in this scrap pile you call a vehicle?" Sofia yelled as she clung to anything she could get a grip on.

Emory grinned like a maniac as she put her foot down harder on the gas. "This baby has a whole heap of surprises under her hood, Captain. You just watch and learn." She grunted as they hit a deep hole in the ground and the whole van groaned in protest. The headlights did little to help find a clear path out of the air base.

"Christ, what a mess," Sofia said, staring out the windshield with wide, disbelieving eyes.

"According to my sources, the rest of the planet isn't faring too well either. They're attacking everywhere." Emory swung her wheel around and got them back on a road she knew would get them out of there. It was mercifully untouched. "Tell me," she looked at the captain's uniform for identification, "Martinez, what the hell is Area 51 hiding because it sure as hell pissed something off. Enough to bomb the place to smithereens and then take its show on the road and make us all pay for your sins."

"That's classified information."

"Bullshit. Look around you. Does this look classified to you now? Someone opened up the earth to expose Area 51's secret lair and lay waste to it. This looks like someone is really determined to wipe Dreamland from the map, Martinez."

"That's Captain Sofia Martinez to you, civilian," Sofia snapped.

Emory laughed at her. "Really? I pull your ass out of the fire and you still expect me to salute you? Pull that rank all you like, lady, but it means nothing now that we've got flying saucers bombing the hell out of the planet. So, I'll ask again. What are we up against, because I'd say it's a safe wager you know exactly what those things are."

Sofia pointedly ignored her and kept her eyes trained out the window.

"I don't think she's going to spill her secrets just yet, Emory," Dink said in her ear. "She's pretty though, don't you think? She's got that sexy Latino thing going, all dark hair and darker eyes. Feisty too. And her name, Sofiaaaaa. Listen to how she says it with that voice of hers. God, she sounds like aged old whiskey personified with that husky tone."

Emory sighed inwardly at Dink's dreamy tone. She had noticed how pretty Sofia was, even when she'd had a gun pointing at her. The gray camouflaged battle uniform she wore did nothing to disguise her feminine curves or the strength with which she held herself. Emory admired the way her dark brown hair was cut short and blunt around her face. But not even the standard camo air force peaked cap she wore could hide or tame the natural wave to her hair. Sofia's skin tone was a shade darker than Emory's and her eyes a deep brown. Her face was austere, trained to give no secrets away. Emory knew Sofia was beautiful, and her eyes slipped to the full lips that were pursed in annoyance as the van raced to anywhere but here. The fact she found Sofia attractive was not going to help her find the answers they desperately needed this night.

"You're staring at her instead of the road, Romeo. Eyes ahead, and for God's sake, turn your lights off. You don't want to alert anything to your presence. There are some dwellings just over the next ridge, head toward them. We need to evacuate anyone living near that damn place."

Emory switched the headlights off.

"Why did you do that?" Sofia asked sharply. "The road is hardly drivable as it is."

"The voices in my ear say not to alert those things above," Emory said, squinting at the road to try to see something in the light cast by the moon.

"These voices. Heard them long, have you? What else are they saying?" Sofia was looking Emory over with a suspicious eye. Her hand was inching toward her holster.

"Nothing much. Just that maybe I should dump you on the side of the road for being so uncooperative and let you fend for yourself against whatever is out there flying above us."

"Actually, I never said that," Dink argued.

"Why? Because I won't spill military secrets to someone who has already proved herself to be a liar and had fraudulently worked her way onto a restricted air base? I should be arresting you. In fact, consider yourself under arrest for crimes against national security."

"This isn't about me. This is about you telling us what the hell you have released above us that is now systematically bombing the planet."

Sofia crossed her arms firmly across her chest. "I'll give you my name and rank. That's all you're going to need before I arrest you for trespassing on government property. Also, if I find out that laptop bag you squirreled away in this wreck of a vehicle does not belong to you I'll be adding theft of military property on top of the list of charges I'm compiling against you."

Emory slammed on the brakes, forcing the vehicle to slide to a halt. "Fuck this. I don't care how pretty you are."

Sofia lurched in her seat. She gasped out loud as the seat belt dug painfully into her chest. Emory unfastened her own seat belt and reached across Sofia to push the door open. "Get the hell out, *Captain*." Shifting in her seat to literally kick Sofia out of the van, Emory spotted something and hastily slammed the door shut again to extinguish the interior light.

They were both startled into silence by the saucers that flew over the van, heading toward the ridge Dink had just directed them to go.

"Where did they come from?" Sofia craned her neck to watch the crafts fly by.

"That's the thing, Captain; they just appear out of nowhere. But I think you're already aware of that." Satisfied that the crafts were well ahead of them, Emory started the van back on her course.

Sofia was shaking her head. "Those aren't our crafts."

"You sure about that?" Emory didn't believe her. "I mean, the military have suddenly revealed high-tech crafts before that they had kept hidden for years while they were tested and had proved their worth on the battlefield."

Sofia nodded distractedly. "Area 51 houses many projects of advanced technology. Aircraft just happens to be one area among many. But I'm telling you, those things aren't ours."

Emory huffed in barely restrained annoyance and crested the ridge so they could look down on where Dink had directed her to get people out of their homes.

They were too late.

The saucers hung above the rough dwellings that were the rare few that skirted the edges of the Area 51 lands. The white beam was sweeping over the ruins of the buildings, picking through the survivors and taking their spoils.

Sofia's choked gasp made Emory startle from what she was witnessing for the second time that night. Multiple human abduction by unidentified means.

"Those aren't ours," Sofia said in a shaky tone, "because *our* crafts don't have the capability to do *that*."

Chapter Five

Emory and Sofia sat in stunned silence watching as the saucers finished recovering the living from the area and then sped off toward Area 51. Before Emory could open her mouth to speak, there was an almighty explosion from miles away. The force of it shook the van and the ground beneath it. Emory felt her teeth rattle as a shockwave battered them, the force of it penetrating through to her very marrow. It felt like an earthquake had hit, and they were sitting right on top of the epicenter. The noise alone was deafening, and it took a while for Emory to get her senses back.

"What the fuck was *that*?" Emory twisted in her seat to look over her shoulder to where a huge plume of smoke was rising from the direction they had just fled. Lit by a raging fire, it was unmissable against the darkness of the night.

"That was Area 51 being wiped from existence before the cameras I was viewing it on were destroyed. It's gone, Emory. A big black ship blew it all away. Literally." Dink's voice sounded hollow. "We are seriously screwed if they have that kind of firepower at their disposal."

Emory shifted in her seat to face Sofia. "Let's rewind to your last comment, Captain. Something along the lines of 'our ships don't do that.' So, for *our* ships *not* to do that, I'm taking that to mean we have flying saucers of our own."

Sofia wouldn't look at her. "No comment."

Emory smiled. "Too late. You've already let the saucer-shaped cat out of the bag. You, the military, have flying saucers. Dink, I damn well told you they did." She slapped her hand against the console in victory. She noticed that Sofia jumped at the noise as it pulled her from her daze.

"Yes, you did, Emory. But remember, she inferred that whoever or *whatever* is piloting those saucers has the same technology too."

Emory sighed. "Captain Martinez, just give it to me straight. Are the bastards abducting people by some means *we* don't allegedly have, human or something else?"

Sofia turned slightly to look Emory over with a considering eye. "I'm sure you're full of theories as to what the answer is to that."

"Oh God, lady, don't ask her that," Dink said softly.

Pointedly ignoring him, Emory smiled at her. "I'm saying human. Yes, technology has come along in leaps and bounds after the Second World War, but then the military scored some major players when it took Germany's rocket scientists on board. I guess not all the Third Reich were considered the enemy when they had the knowledge to create rockets and bombs. Switching sides must have been a no-brainer when that information was in exchange for no prosecution for their war crimes."

"You know your history." Sofia sounded surprised.

"It's easy enough to research, and besides, history is a bit of a blabbermouth once enough years have gone by. I also know that the government loves to mislead the masses. You've got spy planes and stealth craft whose specifications you wouldn't want to fall into enemy hands. So when we see them being tested we get fed misinformation. Every time there's something bright traveling fast, it's got to be reported as something alien. That way, you kill two birds with one stone. Hide the truth and terrorize the population. Keeping us in fear of an invasion from outside the planet keeps us in line. It also lets you build up your weaponry without us making a peep. You're keeping us *safe*."

"You have a vivid imagination," Sofia said, her eyes stony. "And we need to leave here now and get to a military base. I need to report in."

Emory removed the keys from the ignition and palmed them. "I have a mind that's my own, and we're not going anywhere until you tell me who's piloting the saucers."

"I have no idea. And I am ordering you to take me to the nearest base."

Emory snorted her derision at Sofia's commanding tone. "You can't order me anywhere. I'm not one of your subordinates. Besides, while the military is scrambling to fling every airplane they have at those things, nothing is working, so they exactly won't miss one captain for the moment."

Sofia folded her arms over her chest and stared out the windshield. "I'm not saying another word."

"That's okay, I have more than enough to say. Like how I watched the people from Area 51 be hoisted up into the beams from the saucers that 'aren't ours.'" Emory made air quotes around her last words. She was pleased to see how much that riled Sofia.

"You saw the civilians escape?"

"No, I saw them being captured by whoever or whatever was piloting those saucers that you claim to know nothing about. Something is harvesting us. It's capturing humans in a beam of light and sucking them up into the ship. I have no idea what happens to them next. Do *you*, Captain?"

Sofia shook her head.

Emory scoffed at her. "Now why don't I believe you? Who else got their hands on the blueprints for your crafts so they could build their own?"

"No one could steal the plans because there were none in the first place." Sofia sat back with a resigned sigh. "What do you want me to say? What would you like me to tell you? I don't know who's flying those things. Do you really want me to just guess? Because my guess, according to the rumors you probably believe in, is that the only other ones who could build those craft were found dead years ago in a wreckage back in 1947."

Emory could hear Dink's excited noises in her ear. He sounded like he was in the throes of a seizure.

"You mean Roswell?" Emory watched Sofia's face and barely caught the shrug in reply. Dink screamed in excitement and nearly deafened her. "So much for it being a weather balloon."

Emory couldn't believe what all this meant. She felt overwhelmed by something she knew so much about but had never believed. It was like being hit by a tidal wave, and while she was floundering, Dink was whooping like a five-year-old through her earpiece. He was probably doing cartwheels in his underground bunker and breaking out his victory dance. She'd seen him do it; it wasn't pretty.

"We really need to get to a military base. I have to report what I've seen."

"Captain, the whole world is aware of what's happening so I think your superiors know exactly what is going on and who has come knocking to get their technology back."

"Aliens, Emory! We're being invaded by aliens!" Dink sounded almost giddy with excitement. Emory shook her head at him. Even if that was the case, it didn't exactly make the situation any better.

"I heard, Big Brother. Now we have to figure out how to stop them."

"*Now* do you believe?" he asked.

"You know me, I go by the facts. I haven't seen anything yet that points conclusively to little gray aliens from Mars or wherever. But I assure you, the moment I do? I'll be sure to eat my words." She fit the key in the ignition and started up the van. "Captain, I know you want to be reunited with your air force buddies, but I need to get to Las Vegas first. My family is there and I need to know they're okay."

"The military could help," Sofia said.

"I'm sure searching the rubble for my family is high on their list of must-dos for today. *I* need to do it. I can't reach them on the phone. I have to try to find them. Then I promise I'll drive you anywhere to regroup with your squad or whatever you call them." Emory could feel Sofia's eyes on her.

"We need to be careful. We can't be seen by the saucers."

"Good thing I'm not night blind, isn't it? I'll keep the lights off, and we'll drive by the light of the moon."

Sofia faced forward again. She was silent for a long while until she broke their silence. "The ones who evacuated Area 51? The civilians and the staff? You really saw them being abducted?"

"Yes."

Sofia's jaw clenched, and she brushed a hand over her eyes. "I'm going to need more weapons. I've only got my service revolver, and we're going to need stronger firepower than that."

"*After* we find my brother. It will take us about three hours, a little more if the Vegas Strip is a nightmare like it usually is. Winchester is literally on the other side of the lights. Let me do this and then I'll follow your orders."

Sofia laughed. Emory thought the sound was surprisingly beautiful for such a serious looking woman.

"Why do I get the feeling you doing what I say is going to drive you crazy?" Sofia smiled just enough for Emory to catch sight of it in the moonlight.

"Because you didn't reach the rank you have by not being astute."

"I'm still arresting you for impersonating a CIA agent."

"Let's see what happens first. You might find I'm of better use to you in the field than locked up behind bars." However much safer that sounded to Emory's ears.

Emory's head was whirling. All her beliefs were wavering and crumbling before her. Were all the stories of aliens true? The cave drawings that depicted star creatures, or the visitors that rode the sky on fiery dragons told in all those ancient tales? And what about the leaked stories from Roswell itself and the endless other sightings? She knew of them all, had studied them, but never fully believed. If they were true then it challenged everything she had built her world of theories on.

But she couldn't deny that there were unidentified flying saucers in the skies. And she'd just been told by someone in the military that bodies were recovered at Roswell and the craft had been scavenged for its secrets. Secrets the military now had at hand in saucers of their own.

But could their saucers stand up against the might of the originals? For now, Emory couldn't think about that. She had to see if her idiot of a brother was still alive to make her life a misery over the fact he was right as always.

She hoped he got that chance.

❖

It was only by following her GPS that Emory knew she was driving into Las Vegas. The once iconic landscape of bright lights and fantastical buildings was all gone. Its endless Strip of decadence lay before them in ruins. The hotels were broken, empty husks of their former glory. Shattered signs blinked erratically and sparked through broken bulbs. The Statue of Liberty had been broken off her pedestal and melted so she was bent out of shape and leaning over. It looked like she had been forced to bow down to a more powerful being. Caesar's Palace, the Bellagio, the spectacular fountains, all were gone in endless mounds of rubble and massive craters. Vegas was closed to business indefinitely.

Emory drove down the middle of the Strip, trying desperately to dodge the screaming people running everywhere. A dance troupe from one of the many shows ran out in front of her, blind in their panic. The bright and gaudy dresses the women wore were ripped to pieces, blood-soaked, and stained. The once shiny sequins were now hidden under layers of dirt and dust. Emory careened the van around them, desperate not to hit them. The road crunched beneath her tires as she steered over debris of what was left from the surrounding buildings. Scattered cars were everywhere. Many had been flipped over onto their roofs, while others had been thrown a great distance. Emory saw one that had impacted with the remains of a building front, shot like an arrow straight through the wall. Other cars were ablaze; some were blackened or already gutted from the force of whatever had hit them. Emory could only imagine where the drivers had ended up. For a bustling monument to gambling and fun, Vegas was now filled with the screams of both the living and the dying. The surreal sight terrified Emory. The glitz and glamour that Las Vegas was famed for was all gone. Now it resembled a war zone.

"We have to help them." Emory looked for a safe place to park. The earth rumbled and shook beneath her tires, and Emory felt the road *shift*. She and Sofia watched with horror as one of the hotels shook with an almighty tremor and then collapsed with a deafening roar. The dust and debris from it spread across the already wrecked landscape. Pieces from it flew through the air, and Emory instinctively ducked as a large chunk of balcony flew past the windshield.

"Get us out of here," Sofia ordered. "There's nothing we can do. If we try to mount a rescue attempt we stand the chance of being killed ourselves. The area isn't safe."

Emory gunned the engine, fixed her gaze forward, and didn't look back. It killed her to drive away, but she recognized the futility of staying in such an unstable area. *And I need to find my family. I can't save the world...*

"Any ideas what weapons they might have, because we need something to match them to stand a fighting chance," she said, desperate to have any kind of chatter to drown out the noise of the screaming and the booms from collapsing buildings they were driving away from. Vegas was falling; its loss was catastrophic.

"We have some of the same technology," Sofia said quietly. She was scanning the area just as Emory had, obviously taking in the carnage but distancing herself from it. Emory wondered what Sofia had seen before that made her able to put up such a wall to block it all out. She dreaded to think.

"Then why are they sending up planes instead of saucers?"

"Because our saucers were in the hangars at Area 51, and now there's no Area 51 left."

"Sabotage," Dink said in Emory's ear. He'd been quiet for most of the journey except to tell her where the ships had moved to next. Planet Earth was under attack on all corners.

"Do you have any more hidden somewhere?" Emory asked.

"Not to my knowledge."

"Would you tell me if you knew?" Emory cut Sofia a look. She was surprised to see Sofia crack a small smile.

"There's not much point in me hiding it anymore, is there? You've seen the saucers; you've seen what they can do. We need to get to a military base so I can liaise with my superiors. Maybe they have a better idea what we're up against and how we can fight back."

"My brother is in Winchester. It's not far out of Las Vegas. I just need to know—"

"I understand you wanting to reach family, but what if he isn't there?"

Emory froze as that sunk in.

"We can't stay, Ellen. We have to find help. Military might."

Emory released a shaky breath, railing against the truth but knowing that Sofia was right. "It's Emory."

"What?"

"My name is Emory Hawkes. Ellen Mays is my CIA ruse." She gave Sofia a weak smile. "If you're going to arrest me as you keep threatening to you might as well use my proper name to do it." She looked out into the darkness. "I don't think my brother will be able to bail me out this time anyway."

"He might still be okay," Sofia said.

Emory knew that tone of voice. Sofia didn't believe her own words any more than Emory did.

"I think you need to find a way to get to me, Emory." Dink's voice startled Emory in the lengthening silence. Sofia was brooding beside Emory, her eyes fixed out the windshield as if all the answers lay outside in the darkness. "Once you ditch the captain, you need to come find me. You're not safe out there."

"Are there any saucers in Winchester?" That caught Sofia's attention. When Dink said no, Emory shook her head. "So no saucers *yet*."

"We don't have a base there," Sofia said.

"So you think they're hitting military bases on purpose?"

Sofia shifted in her seat to face Emory. "Wouldn't you?"

"Ask her about the nuclear stations," Dink said.

"Is it true the saucers are powered from the nuclear reactors, or are they just scoping them out because we have that tech?"

"I don't know. Before tonight I didn't know there were any other saucers other than ours. That's why I need to get to a base so I can find out exactly what's going on."

Emory wasn't sure she believed her, but she didn't believe anything the military or government said. She hesitated.

Sofia glanced over at her. "That laptop you squirreled away behind your seat, is it yours?"

"Yes," Emory blatantly lied without conscience.

Sofia shifted in her seat. "It had better be. Because if it isn't you're facing years in a military prison for stealing government property to no doubt try to hack into highly classified military—"

Emory interrupted Sofia's tirade. "I took that laptop in with me. You can check the base's cameras to prove my story." Emory snapped her fingers as if a thought had struck her. "Ah, that might be a problem now seeing as the cameras, along with the rest of Area 51, are currently going up in smoke. Guess you'll just have to take my word for it."

"And if I don't believe you?"

"We have a choice, soldier. We can sit here and become saucer bait—"

"You still won't say alien, will you?" Dink said, but Emory paid him no attention.

"Or, hypothetically speaking, if we *could* appropriate something that maybe has answers on it that you weren't privy to, wouldn't that be a help instead?"

"There might be a reason for whatever is on there not being made public. I'm going to ask you to hand over the laptop before I make you give it to me." Sofia's voice was harsh and authoritative. Emory paid little attention to that too.

"What kind of reasons can't be made public knowledge? Like there's flying saucers that could potentially destroy the earth? I think we're all aware of that secret now."

Emory didn't want to burst her bubble and tell her that Dink was already knee-deep into the memory of the laptop and was using it to hack into the government and military systems linked to that one machine. Once he'd remote accessed it there was no stopping what he could do with the information the laptop held.

"And what if you had found something that isn't intended for the eyes of the general population?" Sofia asked. "What good is that information to you?"

"You're asking the wrong person, Captain. I'm due in court in a few weeks because I posted to a site details from a reliable source that there is a secret military agency serving alongside the military that governs Area 51. I was just waiting on this source to furnish me with names and job descriptions, but the site got busted."

Sofia swung around in her seat and fixed Emory with a hard glare. "There is no secret military agency. Your source was lying." Sofia's voice was harsh as she bit the words out.

Emory wondered at the tone and the vehemence behind it. *Me thinks the lady doth protest too much.*

"Well, I never got the chance to see definitive proof or name names, but I'm going to be prosecuted for not revealing who my source was. So I'm the wrong person to ask about keeping secrets a secret."

Sofia's shoulders dropped. "Your pursuit of these crazy fantasies is going to get you into serious trouble one day, Emory. And not just with me."

"But they're not so crazy, are they? There *are* saucers invading us as we speak. So who's crazy now? The one who believed in their existence but got ridiculed or the one who didn't believe because they were told the rest of us were making up stupid conspiracy theories for our own ends?" Emory said. "They're only classed as crazy because people who are frightened for the truth to come out label it as such and the name sticks. Otherwise it's just a theory. Like the theory centuries ago that the earth was flat. How crazy a theory was that, hmm? This is how I've chosen to live my life, not taking things at face value because I'm told I have to. But you'll find I'm a relatively minor glitch in whatever security there is left on this planet thanks to the invasion. Besides, aren't you just a little bit curious as to whether we'll find out if this is all some great big setup? A theatrical display run by the military and the government to keep the general population under control?" Emory flashed her a toothy grin. "Go on, Captain, rebel a little. Come see the world from our side for a while. I promise you, you'll be amazed at the view."

CHAPTER SIX

Sofia grimaced at Emory's words. She was well aware of a great many times disinformation had been sent across the wires and played out on the field. She feared this threat from above wasn't man-made and therefore was in no way under anyone's control. *No, this is something different entirely. Something that I was never briefed on.* "So, just who is this voice in your ear?"

"Big Brother. You're in safe hands though. He is a man of principle."

Sofia caught the smirk that ghosted across Emory's lips before it disappeared just as fast. "And what are *you*, Emory Hawkes?" She watched Emory's face closely and saw a myriad of emotions run across her features.

"It depends who you talk to. I'm the crazy conspiracy theorist with subversive tendencies if you listen too long to my brother. He's probably right. You would see me as the intruder who set eyes somewhere I was never meant to see. I see myself as someone who uncovers the secrets and lies of those in positions of power. I'm a privacy advocate because Big Brother is everywhere, and I don't just mean the one in my ear." Emory paused a little and smiled. "He says I missed the part where I'm the best friend he has ever had. I like that description best of all."

Sofia was surprised to see a faint blush color Emory's cheeks, visible even in the pale lights of the van's interior.

"Well, I'm just glad that Big Brother exists so that I don't have to worry you're not as insane as I first thought with you talking to yourself. Any chance I can be patched into his chatter, or is this a marriage of just two minds?"

Emory must have been listening to the reply in her ear because she laughed. "He says he's all for a threesome but knows he's not my type." Emory started the van back up. "He says he'll talk to you though. He hates to keep you out of the loop. He'll get chatty while we still have communications working." Emory set them in motion again. "And why is that, I wonder? We have a whole ton of scrap metal orbiting the planet, an endless stream of satellites sending out information and defense systems guarding the planet. The invaders didn't think to cut off our main source of communications as they passed by? Color me curious that we can still see lights shining and our phones work." She fished her phone out of her pocket and handed it to Sofia. "For now, press 'speaker.'"

Sofia did so and the deep tones of a man's voice came from within.

"Captain Sofia Martinez, I am pleased to make your acquaintance. You may call me Dink."

Sofia frowned. "Dink? What kind of name is that?"

"One well deserved and preserves my air of mystery, wouldn't you agree?"

Emory smiled and shook her head.

"So, now that the introductions are in place, let's talk. I hope you're ready to talk about aliens. You see, Emory won't commit herself until she's seen concrete evidence. I, on the other hand, want to hear all about Roswell."

"You know that is classified information," Sofia said. "Even I'm not privy to all of it. All I know is a craft was found and we learned from its technology. I know nothing more than that." She'd already told them as much when she'd laid eyes on the saucers for the first time. And with what was being seen worldwide, there wasn't much point trying to keep that secret hidden any more.

"I'm sure you can try harder than that. It's presumably a long drive between where you are and where you want to go. We'll need something to talk about to while away the hours. You have no idea what is happening in the big wide world, Captain. Let me be your eyes and ears for a while and share with you what I know. You'd be surprised what Big Brother can see from in hiding."

Sofia had the horrible feeling he was right about everything. She hadn't been truly aware of the situation since the evacuation siren had pealed through the complex and she'd been left behind to…do what? Sofia had no idea. She couldn't lock down the underground base because it had been compromised from above. And now she knew there was no base to secure at all. *And I would have been among the dead too if it hadn't been for Emory coming in and getting me out in time. With my rank and position, I shouldn't have been left behind.*

So who can I trust now? The military I have given my life for but who left me to die? The government I have pledged to serve? Or the crazy woman driving an old VW Bus who talks to a mysterious voice in her ear?

"Why did you save me?" she asked, curious as to what excuse Emory would give her. Sofia had no reason to trust anything this pseudo CIA agent said. *But I do trust her for some reason, and I don't know why. Especially since she is against everything I stand for.*

Emory stared at her. "Why wouldn't I have? The base was about to be blown to smithereens and we needed to get out."

"But you could have just saved yourself."

Emory frowned at her. "And left you to die in there? That wasn't ever an option, Captain. I couldn't stop the others from being taken up into the saucers, but I could get you out. I would never have thought to leave you behind once I knew you were there, and with the knowledge I'd been given, we needed to get out fast."

"And it's just a lucky bonus that you're so pretty!" Dink said.

Emory shook her head. "Dammit, man, I should have left you off coms."

Sofia laughed softly. "Thank you, Dink. So I'm guessing you can see as well as hear everything, yes?"

"My glasses aren't prescription lenses," Emory spoke instead. "But they are equipped with a handy-dandy camera that lets Dink see what I see."

"So there were really two trespassers on the base?" Sofia made sure she had a stern face on when Emory turned to look at her.

"But only one who could be jailed for it," Dink said with little compunction. "If I switch off the feed, those glasses are just another fashion accessory for the up-and-coming agent under false pretenses to wear."

Sofia wondered just what or who she had gotten herself mixed up with.

"This laptop in the van? How involved are you in that, Dink?" she asked, determined to get to the bottom of it.

"Oh, that's nothing to do with me. That's Emory's machine, and she will insist on lugging it everywhere with her. She's unashamedly addicted to Facebook."

Emory choked on a burst of laughter but kept her eyes fixed firmly on the road ahead. Sofia had a feeling there was a lot more going on in this conversation than she was hearing.

"I'm certain that your military laptops and computers are fitted with highly specialized software and firewalls to keep someone like me from delving too deep. I'd probably only be able to get as far as seeing that the owner has some primo porn sites listed on his browser, all with his password and credit card details saved for easy access. But then it's amazing what you can find out about people if you dig deep enough, isn't it?"

Sofia wondered at his tone. "Please tell me you're not the sort to attempt to hack the Pentagon?"

Dink's laughter filled the van. "Oh, my dear Sofia," he said devilishly, "I did that parlor trick *years* ago."

Sofia sighed. "You do realize I will be required to arrest you both for treason when we reach a base?"

Emory pulled into an empty gas station. "Let's save the world from the so-called aliens first and then we'll talk about how much trouble Dink and I are causing you." She stepped out of the van to go fill up the tank.

Sofia sighed again and looked out into the darkness. "Dink? Why is there no one on the road? It's never this empty."

"They struck at night. It's obviously caught everyone unawares. Also, think about it. There are saucers in the sky. Who in their right mind is going to escape on the road that leads *toward* Area 51?"

She had to concede that point to him. "What the hell are they going to do with us?" Sofia was worried by what his answer would be.

"I was hoping you'd know."

"I have no idea. This wasn't anything I was made a party to. I'm as clueless as you are."

"Then we're in trouble, Sofia, because we need to see what and who we're up against before we can fight back."

Sofia had never felt so powerless. All the might of the military behind her, and still the saucers kept coming. "What are we going to do?" she said, her voice barely above a whisper.

Dink heard her. "Survive. It's all we can do."

❖

The sound of pumping gas echoed across the forecourt. Emory barely watched what she was doing; she was too busy looking around her. Something felt wrong. As wrong as an empty gas station in the middle of the night with flying saucers bombing the planet could feel. Her nerves were already jangling from what she'd witnessed at the base and beyond. The eerie stillness of the gas station was sending her warning signals. There were three other cars at the pumps, but their doors were open and no one was around. Oddly, there was a car door on the ground, just lying there. The metal looked strangely twisted and bent. The lights were all on, but the store part of the station looked deserted. Emory finished filling up her tank and removed some bills from her wallet. Belying her fear, she walked as confidently as she could toward the store to leave her payment. She couldn't shake the feeling she really shouldn't step one foot inside.

Emory was a frequent visitor to this station. It was on her route planner when she went to see her brother, so she was friendly with the elderly owner. She couldn't see him anywhere in the store, and that only made things worse.

"Mr. Sudzin?" Emory left her payment beside the cash register and braced herself to look over the counter. She was half expecting to find a body there. It was empty. "Mr. Sudzin? It's Emory Hawkes. You remember? The crazy lady who keeps getting chased off from Area 51? You let me hide in your car wash the last time when they followed me all the way down here?"

Emory nervously looked up and down the aisles of goods. There were items scattered all over the floor, as if someone had come in and thrown a fit, knocking the chips and popcorn all over. The soda fountain was running. Coke was spilling in an endless sticky stream to create huge puddles of bubbling brown on the floor. Emory stepped around it as best she could and switched it off. "Mr. Sudzin, I left my gas money by the register for you."

A noise from behind her made Emory spin around. Blindly, she reached for something, anything, to use as a weapon. A window washer was all that came to hand, but Emory brandished it, poised for whatever was coming.

A trap door in the flooring slid open, and a pair of frightened eyes peered out at her, along with the twin barrels of a shotgun aimed at her legs.

"Alien lady!" The gun was mercifully withdrawn.

Emory bit back a sigh. She wished he'd call her Emory.

"Hi, Mr. Sudzin. Are you okay?" She lifted the door up a little, but he refused to come out.

"Are they gone?" he asked, his eyes darting back and forth over what little he could see of his store.

"Who?"

"The weird children. What looked like a whole school bus load of them suddenly appeared out of nowhere."

"Kids did this and made you hide?" Emory was a little skeptical. She knew he kept the shotgun behind the counter for protection and wasn't afraid to brandish it.

"They weren't real kids, just looked kid sized. There was so many of them. They all had these huge heads with large black eyes. They terrorized what few customers I had this morning, dragged them out of their cars and took them off to who knows where. They ripped the door off one car to get in at a guy. He managed to drive off though, screaming and yelling at them to keep the hell away from him. When I saw them coming toward the store, I hid. I'm too old to wrestle with young 'uns. Are they still out there?"

Emory shook her head. "No one is out there except for me and…a friend." Emory was loathe to leave him there. "How about you come with us and we'll take you somewhere safe?"

"We'll never be safe now that they're here. You need to go hide too, otherwise they'll take you as well. They weren't anything I've ever seen before. These old eyes have seen a whole lot in my lifetime, but I have never seen anything like what they were. They weren't human, and they didn't look like any critter either." He tightened his hold around the edge of the door he held up. "Thank you for being a good customer and for not stealing the gas. But you need to go now before they decide to come back." He ducked his head back down and began closing the door behind him. "Take some food with you, on the house. Who knows when you'll get a chance to eat again? And don't just take chips. I sell healthy stuff too. Grab you some of the fruit roll-ups by the counter."

Emory watched as Mr. Sudzin disappeared back under the floor and closed the trap door. She heard a bolt slam firmly into place. Hastily, Emory grabbed up cans of soda, a couple of bags of chips, and handfuls of candy bars. Stuffing everything into a paper bag, Emory then dug out some more money. She put it on the counter because no matter whether the world was coming to an end or not, she was not shortchanging Mr. Sudzin for his kindness. Lastly, she scooped up a few packets of the fruit roll-ups as directed. She then fled the store.

"What the hell?" Sofia squealed as she was alarmed by Emory throwing herself into the van and tossing the grocery bag at her. Sofia barely caught it in time.

Emory started up the van and peeled out of the station with a horrendous squealing of the tires. The van lurched onto the road in her haste to get as far away as possible.

"You look like you've seen a ghost." Sofia shifted the bag in her lap and peered inside. "Oh, for God's sake. Please tell me you didn't just rob the gas station. I'm already staring at a long list of offences against you without adding not paying for gas and groceries to it as well."

Sofia's sarcasm was lost on Emory as she put her foot down heavily on the gas and drove.

"Emory, get the fuck out of there before what he saw comes back," Dink said.

"Whoever is in the saucers, they're not just in the sky now," Emory explained to Sofia. "He said they'd taken some of his customers, and not by using the beams this time. They physically pulled them from their car."

"They've landed?" Sofia's grip tightened on the grocery bag.

"He called them children with misshapen heads and black eyes. Dink, I don't want them to be Grays." Emory couldn't help but sound whiney. "Mr. Sudzin saw them. They trashed his place, took his customers, and ripped a car door off its hinges, so they might be the size of kids, but their strength is something else entirely."

"They're obviously not content with dominating the skies; they're invading on the ground too. How many abductees do they need for whatever purpose it is they seem to have for us?" Dink asked rhetorically. "From my news feeds, the rest of the world is being attacked from above. There are reports of the huge mother ships, those big black triangles, hovering all over the major cities."

"Hitting Area 51 seems mighty personal," Emory said, sliding a look in Sofia's direction. "Without me getting your standard 'that's classified' comment, Captain, do you have any ideas as to why that base was not only attacked but wiped from existence?"

Sofia clung to her seat as Emory took a corner a little too fast. "We need to be in one piece to go save your family, Emory. Killing us before we get there isn't going to help them."

"*Do* you have any ideas, Sofia?" Dink said.

After a long moment of silence, Sofia finally replied. "Perhaps it's because that's where it all began. The original saucer was moved there, as were the bodies. Or so rumor has it. You know the history as much as I do. Probably more with your research." She returned Emory's look steadily. "I have never seen anything to corroborate those stories. I just know we have the technology from a craft that crash-landed. For all I know it could have come from Russia as a spy craft and we've taken their technology and made it our own."

"And the bodies that were said to be found?" Dink asked.

"Could have been children, could have been monkeys," Sofia said. At both Emory's and Dink's disbelieving noises she added, "I wasn't there. I didn't see it. I just know about our saucers that were kept at the base."

"And you never asked where they came from originally?" Emory couldn't believe that Sofia had no knowledge of the genesis of the crafts that had been hidden away in the hangars on Area 51.

"You know the old adage, Emory: don't ask, don't tell. My job is on a need to know basis, and what those crafts were I did not need to know." Sofia reached into the grocery bag and rummaged inside. "Tell me this isn't your regular diet."

"What's wrong with it?" Emory said, taking a can from Sofia's hand and managing to pop the ring while still driving.

Sofia puffed out a sound of disgust. "You eat like a child."

Emory shook her head. "You sound like my mother, and I listen to her even less than I listen to my brother."

"That's probably why you're a magnet for trouble," Sofia muttered, opening up a bag of chips and staring back out the window.

"She's got your number, Em," Dink said.

"Switching you back to silent, Big Brother, or as it's technically known, shut the fuck up!" Emory tapped the phone screen and took him off speaker.

"I'm still in your ear," Dink sing-songed.

"And I'm not listening to you either until you tell me something I want to know."

Emory knew this leg of her journey by heart. She just hoped that by the time they reached the quaint little suburb Brad and his family lived in there was still something left to save.

It was time for her to bail her brother out this time.

CHAPTER SEVEN

Winchester was in pandemonium. All of Emory's fears and dreads were realized. Multiple saucers were plainly visible in the predawn light, darting back and forth above the neighborhood where her family lived. They'd just appeared out of nowhere, with no warning and no sound. Until the humming started, and Emory knew that sound all too well.

"Oh God no," she moaned as a large black craft swept over entire blocks and shut out the fading stars. The light it emitted lit everything up in a blinding white intensity. The brightness was too much to look at directly. Even from the short distance Emory still had to cover to reach the suburbs, she knew she wasn't going to get there in time. There were too many silver saucers, hovering in the air like a swarm of angry bees.

"Dink? Tell me what is happening there because I can't drive this thing fast enough. Traffic is starting to choke the roads too. People are awake now; all hell's breaking loose. They're evacuating but have no idea where the fuck to run to."

As she steered them down a block, frantic people were running from their houses. They were tossing everything and anything they could carry into their cars. They were jamming the neighborhood roads as they tried to escape in droves.

Just where the hell *can* they escape to? Emory joined the frenzied drivers and tried to find her brother's street. The other cars were testing her already nonexistent patience. She had to get to her family, and short of ramming through every car in her way, she was stuck in a long line that wasn't going anywhere fast.

To hell with being polite. Emory swung the wheel around and drove up onto the sidewalk, not caring that she was digging huge ruts into the perfectly manicured lawns.

"What are you doing?" Sofia clung to her seat as they bounced over an ornamental pond and her head nearly came in contact with the roof of the van.

"The saucers aren't waiting and neither am I." Emory winced and feared for her tires as she drove straight through fences and walls. She bumped the van back down with a bang onto the road again. She spotted the street she needed and careened around a reversing car to tear down the road toward her brother's home.

"Emory! Saucers are everywhere. For fuck's sake, do not get taken!" Dink was frantic. "There's too many to count. I can't keep track of them all."

There was a strange unearthly whine and then the van was hit. The next thing Emory knew, the vehicle was lifted off its wheels and tossed aside as if it weighed nothing. The near miss by a saucer's laser flung the vehicle into an adjacent driveway. It slammed against a trailer-bound speed boat and mercifully remained upright. Emory heard the sickening sound of Sofia's head hitting the passenger side window as the van's flight stopped so abruptly. Emory's own head whipped back making her cry out in agony. Half blinded by the pain and dizzy from the whiplash she'd no doubt sustained, Emory barely had the chance to gather her wits about her before the beam of light struck the buildings on the other side of the road. Realizing that one of the houses bathed in light was her brother's, Emory screamed.

"NO!"

She struggled to release the seat belt keeping her trapped in her seat.

Sofia grabbed her arm. "You can't go out there!"

"It's going to take them." Emory wrenched her belt free and scrambled for the door handle. Sofia lurched out of her own seat and tightened her grip on Emory.

"Don't be a fucking idiot! What use are you to them if the goddamn saucer takes you too?" She tried to pull Emory back into the van.

Not thinking about anything but getting to her family, Emory wrenched herself out of Sofia's hold. She flung open the van door and fell out, crashing to her knees on the hard concrete driveway. The jolt shocked her but didn't deter her from trying to get up and run toward the light.

She never heard Sofia chase after her over the sound of the screams coming from the residents who were streaming out of their houses, terrified by what they were witnessing. Everyone watched in horror as the light beam literally drew people up and out of their homes.

Emory ran until she was just about to step foot onto her brother's driveway and into the cool white beam. She could feel it, the temperature was immediately different from the dawn's September air. The chill of the beam barely brushed her skin before she was bodily yanked off her feet and flung to the ground out of the light's path. Sofia wrestled her down and rolled her out of the way to safety. Emory fought her, swinging with wild punches and kicking her legs to try to get Sofia off her. They ended up with Sofia holding her firmly in some kind of restraining hold. Emory could feel Sofia beneath her, her arms and legs wrapped around Emory's, stopping her from escaping.

"Stop it! I'm trained to do this. Don't make me hurt you any further."

Sofia's harsh words eventually made Emory stop struggling, and she was left lying on her back, held firmly in Sofia's strong arms, looking up at the sky. Above her, the white beam sparkled as if alight with tiny diamonds. Or with millions of tiny snowflakes, Emory thought, as the cool beam lit a pathway into the sky. The widest end of the light enveloped the houses, blanketing them in the glow. Emory watched helplessly. She was unable to tear her eyes away from the horror unfolding, as limp, lifeless bodies were plucked from the buildings as if the walls and rooftops were not even there. From her vantage point, Emory could see each person pulled up into the beam then sucked out of existence into the saucer.

Emory was able to recognize the tiny body of her youngest niece, Ellie. The five-year-old was still in her nightdress. It flowed around her ankles as she was pulled up in the paralyzing beam. Emory could see the look of terror on Ellie's face, her mouth fixed in a silent scream. Emory never took her eyes off her as Ellie disappeared into the air to be swallowed up by the saucer.

The light cut off abruptly, and the saucer shot up like a bullet shot from a gun. It went so high into the sky to become lost to the fading night.

Emory could hear wailing. It was a mournful, distressing sound of utter loss.

She didn't realize it was coming from her.

The cloth against Sofia's temple came away bloodied. She gingerly dabbed at the ragged cut, catching her breath as it stung like crazy. She had managed to clear out all the glass that had come from the fractured window she'd smacked her head against. She was just thankful she'd been alert enough to get out of the van quickly to stop Emory from her insane plan to stop the invaders from taking her family while they were in the process of *being* taken. Sofia shook her head at herself in the mirror. The sooner she had Emory Hawkes behind bars the better, and the military courts could take care of her.

She wiped her hands off on the towel that hung beside the sink and paused to gather her bearings. She was standing in the bathroom in the home of Brad and Callie Hawkes. The saucers had all gone once the harvesting had taken place. Only then had Sofia felt it safe to loosen Emory out of her hold. Emory had headed straight for the house. She'd used her key to get in and then torn the place apart in case anyone had been left behind. There was no sign of Brad, his wife Callie, or seven-year-old Missy. Sofia had seen the numerous family photos scattered around the home; she'd recognized little Ellie from them and knew that had been the child she and Emory had seen taken right before their eyes.

Sofia shook herself to try to clear her memory of that scene. It would haunt her for the rest of her life. Which wouldn't be long, if the aliens had their say. She really needed to get to a base and regroup with the military.

"Emory?" Sofia wandered from empty bedroom to empty bedroom until she found Emory on her knees beside a little bed. In her hands was a teddy bear dressed in a princess gown. The look of agony on Emory's face made Sofia pause.

"Emory?" She softened her voice and she took a tentative step nearer.

"Ellie won't go anywhere without Elsa bear. I bought it for her last Christmas after she'd made me sit through *Frozen* three times in a row one night I was babysitting." Emory clutched the bear to her. "She's only five years old. She takes this bear everywhere with her, and my brother bitches to me about it because she throws a fit if Elsa gets left behind."

Not letting go of the bear, Emory swept past Sofia and hurried onto the landing to pull down the ladder to get up into the attic. Only then did she entrust Sofia with the bear with a look that warned her not to let it out of her sight. As Emory clambered up the ladder, Sofia stared at the bear. The pretty blue dress was covered in snowflakes and sparkled. The bear was a soft cream with a feminine furry face. Sofia recognized the make; she had friends who took their kids to the store to build their own bears. She held it close for comfort.

"Dink, they're not here."

Sofia listened as Emory tore the attic space apart. She looked at the phone in her hand. "Dink? What can I do?"

"Let her look until she can't anymore."

"I can fucking hear you, Dink." Emory's voice carried down from the attic.

"I know you can, Em. Come out of the attic. You can see they're not there."

"Then *where*?" Emory climbed down the ladder and landed with a tired thump at the bottom. She reached out for the bear.

"Check the garage," Dink said and Emory thundered off down the stairs at his bidding. Sofia followed at her heels.

A very expensive looking sporty red car was parked beside a more staid family vehicle in the spacious garage that housed the children's bicycles and a myriad of tools.

"This is his pride and joy." Emory trailed a finger over the hood of the car then laid her palm down. "It's cold. They never had a chance to escape." She kept her hand on the shiny paint job. "This is the car he throws in my face when I park my VW Bus in his driveway and scandalize the neighbors with its vintage."

"Emory, do you think you can salvage anything from that house? Tools, fuel, food?" Dink asked.

Emory nodded and opened the garage door. She handed the bear to Sofia again who took it silently. She was very aware that Emory was skating on thin mental ice. She'd held on to Emory tightly while she'd cried and mourned for her loss. It had torn at Sofia's heart to witness Emory so broken as the saucers left the area as if they'd never been there. This was the woman who had rescued her from Area 51, the fearless idiot who searched where she ought not to be looking. Listening to her sob her heart out had been distressing and had made Sofia see another side to Emory Hawkes. The sister who risked her own life to save a brother who wasn't the best of brothers to her. The aunt who loved her nieces so much she was prepared to be abducted to get them back. Sofia looked at the teddy bear in her hands.

"We'll get them back," she muttered.

"I hope to God you're right," Dink said over the phone.

Sofia jumped, forgetting that he was listening in at all times. Big Brother at his best, she mused. She heard the familiar sound of the VW Bus being started up and then a teeth jarring screech of metal on metal as Emory pried it free from the boat they had been slammed into.

"Ooh, that's going to leave a mark," Dink said.

Sofia watched Emory reverse the van onto the driveway and backed it into the garage. Emory got out and opened the one undamaged side door. She made a grabby hands gesture toward Sofia, and Sofia obediently handed over the bear. Emory set the bear on the empty seat and fastened a seat belt tightly around it. Sofia realized that Emory's priorities had now dramatically changed.

Emory turned to go back into the house. "Captain, take whatever you think we'll need from anywhere in the house. My brother and his family are all gone so feel free to loot the place. You have my blessing."

Sofia trailed after her, curious as to where Emory was going. "And what are you going to do?"

"I'm going to find my brother's stash of fine wines and whiskey, steal his cigars, and make up a care package for Dink."

"Don't forget my chocolate," Dink reminded her.

Sofia looked down at the phone with a quick smile.

"How did I come to be partnered with the weirdest pair in the whole of Nevada?"

"Technically, I'm not *in* Nevada," Dink said.

"Where are you exactly?" Sofia asked.

Dink just laughed. "Like I'm going to reveal that while you're still threatening my best friend with this whole national security nonsense and the brandishing of handcuffs. And not even the fun fuzzy ones either."

"I'll find out who you are. I can promise you that," Sofia said, her words for Dink but her eyes following Emory who moved around the kitchen picking through the cupboards as if on autopilot.

"You can try. But for now, I need you two to stay alive, so you'd better keep my friend safe, Captain. Otherwise I will be forced to leave my hole to hunt you down and kick your ass."

Sofia heard Emory snort at that, but she continued to mindlessly gather food and stuff it into bags. Sofia wandered off to see if Brad Hawkes had any weapons lying around. She would feel safer with a little more firepower by her side. Her thoughts drifted to the sports car left in the garage. She wondered if Emory would consider swapping that for her beat-up van. She had a feeling Emory wouldn't want to be seen dead driving her brother's car. Pity, because it was much more Sofia's style than the vintage VW she was currently traveling in.

Chapter Eight

The shotgun in the study had been a surprising find for Sofia. It barely looked used and was in pristine condition. She quickly collected all the extra shells for it and picked up the small handgun that was also in the makeshift gun case. She didn't feel too bad that she'd had to bust open the rather flimsy lock to get into them. The vandalism had yielded a nice cache of extra weapons.

She sat at Brad Hawkes's desk and checked the shotgun over before loading it. Eventually, her eyes were drawn to a framed family portrait that sat on the desk. Brad looked every inch the successful businessman in his suit and tie with his picture-perfect wife beside him. Callie was expertly coiffured from top to toe. Obviously no expense had been spared for her to fulfill her role as a trophy wife. The two little girls were the only ones genuinely smiling for the camera. Ellie was sporting a gap-toothed grin while Missy tried to match her mother's poise. Sofia could spot traces of Emory in both little girls. An older lady, stern looking and stiff, had a proprietary hand placed on Brad's shoulder. Sofia hazarded a guess this was their mother. Emory was also in the photo, her unease of being a part of the portrait obvious. Not for the first time, Sofia wondered why she'd fought so hard to reach a family that were so obviously uncaring of her. Then she remembered the bear. It wasn't so much the adults Emory had been desperate to get to; it was her nieces.

Sofia snapped the barrel of the shotgun closed and rested it comfortably in the crook of her arm. It was a nice weapon, obviously one more for show than for use judging by its wear. She could hear faint sounds coming from the garage as Emory worked on the van to make sure it was road worthy after all the damage it had sustained on their wild ride away from the base.

But it was the unexpected noise from outside that drew Sofia's full attention away from everything else. The street where Brad's home lay was now deserted. Everyone had packed up and driven off to anywhere in their fear and flight modes. Those that had stayed had locked and bolted their doors, drawn their curtains, and were probably hunkered down in their basements to wait out this storm. Sofia and Emory had stayed behind to gather what they could before setting off again on their own road trip. Sofia still had to work out where she needed to go next to be of the most use.

Sofia rose to investigate the noise. When she stepped into the kitchen she found Emory already at the door, nervously peering out the window.

"You heard it too?" Emory looked at the gun in Sofia's possession. "Oh, I see you found Brad's big bad bear gun."

"He hunts?" Sofia couldn't quite see him as someone who got his hands dirty.

"No, it's all just for show. Like everything else in his world." Emory slowly opened the door to look out at the backyard. "It's probably just a dog or something that got left behind in the panic." She looked at Sofia for agreement. "Right? I mean, what else could it be?"

Sofia instinctively stepped in front of Emory to shield her and scoured the area. She could see some definite movement in the bushes at the back of the yard. She raised the gun automatically. Her senses were on high alert. Something was definitely there and she wasn't taking any chances.

What came out of the greenery screeching at them like a banshee was no stray animal. It was small, gray-skinned, with the biggest soulless black eyes Sofia had ever seen. Its small lips were drawn back in a snarl, and there was a very strange high-pitched sound coming from it. A noise like an earsplitting electrified static. It grated on the eardrums and set Sofia's teeth on edge. Whatever it was, it was definitely not human. The creature rushed toward them on spindly legs that looked barely strong enough to hold it up. Its hands were shaped into lethal looking claws.

This wasn't going to be a polite first contact.

Sofia never hesitated. She released both barrels of her gun at point-blank range into its scrawny little chest. The impact blew it high into the air to land with a thump on the ground.

"Butterfingers," Emory muttered beside her.

Sofia noted Emory's face was even paler than before. At Sofia's puzzled gaze, Emory smiled weakly.

"I owe Dink chocolate. He was right. There are aliens after all." She let out a breath. "That fucks up years of arguments I have had over their nonexistence." She rubbed at her forehead with a very shaky hand. "I hate being wrong."

Sofia ejected the shotgun shells from the gun and swiftly reloaded it. Then she took a very cautious step forward to check on what she had shot.

"Dink wants to know if it's dead," Emory called after her, not moving from her position at the back door.

Sofia made sure to check the surrounding area just in case this wasn't the only intruder in the yard. She leaned closer to the corpse and reached a hand out.

"Don't touch it!" Emory screamed. "It could be carrying all kinds of space borne diseases that we have no cure for. Don't touch it to see if it's dead."

Sofia gave her an impatient "then how the hell do I find out" glare.

Emory shrugged. "Shoot it again and see if it flinches."

Sofia spared her an incredulous look but didn't touch the body. She nudged it with the barrel of her gun instead. Mercifully, it didn't move. Sofia wasn't wholly surprised considering the damage the shotgun had done to its body. Whatever innards it had were now ripped apart in its chest. It didn't seem to be bleeding blood; instead, the secretions were a strange mix of a gray/black substance. It resembled an oil patch, the shiny black viscous fluid was shot through with a rainbow tinge. Sofia moved to study the creature more closely.

"Hey, Captain?" Emory had stepped out from the house but seemed reluctant to go any farther. "Dink is giving me all kinds of hell for not letting him see the alien. Is it safe for me to come closer?" She took another tentative step and muttered, "Even though I really don't want to get anywhere near that thing."

"I'd have thought you'd have been excited to see a real live alien."

"Nooo," she drew out the word as she finally came to Sofia's side. "I prefer Wookies, or Sullustans, Betazoids or Bajorans. Fantasy over reality is my mantra. These things aren't supposed to exist in my world."

Sofia couldn't resist watching Emory's face as she saw her first real, true alien in the flesh. Emory's movements were slow and deliberate, obviously making sure Dink got to see his fill.

"I don't think it's something I can stick into a Ziploc bag," she said and Sofia frowned at her. "Dink wants me to bring the alien along with us. He wants it." Emory stared silently at the body. "One of the last things I said to my brother was that raging at the stars wasn't any use because the threats I saw didn't come from there. At least, so I believed."

She shook her head at the dead creature before her. "I've never believed in the existence of aliens." She frowned and crouched down to get a closer look. "I guess I could squeeze it in the cooler Brad keeps for his fishing trips with his boss. We've just got to work out how to get it in without touching it. I've read one too many reports of people supposedly touching aliens' skin and were found to have contracted radiation poisoning. Which led to them receiving the diagnosis for an aggressive form of incurable cancer. I'm not taking that chance."

"But you didn't believe their stories."

"I believed they were experimented on by humans for purposes known only to the military and the government."

Sofia tempered her need to roll her eyes at Emory's endless rage against authority. "And now that you've seen this with your own eyes?"

"The jury is still out on certain theories I hold, but I'm more open to new ones now." She took a step back from the dead alien. "But new discovery or not, that thing is *not* coming in my Bus."

❖

The house was oddly still when Sofia wandered into the living room. She found Emory fast asleep on the settee, her mouth open slightly and her soft breathing the only sound in the room. Sofia couldn't help but think she looked less confrontational when she was asleep. Carefully, Sofia removed the glasses from Emory's face and set them on the coffee table. Spy glasses, she thought with a sigh. *Thank God this damn woman never got any farther into the base.* Sofia wanted to check them over to see if she could see where the technology was hidden but knew that Dink was on the other side of that camera and would be watching her every move. She purposely turned the lenses away from the door and tiptoed out of the room to let Emory sleep while she could.

Outside, the early morning had dawned clear and bright. Sunshine, with a good chance of saucers, Sofia mused as she stealthily slipped away from the Hawkes property and jogged toward the next block. She made sure she was well out of sight of prying eyes as she hid out in an abandoned carport. Only then did she remove the radio she had hidden on her belt. She prayed there was still someone out there to answer.

"Damocles Five reporting in. Do you read me? Over."

She waited then repeated her message again. She jumped as the radio spewed forth a burst of loud static. Hastily, she tried to turn it down before it drew any unwanted attention her way.

"Damocles Five, we copy. State your location."

Sofia let out a relieved breath. "Winchester. Hiding out in the suburbs. The sky is clear here. Requesting relocation orders." Sofia chewed at her bottom lip pensively as she waited for where she needed to go to next.

"Damocles Five, request you join your group at Mirror Base East."

Utah. Sofia closed her eyes and let out a relieved breath. That meant the secret base there was still intact; she just had to get to it.

"Roger that. Driving to location. Will inform you of estimated arrival." She paused for a second. "Fifty-one is gone."

The air silence spoke volumes. "Acknowledged."

Sofia's thoughts went to Emory's VW Bus and the peril from above. "Air traffic is a problem. Are you aware of the abductions?"

A longer radio silence made Sofia almost wish she hadn't asked. Then she heard the mic being keyed twice as a nonverbal yes. It was followed by a terse "Out," and the radio fell silent.

Sofia stared at the now silent radio in her hand. "That's all you're going to say? Yes, we know?" She sighed and got back to her feet. "Goddamn priorities. What good is protecting and serving if there are no people left on the fucking planet to protect?" She jammed the radio back under her jacket and hid it again. With watchful eyes both on the ground and to the sky, Sofia made her way back to the Hawkes house to let Emory know they needed to go to Utah. To a top secret, underground base. A mirror base, so called because it was the mirror image of Area 51. This time its secrecy hadn't been compromised by flying craft taking photos from above to expose it. This would be Emory's dream base.

Sofia considered how far she could trust Emory, and Dink by extension, with the knowledge of this hidden fortress. It would be like releasing a chocoholic into a candy store. She certainly couldn't entrust Emory with that kind of information, not given her whistleblower mentality.

Sofia knew what lay deep underground there. Emory's theories had more truth to them than she could have ever imagined. But Sofia still couldn't let that be revealed.

Chapter Nine

E mory?"
Dink's voice woke Emory with a start. She dimly remembered sitting down for a minute to process all she'd seen and had obviously fallen asleep. Woken up by the ever present voice in her ear, Emory was brought crashing back to the here and now.

"Sorry to wake you, but you have to see something. Can you check if the Internet connection is still working in your brother's home? If so, go grab *your* laptop." He deliberately emphasized which laptop he wanted. "It's time you and Sofia see what's going on outside of Nevada. Put me on speakerphone when you're ready. I'll disconnect if I just want to talk between us."

Emory reached for the glasses that aided Dink in seeing through her eyes and put them back on. She had already tried to see if the TV in the house still got a signal, but only static had shown up on the screen. Still half asleep and feeling sluggish, Emory dragged herself off the settee and padded out into the garage.

Sofia was out there, attaching a small trailer to the back of Emory's VW. The trailer held a cooler that now housed the dead body of one alien invader. Emory walked past to reach inside the van and pull out her laptop.

"That's not the one you had at the base," Sofia said, her voice soft but still a touch accusatory.

"That's because this is my personal laptop. If I'd taken this inside the base and booted it up, the vast amount of conspiracy sites and my Bubble Witch games might have given away my non-CIA status, don't you think?"

Sofia didn't look convinced but followed after Emory at her beckoning. Emory led them back into the living room, laid her laptop on the coffee table, and opened it up. She called Dink on the phone and laid it on the table between them.

"Why is there a piece of colored tape covering the camera on your screen?" Sofia asked.

Emory couldn't hold back her disbelieving stare. "You really have to ask? I'd prefer not to have anyone using my camera feed to remote view me."

"Do you really think that someone can do that?" Sofia sat next to Emory.

"Do I really believe certain factions can use their tech savvy to break into computer cameras to watch what the unsuspecting public do in the privacy of their own homes? Hell yes, I do. Do I think it's a huge invasion of privacy hidden under the title of *security* concerns? Hell yes, again. Web cams, gamer cameras, baby cams, security cameras, in the right hands any of those can be used for less than innocent means."

Sofia shook her head at her. "You're paranoid."

"And you're military and therefore know damn well I'm right. You know there's surveillance on every street, that every Google search we make is catalogued, and that through these web cams you can watch us masturbate to the porn we've just illegally downloaded."

Sofia looked disgusted.

"Yeah yeah, like you know that doesn't happen." Emory faked some orgasmic groaning as she booted up her laptop. She enjoyed the displeasure on Sofia's austere face. Emory wondered what noises Sofia would make while in the throes of passion. She amused herself with those images while the laptop came on. The screen lit up with a picture of Emory and her nieces all smiling brightly at the picture taker. She hesitated on the desktop theme, soberly brought back down to earth. "I can't get these girls back if you're hell-bent on arresting me, Sofia."

Sofia's eyes widened at Emory using her name for the first time. "I don't know if there is a way we can even get them back," she admitted.

Emory shook her head harshly. "No, no, no. You don't get to decide that. I'm finding those girls and bringing them home. Then you can arrest me and lock me away if you have to."

"And if you die while executing this crazy plan?"

"Then there'll be an extra cell open for someone else who bucks against the system. I'm going to do everything in my power to get my family back." She opened a file and watched as the cursor moved around without her help.

"What the hell?" Sofia edged closer to watch it too.

"Remote access at work," Emory said as she watched Dink upload a player for her. When it began to play, she was stunned into silence.

"Is this happening now?" Sofia asked as they watched saucers flying over Washington, DC.

"Going live as we speak," Dink said. "Those ships are parked over the Capitol."

"Any news on the president?" Sofia said.

"No sign of him on any broadcasts yet. He's probably deep underground with the other leaders, all hoping that the beams can't stretch that far to yank them up and away." Dink switched feeds. "That's what the networks are showing. But here's what the upload generation is posting online."

The videos changed to clips filmed from cell phones. There was more footage of aliens shown and the terror of the population being targeted from both above and on the ground. Not all the humans were being abducted. One film showed aliens attacking a man. They tackled him to the ground and killed him by clawing him to shreds. The ones filming it all shook and sobbed at what they were witnessing from their hiding place. There was also a compilation of people who were shooting aliens en masse, crowing over their kills and displaying them like trophies.

"We need to get rid of the ships and saucers," Emory said, watching a clip of the saucers appearing from a black triangle craft and speeding off across the sky. She remembered that sight all too well. "The trouble is, we need to do it without bringing them down on our heads." She rubbed her chin as she considered their options. "Nuclear warheads, maybe?"

"Sure," Sofia said. "We could send them up, but the fallout from the blast would come right back down on us and radiate the earth for years to come."

Emory made a face. "Invaded or irradiated. Not exactly a win/win situation there."

"The navy is drawing them out to sea to shoot them down away from land, but there are too many of the smaller crafts for the ships to handle, especially with the saucers firing at them. We did get one though somewhere over Maine." Dink flashed up the still of a huge black triangle shaped ship on the coastline of rocky cliffs. Three quarters of its massive bulk was submerged under the dark, foreboding water. The rest had obliterated the cliffs it was smashed into while the remainder of the surrounding area was flattened beneath its bulk. It resembled a humungous beached whale, lying dead in the water. Its unbelievable size dwarfed the coastline and looked distinctly ominous against the surrounding landscape. Military helicopters were swarming over it, like flies buzzing around a rotting carcass.

Emory couldn't believe what she was seeing. "Did no one stop to think that bringing something down of that size might end up pancaking whatever the fuck it falls on? It's going to take forever to dig that thing out of the cliffs it's embedded itself in. Jeez, obviously our leaders are taking their lead from the movie *Independence Day* and think that going in all gung ho and bringing the big ass ships down on our heads is how it's done."

"It didn't prove to be the smartest of moves either because the saucers retaliated," Dink said. "And the big ship with the big guns? That's now at the bottom of the sea too. Word on the Dark Net is it's been decided not to do that again anytime soon until a better idea comes along."

"But they can be stopped. It just takes immense firepower and a better area to bring them down in," Sofia said. "I need to regroup with my squad to get into the fight and work out a better strategy." She looked around the room. "Though there's a big part of me that wishes we could just stay here for as long as possible and ignore what is going on out there. This isn't a normal call to war."

"So where do we go, Captain Sofia Martinez?" Emory purposely used her full name. "You're in charge, so where do you suggest?" She watched as Sofia considered her words before she answered. "We're on your side, Sofia, odd as that sounds coming from me."

"We head to Utah. The directions are already programmed into your GPS."

Emory's mouth dropped open a fraction. "You were so sure I'd take you there?"

"I can just as easily switch the GPS to your brother's car and make the trip on my own. Actually, I'd prefer that than driving in your Mystery Machine." Sofia gave her a smile that didn't exactly reach her eyes.

"Dink, she just Scooby Doo-ed my Bus."

"Ruh roh," he deadpanned. "I'm just hacking into your GPS and….the coordinates she's put in don't lead us to a known air force base. How curious is that?"

Emory was intrigued. "So just where am I driving you, Miss Daisy?"

Sofia's smile was not much warmer this time. "Just follow the directions and you'll see soon enough. Let's just say if we get there in one piece, it will be all your Christmases come at once."

That really sparked Emory's interest. "Conspiracy road trip!" she sang and waved her hands in the air. "Just let me hit the bathroom and then we can go because who knows when we'll find a bathroom again that hasn't been hit by saucer fire." She ran up the stairs noisily, deliberately sounding like a five-year-old. "Camera and radio silence, Dink," she ordered. He didn't need to see and hear *everything*. She took a slight detour first into Missy's bedroom and lifted a photo off the wall. It was a shot of Emory, Ellie, and Missy eating from a large ice cream sundae bowl together. Emory slipped the photo out of the frame and put it in her pocket.

I'm going to find you all if it's the last thing I do, girls. I promise you.

❖

The small trailer appeared rather incongruous attached to the back of Emory's VW. It looked like a little red Radio Flyer being pulled behind the large black van. The trailer usually housed Brad's fishing equipment, his golf clubs, or sometimes the family's rare camping trip necessities. Today it housed a large cooler stuffed to the brim with ice and the body of one dead alien wrapped in a tarp. Emory had rolled and poked the creature onto it using various garden implements with Dink in her ear berating her not to damage the goods.

Sofia sat in the passenger seat with the shotgun across her knees and a backpack by her feet with the other gun she'd taken and all the ammunition stored inside. Emory drove in silence beside her, her senses all on high alert searching the road ahead and the skies above. She was twitchy, craning her neck to look in every direction for incoming saucers. Her eyes were burning from staring too much into the sky in case saucers just dropped in. There was a box of frosted doughnuts on her center console, and she ate them without even tasting them. She knew she had to eat and drink to refuel her energy, but she was so nervous of what was going to happen next. She'd been watching cars drive past them, many overtaking the van at speed, all in their rush to get somewhere, anywhere but *here*. But every city was a *here*, and the saucers had made their way through and destroyed what they wanted. It had left the people of planet Earth running mindlessly in all directions with nowhere truly safe to hide.

Emory snuck a glance over at Sofia. Her head was back on the headrest and her eyes were closed. Emory didn't begrudge her the chance to sleep. They'd decided to drive in shifts for the Utah Exodus, as Emory had entitled it. Sofia looked so pretty without her military mask on. Her lips were curled in a soft smile. Emory hoped she was having good dreams. She wished they could have met under different circumstance because Sofia was definitely Emory's ideal. Dark hair, those dark eyes, a voice that did curious things to Emory's insides, even when it was being snarky. Unfortunately, as first meetings went, having Sofia's accusations of her being a risk to National Security were not the sweet nothings Emory would have preferred to hear coming from Sofia's lips.

"Eyes on the road, Em."

Emory sighed at Dink's laconic voice in her ear. *And then there's the ever present third wheel.*

The sun was shining brightly, and Emory flipped down the visor so that it shaded some of Sofia's face from the glaring light shining through the windshield. In the daylight, the full horror of what had happened the previous night was impossible to ignore. Not all the towns and cities had been left untouched. Blast sites were scattered along the landscape as Emory drove through ruined streets. Terrified people were huddled in what was left of the buildings that remained somehow standing. Above, military aircraft flew, but Emory guessed they were just surveying the damage to report it back in. Against the immense might of the black crafts and the firepower of the silver saucers, the aircraft piloted by humans were proving no match.

"Dink?" Emory spoke quietly so as not to disturb Sofia. "Are you still getting reports from the TV?"

"They're patchy. Some of the stations have been hit in the fighting. I've been trying to get a link to Europe. From what I see and hear, there's a lot more aliens on the ground there."

"Are they abducting from there too?"

"That's a worldwide occurrence. Seems to be something very high on their agenda to gather up as many humans as possible. But no word yet on where they are taking them."

"I want to know if the Space Station saw this invasion coming," Emory said. "It's not like you could have missed that many ships doing a flyby past the Station's window on the world."

"No official word from NASA yet, but my sources tell me there was nothing on the radar, and nothing was seen by the astronomers I've contacted online."

Emory considered this. She knew Dink had numerous spies in many interesting places; that's how they got so much of their information. "The fact we still have satellites letting news reports be broadcast means that they haven't been destroyed yet. We have communications. I can still phone you. All that is above our heads, floating above the planet. If they didn't come from outer space to knock out our communications satellites on the way in then that can only mean…" Emory balked at the inference she was making.

"They were already here," Dink said.

Emory felt the cold shiver run through her body at that obvious conclusion. It shook her to the core.

Emory's gaze shifted to the rear of the vehicle where she knew the trailer was. "Dink, there's a fucking alien life form in my brother's 'catch of the day' cooler."

Dink chuckled. "Thanks to Sofia being an excellent markswoman. I can't help but wish she'd used a smaller caliber though. That's a big ass hole in his belly. I'd have preferred him a little less battle worn."

"Do you really think she's going to let me just drive off with this specimen so I can bring it to you so you can mount it on a wall? For that matter, do you think she's honestly going to let *me* go free for breaking and entering Area 51?"

"Technically speaking, the saucers did the breaking and entering. You merely took advantage of the opportunity that arose from that situation."

"Remind me to have you speak up for me in court. My brother is currently unavailable to speak as my counsel."

"We'll get your family back, Emory. I'd do my damnedest to get those girls back for you."

"I hope so because they are the only members of family I have that give a damn about me." Emory looked around her. "Are we still broadcasting a picture clearly from the van's rooftop, Dink?"

"Amazingly so considering how you drive. The mounted camera is still attached, even after the van was nearly shot off its wheels by an alien laser beam."

"I'll be sure to write the manufacturer a glowing review."

Emory's attention returned to the road. She couldn't believe the devastation spread out for miles. The crafts had obviously blasted through most of the surrounding area and had just laid waste to it. The once vibrant towns were now reduced to rubble, leaving the landscape flattened and desolate.

"Any clue what planet Earth is doing to fight back before they destroy everything?" Emory scoured the skies again; they were empty of either human or alien ships.

"There's been some chatter about how useless our planes are against the speed of the saucers. Conventional weapons aren't cutting it against their technical might."

"You and I both know there are unconventional weapons that could be employed." Emory risked a glance in Sofia's direction, but she was still sleeping soundly. "What we need are the saucers that Area 51 had tucked away. At least that would have given us a fighting chance."

"I wish we could have seen one," Dink said. "And I wish you'd have been able to see more at the base before you had to rush back out."

"I'm just glad you gave us fair warning before they blew the base off the map. Thank you for that."

"You're welcome. I will always have your back. Mainly because you owe me candy."

Emory grinned. She made sure to look at herself in the rearview mirror so Dink could see it. "I know, Dink. Believe me, that little gray corpse riding behind my Bus is a big reminder of my debt to you."

CHAPTER TEN

Sofia woke up slowly and squinted at the sunlight that poured through the windshield. She sat up, winced, and then carefully stretched her spine. She sighed as she felt something pop back into place.

"Getting too old for falling asleep in the front seat, eh?" Emory said from beside her.

Sofia shot her a dirty look. "I am not too old for anything." She rested her hand on the shotgun and Emory laughed.

"Hey, no need to shoot the driver. I was just making conversation now that you're not snoring and drooling on your uniform."

Unconsciously, Sofia's free hand went to the corners of her mouth. Her face was drool free and dry. "You are such an ass. And for your information I do not snore."

"Then that alien lagging behind us must be emitting a loud hum because I could have sworn I heard something." Emory grinned at her. "So how old *are* you?"

Sofia frowned at the meaningless conversation Emory was trying to engage her in. "Why does my age matter to you?"

"Just shooting the breeze with you. You've been out like a light for a few hours. All I've had was Dink to talk to, and even he needs to sleep sometime. And I've had to watch out for saucers. And let's not forget I've also had to keep an eye on the road for the damn fools driving like maniacs who are more likely to die in an accident due to their fleeing than they are at standing a chance of being abducted."

"How old do you think I am?" Sofia asked, deliberately giving her voice a more sensual tone.

Emory chuckled at her. "Oh no, I'm not playing that game. That way leads on a dangerous road to tread. I haven't been with a great many women in my life, but I have learned that you *never* guesstimate a woman's age. It's a surefire way to get left at the restaurant with the bill and no kiss good night."

So that answers that speculation, Sofia thought. She'd had a feeling Emory was gay. If for no other reason than the looks she shot Sofia's way when she thought she wasn't looking. Subtlety didn't seem to be a trait Emory had mastered. *Trapped in a VW Bus with a lesbian conspiracy theorist, who is a known military threat with her whistle blowing attitude, all in the midst of an alien invasion. Fate is surely laughing down on me.*

"I'm thirty-four," Emory said. "An age which my brother says means I should be settling down in a real job, getting a cat or two....or three, and driving some poor woman mad with my theorizing. That's his view of my future. It's not exactly mine."

"I'm forty," Sofia said and saw Emory's eyes widen a fraction.

"Wow, you don't look that old." Emory grimaced as she no doubt realized too late how bad that sounded. "I mean, you don't look your age. Not that forty is old...well, it's older than me. Six years older than me in fact."

Oddly amused by Emory's ramblings, Sofia ignored her and reached into the bag behind her seat for something to eat. She pulled out one of the sandwiches that Emory had grabbed from the gas station hours before and checked to see if it was still edible.

"You'd have left me at the restaurant staring at the bill by now, wouldn't you?" Emory sighed, finally shutting up.

"My dear, I wouldn't have gone out with you in the first place." Sofia took a big bite from the sandwich and savored the taste of plentiful mayonnaise slathered on tuna. Not exactly the breakfast she was used to, but it filled her empty belly.

"Not even if I was the last woman on earth? Which, judging by the way things are going, might be bordering on truth soon."

"Not even then." Sofia was delighted to catch Emory's nonplussed face. "I'm a captain from a top secret base. You broke into said base and misappropriated a military laptop." Sofia raised a hand to halt any of Emory's arguments on that accusation. "I don't see us being star-crossed lovers any time soon, do you?"

"Han Solo was a pirate and he ended up marrying a princess," Emory said.

"You're using Star Wars characters for your example of true love?" Emory's face lit up. "You're familiar with Star Wars? Of course you are. You're old enough to have seen them during their original releases."

Sofia's teeth clashed together as she bit harder into her sandwich than she meant to. Fuming, she cut an evil eye at Emory and found her silently laughing at her, her eyes alight with mischief. Sofia glared at her but realized something. She was being *teased*. It wasn't something that she often had cause to recognize at work, and none of her friends would ever do it. But Emory obviously felt she could.

"Has anyone ever told you you're beautiful when you're angry, Major?"

"That's Captain," Sofia bit out, "as you're well aware."

Emory nodded. "Yeah, but I think the title Major suits you more because you're going to be a *major* pain in my ass."

Sofia grinned at her evilly. "Oh, you have no idea, *Agent*. But, by all means, keep poking the bear and see how long it takes before it bites you."

Emory's smile grew wide. "I'm glad I saved you, Sofia. You know, from that top secret base I was in illegally but mercifully saved you from certain death there anyway? I can see it now. You and I are going to have so much fun." Emory took a hand off the steering wheel and gestured to the food bags. "Pass me something sugar laden, Major, and let's talk about what is so important in Utah for us both. And skip the 'no comment' route. We're way past that nonsense now, wouldn't you agree?"

Sofia didn't. Instead she deliberately took another bite from her sandwich to stall the conversation. Alien invasion or not, she knew her position.

No handsome blonde with a devastating grin was going to sway her from her duty while the world was under attack. Especially one who was way too clever at finding out secrets that should never be uncovered.

❖

Sprawled out on the long seat in the back of her van, Emory jerked awake from a deep but restless sleep. She lay paralyzed, the nightmare she'd experienced still clutching her tight in its hold. She willed her heart to calm its furious beat until she could once again hear something other than its frantic pounding in her ears. The rhythmic sound of the tires on the road almost lulled her back into slumber. It was only the dawning realization that what she'd seen in her dreams hadn't been the conjuring's of a tired mind. Her gaze fell on the teddy bear strapped into the seat opposite her and she remembered. She bit back the moan that clawed to escape her chest as the horror engulfed her all over again.

Ellie was gone. It hadn't been a dream.

Emory could only guess that the rest of her family had been taken as she had. All except for her mother who had been vacationing somewhere in Florida. Emory had a feeling not even alien invaders would touch that old woman with her disapproving mindset. They'd soon beam her back to Earth and the hell off their ship. Her mother could take care of herself, there was little love lost between them, but Emory wanted her nieces back safe and sound. She didn't have a clue where to start or even what to do. Dispirited by feeling she failed before she could even start, she laid her head back down on the cushion she'd been sleeping on and curled up into a little ball of misery. She hoped that if she held herself tight enough she wouldn't fall apart.

Blindly, Emory watched the scenery go by the window. She guessed it was early evening, but she had no idea how long she'd slept. They had obviously reached Salt Lake City in that time.

Tall buildings obscured her view, the endless row upon row of windows and metal that usually housed people in their mundane jobs. Emory had a feeling no one was manning those desks today. The dark buildings cast shadows into the van's interior and made it far cooler than Emory liked. She shivered and then her stomach let out a loud grumbling noise that drew her from her musings.

"I guess your belly is awake even if you're not," Sofia said from the driver's seat.

"How long was I asleep?" Emory forced herself to sit upright and brushed her hair back off her face.

"About three hours. I wasn't expecting you to stir just yet. You seemed out for the count."

Emory rubbed at her face wearily. "I had a nightmare that woke me. I dreamed my nieces had been taken up into a large flying saucer. Then I woke up remembering it was true. I don't know which is worse, seeing it happen in reality or having to relive it when I close my eyes." Emory stared at her hands. She wasn't surprised to see them shaking. She barely had time to acknowledge that before she felt something else. Weird vibrations that made her shake all the more.

She shouted out her warning at the exact same time Dink's came over the cell phone Sofia had resting near her.

"Incoming!" Dink screamed.

In the distance, a huge black triangle craft descended from the clouds. Majestically, it lowered itself to rest above the buildings, where it waited, menacingly.

Emory scrambled over the seats to join Sofia in the front. They both peered up between the surrounding buildings that hid so much of the sky.

An explosion ripped through the air. Emory braced herself for the blast. A large building, two blocks ahead of them, blew apart. Huge chunks of debris were blown from the point of impact and smashed to the ground. The rubble landed directly in the path of the busy traffic in the streets. Cars and buses, full to the brim with people trying to evacuate, were hit with devastating results. Cars were crushed beyond recognition and people on the sidewalks were obliterated. It all happened in the blink of an eye, then everything cascaded into chaos.

Sofia managed to keep the van going while swerving around the cars in front of them. All had either slammed on their brakes or were trying to turn around to get away. She swore loudly as one car nearly took out the front of the van in its driver's desperation to escape. Sofia deliberately used the bulk of the van to nudge past other vehicles. She gave Emory an apologetic look.

Emory shrugged. "What's a little chipped paint in an apocalypse?"

The van inadvertently mounted the sidewalk as another car sideswiped them as the inevitable domino effect took place. Car after car slammed into the one in front, and the pileup that resulted began to release smoke into the air.

"We're going to get trapped," Emory said as another explosion deafened them with how much closer it was. The resulting damage from that hit smashed another building to smithereens and blocked the road ahead completely with the falling debris.

Sofia searched for what little escape they had available. She ruthlessly pushed another car out of their way so they could drive into an alley between two separate buildings. She smashed through a wrought iron gate in her bid to get them off the road. The trouble was, it wasn't a roadway, but a very narrow alley that was littered with garbage cans and more gates that Sofia plowed through without ever slowing down. Suddenly, she slammed on the brakes. Emory grabbed for the console in front of her even though she was belted in.

"What's wrong?"

"I can't tell if this alley is narrowing at that end."

Emory squinted to try to see what Sofia meant. The buildings looked like they were built at an angle; the alley they were in seemed to be tapering to a point. They'd never get the van out.

"Fuck, looks like you're going to have to reverse all the damn way back," Emory grumbled. "And there's nowhere to go back there." She took off her seat belt and got out of the van. "Let me see if there's room for us to squeeze out down there before you drive us any farther."

Emory set off to check it out. She heard the other van door close and Sofia was soon beside her.

"We shouldn't…" Sofia began, but her words tapered off as the alleyway was plunged into darkness. Total darkness.

Sofia grabbed onto her arm as they both looked up to see what had blocked out the already meager light that managed to shine between the two buildings.

Oh, crap.

Emory was able to make out every detail on the black triangle's undercarriage. There were no visible panels, no nuts or bolts keeping the ship intact. The whole craft looked like it was made from one seamless piece of material. And just what kind of material that was Emory couldn't even begin to imagine. This close under it, the craft shimmered like a fluid, as shiny as an oil slick. Nothing reflected on it, for all the shine of its skin, nothing it hovered above was reflected back on its sheen.

"Whoa." Dink's voice was hushed in Emory's ear. "Em, if you can bring me one of those babies back too I'd love you forever."

"I'll need a bigger trailer," Emory whispered, terrified that the ship above would hear her. Her whole body trembled from the vibrating hum that the black triangle emitted. She couldn't move; she was mesmerized by the alien ship that was very likely going to kill her. Abduct her, experiment on her, *then* kill her. She was beginning to wish she'd never woken up.

Sofia's crippling grip on Emory's arm broke her from her paralysis. "Have you ever seen one of those before?" Emory asked her, her mind always full of questions.

"We can't just stand here and stare. Let's get back to the van and go."

Emory didn't budge even when Sofia tugged at her roughly. "Have you?" she asked again.

Sofia huffed out a grumble. "I've heard about them just like you have, but I have never seen one this close."

"So you guys haven't got your own versions of *these* hidden away in a base somewhere?"

"Unfortunately not."

Emory couldn't mistake the disappointment in Sofia's tone. "Did you know about these being here?"

"Emory, this isn't the time or place for you to pull a Fox Mulder! We need to go!" Sofia spun Emory around and pulled her back toward the van.

They never had a chance to reach it.

CHAPTER ELEVEN

A n explosion hit one of the nearby buildings. It was way too close to where they were sandwiched in the alley. The power of the blast, even from a distance, blew Emory clear off her feet as it exploded through the narrow alley opening. She landed ungainly, flat on her back in a pile of garbage bags situated halfway down the alley. Emory rolled off and landed with a thud on the ground. Her arm twisted under her and made her cry out in pain. She could feel the steady rain of tiny pieces of rubble and glass pelting her from above. She covered her head with her hood quickly to stop herself from being hurt more. Whatever weapon had hit this time had pulverized the building which, in turn, had damaged surrounding structures. Emory was still being showered by the debris. In her haste to get out of there, she barely registered when a larger piece of brick struck her head and knocked her down. The resulting ringing in her ears and the blurring of her eyes let her know that it had been more than a glancing blow. Emory blinked repeatedly, desperately trying to clear her vision. The black craft had moved on and a weak light, dust-laden and smoky, gave her some sight back in the alley. She had a brief moment of panic checking that she still had her glasses on and that they were undamaged. Then she rummaged in her pocket to make sure her phone wasn't smashed. She let out a sigh of relief. She couldn't lose Dink too.

"I can see, Emory, but I can't see you. Are you okay?" Dink's frantic voice echoed through her head. At least she hadn't lost the earpiece either after being thrown halfway down the alley.

"I think so. Just got my bell rung by something." Emory coughed and hacked at the dust, trying to yell over the din as another explosion rang out and the building to her left seemed to shudder and shake. She realized they were not safe anywhere. Emory scrambled to her feet. She rocked as if drunk and tried to get her bearings in the heavy blanket of dust. She needed to find Sofia.

"Sofia? Sofia!"

She finally spotted her, lying curled up and motionless against a wall. Emory rushed over to her just as another earth-shattering explosion hit. The blast made Emory throw herself over Sofia's smaller body to try to protect her as best she could. Eventually, she realized that explosion had happened much farther away from where they were trapped. However, the violent aftershocks from it made the ground quiver beneath her. Carefully, Emory eased back to see if Sofia was okay. Her face was bloodied, and there was a deep cut on her cheek that bled through the thin layer of dust that seemed to cover everything now. Emory hadn't even realized she was shedding layers of dust every time she moved. There was then one more boom that sounded too close for comfort.

"That last explosion was a tank shell," Sofia said, barely shifting in Emory's hold. "We're fighting back with our own weapons. Someone's brought in the big guns."

Emory flinched at every explosion and sound of buildings being blown apart that thundered loudly in the distance. Now it was joined by the sound of big military guns shooting back. She never once released Sofia from her arms as she bent over her, shielding her from whatever was going to happen next. She could feel the warmth of Sofia's breath tickling her skin. The destruction courtesy of the black craft seemed to be moving farther away, but Emory was loathe to leave Sofia uncovered. Only when noise filtered in from the street behind them did Emory realize that the alien threat had shifted away from where they were. She finally felt like she could breathe again. Gingerly, and only when she was certain Sofia hadn't broken anything, Emory shifted from her cramped position. She moved to cradle Sofia in her arms. The all too quiet, almost unresponsive reactions she was seeing from Sofia were unnerving her.

The steady noise of gunfire, a uniquely human sound, erupted around them again. Reinforcements had arrived. It was so loud Emory could no longer hear Dink in her ear as he tried to tell her what he was seeing on what few street cameras were still functioning amid the chaos. The military was riding in on tanks and huge vehicles, firing on the silver saucers that Emory hadn't even realized were also in on the attack.

Emory noted that Sofia barely flinched at the sounds of the battle raging. She wondered what kind of service Sofia had seen to be almost immune to the constant noise and the screaming. Emory wished the screaming would stop most of all. She was thankful to be trapped in the alleyway and not on the street where the people were out in the open and exposed. She dreaded to think what she would see back there. The sounds of terror in between the gunfire made Emory all the more frightened for them all. She held Sofia tighter. She was so lost in her own head that she started when a hand brushed at her face, wiping away the blood that was running down along her jawline.

Sofia spoke against Emory's ear causing her to shiver. "I could probably sit up now," she said. "I just had the wind knocked out of me hitting the wall."

"I'm not holding onto you for *you*, I'm holding onto you for *me*," Emory said, incredibly aware she wasn't lying either. She'd been terrified that something had happened to Sofia, and she didn't know what she would have done if she'd found her dead instead of just dazed. Unable to help herself, Emory stared down at Sofia. Even covered in dust, Sofia was beautiful, and the fire in her eyes was still plainly visible through the pain she obviously felt. True to her nature, Emory didn't think; she acted. She gently wiped off a smear of dust from Sofia's bottom lip and lowered her head to kiss her. It was a soft kiss, a gentle pressing of their lips together. In that one sweet kiss was wrapped a benediction, an honest expression of relief, and for Emory, a recognition that Sofia was someone special to her, for all their differences in a very crazy world.

Sofia looked suitably surprised when Emory pulled back.

"What was that for?" Sofia asked huskily.

"I couldn't stand the thought of me dying here in this alley and never having felt your lips on mine."

The corners of Sofia's eyes crinkled as she smiled. "You really are a scoundrel."

Emory smiled in recognition of the term. "You like me because I'm a scoundrel." She wondered how much further Sofia would take them in reciting the love scene from *The Empire Strikes Back.*

"You haven't forgotten I still have to arrest you, right?"

Oh, not much further at all, Emory lamented, but enjoyed hearing the authoritative tenor back in Sofia's voice. "Yeah, I know. Just add my kissing you to my list of charges. At least this way I'll have something wonderful to remember when I'm in my cell trying to dig my way out with a spork."

Sofia laughed but hissed as the movement pained her. Emory hugged her closer.

"Keep still, Major, please."

"It's Captain."

"You know I don't do well with authority, so you might as well get used to it." Emory looked around them. The alley was unrecognizable from what they'd first entered. Emory was unsure whether to be claustrophobic from the enclosed space or thankful for its shelter.

"Captain Martinez?"

Emory's heart nearly shot out of her chest in fright. A soldier, gun drawn, appeared almost over her shoulder to peer down at Sofia. Sofia laughed then winced again.

"You confound me. You run into danger trying to get abducted, but you scream like a little girl at the cavalry arriving."

Emory was silent, still shaking, as she watched the soldier holster his gun and kneel beside Sofia.

"What are you doing this far north, Captain?" he asked, reaching to help Sofia to her feet.

Emory immediately missed the warmth of Sofia's body from her own.

"Let's get you both somewhere safe." He slung an arm around Sofia's waist.

Is there such a place? Emory fell into step behind them, her eyes constantly darting to the sky above.

❖

The vehicles blocking the alleyway were moved aside with little preamble by the military so that Emory could reverse the van back out and onto the road. Sofia was bundled off into a military truck, and Emory was given instructions to take a place in the convoy. Sofia didn't seem all too happy to leave Emory to her own devices, especially as Emory had introduced herself as CIA Agent Ellen Mays. She'd flashed her false credentials too and hadn't missed the furious scowl Sofia had directed at her. Emory had dared her to reveal her true identity. Instead, Sofia had glared at her, threatening silent retribution, then had been escorted to the medical truck.

Emory's head wound had been given more than just a cursory glance, but she'd argued she was more than capable to drive her own vehicle. The soldiers had given her some strange looks about the VW Bus, but Emory had muttered something about ending up with an undercover car and they'd just shrugged it off with comments under their breath about how odd the CIA was.

Emory was relieved to see how many huge armaments this force had brought with them to chase away the saucers. Large anti-aircraft guns were mounted on the back of trucks, soldiers carried handheld rocket launchers, and there were some weapons Emory had never seen before. And then there were the tanks. Huge behemoths with their turrets aimed at the sky.

The saucers had vanished, leaving behind them a swath of destruction through the buildings. Now was the time for the military to make a strategic retreat back to base to fill up on more ammunition before heading out again. Emory realized that having the tanks roll in meant that this time the saucers didn't get a chance to land or to start their abductions.

"Emory, this Euphoria they're taking you to isn't a listed base on any of my records," Dink said in her ear. "I also have a feeling you are going to have to go in blind because Sofia knows about me and the fact I've got you kitted out so I can see all."

"If I have to hand over the phone I will. I'm not taking chances in there arguing and ending up behind bars because I piss off people other than Sofia. If I can keep it all though, for God's sake, make sure you keep an eye on where I am in case I disappear."

"I'll do my best. If it helps I have gotten some new keys for padlocked doors that usually keep me out on the net. That laptop you got me into is opening up some new areas for me to investigate. I'm using it to check out Euphoria."

"Sofia isn't going to let it drop about the laptop. She knows it's not mine."

"You can give it back to her. I've gotten off all that I need thanks to you patching me in before she found you. Just get the USB off it without her seeing and she can have it back and it will look untouched. Thanks to it I have passwords for top secret clearances and enough files to peruse for a long time. Also, its owner, Lt. Commander Garner, very kindly revealed a new word for me to look into." He paused dramatically. "Dionysius. Sound familiar?"

Emory's memory began sparking. "That sounds a lot like the name our source was getting ready to furnish us with before the site got shut down and prosecution was threatened."

"That's what I thought, so I'll check into this a bit more now that I have more than my foot in the door."

"Talking of being let in, there's a part of me worried we'll reach this base and they won't let me through the door for some reason."

"Like the fact you're not who your credentials purport you to be?"

"Sofia can verify that. Man, it's hard sneaking around the military when there's so many of them to get past."

"I can't see them leaving you outside in the van while they all traipse inside. For one thing, Sofia is going to want to keep you where she can see you." Dink chuckled. "Speaking of which, Casanova…"

Emory had wondered how long it would take for Dink to mention her kissing Sofia. She knew all too well he had had a front row seat—literally, thanks to the glasses—to what she had done.

"It was sooooo romantic," he warbled. "And seeing it all up close and personal that I could almost taste the captain's lipstick myself was almost a religious experience."

"Shut the fuck up," Emory said, not enjoying having her chain yanked over something that had felt so right. "I thought we were going

to die. And can you honestly blame me? She's all kinds of beautiful."
Emory couldn't stop the sigh that escaped her. "But she's so far out of my league she might as well be in orbit."

"Along with the little matter of her being military and working at the base you were trying to investigate."

"Montagues and Capulets, Dink." She looked over the landscape they were driving in. "I have no idea where the hell I am."

"Off the grid as of five minutes ago. So far off the grid you're no longer on Google maps."

"Are you sure you've never come across Euphoria base, Dink? I've looked into so many, but this name doesn't ring a bell with me."

"Same here, but for every Edwards Air Force base that gets found out, there has to be some that remain secret. This is a golden opportunity. I really want this to be more than just a military base."

"I just want it to have the weapons to bring those goddamn saucers down." Emory followed the truck ahead of her, mindful not to stray out of line.

CHAPTER TWELVE

Euphoria was a nondescript air force base that didn't exactly scream out it was anything special. Emory was seriously disappointed as they drove into its compound. Before she could even get her bearings, Emory was directed to the medical center to have her head wound looked over a little more closely. She could hear Sofia being dealt with behind the curtain drawn between them. Emory sat still and relatively silent except for sharp intakes of breath when the prodding hurt. The laceration on her scalp was cleansed but left uncovered, and she was dismissed with some pills for the headache that was lurking behind her eyes.

Much to her delight, Emory was handed a clean pair of fatigues to change into and was left alone to get undressed. She was happy enough to get out of her debris-covered clothing and into something clean. Especially fatigues that would serve to make her look like everyone else on the base. She quickly washed her face in the small sink and eyed herself in the mirror, knowing Dink could see her as she deliberately smoothed the collar down on her jacket. She listened as Sofia answered something the doctor had asked her. Spying an opportunity, Emory drew back the curtain as soundlessly as possible and checked that no one was in the room except for those behind her. The coast was clear so Emory snuck out as quietly as possible.

"I need you to get out of this building and head across the base to the third hangar," Dink said urgently after being silent for so long.

"How so specific?" Emory muttered under her breath as she nodded at the soldiers that roamed the base.

"Because the roof cam of the van is showing me the hangars and there's a lot of to-ing and fro-ing going on in that specific hangar."

Emory frowned. "So you think there's something in there? It could just be a mess hall."

"You're on a base that isn't in the public domain of known bases. It's got an air of secrecy that is making my Spidey senses tingle. And there's a whole load of military gathered there too, with the big guns. I'm not seeing people coming out of there with bags of chips, Em. Something is happening in that hangar."

"I'm a die-hard conspiracy nut, Dink, and even that's a stretch for me."

"Yes, and you didn't believe in aliens either, and now you're down three candy bars that you still have to furnish me with. Anyway, from what I saw as you drove in and then very kindly stood to give me a three hundred and sixty degree angle of the area, I have made some calculations."

"I love it when you break out your nerd genes."

"I believe the building you need to concentrate on is Hangar Three. If I'm wrong then it's up to you to just look around and not get caught."

Emory spotted a young officer. "I'd better get a decent cover story in case a certain captain realizes I'm AWOL." She took out her credentials and held them up to him. She read his name tag. "Airman Rowe, can you direct me to a private line, please? Aliens or not, if I don't check in with my superiors I'm going to be begging for little green men to abduct me."

The airman gave her an all too understanding look and led her to an office.

"Thank you." Emory stepped inside and walked toward the desk.

"Can't promise you a clear signal," he said.

"That's all right, I can at least try. Can you close the door so I don't get disturbed? Even with what's happening out there some things are still classified."

He nodded and closed the door behind him. Emory could see his shadow move a little to the left of the door as he guarded it against intrusions. She flipped the lock and then hastened over to the window.

"This way, if Sofia comes after me I'm supposedly locked in here."

"She's going to kick your ass."

"Then let's hope my field trip here is worth the wrath I'm going to have rained down upon me by the little Latina."

"You like her though."

Emory eased the window open enough to make an exit. She checked quickly that no one was in sight.

"Yes, I do. But that's not going to stop me from investigating a base that has an exclusion zone above it. Or carries such badass weaponry that can chase flying saucers off."

"Just don't get caught," Dink said. "I can't exactly come and break you out from a base that doesn't exist."

"Sneaky as a ninja," Emory promised as she slid out the window without a sound. "God, it's like being sixteen all over again and sneaking out to go make out with Dana Benson." She closed the window behind her and scanned the area.

"Now walk across that base as if you own it, soldier," Dink said.

Emory tugged her fatigues down and set off determinedly. She hoped that Sofia was being delayed enough to not wonder what Emory was getting up to. Emory knew she was living on borrowed time where the captain was concerned.

She got to the hangar without being stopped and found a very out of place set of elevator doors.

"Ooh, lookie what we have here." Emory quickly looked around her and then hastened toward the doors. There was no button to press to call the elevators. Instead there was a swipe box.

"Damn it." Emory's mood plummeted. Then she brightened. *Please let this work, please let this work.* She opened a pocket on her fatigues and pulled out Jessica Sanders's swipe card she'd found. She ran her fingers over the smooth plastic, took a deep breath, and with a decisive swipe, ran it through the machine.

The elevator dinged and the doors opened. Emory stepped inside and stared at the long list of floors. Just numbers, no descriptions.

She tugged her sleeve over her hand so she wouldn't touch the button directly. She didn't need to leave fingerprints behind unnecessarily. The elevator began to descend. Emory couldn't help but feel that with that one press she had sealed her fate.

"Where are all the secrets hiding at Euphoria base?" Dink asked in an announcer's voice. Emory played along.

"I'll take Level Forty for one hundred, Alex."

❖

Sofia was incensed. She'd already chewed out the medical staff and was now storming the corridors in search of Emory Hawkes. Or more erroneously, one Agent Ellen Mays as everyone here recognized her as. She couldn't believe Emory had walked out of the medical center and disappeared.

"I'm going to kill her," she growled under her breath. She barely registered the man who snapped to attention as she passed him. Sofia stopped abruptly and turned around.

"Why aren't you at the briefing, Airman?"

Airman Rowe gestured back toward the office. "I'm waiting to clear the room. There's a CIA agent in there making a call." He frowned a little. "I think she's calling every active agent going because she's been in there a very long time."

Sofia tried to open the door. It didn't budge.

"She said she needed privacy for classified talks." He shrugged as if that explained it all. "CIA."

"I bet she did," Sofia fumed. "Open this door now."

"I don't have the key, ma'am."

"Then kick the damn thing in," Sofia ordered and stood back as he hurried to do as she requested.

The room was empty.

"But I haven't moved from out here." Airman Rowe entered the room and looked around.

Sofia went directly to the window and noticed that it wasn't locked down. "Direct me to the security tower."

Big Brother indeed had eyes everywhere, including every inch of a secret base that had need-to-know things to hide from far too inquisitive investigative journalists whose theories were too close to the truth.

Sofia's anger fueled her footsteps. She was berating herself for thinking Emory wouldn't abuse the freedom Sofia had allowed her by not chaining her to her side.

I should have smashed those damned glasses of hers when I had the chance.

"Ma'am? Captain? Is there a problem?" Airman Rowe was favoring her with a very apprehensive eye.

"Fucking CIA," she said.

He smiled. "Understood, ma'am, loud and clear."

CHAPTER THIRTEEN

The journey down in the elevator was broken up by people stepping on and off at various floors. It probably would have looked like any other day in the building if not for the grim looks of strain and distress on everyone's faces. Emory couldn't fault that. She knew that even being this far underground was no deterrent for the power the aliens had. She hoped the weapons the military had brought into play earlier were available here. She had no desire to have escaped Area 51's destruction only to die in an undisclosed base.

There were forty levels listed, but the elevator only went as far as floor thirty-seven. The last three could only be accessed by stairs and a card swipe. Emory wished Jessica Sanders hadn't been abducted, but she was grateful she had left her card behind so that Emory could have use of it. She had it hanging round her neck on its lanyard, forever grateful it wasn't the sort that required a photo ID.

Emory quickly pinpointed where the stairwell she needed was as she followed everyone else off the elevator. She walked past a vast array of laboratories. The lab rat in front of her was carrying a stack of files tucked under his arm, so Emory, making sure no one was behind her to catch her, swiped a few out. She figured he'd never miss them until they were needed, and by then she would be well out of range. She halted by a window and pretended to be reading through the file, all the time keeping her head up so that her glasses caught everything she was seeing. She hoped Dink was getting it all. She tried desperately to spot something she could use. Anything that she could have as a leverage toward getting her family back. She had no idea what but just knew she had to do something more than hide out and hope the aliens would eventually leave. There had to be something, *anything*, in the base that she could use to her advantage. *And if I have to search every damn saucer I will until I find those girls.*

She flipped through the file she was using as cover as if it would tell her something. It was mostly schematics of a strange symbol. It had the shape of a mandala. Concentric circles winding into infinity in their intricate patterning. It was a highly stylized design that sparked something in Emory's memory, but she couldn't quite put her finger on what. She stared at it for a moment longer then shoved the file under her arm. One way or another she was taking its contents with her. She spied a sign for restrooms and hurried inside.

After locking herself in a toilet cubicle, Emory took out the pages she wanted and folded them. She then started stuffing them in her bra and down her boxer shorts. She positioned them as best she could for comfort's sake. She'd learned long ago that people were more likely to pat your clothes and make you toss your pockets. Very rarely did anyone ask you to drop your shorts or undo your bra so they could check for stolen paperwork. She just had to live with any paper cuts she incurred.

She stepped out of the cubicle and checked her appearance in the mirror to make sure there was nothing showing. Then, still clutching the files that were a little less full, she slipped back onto the laboratory floor and started to wander around. She was curious what was being researched here. She peered through one of the glass partitions and mourned the fact she'd spent her chemistry lessons at school mooning over Kate Moore more than she had paid actual attention to the subject. There were too many people around for her to be brazen enough to walk in and look through the microscopes. The areas were filled with test tubes, vials, and equipment she had never seen before. Huge fridges housed multitudes of samples of whatever was being tested there.

I'm guessing that's not a place to stick your sandwiches, Emory thought as she saw something large and green growing up the side of one tube. She had to step back as someone nearly knocked into her as they came out of the door at speed. Emory decided it was time to move.

"Dink, I hope you can see this."

The reply was faint and intermittent in her ear. Emory figured it was because she was so deep underground. The fact she didn't have him so readily available in her head frightened her. She decided not to linger and go elsewhere before she was found out. She walked back toward the swipe machine and ran her card through it. She breathed a silent sigh of relief when it opened the door without a problem. Emory slipped through quickly and tried not to run down the stair well while under the watchful eye of the camera poised above the door.

Level 38 of Euphoria base was a hive of activity with people working with lasers and large, noisy weapons. The steady thumping rhythm of gunfire made Emory realize how soundproof the underground facility was. She also got why everyone wore ear protectors and grabbed the first pair she could get her hands on. She really wanted to spend more time looking around the laser weapons being demonstrated. They were like something from a science fiction film and were shooting through solid walls and metal like it wasn't even there.

The appearance of a high ranking official flanked by his minions made Emory turn and get out of there. She could see an officer systematically checking peoples IDs and she didn't know if Jessica Sanders would have had clearance to be around all this firepower. She'd seen enough. These weren't bullets and guns being tested. These were weapons of the future already designed, created, and in action. She couldn't help but wonder what else the military had hidden away.

She followed the steps down to Level 39 and found nothing more than a storage area. Endless packing crates lined the large room, packed one on top of the other, from floor to ceiling.

I wonder if the Ark of the Covenant is in here.

Emory walked around and inspected the markings on the crates. She picked up a clipboard and scanned the pages attached. "How very old school," she muttered, flipping through the sheets that seemed to do nothing more than list the crates. It gave no clue to the inventory inside. She looked around in case anyone was patrolling the room. She couldn't see or hear anyone else in the area so she tried to pry the lid off one of the crates. It wouldn't budge. Emory grunted and tried again, bruising her fingertips trying to lift the crate's heavy wooden lid. Nothing would move it. She shook her hands out to try to ease the ache.

"Guess I won't be finding anything worth exposing here." She doubled back to go back to the stairwell. Level Forty lay just a staircase below. Emory made sure not to turn around and have her face visible on the camera behind her. She'd paid particular attention to only presenting her back to the all-seeing eyes. She paused listening for footsteps. Hearing none, she set off down the steps. She'd never gotten the chance to see what Area 51's levels held, maybe this time she'd find something to satisfy her curiosity.

CHAPTER FOURTEEN

A simple swipe of Jessica Sanders's card and Emory heard the most gratifying sound ever.

I'm in. Oh my freaking God, I'm in!

She looked around, greedily taking in everything as fast as she could. This was a once in a lifetime opportunity, and she didn't intend to miss a thing.

Please don't let it be a storage level for food supplies. I'll be so gutted.

The room was one huge refrigerator. Everything was bathed in a soft blue light. And it was cold. Bitterly cold. So cold Emory could see her breath form a mist in front of her with every exhalation. That went a long way to explaining why there was no one guarding the door here, or inside. There weren't any cameras either, which Emory found odd. She padded around, realizing that these weren't regular refrigeration units all lined up like soldiers. Row upon row of domed, ice covered appliances were laid out before her. They looked almost like pods, but the thick layer of ice on them distorted the actual shape. She could tell there was a glass front, but the ice was too thick for her to see inside. The machines hummed as the electricity was fed to them to keep them frozen. Emory picked her way over the wiring to get a little closer to try to see what was inside one of the pods.

"God, it's freezing in here." Her teeth began chattering as the temperature seeped through her clothing and chilled her to the bone. She wrapped her arms around herself to try to keep warm but continued forward. She had come too far to stop now.

She stopped in front of one pod and began scratching away at the frozen ice clinging to its glass. She didn't get very far. Frustrated, she looked for something tougher to use. She didn't want to use Jessica Sanders's card that was proving to be way too precious to let out of her sight, so she riffled through her wallet and pulled out a store card.

"I doubt this store is still in one piece thanks to the invasion." She dragged the plastic card across the glass and was heartened to see the ice flake off, albeit slowly. She didn't stop until she could see enough to peer inside. She jumped back with fright and then looked around her, embarrassed in case anyone had seen her display of fear. She shook her head at herself; she was alone in the room.

Or, apparently, *wasn't*.

The face of a little gray alien stared back at her. Judging by the mottled appearance of its skin, it had been a long time dead and was now in storage.

"You're not a recent addition here," Emory said as she looked about her and tried to count how many more of this sized pod there were in the room. There were too many for her to fully see. "Aliens on ice, conspiracy theory 101." She spotted a much bigger pod and hurried toward it to see what the difference was. She began digging away at the ice covering the glass, but all she could see was that something was in there. She just couldn't tell what. The refrigerated pod was too tall, well over Emory's reach, so she searched for something to stand on. There was a lone chair that she had to kick at to break it free of the ice welding it to the floor. She carried it back to the pod and stood on it to clear more of the glass. She went through two store cards and three chipped nails before she finally cleared a big enough patch off the top of the pod to look inside. She brushed her hand over the glass to clean away the residue of frost.

"Fuck me!" Emory jumped so much she fell off the chair and landed awkwardly against another pod. She quickly righted herself and stared up in horror at the cleaned off space in the glass and at what stared back out at her.

This wasn't a small gray alien with big black eyes and spindly legs. This was much bigger. Emory estimated at least seven foot tall bigger. The skin of the creature inside was more a navy blue in color. Its eyes were lidless, and even frozen in death, the black eyes were unnerving. Its head was squarer in contrast to the grays' teardrop shape. But it was the mouth that caused Emory to gape. It was wide open and fearsome. This monster hadn't died peacefully; its final moment of rage had been captured in death and frozen in place. In silence it was sending out a terrible roar. Emory stepped back up onto the chair cautiously, afraid even though the beast inside the pod was undoubtedly dead. It was still the most frightening thing she had seen. Its mouth displayed a savage array of teeth. There were two rows of them, each tooth needle sharp and lethal. The torso that Emory had revealed earlier was heavily muscled and covered in what looked like scales. The huge clawed hands only served to make Emory even more nervous.

"How many aliens are we fighting here?" She couldn't tear her eyes away from the monster in front of her. Was this what her family was up against? Taken by the grays but brought before the blues?

She stepped back down to the ground and stared at the pod, her mind filling with terrible scenarios of what her family was facing.

She was brought back to the present abruptly by the sound of the hammer being pulled back on the gun that was pressed to the back of her head. Only then did Emory realize she was no longer alone. She closed her eyes and waited for the shot.

"Give me one good reason why I shouldn't just shoot you now and shove your body into one of these tubes? You'd fit right in with all these other intruders who ventured where they had no right to."

Sofia. Emory was never more grateful that's who'd found her. The gun, however, was a problem. Emory truthfully had no escape now. She was as trapped as the countless dead aliens that resided on Euphoria's Level 40. Dead *aliens*, different *types* of dead aliens, all hidden away in an undisclosed base. Emory came to a realization fast.

How ironic the one time I get caught where I shouldn't be is in a room of honest to goodness aliens that I never damn well believed in in the first place.

❖

Sofia snapped the lanyard free from Emory's neck and held it up to see where she'd stolen it from.

"This isn't like your false CIA credentials," she said, flipping the card back and forth and recognizing its authenticity. "Where did you get it from?"

"I found it," Emory said.

"Who is Jessica Sanders?"

"Someone who was abducted at Area 51 the same night I saved you from probably the same fate."

Sofia stifled the urge to roll her eyes.

"You worked there. Did you ever meet her?" Emory asked.

"There were a lot of people in and out of that base, Hawkes. Including a thieving investigative journalist chasing conspiracies under the guise of being a government agent."

"There's a fine line between coincidence and conspiracy, *Major*." Emory emphasized the rank to deliberately annoy Sofia. Sofia tried her best not to bite. "Such as the coincidence of flying saucers being seen in the sky above Area 51 and my finding out that actual saucers existed there. Not only were they there, they were *built* there. Yet there was a conspiracy to keep that fact hidden from the world. I'm seeing a conspiracy of silence there, Captain Martinez. What do you see?"

Sofia stuffed the swipe card and lanyard into her pocket. She ignored Emory's comment. It was true. That didn't mean Sofia had to acknowledge she was right. "You can't possibly understand what we did there."

Emory had the gall to laugh at her. Sofia spun her around, her gun still trained on Emory.

"Oh, please! Do not Jack Nicholson me!"

Sofia stared at her. "What?"

"You can't handle the truth!" Emory said stridently.

Sofia holstered her gun and grabbed Emory by the lapels of her jacket. She tugged her forward to snarl in her face. "I don't care what mission you see yourself on. I'm having you thrown into the brig once we get to the next base. You're a liability and I'm done covering your ass."

"*I'm* dangerous? We're being attacked by aliens." Emory waved her hands to gesture around the room. "And look what you guys just happen to have on ice like popsicles. Tell me, Captain, the big guy here? He's not like the little gray you shot the guts out of. What the hell is he? What else haven't you told us that we're going to have to face?"

Sofia pulled Emory roughly out of the room. She made sure to lock it securely with her own card. Once in the stairwell, she put Emory in front of her but kept a firm grip on Emory's jacket from the back. She needed the camera operators to see them just leaving, not that she was forcibly removing Emory from somewhere she should never have been at all. She marched Emory up the levels toward the elevator.

"They have cool laser weapons in there," Emory said as they passed a floor. "Does the NRA know you guys have those kind of kickass weapons to add to their constitutional right to bear arms?"

"You were supposed to stay put." Sofia pushed Emory up the next set of stairs.

"I got restless. And I'm inquisitive. You know that about me. It's one of my most endearing qualities." Emory turned to flash a toothy grin at Sofia. "It's also my job."

"Your job was promising a jail sentence in your future for threatening to leak details of a fictitious agency some idiot had conjured up. You're just chasing shadows in the dark. And why do you do it? Are you trying so hard to uncover something secret to gain approval from your mother because nothing you ever do is good enough for her? She's got her golden boy with his picture-perfect family and there you are, chasing secret plans and no doubt fantasizing about plots of a one-world government." Sofia ran into her as Emory stopped dead in her tracks. The crushed look on Emory's face made Sofia regret her cruel choice of words.

"Wow, that was mean," Emory said. "And, unfortunately, probably justified. My mother barely tolerates me. She didn't have time for a daughter because she was too busy grooming Brad to be the best at whatever he achieved. So while he followed a strict and rigid pathway to success, I got to roam free and see the world outside of its narrow minded viewpoint."

"Emory—"

"Don't apologize, Captain. I'm aware you're going to have to account for me for trespassing on yet another base that *you* brought me onto and for me poking my nose into secrets that no one outside the military is supposed to be privy to. I get that." Emory looked behind her to where the elevator doors lay then looked down at Sofia. "I promise you this though, I'll be more use to you by your side than stuck in a cell waiting to be bombed by aliens."

"And what talents could you possibly bring to me except for your amazing talent for sticking your nose where you shouldn't?"

"I have a Dink."

Seeing Emory's bright smile and earnest look almost made Sofia smile back. She sighed instead. "Another subversive meddling in the military's private dealings. Don't think he isn't on my list once I have dealt with you."

"What happened to the woman who was going to help me get my nieces back?" Emory started to walk backward up the steps toward the elevator. "My sister-in-law is okay too, so I'd like her back. I suppose if I rescued Brad, Mother would have to say thank you. It would be so satisfying to see her trying to spit those words out from behind her expensive dental work."

"Where is your mother?" Sofia punched the button to take them back up top.

"Probably still in her California home. She's a spiteful old bitch. If the aliens abducted her they'd soon take her back."

Sofia chuckled softly. "You're a piece of work, Emory."

"You said I was a scoundrel. I liked that. I liked the captain who said she'd help me get my family back. What brought the major pain in my ass back in play?"

Sofia shook her head. "Moments of weakness like that won't happen again." She suddenly had a thought. "Is that why you kissed me? To curry favor with me so you could continue spying on the military up close and personal?"

"No. I did it because it felt good." Emory's look was all self-satisfied smugness. It made Sofia long to wipe it off her face because the kiss had felt good to her too.

"Yeah, well you're not that great a kisser." She was pleased at the affronted look Emory gave her.

"I am too a good kisser! I've never had any complaints."

"I'm sure the information you've gleaned from your many lovers is as reliable as your penchant for chasing after nonexistent secret agencies." Sofia couldn't help the superior air in her voice, but she was enjoying watching the multitude of expressions running over Emory's face.

"That's a lot of fancy words for insinuating that the women I've fucked have probably lied to me about how good my lips are on them." Emory's sulky tone made Sofia laugh all the more.

"Potato, potahto." Sofia stuck her hands in her pockets to try to ease the chill in them from her exposure to the cold storage level. Her fingers inadvertently found the lanyard. "I can't believe you'd steal a dead woman's swipe card." The second the words left her mouth, she regretted it.

"Dead? She was abducted. How do you know she's dead?"

"I misspoke."

"What the hell else do you know about that you haven't told me? I can't deal with them being dead, Sofia. The abductees have to be alive somewhere. I need to find my nieces out there. Don't tell me they're dead already."

Sofia gripped Emory's shoulders and held on to stop Emory's frantic pacing in the confined space.

"I misspoke. I don't know what happens with the abductees because until I saw it happen I didn't even know it did."

Emory stared at her incredulously. "How could you not know? You knew about the saucers, and you obviously knew about the aliens, seeing as you never even flinched when you shot that one in Brad's backyard. Don't expect me to believe you don't know the alien agenda here."

"That's just it, Emory. I don't," Sofia said. She knew enough, though, that she couldn't even begin to trust Emory with.

"Then it's a good thing my ace in the hole is there for both of us, isn't it?"

"Ace?"

"I told you. I have a Dink, and there's nothing buried deep enough that he can't bring to the surface."

That's what I'm afraid of. Sofia had so many secrets of her own that needed to stay well hidden from Emory's investigations. In some ways, the aliens were the least of their problems.

❖

"Tell me you can hear me now? Oh God, tell me you can hear me now?"

Emory was relieved to hear Dink's voice in her ear once she was back inside the hangar. She was following Sofia but wasn't sure whether she should try to make a break for the van and drive out of there. She was uncertain what Sofia had in store for her. Emory let her gaze linger on Sofia's ramrod straight back as she marched ahead.

"Yeah." Emory tried very hard to keep her voice low, but Sofia spun around.

"Are you still in contact with Dink here?" She pulled on Emory's arm and tugged her down to see the small earpiece firmly lodged in her ear where it always was, hidden behind her hair. "For fuck's sake! You're on an undisclosed military base and you're still playing spies?" She flung her hands into the air in annoyance. "It's bad enough I'm so used to seeing you in those damn glasses that I forget you don't need them to see. But Dink does." She reached out to snatch them from Emory's face. Emory swiftly slapped her hands away.

"Hey! No, you don't. You knew I wasn't CIA the second you set your ass in my van. You knew I still wasn't legit when you brought me here and didn't rat me out at the gate. You're an accessory to my duplicity, Captain Martinez, because you *know*."

"Ask her about the aliens!" Dink raised his voice to be heard over the silent staring war going on between Emory and Sofia in the middle of the base's driveway. "Ask her about the big guy. That's no usual gray. That's a whole other race. I thought I was going to have a geekgasm when I saw that!"

Emory grimaced. "Geez, Dink. Too much information, don't you think?" She took a step back from Sofia and her grabby hands. She purposely kept her voice low so no one could overhear. "What was the other alien? That wasn't your standard close encounter alien. He was at least seven feet tall. That's not little green men material. That's a badass blue motherfu—"

Sofia slapped her hand over Emory's mouth and quickly shoved her around to the back of another hangar. "I don't know what that alien was, okay? I didn't know they had all those down there." She shook her head at Emory's disbelieving huff. "What I will disclose is this, and I have no idea why I am telling you at all." She took a deep breath. "I worked specifically with the saucers we were manufacturing and have since I was drafted over to Area 51's aviation department. I knew there were bodies, small alien bodies that were found at the crash site in 1947. Those were the only ones I had heard about. I have never seen them even though they were kept at the base."

"Area 51 had the Roswell aliens?"

"They are the only ones I knew about but never had cause to have dealings with. It wasn't anything to do with my job. I was aviation, not alien sciences."

"So your level forty wasn't a refrigerator for a hoard of dead aliens, including a Lurch?"

"Lurch?"

"That one is *very* tall." Emory grinned at her. She looked down between them. There was barely any space keeping them apart. Sofia was so close Emory could smell the lingering remnants of the coffee she must have had before she came tearing out after her. Emory knew it was totally inappropriate, the timing and circumstances were all wrong, but she was enjoying having Sofia pressed that close to her again while she described her role at a base long gone. She had to ask. "Why were you following me, Sofia? You could have left me wandering until I gave myself away and got hauled out by the guards here. There were cameras on me the whole time. I was going to be found out sooner or later."

"I saw you on the base's security cameras after I found you weren't calling your so-called superiors in a locked room. I knew where you would go. You never got the chance at Area 51, so I guessed you'd be desperate to see what was hidden away on the lowest levels underground. You're nothing if not predictable."

"It's my job to investigate. Why didn't you just send the military police after me? You could have saved yourself a whole heap of trouble."

"Because I needed to get you out before someone realized who you weren't."

"So this time you saved me." Emory was warmed by that thought.

"Don't flatter yourself. I was saving myself. I'm the one who brought you here and let you loose in a conspiracy theorist's candy store. Believe me, what the military would do to you if they found you out is nothing compared to what they'd do to me because of it."

Emory let that sink in. They were both watching each other's backs. Emory patted Sofia's arm as comfortingly as she could. "You didn't seem surprised that there were a ton of dead aliens in Euphoria's basement." Looking back, Emory was intrigued by Sofia's non-reaction to what lay in level forty. Sofia just shook her head and favored Emory with a small smile curving her lips. Emory couldn't tear her gaze from them. She'd tasted them. She found herself not caring any more for Sofia's answer. She just wanted to kiss her again.

"I've learned that there are a great many secrets the military keeps. Secrets it keeps from itself too. It's not my place to ask why. My place is to do my job."

"And keep the knowledge of invaders coming to Earth from the whole of humanity in the process?"

Sofia nodded. "Not everyone could handle that truth."

"And the fact that aliens are now trying to blow us off the face of the planet for some reason?"

"That is something for the government and the military to try to stop."

"You'll forgive me for not putting much trust in either of those concerning that." Emory was surprised as Sofia placed her palm on Emory's cheek and stilled her restless movements.

"Then put your trust in me."

"You want me behind bars," Emory said, not trusting herself to speak while Sofia was touching her. After the cold of the storage level, Sofia's warmth thawed Emory clean through.

"You need to curb your insatiable need to hunt out secrets. Some things are best left unknown."

Emory couldn't tear her eyes from Sofia's. Everything she had dedicated her life to slipped away as unimportant. "Are we staying here?"

Sofia shook her head. "No. I have my orders to reach the other base so we need to head out once I've gathered supplies."

Emory was disappointed when Sofia moved away. She cursed herself for letting her mind be clouded by a pretty woman who stood for everything Emory tried to bring down.

Like having aliens invading wasn't enough to contend with.

"These supplies, any chance they could include a couple of the laser guns I know are available?" Emory was amused to see the spark ignite in Sofia's eyes. The glare leveled at her was just plain adorable too. Now *that* was the Sofia she was starting to know and love. Emory swallowed hard.

She always had to add something else to the mix to contend with too.

"Just how much did you see on the weapons level?" Sofia shook her head in exasperation and walked off muttering to herself. "God, you make it so hard for me not to just kill you myself."

Emory hurried after her, trotting beside her like an excitable pup, deliberately baiting Sofia's temper with her exuberance. She nudged Sofia's shoulder. "Admit it, you like me."

"Don't you dare leave my side again," Sofia ordered, her voice threatening retribution if Emory dared to disobey.

"Wouldn't dream of it." Emory saluted her and added a wink.

"Don't tempt me, Emory Hawkes."

I'll try not to dream of that either, Emory thought with a smile.

CHAPTER FIFTEEN

Emory sat busy stuffing as much of the sandwich she had into her mouth without choking. She was starving, but Sofia didn't seem to have a pause button that meant they could sit and eat like civilized people under the threat of an alien invasion. Emory was watching as Sofia systematically went through the armory piece by agonizing piece. She was picking out suitable weaponry to carry with them on their journey. Around a mouth filled with ham and lettuce, Emory tried to catch Sofia's attention.

"How about that one? The silver one with the scope thing?" She pointed toward a high-powered sniper rifle that looked suitably lethal to Emory's eyes.

Sofia dismissed it. "That's no use against a horde of saucers." She continued sorting through the handguns.

"And those are?" Emory grumbled. "Can you at least pick me one that I don't have to constantly reload?"

"I am not arming you with a machine gun. In fact, I am not arming *you* at all."

Stung by Sofia's words, Emory huffed a disgruntled sound. "Man, you're meaner than mean." She dusted the crumbs from her clothes and slipped down off the box she'd been sitting on. She slowly perused the impressive lineup of weapons of all shapes and sizes in Euphoria's armory as if she knew what she was looking at. Pistols, rifles, machine guns. Emory was pleased to note that Sofia had put one of those aside despite her comment. Then she saw it. Emory's jaw dropped in awe. "Oh, please tell me we're bringing one of these beauties with us."

Sofia looked over her shoulder to see what Emory was referring to. She snorted. "And just where do you expect that to go?" Sofia looked around to make sure they weren't being overheard. "On the trailer to cuddle up against your tarp-wrapped alien buddy?"

Emory ignored her and ran her hand over the missile launcher that fascinated her so much. "I could find room for this. Tell me about it, please."

"You're still not having it even if I tell you its specs. It's a Stinger, a portable surface to air missile launcher."

"What does it launch?"

"The warhead is a high explosive." Sofia touched the launcher with respect. "It has an infrared homing guidance system too."

Emory grinned. "See? You're falling under its spell too, aren't you? We can't leave without it. You can't leave Rooty behind."

"Rooty?"

Emory nodded. "Look at it. This weapon is a serious Rooty Tooty Point and Shooty. It's the ultimate in weapons."

The look Sofia gave her clearly questioned her sanity, but Emory didn't care. She wanted the launcher and gave Sofia her best puppy dog eyes. Sofia stared at her then dismissed her.

"Once you've stopped drooling over the launcher, how about you do something useful and help me get *my* weapons stored away in your van so we can get on the road?"

"I think we're making a huge mistake leaving her behind."

"You've assigned a gender to a weapon?"

"Look at her. Sleek, toned, deadly when fired up. Sounds just like a woman to me." Emory thought about what she'd said. "Pretty sure I've dated a few like that."

"Why am I not surprised you usually hook up with something that ends up going ballistic on you?" Shaking her head, Sofia moved to gather up her guns.

Emory laughed. "Did you just make a joke, Captain? Admittedly, one at my expense, but quite amusing for all that."

"Just take these and put them in that bag." Sofia handed Emory an armful of bullet boxes.

"I'd ask if you were expecting trouble, but I've seen what's in the skies above us and what's invading our backyards." Emory juggled the sliding boxes in her arms. "Which reminds me. Did you ask the guys here what's happening worldwide?"

"They're a little preoccupied with what's happening here to worry about how the rest of the world is faring. Though it has been confirmed that Area 51 was the initial attack point."

"So your base of operations was Ground Zero for the aliens. They probably found out you had a bunch of their buddies on ice like they do here." Emory zipped up the bulging bag crammed with ammunition. "Which doesn't make me want to stay here for any longer than we need to. Have they worked out how many black triangles there are in orbit at least?"

Emory was aware Dink had been trying to figure that out as well. Especially seeing as they were the craft that looked to house the endless stream of saucers inside. Dink was of the belief that bringing down the triangles would slow the saucers considerably.

"Someone else is probably looking into that, and we'll get the report when they're done." Sofia's look of irritation revealed she wasn't too impressed. Emory had been keeping her up to date with all that Dink had found out from his research. It was becoming obvious that Dink had resources Sofia didn't have access to.

Emory could have told her that from the start.

"I'm just thankful they rolled the tanks out for us, otherwise we'd still be stuck in that alley with the saucers buzzing about our heads." Emory leaned against the table Sofia was still working at. "How armored were *your* saucers, Sofia?"

Sofia never looked up. "Well enough."

"Enough to have given us a sporting chance against them?"

"Probably, but we'll never know for sure. The tech was difficult to transfer to our own saucers, but we managed to use it to our advantage."

"Did your saucers have the lasers too?"

Sofia shot her a sharp look over her shoulder before she started packing away the last of the weapons.

Emory sighed. "That's your *classified* face. I hate that face."

"We're at war. That still doesn't mean you're allowed access to all the secrets the military keeps."

"I'll wear you down eventually." Emory tried to pick up one of the bags and grunted at its weight. "Think you have enough ammo here?"

Sofia sauntered over and picked it up with ease, swinging it over her shoulder. She gave Emory such a condescending look that Emory fought the urge to childishly stick her tongue out at her.

"Show off," she muttered under her breath. She followed in Sofia's wake, feeling justified in staring at her ass after that show of superiority. Emory shoved her hands in her pockets and hid her smile as she felt the newly appropriated revolver snug against her leg. She kept her stolen gun hidden as best she could and held on to the purloined bullets in her other pocket so they wouldn't jangle and give her away.

Sofia really did need to learn to keep a better eye on her.

Sofia left her with a warning *not* to move from the van and that she'd be back after she'd had one last word with someone whose name meant nothing to Emory, so she just nodded dutifully. She watched as Sofia disappeared into the main building. The second she vanished from sight, Emory made a beeline toward the armory. She flashed her CIA credentials at the airman who'd been on guard when she and Sofia had been stockpiling their weapons.

"One more pickup and we're good to go," Emory informed him.

"Can I help you, ma'am?"

Emory shook her head. "No, I know exactly which one Captain Martinez wants me to grab, so I'll be out of your hair in a flash."

He nodded and sat back down, leaving Emory to hurry down the aisle where she had seen what she'd come back for. She picked up the rocket launcher reverently, then collected as many missiles as she could carry.

And here's where the fun begins.

❖

Sofia headed back through the base to talk to Major Chilcott, the commander of Euphoria base. She found him in the war room, staring at a set of screens that showed just some of the devastation around the country. It made for chilling viewing.

"Major?"

"Captain Martinez, taking your leave of us so soon?"

He turned to face her. Chilcott looked weary and old. Sofia knew he was nowhere near retirement yet, but seeing him looking so defeated aged him dramatically. Sofia wondered how much of what she'd witnessed in the last few days had written its horror across her own face.

"My superiors' want me elsewhere, Major." She smiled at him. "It's nothing personal, I assure you. I'd be more than happy to stay here and man the tanks with your soldiers. You have an amazing force here. I owe them my life."

"I fear our bullets won't be a match for long against what we're facing. It's as futile as throwing sticks to try to stop a tornado in its path."

Sofia saw her opportunity. "Has there been word of us deploying some of our more powerful weapons, sir?" The shake of his head made Sofia's heart plummet. They had the capability to do more damage than doing ground-to-air attacks or sending up planes that were just swatted aside.

"Between you and me? Word is circulating that there's someone very high up in the chain venting their displeasure at the bringing down of that one black craft over Maine." He leaned forward and switched a camera to the exact point.

At first, Sofia couldn't help but marvel at how huge the black triangular craft was with the military-manned camera sweeping over it live. She recognized the crash site from the photo Dink had sent Emory. The still had been nothing compared to the reality of the downed craft. It was spectacular, and the engineer in her wanted desperately to open it up and see how it all worked. However, as the camera pulled back she gasped at the devastation it had caused where it had fallen. A massive chunk of the coastline of Maine was missing. She tried to pinpoint its location on the map that Chilcott had spread out before him. That area had to have been populated. She couldn't begin to calculate the magnitude of that loss. Whatever had been there was now crushed under however many tons of spaceship.

"Oh my God," she whispered. "We can't shoot those things down. They'll wipe out the whole planet landing on us." She couldn't tear her eyes away from the sight. "How many black triangles are there?"

"We don't know. We're still scrambling for information. We were never equipped to fight something that had such superior firepower *and* the ability to use some sort of beam to abduct the population at will." He rubbed at his face in agitation. "I fear we can't win this fight. We've always been told that aliens didn't exist. I've known respected men who lost their jobs over what they said they'd seen and were discredited for it. Now I have to believe they were right all along and I'd dismissed them as cranks?"

Sofia felt sorry for him, but she knew all too well the secrecy that was perpetrated in the military. No one knew everything; it was never in anyone's best interests to do so. You followed your orders and your superiors without question. You served your God and country. Only the select were ever privy to the fact that aliens had visited Earth. The government had done everything in its power to keep that hidden while they gave the orders to those in the know to use the technology scavenged for their advancement alone. It was as top secret as it got.

Yet it wasn't really a secret when people saw saucers that weren't the military prototypes. When abductions happened but were hushed up in the press or ridiculed. When pilots, military and commercial, filed reports of seeing unidentified objects in their airspace and ended up discharged or benched. Sofia had believed what she'd been told and had ignored the warning signs from outside the protective military bubble she'd been working in. All she had wanted to do was equip the air force with a machine that could combat anything that came at them. She hadn't considered that it would be against more aliens intent on destroying them.

"So, you're being called farther afield?" Chilcott said, eying her closely. "What do you think you'll find there, Captain?"

Sofia straightened her shoulders. "Answers, hopefully, sir."

"Be safe on your journey. Those ships are out over the North Atlantic, bombing the bejeezus out of Switzerland on our last watch. Get to where you're going fast. There's no saying those crafts won't swing back around to finish us off here. All our military might and it's come down to this." He leaned against his console. "This CIA agent you're traveling with. Does she have any better idea what's going on here than we do?"

Sofia held her tongue then had to answer honestly. "Yes, sir, I think she does. I believe her branch of the CIA has some information from places we have no control over."

"The government is dispatching agencies to gather up the population left stranded by these attacks. You don't want to find yourself caught up in that net. Stick with your CIA contact. Maybe you'll both be safer."

CHAPTER SIXTEEN

The drive to the undisclosed base was going to take them well into the night, but Sofia knew the minute she tired Emory would take over the task of driving. She looked over to where Emory was fast asleep in the passenger seat. Sofia had no idea how she could be comfortable or even able to get any sort of rest in the boneless sprawl that she was currently in. In Emory's lap lay the wrappers from numerous candy bars. Sofia was surprised Emory wasn't bouncing around the van on a sugar high. She marveled at how much food Emory seemed to be able to consume. She had to admit Emory probably had the right idea to eat as much as she could when she could because they weren't always going to be able to find food so easily.

It was going dark as she drove along the interstate. She was grateful that the Euphoria base had filled up the van with gas along with extra fuel to aid them on the journey. She didn't like the idea of stopping on the highway. Major Chilcott had told her of the panic that was ensuing. Looting was becoming commonplace, and there had been reports of killings over items that wouldn't be much use to anyone anymore. She'd gotten provisions and gas that would get them to the base. And Sofia was armed and ready to shoot at every bathroom break. No one was preventing her from reaching her destination, human or alien.

Sofia knew exactly where they were heading and how different it was from the last base. Euphoria had been a covert base, and even she hadn't been aware of all that had been hidden there. She eyed Emory again. She wasn't in the least bit surprised that Emory had taken the chance to start snooping around. Finding the frozen remains of dead aliens wasn't exactly going to be breaking news now that there was an invasion of live aliens taking place.

Still, she needed to keep a tighter rein on Emory's wanderlust once they arrived. Euphoria flew under the radar for many reasons. It had alien bodies, something Sofia hadn't been aware of but hadn't been as surprised as Emory had to see them. Except for the large blue alien. *That* one had been a surprise.

Area 51 had seen a wealth of secrets hidden beneath its surface. The original Roswell alien bodies had been housed there; the ship had been hidden there and raided for its technology.

Sofia didn't pretend to not be intrigued by what else went on there, but she'd learned very early on in her career that to rise up the ladder you didn't question your superiors and you kept your eyes and mouth shut. She'd worked her way up the chain of command by being good at both. She'd also been instrumental in refining the design of the aircraft that utilized the technology they had found and made their own. Through the endless incarnations of the alien/human saucer, modified and redesigned over the many years since the crash, Sofia had worked to develop an almost perfect model of the alien ship for use by human pilots. She'd become quite adept at reverse engineering the alien tech, so adept she'd been given the lead on all the subsequent projects and earned her rank with distinction.

She'd watched her saucers take off from Groom Lake and fly under the cover of darkness. The saucers, cloaked in secrecy, raced across the night sky in their clandestine flights. When they had been seen, the witnesses had been either discredited or given some cover story to steer them away from the truth. Saucers had long been flying in the skies, both of alien and human manufacture.

Sofia hadn't been aware that hers weren't the only ones. There was a part of her questioning why she hadn't been informed that aliens were still at large. To her knowledge and training, all the alien crafts that crashed on the planet, and there had been numerous such incidents, left nothing living to tell the tale. She was already working under a tight veil of secrecy. What else was being hidden from her?

She'd taken on the extra responsibility of securing the base once she'd gone as far as she could, for now, in building the crafts. She didn't want what she'd worked so hard on to be vulnerable to outside sources so she was trying to use some of the defenses that the ships employed to defend Area 51. It was that added responsibility that had unwittingly left her vulnerable in helping to evacuate the base. It had also resulted in her being left behind.

There really was more going on than people would believe. Those that suspected anything beyond the "normal" were discouraged from investigating. Fortunately, Sofia knew the majority of the human race didn't want to believe in anything that could tamper with their day-to-day lives. Ignorance is bliss, after all. And the human race had been kept ignorant of a great many secrets. Secrets that some people dedicated their lives to unearthing and exposing. Uncovering the lies and being derided for seeing the world differently while everyone else shied away from what was really happening. All that was in plain sight if they'd only open their eyes to see. Thankfully, the world preferred to be kept in the dark. Just not all, she thought as she looked over at Emory again.

Emory shifted, letting out a soft grumble in her sleep. Then her breathing deepened again as she slipped deeper into slumber.

Then there were people like Emory. People who saw beyond the surface and dug until they uncovered whatever was hidden, no matter how hard The Powers That Be tried to keep those things buried. Secret governments, powerful men pulling the strings behind the scenes, hidden agendas. The reality of every conspiracy theorist. Sofia heard enough to know that such things had long been in play. She didn't question it. Nothing good came of delving too deep.

She had given herself to serve and protect. Even now, with the world invaded by an outside force, Sofia felt the need to do her duty. She just didn't know who she was supposed to serve now in order to fulfil that. She'd been kept in the dark by her superiors. At what point did they feel she was only worthy of seeing a sliver of light in the darkness they dealt in?

Emory shifted again, and Sofia's gaze was drawn inexplicably back to her. Sofia wasn't even sure she could trust her. The fact that Emory had seen fit to sneak a handgun out of the armory when she thought Sofia wasn't looking galled her. Really, just how stupid did she think Sofia was? Emory was a born risk taker. She was foolhardy, always running toward trouble without fear of the consequences. Sofia shivered as she remembered Emory's panicked race toward the saucer's light to do anything she could to rescue her family.

She also wondered who was the source leaking the information of the secret agency that Emory had even been willing to go to jail for to protect? Maybe Sofia could ask and Emory would tell her. After all, Emory believed that Sofia wasn't going to have her thrown in the brig for all the crimes she'd committed at Area 51 alone. Maybe she'd trust her to reveal her sources. Sofia was intrigued by what Emory seemed to think she could expose. It must have been something divisive enough for her to stake her career and her freedom on it. Still, Sofia watched as Emory slept the sleep of the innocent.

Foolhardy and naïve, beautiful yet crazy. Didn't this theorist realize such agencies, by their very definition, were invincible? Powerful, untouchable, whatever they were. Emory never stood a chance going up against them. Closed ranks wasn't just confined to the military.

"So, tell me, what was it the aliens got out of the deal you guys obviously made with them?" Emory leaned back in her seat, hands comfortable on the steering wheel, letting the GPS guide her to the all-important base Sofia needed them to reach.

"Who said anyone made a deal?" Sofia was moving around in the back of the van. She was just getting up after sleeping a few hours while Emory took her turn driving through the night.

Emory watched her in the rearview mirror, fixing her hair and stretching out the kinks that had settled after sleeping on the less than comfortable long seat the van afforded. Sofia had taken off her fatigue jacket to sleep and was clad in a tight T-shirt that Emory found very distracting. Who knew the captain was hiding such delightful curves beneath that shapeless uniform?

Inexplicably flustered, Emory swiftly returned her eyes to the road and to keeping a watchful eye on the sky. Dink had been keeping her company all through the night, but he'd gone to take a quick nap before he'd be back in her ear. Emory was aware he was delving deeper into the military's data bases. He'd told her of some of the information he'd already found out.

Who needed a back door into the Pentagon's systems when emails all too easily gave away top secret plans? Some even came with photographic evidence or schematics attached. These had proved all too easy for Dink to download. When not telling her what he was finding out, he'd been teasing her for hiding top secret documents in her underwear. Thankfully, that had been something she'd told him about and not what he had witnessed through the all-seeing glasses. In a feat of stealth and long practiced sneakiness, Emory had managed to transfer all the folded sheets she'd stolen from the files to a hidden compartment in the van for her and Dink to go over another time. For now, they were hidden in the same place currently housing a Stinger rocket launcher from Sofia's all too watchful gaze. Emory figured she had to have some secrets of her own.

"Come on, *Major*, there had to be some quid pro quo going on. You couldn't have gotten FTFTA for nothing."

Sofia eased herself into the front of the van and sat in the passenger seat. "FT…what?"

"Future Tech for Today's Aviation." Emory deliberately took on the droll tones of an announcer.

Sofia rubbed at her eyes. "Christ, it is way too early for you to be making up shit. Ask me again when I'm more awake and have had coffee."

"That's when you'll just keep repeating your 'classified' routine. I'd rather ask when you're still drowsy and hopefully more loose lipped."

"Dream on, Hawkes. These lips are sealed."

"You've told me stuff though," Emory said. "What's there left to hide now? It's too late. The aliens are here."

"Yes, they are so now you know it all." Sofia shifted to look at the sky. "Have you seen anything while I was asleep?"

"Like the fact you twitch like a puppy dreaming about chasing rabbits or that you drooled on the upholstery of this fine vehicle?" Emory laughed when Sofia slapped her on the arm in retaliation. "No. The sky was surprisingly clear. According to Dink, that's because the majority of the saucers are currently over Europe attacking France and Switzerland." She caught Sofia's attention at that disclosure. "Ooh, I see by that look you already knew that. How intriguing and how disappointing you didn't deem it fit to share with the class. He also says there's at least seven black triangle crafts in orbit."

Sofia frowned. "How'd he work that out?"

"Ways and means, lady, ways and means."

"Which are?"

"I'm sure the same as what your military have but don't use for the same reasons."

"Just how deep is he buried in our tech?" Sofia's eyes hardened as her renowned temper began to spark. Emory found it fascinating and rather attractive to watch Sofia's eyes darken and her lips purse in annoyance.

"Deep enough. But believe me, his aren't the only hands furtively playing in the military's technical undergarments."

Sofia rested her chin in her hand and eyed Emory. "You know you're just handing me more rope to hang you both with."

Emory's smile grew. She loved riling Sofia up. It was like foreplay. The flame that burned in Sofia's dark eyes seared Emory through to her soul and turned her on. "You seem more awake now. Care to tell me what the *live* aliens got out of letting you keep their ships?"

"I wasn't aware there were live ones. You've seen the ones in cold storage the same as I have. That's the story I was told."

"You'll forgive me if I don't believe you."

"You can believe what you like. Your sort usually do." Sofia turned her face back to the road, effectively dismissing Emory.

"*My* sort?"

"Conspiracy theorists. What you can't research you just make up. You and all of your little basement dwelling buddies."

Emory's hands tightened on the wheel for a fraction of a second before she calmed. It wasn't like that wasn't something she'd heard a thousand times before. From the mouths of officials, from the government when challenged, from her own mother who despaired of a daughter who wouldn't toe the family line and get a proper job that didn't question authority. Emory spoke softly.

"Believing in conspiracy theories is like having a different view on religion or politics. People get really angry when you don't agree with their beliefs and purposely won't listen to you no matter how strong an argument you have. They accuse you of badmouthing the country or trying to smear the integrity of those in positions of power. Worse still, if you question a tragedy, they say you're besmirching the memories of those that were lost. That couldn't be further from the truth. But people won't look any further from what they are told, because if they're shown something that doesn't fit into their neat little way of living then they can't cope with what it might actually mean to them." Emory saw she had Sofia's attention so she continued.

"It was once believed that the Earth was flat. That what man lived on was a flat disc that lay in a vast ocean, just floating like a lily pad, surrounded by a spherical sky. The astrologers, way back when, studied the stars and said that it was much more feasible that what we stood on was a sphere. Adventurers like Magellan and Columbus took to the seas and proved the Earth was indeed round. So you had what was *believed*, what was *theorized*, and what was *proven*."

Sofia eyed her dubiously. "You're going to give me a history lesson at this hour?"

"The term 'conspiracy theory' pretty much came into existence after the assassination of John F. Kennedy back in 1963. The report that was published about what happened that day was released to the public…but not everyone believed it. To them, the idea of a lone gunman just didn't seem feasible."

"That's because of the ludicrous 'magic bullet' theory."

"Which has since been debunked, thanks to simply moving the chairs in the limousine to where they were positioned that day. Not everyone believed what the Warren Commission said happened was what really *had* happened. So they theorized on other scenarios that would bring about the same outcome."

"Either way we lost a president."

"True, but isn't it better to know the hows and whys than just sit back and not question the *who* as well? Why was he shot? What was the motive? Who stood to gain from his death? It's a story filed away in the history books now. He's a tragic footnote in time. But his death was believed to have been down to one man. Since then, it's been theorized that there could have been multiple shooters."

"And the Warren Report had what was proven to show otherwise," Sofia said.

"No, that report had what it needed the country to see to keep them in the dark. There are endless reports of evidence going missing, witnesses mysteriously dying. But enough real evidence was left for us to follow the trails that lead to other conclusions."

"You would believe in a cover-up," Sofia huffed.

"And that's why I'm a conspiracy theorist, because nothing has been definitively proven where his death is concerned. I've been told what I should believe, but it's not been proven enough to my satisfaction."

"Believe, theorize, and prove. That seems to be your mantra."

"Better that than to be blind to what is really happening. We're force-fed what to believe about the world through the media. Spoon-fed opinions, brainwashed into believing only what we see and read and are told. We're never expected to look into it for ourselves. And if anyone questions the 'norm' we get the word 'crazy' attached to our title. Crazy conspiracy theorist. If I had a dollar for every time I've been called that, I'd be driving something other than this VW Bus." She reached for the phone in her pocket and dialed it. "Good morning, Dink. I can hear you up and about. Care to join the panel discussion?" She laid the phone down between her and Sofia. Dink's voice soon came through loud and clear.

"Here's my ten cents worth, ladies. If we question going to war, we're branded un-American. Yes, we question the military's motives but not the soldiers who are sent to keep us safe from those who mean us harm. Those we are proud to acknowledge as the heroes they are and we pray for their safe return. I've lost too many friends to wars that weren't our fight. It's the *secret* military I despise, the covert ones who use those brave souls to chase after shadows instead of our real enemies. The leaders with other agendas to fulfill are who I'm after, and you know well enough, Sofia, those agencies exist. There have been enough disclosures and documents declassified that point to things happening that weren't all for the greater good of the country. Or our brave soldiers' welfare."

"You know I'm not at liberty to comment on that."

"Yeah, well, no one saw fit to comment much on the death of my brother either. He went out to fight for right and came home to his family in a wooden box. National security hid his death from us. I soon found all the answers I needed to my questions by looking into it myself. And there I found a whole lot more besides. His body had been pumped full of a crazy cocktail of drugs, the likes of which and the origin of them no one outside the military could even guess at. Who knows what they were doing to him when he died. The truth will out, Sofia. It was a crazy conspiracy theory that there were no Weapons of Mass Destruction. The war raged, innocents died, and we were labeled as unpatriotic to imagine such a thing."

Dink sighed. "And then what happened? Turned out we were right. There were no weapons after all. But no one except us questioned it because the propaganda surrounding the search had whipped the country into a fever. And if you can blind enough to the truth often enough, then they'll come to believe anything you damn well want them to believe. Blind faith isn't relegated to just the church, sadly."

Emory shook her head at Sofia's defensive posture and angry silence. "Just how crazy are people like me and Dink? How about this for another example? People have believed for a long time something crashed to Earth back in 1947. It put a little place called Roswell on the map. Whatever it was, it was initially reported to be a spaceship from outer space. That was swiftly covered up with a denial. Nothing to see here, folks, just your common weather balloon."

Emory glanced up at the sky reflectively. "But the saucers kept being seen. Those bright lights in the sky didn't stop coming. The public was told they were hallucinating, or seeing a particularly bright star. Or that it was just a normal airplane seen at a curious angle. Mysteriously, our technology suddenly started to grow in leaps and bounds. We developed stealth aircraft and weaponry way ahead of anything we'd had previously. For those who believed the flying saucer story, they theorized that maybe we were using what was found on that ship for our own uses. The proof? Look at how far we have forged ahead in technology."

She watched Sofia's face reflected in the windshield. She could tell Sofia knew where Emory was going with this. "As a conspiracy theorist, I have to believe in a hidden agenda. It's kind of in the title, you see. It's what conspiracy means." She knew she was deliberately goading Sofia, but everything she was saying was the truth. And Sofia *knew* it. "So, the hidden agenda. Let's see, does anyone stand to gain from hiding the technological advances that could come from such a craft? Well, there'll be weaponry far superior to anyone else's to have. And what about the government that has that power at hand? Fuck, they'd be gods among men."

"But you didn't believe in aliens," Sofia said stonily.

"No, I didn't. I needed that proved before I could get one hundred percent behind that idea. I subscribed to the crafts being secret military weapons and the use of the 'aliens from another planet' angle was to keep the masses in fear. We grow up fearing the boogie man under the bed, but at least he's a localized terror. Invaders from another planet coming to destroy us? That's a nifty little control technique."

Emory laughed softly under her breath. "All this time we've been told there are no saucers, no aliens, no futuristic weaponry being built and tested in secret bunkers miles underground. And then the aliens struck and blew that lie wide open. So, yes, I'm a conspiracy theorist because I look for proof of a lie. And, honey? You are up to your pretty little neck in all the fucking bald-faced untruths *your sort* have told us. The proof is laid bare ass naked for all of us to see now." Emory looked away from the road to capture Sofia's gaze.

"Try explaining this away with a goddamn weather balloon."

CHAPTER SEVENTEEN

Please tell me you're not sulking." Emory looked over at Sofia who was pressed up against the van door as close as she could get. Her arms were folded over her chest defensively, and the look on her face had almost made Emory hold her tongue. Unfortunately, Emory wasn't exactly known as one who feared to tread where angels wouldn't.

"I'm not sulking."

"Kinda looks like you are," Emory singsonged just to be even more annoying.

"I am not sulking. I'm selectively ignoring you. Just because we are trapped in this van together doesn't make this a jolly little road trip we're sharing."

Emory heard the sound of Dink coming back online. She dialed the phone so he could be heard in the van. He'd been absent for a while, and Emory was relieved to hear his voice.

"You ladies okay out there?" he asked.

"Sofia's sulking," Emory said. She kept her eyes fixed on the road. She had a feeling the look Sofia was shooting her way would kill on contact.

"You are worse than a child," Sofia said. "The first saucer we see? I'm throwing you under it."

Emory just laughed.

"Okay then, so this is what happens when I'm not here to keep an eye on you. Consider both of your heads banged together. Sofia, I have a question for you. What do you know about a mass evacuation underway?"

"Major Chilcott mentioned that the government had ordered agencies to start gathering up the survivors. They're probably going to start scouring the devastated areas first then will start evacuating as many as they can."

"Evacuating them to where?" Emory asked. "This isn't like a hurricane or a tornado breezing through. You can stick a ton of people in a stadium for their safety, but that isn't going to stop the aliens from sucking them up and out of there."

"The missile silos under the mountains would be a much better place to hide humanity," Dink said.

Sofia scowled more. "God, I forget how much you know." She rubbed at her face.

"Knowledge is power, dear Captain. I'd hope with the knowledge the government and the military have accumulated over many years knowing about the aliens that they had a contingency plan set up just in case the peace accord turned sour. I'd like to believe that all the safe zones built deep under the earth and the vaults set up to escape a nuclear attack aren't just hiding the rich and the elite while the rest of us are sitting ducks."

"The government is doing all it can, I'm sure," Sofia said.

"I'm sure they are. All from the plush seats so far down underground that their asses are roasting off the center of the earth's core," Emory said. She checked the sky for any signs of movement. It was becoming a nervous tic. "Dink, what have you heard?"

"Word is people are being rounded up off the streets and herded into trucks. No one knows where they are being taken to. The soldiers aren't telling anyone what's happening. Families are being split, and they can't find out where their husbands or children have been taken to. People are frightened, both by the invasion and the disappearance of their loved ones to God knows where."

"They're not the Gestapo, Dink," Sofia said tersely. "What do you think is happening?"

"Worst-case scenario is people are being rounded up to be used as alien bait."

Sofia slammed her fist against the side of the van in a burst of anger. Emory winced in sympathy because that had to hurt.

"Stop the van." When Emory didn't immediately pull over, Sofia screamed the order. "Stop the fucking van right now!"

Emory pulled the van out of the slow stream of traffic she'd been negotiating. She didn't even get to put the parking brake on before Sofia was out of the van and slamming the door so hard it shook the vehicle. Emory purposely looked in the mirror so Dink could see her.

"Now look what you did. Told you she was sulking."

"There's nothing worse than when you expose a conspiracy theory as something that is irrefutable fact. To be honest, she's taken it better than I thought."

"Really?"

"Well, she hasn't shot you yet so I'm taking that as a good sign."

Emory couldn't argue with that logic. She looked outside to see if she could see where Sofia had stormed off to.

"You don't think she's out there slashing my tires, do you?" She craned her neck out the window.

"I think she's starting to realize that there's more going on here on the ground than there is above us."

"None of which is going to matter if the aliens continue to lay waste to the planet."

"I'm trying to make a list of all the places they have tried to annihilate completely. Las Vegas was bombed but left in ruins. Area 51 no longer exists. The same has happened in Europe in certain areas, but I'm still waiting on the exact details. We're starting to lose connections with the people over there."

"I'm thinking Area 51 was personal. The rest may be just a show of their power, but bombing the base was a blatant act of revenge." Emory rubbed at her eyes. "Dink, you don't really think the government is corralling people to be sacrificial lambs, do you?"

"I just need you to get here as quick as you can once you've deposited the good captain wherever it is in Utah she's aiming for. I can't promise you'll be any safer here with me but I'll be happier with you back in the bunker. It's got to be safer than you touring the highways exposed to the aliens' lethal weapons." Dink was silent. "It's time to come home, Em."

"I'd like to get a look at this base we're going to first. I've got a feeling with it being so off the grid that there's something there worth exposing."

"Like Sofia's going to let you anywhere near it after you found the dead aliens' winter wonderland at the last place."

"Do any of your pals know what the hell the blue alien is?"

"Some I've contacted believe it's proof we've been visited by more than one species of alien. Perhaps Marvin is one of those."

"Marvin? As in the skirt-wearing animated Martian?" Emory smiled. "I think my calling him Lurch was way more appropriate."

"True, he was a rather large dude. Fugly too."

"There being more than one species involved makes this worse than I ever imagined."

"You imagined an alien invasion, Little Miss Sceptic?"

"I've done all the research into aliens, Dink, just like you. I know all the sightings, the history, the abduction stories. I've studied it all and can see how feasible the idea of there being ancient aliens, ones that visited us hundreds of years ago, is based on what we see in the legends from other cultures. You know Roswell has always been a sticking point with me. Something happened there, but I wasn't one hundred percent behind the 'aliens crash-landed' story. There was more proof I was digging up about what this secret military group was up to than I was finding proof of alien existence." Emory thought about what she'd seen. "But then I watched the one thing I never believed in steal my family right from in front of me. I couldn't do anything about that, but I can do my damnedest to try to get them back. I'll fight to get them back from whatever alien, blue skinned or gray, that has them captive."

"You'll need more than the guns Sofia packed in her bag."

"You and I both know there are undisclosed weapons that the military has access to. One of them has to be more effective against the saucers and those triangular craft. We've got to be able to do more than just send planes up to spit bullets at them."

"You're looking for a big gun to bring them down like the ship did?"

"I want them down in one piece so I can find my nieces. But if my family is really gone? I want those saucers blown from the sky in the smallest pieces possible. And then I'll go after the humans who knew the aliens weren't just a myth. The ones who knew they were very much active and yet kept it secret from us all."

"We don't know exactly how deep that rabbit hole goes, Alice."

"Then I'll go as far as I can and bury them all with me if I need to."

"You're not doing this alone. You're going to need help."

"Then call all our basement dwelling buddies, Dink. Tell them it's time we put our own theories to the test."

Sofia managed to keep her anger in check just enough to be mindful where she was stomping to. She was heading somewhere, anywhere, as far as she could get away from Emory. Her hands were flexing on her weapon. She was furious at Emory for her accusations and theories. Sofia was just as angry at herself for knowing a lot of what Emory believed in was actual truth. Truth blanketed in half-truths, shrouded in deception. That wasn't what she signed up for. But somehow she'd managed to get dragged into all the misinformation and lies concerning the saucers.

She flung herself down to sit on an outcrop. She stared blindly out at the fields below, lost to her thoughts. She'd been drafted to work on the saucers very early on in her career. Her engineering skills had singled her out as something special. Her orders were to decipher the technology to see what else could be harnessed for use in aviation and weaponry. So much had already been learned from that one downed craft. It had been a treasure trove of information and opportunity.

Sofia had taken over from one of the original technicians who was getting too old to continue. She'd learned from him then simply replaced him. She'd been working on deciphering the alien code behind the saucer's ability to cloak itself. The beam that she'd devoted so much time to discovering had never given up the secret behind its mechanics. Sofia had never seen it in action until she'd watched people being abducted.

She'd watched Emory throw herself into the cold white light in desperation to get to her family. A family that didn't treat her with much respect. *And I've been guilty of the same derision. What she sees happening in the world that people call her crazy for, I know all too well is true. I've been a part of it. I've helped perpetuate the cover-up of flying saucers under our control. Saucers we copied from an alien craft, something else I helped cover up. So many years from when they first pulled alien tech from out of the wreckage at Roswell. Technology so advanced it was light years ahead of anything the military had at its disposal. And I'm still learning from it.* She came to a realization. *Well, I was, but now all the saucers are gone. Reduced to ashes in the deep crater that was once Area 51.*

She rubbed her forehead where a headache was brewing. *So many secrets, so many lies told to cover up the truth. We knew about the existence of aliens all along.*

She looked at the sky. It was surprisingly clear, and the day felt normal again. She still searched for the sign of saucers. She'd believed that the only saucers that flew their skies were the ones tucked safely away in her hangars at Area 51. She had believed the aliens were dead. She'd been told that any other sightings had been fraudulent, a result of mass hysteria or of deliberate fabrication by the military. That only one craft had landed and aliens had never seen fit to try to come to Earth again. She didn't need to worry; she was just needed to exploit the technology and adapt it to saucers for human flight. She'd seen no evidence to point to anything otherwise. She'd just heard of the dead bodies of the aliens recovered at Roswell suspended on ice deep under the ground at Area 51. Out of sight, out of mind.

Sofia wondered if she'd been deceived as much as the public had been. She'd been let in on part of the secret yet not even she'd been told the full truth behind it.

Have I really been that close-minded to following orders that I let myself be blinded to what really lies in the shadows that I've been working in?

Her fingers twitched on the gun in her hands as she caught sight of movement down in the field. She slipped her finger onto the trigger and slowly rose to go investigate, grateful for the distraction from her own disquiet.

❖

The sound of gunfire startled Emory from the inner argument she was having about whether she should go find Sofia or leave her until she'd cooled down. She scrambled into action, clambering over the seats into the back of the van. She tore open the bag of weapons that were stored there. All the guns were preloaded. Sofia had prepared them for every eventuality. Emory pulled one out and reached for a few other supplies. She left the van, locking it automatically because she didn't trust anyone now, especially with what they had on board. Then she sprinted in the direction she could still hear shots ringing out from.

"Sofia! Sofia!" She careened down the ridge, arms flailing to keep herself upright on the loose dirt. She spotted Sofia at the bottom reloading her weapon. Emory skidded to a halt at Sofia's side, nearly losing her balance in her haste to reach her. "What the hell are you firing at?" She looked to where Sofia pointed across the field. Emory raised her own gun at what she saw.

Aliens were skittering en masse across the ground. Emory couldn't count them quick enough to get any idea of how many there were. She just knew there were more than she wanted to have a close encounter with. She fired, nearly deafening herself in the process with the unfamiliar weapon.

Sofia eyed her with derision. "You brought the machine gun?"

"I just grabbed whatever was first to hand in my rush to come to your aid."

"I don't need rescuing," Sofia gritted out, firing at the aliens and proving herself the much better shot. The aliens fell one by one to Sofia's well placed headshots. "Stop wasting bullets. You're just firing into the air."

Emory bristled at Sofia's condescending tone. She noticed the aliens hadn't changed direction, even in their panic, and were still heading toward a half covered drainage pipe that looked out of place amid the undergrowth. "They're seeking cover. They're damn well trying to escape." She took off after them.

"Emory!"

Sofia used her officer's voice, but, like always, Emory paid it no heed. She just ran toward the grays.

"Where does that pipe go, Dink?" Emory asked.

"It's not for drainage, that's for sure," he replied. "I'm just bringing up the lay of the land. I've found some old geographical maps of that area. It looks like we may have some sort of hidey hole out there for something hidden much deeper underground."

Still running, Emory managed to wrap the gun's strap over her shoulder to free up her hands. She pulled something out of her pocket.

"Oh my God! Don't you dare fucking drop that!" Dink screamed in her ear. He'd obviously caught sight of what she was holding via his view through her glasses.

Emory could hear footsteps rapidly gaining behind her. Sofia was heading across the field. She was still dropping aliens with expert head shots that Emory was totally in awe of. Before she could change her mind or chicken out, Emory pulled the pin from the grenade.

"Fire in the hole!" she yelled as she threw it as high and as hard as she could. It flew through the air, well across the field to where the aliens were congregating trying to squeeze down the narrow pipe. The grenade landed among them as they crowded together, taking it in with them.

The fierce explosion blew apart the pipe and ripped the surrounding land to shreds. Pieces of alien flew high into the air. The force from the blast knocked Emory on her ass. She was sitting there watching the dead alien bodies hit the dirt with dull thuds when Sofia reached her side. Sofia grabbed at her arm and shook her roughly.

"Are you crazy?" she shouted as debris still rained on the ground.

Emory was pleased to note there was very little left of the pipe and that the rubble had buried it. That hidey hole was blocked to anything now. The explosion had also wiped out most of the aliens. All that was left were ones torn to pieces on the ground, screeching as they died in agony. Emory shifted the gun back into her hands. "I won't waste any bullets this time." She stalked over to where the few remaining aliens lay writhing in the dirt.

"Where did you learn to throw a grenade like that?" Sofia asked, keeping up right beside her, her own gun at the ready.

"Softball, of course. The start of many a young girl's lesbian leanings." She turned the gun so its butt was facing downward. "Time for a different game." She held the butt above an alien's bulbous head. She stared into the black eyes, seeing nothing but herself reflected off the lens. It's squealing was reaching an ear-splitting high as it writhed on the ground. "Do you understand me? Do you understand English?" It showed no comprehension at all at her voice. "Where are the abductees? Where do you take the humans you kidnap?" Emory's short fuse was rapidly burning out. She knew she wasn't going to get any answers. "Then it's time we play 'Whack a Martian.'" She slammed the butt of her gun down with a satisfying crunch that stopped the creature's terrible wail. Emory wiped the oily residue off the gun on the grass.

"That's for Ellie."

CHAPTER EIGHTEEN

The field was full of the prettiest buttercups and daises Emory had ever seen. She plucked a bright yellow bloom from its stem and twirled it gently between her finger and thumb. The sunlight sparkled off the yellow petals. Emory turned her face up to the sky. Picture-perfect clouds drifted by. Everything was beautiful.

Then the sky darkened and the clouds began to shift in shape. They stretched until they morphed into the familiar shape of flying saucers. They blotted out the sun, turning the air cold. The shadows they cast left Emory straining to see. Like a sudden shower of rain, little gray aliens began falling from the saucers. They hit the ground and quickly covered it. They landed all around Emory, filling the field completely with bodies. The saucers took off and the blue sky returned. The buttercups and daises were all gone, buried under the writhing, squealing corpses of little gray aliens.

Emory slammed her hands over her ears, desperate to block the sound out as the screams burrowed through her brain until it was all she knew. She took a step, stumbling over the bodies before her.

"Tell me where my family is," she demanded over the row. She stared into their black eyes, searching for one who'd give her what she needed. "Tell me where they are." She kicked out at one. Its screaming escalated. The noise was excruciating, like nails dragging down a chalkboard.

"Tell me! Tell me where my family is!" Emory screamed, climbing over the sea of bodies shifting and undulating like waves on an endless sea.

She slammed her boot across the neck of one alien, cutting off the pitiful noise it was making. "Where are my family?" Emory said again. "Or I promise I will blow this whole field up and all of you with it." A grenade appeared in her hand and she wiggled the pin.

The black eyes stared at her, expressionless and empty. Its fingers scraped at her boot. Emory eased the pressure off of its scrawny neck.

"Where is my family?"

Its eyes never altered as it gasped for breath. She watched as its mouth appeared to form words, its lips moving, making shapes. It even appeared to smile. A cruel curling of its mouth, a sneer of self-satisfaction.

"Where are they?" Emory asked one last time.

It finally hissed out an answer. Its voice had a chilling tone.

"*Dead.*"

Emory woke with such a start she ended up being slammed back into her seat by the seat belt fastened across her chest. Her hands were outstretched, grasping at something, still caught up in the dream. She realized her fingers were fumbling to pull out an imaginary pin.

"Fuck!" she panted, trying desperately to wake up completely and leave the dream behind.

"You okay over there?" Sofia asked from the driver's seat. "I was just getting ready to nudge you because you seemed to be getting agitated."

No shit, Emory thought as she scrubbed at her face to try to erase all traces of her slumber. "Who knew killing an alien would be like eating cheese before bedtime? I hate having nightmares. I was just revisiting my less than finest moment losing my temper over that freaking alien."

"It did hold a crazy kind of heroic charm. Except for you promptly throwing up after it."

"Yeah, there's a reason why I was never invited along on the hunting trips my dad and brother went on." Emory was trying to remember how she even got back in the van. She vaguely remembered Sofia escorting her away from the battered remains of the alien and dragging her back up the ridge. She'd been silent the whole way and had collapsed into the passenger seat. Eventually, she had drifted off into a fitful sleep, exhausted after the adrenaline rush of her first ever up close and personal kill.

"I hate to say it, but you'll have to come to terms with it sooner rather than later. It's probably not going to be the only alien you'll kill point-blank given the chance. We're at war here." Sofia pushed a bag into Emory's lap. "Eat. I haven't seen you stuffing your face for at least an hour. You must be starving."

Emory opened the bag of chips and ate automatically. "How much longer to the base?"

"You weren't asleep that long, Emory. There's still a few hours to go in the journey."

Emory nodded, still shaken by her dream. "Are *you* okay?" She had to ask. Emory didn't know which was more unnerving—the Sofia she'd seen in a full-blown rage earlier, or this Sofia driving the van who seemed uncharacteristically calm now.

Sofia looked at Emory. "I'm not the one who's risked her life three times in as many days. Do you have some sort of a death wish, Emory? Because I'm seeing a peculiar pattern here."

Emory considered what Sofia was getting at. "Three times? Really?"

"Your foolhardy foray into Area 51 for starters. Then there's you throwing yourself at an abduction beam. And now you're running with grenades in your pockets and blowing up drainage pipes." Sofia shook her head at her. "Not to mention you cracking open the skull of an alien. Which was totally badass, but I'm guessing is something that's not sitting well with you?"

Emory deliberately crammed more chips into her mouth so she wouldn't have to answer immediately. She was able to think while she chewed and finally swallowed. "I feel like I'm losing my mind and you already think I'm crazy. I was angry. So angry I couldn't think straight. I'm scared I won't get my family back. Those girls don't deserve whatever the aliens have in store for them. And I can't even let my mind go there. I guess I don't really care what happens to me." She shrugged it off. "It's not like I have anything else to tie me to the planet. Might as well go out with a bang."

Sofia's gaze softened, and Emory felt herself grow warm from the silent scrutiny. "You're a major pain in *my* ass, Emory Hawkes, but you're not sacrificing yourself until you've outlived your usefulness to me and I can find a way to get rid of you myself." Sofia's sly teasing grin made Emory laugh. "I've promised you, if there's a way to get them back, I'll do all I can to help you. Whether I think you're crazy or not. Because that is a given."

Emory noticed that the phone was unusually silent and grabbed at the chance to change the subject off herself and her stupidity. "What's Dink up to?"

"He said he was doing some digging, figuratively speaking. What he's found so far are plans for a series of caverns and tunnel systems under that field you charged into. Oddly enough, that led him to unearthing tunnels under Las Vegas for me. According to your friend, there's a whole series of them running deep under the Strip."

"I'd heard about that. And does he think the aliens bombed Las Vegas because of them?"

"Dink seems to think the tunnels might reach as far as Area 51." Sofia rolled her eyes. "So he's wondering if the aliens we saw at Euphoria were smuggled out by such means. He also said that some of the tunnels known to run underground could fit something the size of an airplane in so he's hinting other sizeable objects could also be moved that way too. I'm reserving my own judgment on that."

"Are you ever going to buy into our justified paranoia, Sofia?"

"I don't buy into your fears that the rescuing of stranded people has any nefarious connotations, if that's what you're asking. But I'm not starting that conversation again because it pisses me off as you have already seen. But I apologize for storming off like a child." Sofia looked out the window at the road ahead. "You've got to admit, you two have some pretty out there ideas."

"Tootsie Rolls," Emory said, enjoying the look of complete and utter confusion on Sofia's face at her words.

"Excuse me?"

"The day you finally admit I am right about something theory based, I will expect a big bag of Tootsie Rolls as an apology." She smiled at the scoffing noise Sofia made under her breath followed by a mumbled comment that Emory thought sounded something like hell freezing over first. "Which reminds me, can you find us bathrooms by a store or something? I really don't fancy a trip off road. If we can find a place that hasn't been damaged or looted, I also need to make good on my debt to Dink."

"You and he bet with candy bars about the existence of aliens?" Emory nodded.

"Like I didn't think you two were crazy enough before this." She turned her attention back to the road.

"He was right and I was wrong. I can honestly say that this was candy I never wanted to hand over." Emory stared out the windshield, her mind awhirl.

"Do you want to talk about what tipped you over the edge from mild-mannered reporter to a gun-toting alien killer?"

Emory smiled at Sofia's description of her. "No, not really. I guess I'm realizing I have more than one role to play now in this invasion. I have to believe in something I'd dismissed as false trails and misdirection. Now I need to believe we can win against the worst odds, and I know we can't do that by me interviewing them. The journalist I am is going to have to take a backseat while I process all of this madness."

"I said I wouldn't arm you. I admit that might not be an option now."

Emory twisted in her seat to watch Sofia drive and see her reaction. "So I get to keep the machine gun?"

"You need to damn well practice with it. I think you might need to swap to something with a few less bullets to spray. You're a loose enough cannon as it is." Sofia fixed her with a look. "And a little scary."

Emory knew that feeling all too well. "I scared myself, to be honest. I didn't know I was capable of killing."

Sofia favored her with a sad smile. "That means you're still human. And that is how we'll win."

Emory was glad to be able to stretch her legs as she hopped down from the van outside a small row of stores Sofia had pulled alongside of. The area was empty and quiet. Not even birds were singing. After looking around outside for anything small and gray, Emory shoved her gun over her shoulder and walked into the store to gather more supplies. She wasn't just after food this time. That didn't stop her from gathering as much candy, including the bars for Dink, that she could lay her hands on. There was always room for chocolate. She found an unopened box of Dink's Butterfinger bars and thought he'd appreciate the sentiment. She filled her basket then wandered off down another aisle. She was surprised to find three teenaged boys huddled in the back of the store, drinking milk straight from the cartons. They took one look at her uniform and the gun she carried and ran.

"Hey, it's okay, I'm not—" Emory jumped out of their way as they sped past her, their arms full of whatever they could carry. "You'd better have something green and leafy in those bags!" she called after them as she watched them race past Sofia and bang out the door. Sofia followed them, presumably to make sure they stayed away from the van.

"I guess we're still not picking up strangers," Emory said when Sofia returned.

"We don't have time to babysit." She gave Emory a pointed look. "Besides, I have enough to deal with watching after you."

Emory snorted at her dig. "Funny that they're the only ones we've seen. This place is like a ghost town. I know we've strayed off the more traveled roads, but I didn't expect this. I just hope they've found somewhere reasonably safe to hide out."

As safe as you can be when the aliens can just beam you up at any given moment.

She wandered up and down the aisles, searching for something specific. She soon found what she was after and began gathering up as many tampons as she could carry. Feeling mischievous, she called to Sofia who was over in another aisle.

"Hey, Sofia? You're way older than me, right? Do you use Tampax or should I just pick you up a load of Depends?" Emory jerked when Sofia spoke directly in her ear.

"Give me one good reason why I shouldn't just stick you in a freezer and leave you there?"

Sofia was standing so close Emory could feel the heat radiating from her. The warmth from Sofia's breath caused her to shiver as it caressed over her flesh. "I can't honestly think of anything when you're this close to me, Sofia." Emory knew her voice wasn't as strong as she'd have liked in Sofia's close proximity.

"Do I make you nervous, Ms. Hawkes?" Sofia's low tones rumbled over Emory's senses, and she had to stifle a moan.

"You make me a lot of things. Nervous isn't one of them."

"You need to stop teasing me. I don't like being teased," Sofia said.

"I'll try to remember that, but you're so much fun to rile up, Major." Emory grunted as she was pressed into the shelf, Sofia's body crowding her. She could feel the softness of Sofia's breasts pressed into her back. It was a marked contrast to the sharp edge of the shelving. Emory closed her eyes and savored the touch.

"It's *Captain* Martinez. Don't make me hurt you." She deliberately pushed Emory harder into the shelves.

Emory dared to peek over her shoulder at Sofia who had her cap low over her eyes. She looked authoritative and, to Emory's eyes, all kinds of hot. *Who knew I'd find the bossy type attractive? Live and learn.*

"And really? Tampons? I'd have expected you to be raiding the chips and dips aisle. That does seem to be the staple of your dietary needs."

"You don't know when we'll get the chance to pick these things up again. I don't expect my periods are going to stop because there's an alien invasion happening so I'd rather be prepared." She eyed Sofia. "Are you going to help me get the right ones for you or are you holding me like this because you intend to pat me down? Believe me, I'm more than up for that."

Sofia stepped back, and Emory winced as she peeled herself off from the hard metal shelves. She immediately missed having Sofia's breath on her cheek. Sofia somehow managed to switch back to the mission while Emory was left trying to stop her legs from shaking.

"This whole place looks deserted. I wonder if the evacuation trucks have been through here," Sofia said, eying the empty store. "And the place is pristine. Even those boys kept their rifling tidy. It hasn't been looted." She gave Emory a pointed look as she gathered as many boxes of Pop Tarts as she could fit in the basket. "Except by your hands."

"We didn't see anything when we drove in. I'm sure we wouldn't miss an evacuation underway. We'll probably run into them on the road, but I warn you, I'm not going anywhere with them. So don't even think about handing me over." Emory flashed a glare at Sofia who pretended to look surprised at such a consideration. Emory's attention shifted quickly as she spotted a freezer full of ice cream. "I'm declaring today an 'eat your feelings' day." She picked through the small tubs of Ben and Jerry's until she could find her favorite.

"Are you expecting me to braid your hair too?" Sofia shook her head at her as she walked past holding a more practical item in her possession.

"You found their camping aisle?" Emory was surprised to see Sofia had an axe angled rakishly over her shoulder. "What are you aiming on doing? Chopping down trees so we can hurl logs at the saucers? Splinter them to death?"

"I'm looking for the gift wrap aisle. I want to stick a bow on this for you so that the next time you want to crack some skulls you'll use this and not the butt of a valuable gun." She smirked at Emory as she sauntered off, obviously pleased with herself.

"Well, aren't you just hysterical," Emory muttered, watching her leave the store. "You can get your own damn ice cream."

CHAPTER NINETEEN

Back on the road, barely five minutes after leaving the store, Sofia was surreptitiously watching Emory drive. She had never seen her look so antsy. Finally, she had to call her on it.

"Okay, you're twitchier than a kid who's been let loose with Red Bull. What's wrong?"

"I can't raise Dink on the phone."

Emory looked almost...terrified. Sofia stared at the phone that lay on the center console between them. She acknowledged it had been quite a while since she'd heard his voice. Emory hadn't been talking to herself either so he'd obviously been silent in her ear.

"Maybe he's asleep," Sofia said.

Emory made a face, and Sofia could tell she didn't think that was the cause.

"It's just so...quiet," Emory said.

"What? Without the voices in your head telling you to do stuff?" Sofia couldn't help but tease her a little to try to get a rise out of her. The fear in her eyes made Sofia feel uneasy.

"With all that's happening, I have no idea if the saucers have been where he is and wiped him out too. He's my best friend, and I'm worried about him. In fact, I think it would be safe to say he's my *only* friend."

"You don't strike me as the antisocial type."

"I'm not, but it's difficult to keep friends once they realize you believe the government is Big Brothering you and has hidden agendas going on. It starts out as great after-dinner conversation, but soon friends start rolling their eyes and changing the subject if you say anything. It's hard to be among people who don't see the world the same way as I do. They'd rather stay oblivious. It's easier for them to just go with the flow." Emory shrugged. "I had one woman tell me she believed what I was saying but didn't want to think about it because it made her depressed. She said she'd rather ignore what she could see because she didn't want to bring her children up into that kind of world. What kind of parent sees what the world is doing and doesn't even warn her kids about it?"

Sofia didn't know how to answer that. She was guilty of the exact same thing but in reverse. She hid the truth. She lied to keep it from being exposed. She helped perpetuate a view of the world the government wanted to be seen. A smokescreen to hide what really lay behind. For Sofia, that was the existence of manmade alien saucers. She couldn't help but wonder what other lies were also being kept from *her*. With every layer of command, there were secrets untold.

She checked her watch. They were roughly two hours away from the base. The roads they'd been on had traffic, but the other vehicles had been few and far between. Sofia found that curious. A convoy of large trucks passed them a while ago. They appeared to be military… but not the usual vehicles. There was no insignia to give any clue as to their affiliation. Sofia wondered just who exactly had been drafted to gather the population. So far, Emory hadn't commented on them, though they could just be seen in the distance. She was too busy checking her phone for a signal and looking to the sky. Sofia chewed at her lip as she wondered just who really was rounding up civilians to take them who knows where. She glanced at a silent Emory. *I've been in her company too long. She's got me seeing conspiracies in everything too.* She wished she could talk to her superior officer, but she hadn't had the chance to call in and he hadn't made contact with her.

She'd see him soon enough.

Emory was still fussing with her phone. "The signal's gone. We're cut off from him." She shot Sofia a nervous look. "That's not a good thing."

"You don't have him in your ear *all* the time, do you?"

"No, of course not. But at this moment? We need him there. He's got a much wider view on the world, Sofia. I need him watching over us, telling us what's going on."

Sofia was surprised to realize how upset Emory was getting. "Hey, look. We're heading to a high security air force base. You'll be safe there. Wherever it is Dink hides out, let's face it, he's not *here* with you. He can't fight by your side like I can."

"I know that, but your base isn't safe, Sofia, no matter how many guards it has on its doors. Without Dink we have no early warning system if there are saucers in our area. You got your orders from somewhere, but you haven't been in contact with them since. I'm with you constantly, Sofia. You're more isolated than I am. What's to say we're not driving toward a base that has suffered the same fate as Area 51? Then what? How safe are we then, both of us cut off from our intelligence?" Emory picked up the phone again. "Goddammit, Dink, now is not the time to go radio silence on me." She lifted her eyes to look up at the sky.

"Oh fuck! Saucer, twelve o'clock."

Sofia could see the bottom of the saucer descending from the clouds. It looked huge in the sky even though it was miles away. She grabbed hold of her seat as Emory quickly swung the van off the road and raced across fields that led to a homestead spread out in the distance. Sofia looked back and could see the familiar white beam being emitted from the saucer. It was directly over the convoy that had been stopped dead in its tracks.

"We need to hide fast," Sofia said, not wanting to see more people abducted when there was nothing she could do to stop it.

"Working on it, Major." Emory swung the wheel harshly. They skidded out of the field and onto a dirt road that lead up to the house that was surrounded by apple trees. "They've got to have a storm shelter, right? Or at least a cellar, somewhere to stick all those apples?" Emory gunned the van up the driveway. "When we get out, grab the guns. I swear, if I get beamed up I'm going with grenades in my pocket and I'm blowing those bastards sky high."

"I should never have let you near the armory." Sofia grimaced as they hit a deep rut in the ground. The van slammed into it and bounced them back out. Sofia's hand flew up to brace herself against the roof to stop her head from banging off it. "We also need to get you some counseling for the crazy kamikaze thoughts inhabiting that brain of yours." Sofia barely hesitated before asking, "Will there be enough grenades for both of us?"

Emory flashed her a big grin and nodded. She directed them into a barn that had been left with its doors wide open. "Somebody sure left in a hurry," she said as she drove in. She turned the engine off and rushed to grab anything she could use to try to hide the large VW Bus from sight.

Sofia grabbed all she could from the back of the van and then helped Emory close the barn doors. They ran around to the back of the house, and Sofia was never more thankful to spot a storm shelter. She had to shoot the lock off the doors to gain them entrance. She led the way down the steps inside. Sofia felt her way down along the wall until she found a space where she set up a base to put the camping lantern on. She lit it and only then did Emory close the hatch above them. The lantern gave off a bright glow and revealed the inside of the shelter to them. Various old bicycles were lined up against the back wall and tubs of apples were stored in hay. A light fixture hung from the ceiling, minus its bulb.

Emory came down the steps and got a gun out of the bag. She sat on one of the old padded seats in the shelter. She didn't take her eyes off the hatch door as if expecting it to come flying open.

Sofia picked her own weapon and took the seat next to Emory. "I thought the saucers had moved overseas," she said, careful not to raise her voice above a whisper.

"Looks like they're back. Maybe the climate wasn't to their liking." Emory rolled back the sleeve of her fatigues. Even in the light thrown by the lantern, Sofia could clearly see Emory's arm hair was raised.

"What is that?" she asked.

Emory rubbed at her arm. "That's my early warning signal. The saucers and big ships must have some kind of static thing going on because this happens to me every time they're close."

They sat in silence, eyes trained on the outer doors. Sofia strained to hear anything from the outside. She kept her breathing quiet and her eyes focused on the shelter doors. Sofia waited, her gun aimed and her finger on the trigger.

After a long while, Sofia heard something, a faint rustling noise. *There'd better not be rats down here.* She looked around nervously. The noise was a little louder, and she realized it was Emory messing with a bag at her feet. Emory took out her tub of ice cream and then pulled a spoon from one of her pockets. Sofia stared at her as Emory popped the lid off, licked all the ice cream off it, and began digging in. She couldn't believe what she was seeing. "Really? You're eating that *now*?"

"It's melting. It would be a shame to waste it while it's still semi-frozen." She held out a loaded spoon to Sofia. "Want a bite?"

Sofia shook her head. She was amazed by how Emory's mind worked at the most stressful of times.

"I eat when I'm nervous," Emory explained around a mouthful of Caramel Chew Chew. "And look at it this way. If I get beamed up right now maybe I can take an alien's eye out with this." She licked her spoon clean and brandished it.

Sofia leaned against Emory. She was understandably frightened and too tired to care anymore. "Don't ever change, Emory Hawkes. Batshit crazy suits you all too well." She returned the goofy smile Emory gave her and accepted a spoonful of ice cream while they waited to see if the saucer was going to find them and whisk them away.

Emory didn't know which was worse, being outside and watching the saucers do their worst, or hiding and waiting for them to come find them. She checked her watch again for the umpteenth time.

"Do you think they've flown to new pastures?" she asked.

"It's been an hour and we haven't had a visitation so I'd say so. How's your early warning system?"

Emory checked her arms. "The hairs aren't standing up. I think they're long gone. We dodged a bullet there, Captain. Pity those trucks in front of us weren't as fortunate. I have a horrible feeling they flew right into the saucer's path." Emory shook her head at the thought. The trucks hadn't stood a chance. The saucer had literally dropped from the sky above their heads. "Do you think they were military?"

Sofia's silence made Emory turn to look directly at her. "They *weren't* military?"

"They were probably an evacuation convoy. I recognized the trucks from Hurricane Katrina."

"FEMA? So the saucer abducted evacuees?" Emory screwed her eyes shut and willed herself not to lose her temper. The trucks were supposedly carrying people to safety and instead had driven them into the path of their abductors.

"It was an unfortunate incident. If we hadn't stopped at that store or you hadn't deliberated for a while over which ice cream to choose, we might have been farther down the road. The saucer could have taken us just as easily."

Emory felt her blood run cold at that sobering thought. She glanced around their shelter. "This place looks like it was left in a hurry. The folks who own this place could have been in one of those trucks if they'd asked to be taken to safety."

Sofia nodded. "They could. For now we need to concentrate on the fact we're *not*. We have a job to do to try to get all those people back." She stood up, laid down her gun, and stretched languorously.

Emory watched her, admiring her beauty once more. She was striking, in a tiny spitfire kind of way. It made Emory want to rile her up to watch her explode. Because when her eyes flashed their fire, Emory was more than ready to burn. "I bet you knock people out when you're dressed in something other than your fatigues. Which is saying something because you totally rock the camo look."

Sofia eyed her. "Are you flirting with me?" She lowered her arms from where they'd been over her head, stretching out the kinks in her shoulders. She brought them to rest on her hips. It was a defiant stance.

It made Emory smile all the more.

"You bet I am. You're gorgeous. I realize in the real world, B.A., Before Aliens, you wouldn't have given me a second glance." Emory shrugged. "It's not like we would even have met in the first place."

"Seeing as I'm career military and you're nowhere near the CIA agent you purport to be."

"There is that." Emory moved closer. "But here we are, fighting side by side. Taking on the invaders together, despite our differences. How cool is that?"

"You're still just one more screw-up away from being thrown in the brig."

"Be honest. You'd miss me if you had to lock me up." Emory moved closer still and reached out to snag a piece of Sofia's hair between her fingers. It felt silky smooth to her touch.

Sofia stared at her. "I probably would, but I'd stand less chance of being court-martialed for being guilty of colluding with a scandal-stirring journalist who is out to expose military secrets."

Emory didn't take offense at Sofia's words. She could see the faintest glimmer of humor in her eye. "Ignoring all that though, here it's just you and me." She gestured around the small room. "A secluded hideaway," she pointed to the lantern, "romantic lighting. I'd be crazy not to admit I'd really like to kiss you again without the fear of either one of us dying in the next second to instigate it."

She looked at Sofia's lips and watched as her tongue came out to nervously moisten them. "I'll back off if you want me to. I understand the policy of 'don't ask don't tell,' and I might be assuming where I shouldn't be, but if you're straight, for God's sake let me down quickly and painlessly."

"Your gaydar works better than whatever it is you use to detect danger," Sofia said wryly.

Emory muttered a "Thank God" under her breath. "If you're feeling this"—she waved her hand between them—"thing between us, then I'm sure you'll agree time is too precious to waste. What with all that's happening outside in the crazy place the world has become." She purposely let her hand fall from where she'd been running Sofia's hair through her fingers. She saw it as a good sign when Sofia grabbed for it and held on.

"You drive me to madness. You know that, right?" Sofia squeezed Emory's hand.

"I can't honestly see that changing, to be honest." Emory tugged Sofia closer.

"And your breath smells of ice cream."

"So does yours. You did share my spoon once you realized I wasn't going to stop making orgasmic noises until you sampled some of its creamy goodness too." She slipped her hands around Sofia's waist and pulled her closer still. "Watching your tongue lick the spoon clean tested my sanity."

"Oh, you can't blame me for that. You're already certifiable." Sofia's smile was a tad cruel. Emory wanted to kiss it off her face.

"You're very mean to me," Emory pouted at her playfully. She did so love a woman with spirit. And Sofia was proving to be the feistiest she had ever met.

"And you talk too much." Sofia grasped Emory's collar and pulled her down to kiss her into silence.

Lost in the feeling of Sofia's soft lips against her own, Emory closed her eyes and reveled in the sensation. Sofia felt so good in her arms. Sofia's hands cupped Emory's cheeks as she deepened their kiss. Their touch kept Emory exactly where Sofia wanted her as she overwhelmed Emory's senses. Emory groaned as Sofia took teasing nips at her lips, tugging at her lower lip just enough to make Emory chuckle at the show of dominance before she was kissed senseless again.

Emory ran her hands over Sofia's back, but the heavy fabric of her jacket hindered her from feeling more. Emory tugged at it, wanting desperately to explore Sofia's shape.

Sofia was the first to pull back, her eyes burning with arousal. She panted softly as she fought to catch her breath. "We should go."

Emory whined pathetically. "Fuck saving the world for a moment! I just want you kissing me some more."

"At ease, soldier." Sofia pulled out of Emory's arms. She kept her head down as she fussed to straighten her clothing.

Emory purposely stepped back into Sofia's personal space. "Oh, I'm no soldier, but I'd gladly serve *under* you, Captain." She leaned in closer to whisper in Sofia's ear, "And I'm very good at taking orders…especially in bed."

Sofia moaned. It was a sin-laden, breathy sound. She tugged Emory to her and kissed her forcefully once more before roughly pushing her away again. "God, you're more addictive than the damned ice cream." She ran her fingertips over her bruised lips.

Emory was surprised to note that Sofia's hands were visibly trembling. Though it killed her to do so, Emory took a step back to give Sofia some space.

"I guess the outside world is waiting for us to rejoin it so it can start spinning again. Kissing you made everything grind to a halt for one purely magical moment." She smiled at Sofia's shy smile. "Come on, Major Turn-on, let's get back on the road before either of us changes our minds."

Chapter Twenty

Emory gladly let Sofia take point and lead the way back up the steps. She watched Sofia slowly ease open the doors, her gun drawn ready for whatever lay out there.

"All clear."

Emory clambered out after Sofia and was glad to breathe fresh air again. She closed the doors behind them and wedged a piece of broken bark under the handles to fashion a poor man's lock. Then she followed Sofia back to the barn to retrieve the van.

Emory took the time to top up the gas with one of the canisters from the previous base. She was so glad to get back in the driver's seat of her vehicle. She waited for Sofia to fasten herself in before starting the engine.

"So, second star on the right and straight on to Mirror Base East?" Emory pulled out from the barn.

"I advise you keep your foot on the gas because that saucer couldn't have been on its own. Let's get to the base ASAP. Have one eye on the road, the other trained on the clouds. The GPS will guide your route, but it won't warn against saucers."

"No, that is Dink's job." Emory picked up her phone again and dialed Dink's number. It still didn't connect. "What the fuck is going on with this?" She resisted the urge to throw the phone in a fit of annoyance. "We need him."

"You have a lot of faith in him."

"He's never steered me wrong so far. He's my partner and I trust him with my life."

"Partner in crime, is that?" Sofia gave her such an innocent look Emory had to smile.

"Yeah, I guess so. He's always the first one I call when I'm arrested. He calms my brother down a lot faster than I can."

"Have you been arrested much?"

Emory shrugged. "Once or twice. I had to learn the hard way how close was *too* close when parking out by Area 51."

"And then there was this latest brush with the law you were telling me about. You were heading to court over not revealing your sources, correct?"

"Something like that. I may be guilty of sneaking into government buildings or the occasional military base, but the only person I put into danger is myself. The people that Dink and I talk to have to know we will keep their identities safe. They are sometimes leaking highly classified information for us to expose. I don't want their blood on my hands if I let myself run off at the mouth and reveal them."

"What was so important about this disclosure that you were willing to lose your liberty over it?"

"We were going to expose the boss and his minions of the highest level cover-ups. It was to be a career building exposé and would have finally proved what we've said all along. There are people behind the scenes pulling the strings that make the government and military perform to the tune they are playing."

"What made you believe in this person telling you these so-called secrets? They could have been feeding you false information. Seducing you with exactly what you wanted to hear to have you tangled in their web of lies and get you prosecuted to shut you down."

It galled Emory to have to agree with that. "You're right. There's always that risk, but this time they were supplying names and faces to the players. If nothing else, I could have caused a big enough rumble to shake the ranks a little." The silence from Sofia was telling and Emory looked over at her. "You've worked at Area 51, Captain. You can't tell me you weren't aware of how many secrets were covered up there."

"The base was huge. Sometimes I wasn't even aware of what was going on in the next hangar."

"Nice deflect there, sweetheart."

"*Sweetheart?*"

"Well, you did kiss me. I'm seeing that as a positive step up from you threatening me with the brig."

Sofia laughed at her. "No matter how many times I kiss you, you have to know I can't tell you everything my job entails. If I did..." She purposely let the sentence dangle.

Emory finished it for her. "You'd have to kill me. Like you need any more incentive for that."

Sofia was quiet. "I worry about you." She reached to put her hand on Emory's thigh. "You keep looking into things where you have no business to be looking. It will come back to bite you in the ass in time."

Emory didn't miss the thinly veiled warning in Sofia's tone. "You know that stern voice of yours turns me on, don't you?" Sofia dug her nails into Emory's leg. The sharp pain made Emory jump and let out a yelp.

"I'm being serious. I need you to tread carefully at the next base. I can't have you pulling a disappearing act again to go Nancy Drewing around locked doors. You'll endanger both of us if you follow your usual M.O."

"You know having to be good is going to kill me."

"Better that than them actually doing it."

Sofia wasn't joking. Emory's eyebrows shot up. "Are you serious?"

Before Sofia could answer, the sound of Emory's phone ringing frightened them both. Emory nearly drove off the road in her shock. She fought to keep the van straight while she fumbled for the phone to answer it.

"Emory!" Dink's voice came over loud and clear through the speaker.

"Dink! Where the fuck have you been? Are you okay?" Emory had never been happier to hear his voice.

"Something strange happened. The Dark Net got corrupted right after chatter started about an alien hit directed on Geneva. We're talking about an Area 51 kind of hit. As word spread, we started losing phone lines, and then the Internet connections were mysteriously wiped out in a domino effect. I was watching the connections fail in a cascade, winking out across the planet. Then mine died too. Damn weird."

"Was it specifically Geneva or was it the whole of Switzerland targeted?" Emory was worried about Dink losing communication with his contacts scattered around the planet. That's all some of them existed for. The theorists, the watchers, and the activists, all poised to do their part in uncovering the truth. They were all each other had to stand up against a disbelieving world. She turned to Sofia. "Had you heard about this cascade?" Sofia shook her head. Emory decided to think about those implications later and just be thankful Dink was okay. "So, how'd you get back in touch with me?"

"I put my faith in the hands of the Lord," Dink said.

Emory smothered the smile that would have made Sofia all too suspicious. She knew exactly what Dink meant. "Have you lost all Internet connection?"

"It's patchy, but I have friends working on it. I have a feeling someone didn't like what we were finding out." He paused. "Sofia, back at Euphoria, did you by any chance tell anyone about me?"

"No. Under different circumstances I would have, but nothing about now is normal. You're somehow keeping us safe so I'm selfish enough to want to keep you on my side. However much I despair of your methods."

"Well, someone reached out and pushed all of us out of the Dark Net and off the airwaves completely. I've never seen that happen before," Dink said. "And I don't think it was the aliens."

"Dink, you know the old saying when you look into the abyss, the abyss looks back? If you keep delving into governmental and military software, sooner or later, you will be found. You hack those systems, they *will* turn the hack back on you. Dark Net or not, there's nowhere to hide online," Sofia said.

"Now there's a sobering thought. Good thing I've learned not to leave footprints leading back to my own door." Dink could be heard clattering away on a keyboard. "So, ladies, catch me up on your news while I was M.I.A. What did you two get up to?"

Emory tried desperately not to look at Sofia who was blatantly staring at her, daring her to tell her best friend exactly what they had been doing. She hesitated. "We saw a saucer and had to take shelter."

"Damn it. This is what happens when I'm not available to give you guys a heads-up." Dink sounded furious and a little frazzled. "You're okay though, right?"

"Yes, still all in one piece. Oh, and we had ice cream," Emory grimaced at how lame that sounded.

"You had a close encounter *and* you had ice cream? Man, I leave you alone for a little while and you're tucking into the sweet treats like you're at an amusement park. On the next adventure? *I'm* riding shotgun."

"Let's live through this one first and then you're on," Emory said. She didn't look down as she felt Sofia's hand on her leg, not wanting to give Dink fuel to his fire. But she covered it with her own hand and squeezed. "We're heading to the base now."

"The base that doesn't exist on any map. Wish I could see it, but your feed is down."

Emory saw Sofia react to that nugget of information. Dink's view on the world through Emory's eyes was out of commission. Emory wondered at the relief she spotted on Sofia's face before she quickly masked it.

Just what in the hell are we heading to, Emory wondered.

Huge warning signs were liberally spread around the perimeter of the largest military base Emory had ever seen. It was a weird oasis stuck in the middle of nowhere, surrounded by a massive mountain range that shielded it from view. It appeared to be twice the size of Area 51. It housed many more hangars, triple the amount of buildings, and more security measures than Emory had ever witnessed. Every guard was armed with machine guns. Sentry posts had gun turrets poised and ready. Armored tanks flanked the fencing as an extra show of force.

"Let me guess. If none of this hardware is a deterrent, they send out a squad of guys to piss on you."

Sofia was not amused. "Stop gawking. You're supposed to be a CIA trained official, not some crazed fangirl jonesing at all this."

Emory grinned and smothered it quickly at Sofia's look of displeasure.

"Best behavior here. I'm warning you, Emory."

"Then you'd better start calling me Ellen Mays because she has the credentials to be professional."

"No! You are not going in there pretending to be your CIA alias."

"That's who's going to get me through the gate. You've got to have me identified as her. I have to be her. I have no business being here as a civilian known for having a dubious background in causing trouble in places such as this. You need me to be seen as Ellen. Besides," she added flippantly, "Ellen rocks. You'll totally dig her. You forget, I've played this game before. I can pass as an agent and have."

"That remains to be seen. I should just leave you out here for my own sanity."

"What? And leave me to the mercies of the aliens? I don't think so. You kissed me, Captain Martinez. You know you're not letting a gorgeous gal like me out of your sight after we shared that tender moment in a dank and dark storm cellar."

"I'm not letting you out of my sight, period," Sofia said. She pulled up to the front gate and dutifully showed her information to the guards. With a brief moment of reluctance, she accepted Emory's falsified ID and passed that over too.

"We don't appear to have Agent Mays on our list, Captain." The guard ran his eyes over his tablet again.

"You won't. She was at Area 51 and saved my life there. I'm returning the favor." She accepted their paperwork back and listened while he gave instructions as to where they were to park.

"Unusual mode of transport, Captain," he remarked, smirking at the Volkswagen Bus with some distain.

"It got me here in one piece," Sofia said. Emory saw her stare down the guard until he took a step back and waved for the doors to open. Sofia drove them through with barely a word.

"Wow, get you pulling that old Jedi mind trick on him." Emory waved her hand as if employing the Force. "This is not the conspiracy theorist you're looking for."

Sofia smirked. "He maligned your Bus and I'm growing quite fond of it." She cut Emory a look. "You, not so much."

Playing to her audience, Emory clutched at her heart. "You wound me. But don't think I won't try to run him over on our way out of here." She switched her attention to where they were going. She was astounded by how immense the base was. "They're a cautious lot here. Anyone would think they had something to hide." Sofia's silence tempted Emory to take a further dig, but she resisted. After all, Sofia was risking everything bringing her here. "So, what's the deal with there being no name over the door? I've never known of a base not even getting a number attached to it. Or is this place so secret it's the Voldemort of secret bases? No one dares speak its name."

"Maybe they like the anonymity."

Emory eyed her suspiciously. "Have you been here before, Sofia? Do you know its proper name?"

"I've never seen this base, and I've visited quite a lot in my service. I know it only as Mirror Base East. Imagine that though, a base that has slipped under your guys' radar. Someone must be doing something right here."

Emory wondered how that had happened. She heard a noise in her ear, but before she could speak Dink spoke instead.

"Do not react to my voice. We're deep into unknown territory here, Em. This base does not exist to the outside world. One of my sources says a mirror base means it reflects what's seen on another. He speculated it's a mirror to Area 51 considering all the secrecy. Add to that, an Area 51 officer has been called to it. As much as I like Sofia, she's a part of what we've been seeking to uncover. She worked on the saucers; she has to know more than what she's revealing. She's now working on their security. Security means you have something precious to protect. Clear your throat if you understand what I'm saying."

Emory coughed and purposely turned out of Sofia's eye line.

"There's so much to see here," Emory said, hoping Dink got the hint.

"I can see it. I'm back online and your glasses are broadcasting. I will see whatever you show me. Keep that quiet too for now. I'm back in business and watching over you."

Emory let out a quiet sigh of relief. She caught sight of the building Sofia had been directed to and they soon pulled up in front of it. Before Emory could do anything, Sofia reached over to touch her face. Then she kissed her. Emory blinked in surprise when Sofia pulled back.

"What was that for?"

Sofia wouldn't meet Emory's curious gaze. She hopped down from the van and only then looked back at Emory who was still seated, stunned from the gentle kiss.

"You might not be so inclined once we go inside and I have to do my job."

Emory froze. "You're not going to arrest me, are you?"

Sofia shook her head. "No. But I'm military born and bred, *Ellen*, and orders are orders. I've been playing by your rules and mine on the road. In here, I have to follow someone else's. It's my job and you might not appreciate what that exactly entails. And you might not like what you see."

Emory nodded, not understanding but trusting Sofia enough to want to be very vigilant among the other officers and mindful of what Sofia might have to do.

She was about to set foot inside a top secret military base, one that was invisible to the outside world. She didn't want to be someone who disappeared right along with it.

CHAPTER TWENTY-ONE

Emory knew she was no safer from the threat of aliens on the base than she was driving on the highway. That didn't stop her from being relieved to finally be inside again in a building surrounded by people with a multitude of weapons at their disposal. She stuck close to Sofia's side, watching as she ran the gauntlet of officers all coming to ask her questions about their journey and what she had witnessed out there. Emory was surprised how cut off from the outside it made them sound.

She tuned their repetitive queries out and fixed her attention on the myriad of wall mounted monitors. Each one showed a key area in a different state. So many landmarks had been destroyed, the devastation a stark vista. The one black triangle craft that had been shot down was looming large on one of the screens. Emory counted at least three different agencies, judging by their uniforms, clambering all over the unsubmerged part of the downed craft. They appeared to be trying to break their way inside the ship. Nothing they were attempting seemed to be making any difference to the impenetrable shiny hull.

"I could have told them using those tools wouldn't make a dent on whatever material that craft is," Dink said quietly in Emory's earpiece. "If it takes a barrage of ballistic weapons to shoot the thing down, it's not going to take something akin to a can opener to pry the metal open so we can take a sneaky peek inside."

Sofia tugged on Emory's arm to capture her attention away from what she was seeing. They barely took a step before Sofia was waylaid again.

"Captain Martinez, glad you made it out of Area 51 alive."

Sofia smiled at his earnest relief. "Airman Douglas, nice to see you again. Can you tell me how many saucers we have shot down since the attack began, please?"

"The saucers are proving quite tricky to pinpoint. You know all too well the speeds they can generate. We've tried to get a missile lock on them, but they have incredible maneuverability."

Emory looked back and forth at them both. "Why are you even considering shooting the saucers down when they might have humans on board?"

The officer stared at her. "And you are, ma'am?"

"CIA Agent Mays. I've seen what these saucers can do, both in firepower and in abduction techniques. I've lost family on one of those saucers. I, for one, would appreciate they're not shot down if there's a sliver of a chance they can be rescued."

"I'm sorry for your loss, ma'am, but in all wars there is always some collateral damage."

Emory saw red. Her instant rage blinded her to everything in that room but the face of the officer as she lunged for him. Dimly, she could feel someone fiercely trying to pull her off him. Sofia was wrenching Emory's arm back, stopping her from punching him in the face.

"Agent! This won't bring them back. Stand down." She struggled to keep Emory back.

Judging by the look of surprise on his face, Douglas hadn't expected quite the reaction his words received either. "I apologize," he said, sounding sincere, but Emory wasn't mollified. She jerked her arm from out of Sofia's grip. She took a step forward and got into Douglas's face.

"If a saucer comes flying over this base, I will personally push you out the door to meet and greet them."

His eyes widened a fraction at the threat. Sofia tugged Emory away a little harder.

"*Agent.*"

Emory stepped back, but she didn't stop glaring at Douglas who looked at a loss as to what he should do now. "I could make you disappear, and I wouldn't need a fucking alien beam to do so," she said with a snarl in her tone. She looked around the room at everyone watching them. So much for keeping a low profile. "Do any of these monitors reveal where the saucers are taking their abductees?"

"Captain Martinez, if you'd care to bring Agent Mays with you I might be able to give you some more information."

Sofia's head shot up at the sound of the man's voice. Emory quickly read his name tag. General Russom. He was an inspiring figure. His gray hair belied his youthful appearance, and for someone who probably spent a great deal of time tied to a desk he looked as fit and lean as the younger officers in the room.

"Ohh, that's none other than Ronald Russom. He's the big man on campus. I bet you that's Sofia's boss," Dink said.

The look Sofia shot her warned her as much. Great, Emory thought, and he's just watched me trying to tear the head off one of his men in the war room. Emory sighed. *Maybe Sofia should have left me in the parking lot after all.*

Emory tried to pull herself together and walked away. She couldn't help but direct one last dirty look in Douglas's vicinity. Sofia discreetly nudged her to stop it and pushed her forward, striking up a conversation with her superior to no doubt deflect the attention Emory was on the receiving end of.

"Sir, it's nice to see you, though I really wish it was under different circumstances."

"Yes, it's strange to see you out here. You're usually firmly entrenched in Hangar One."

"I was lucky to get out alive, sir. I have Agent Mays here to thank for that."

Russom looked Emory over. "CIA, right?"

Emory nodded and held out a hand to shake his. "Ellen Mays, sir. It's quite the setup you have here." She smiled a little. "And well off the beaten track if I may say so."

Russom smiled back. "It's very much a 'need to know' base. Once Area 51 was outed, we decided to find somewhere else to camp out of the sight of prying eyes. It's amazing what a natural mountain range and a big ass exclusion zone above can hide."

"Well, I thank you for your hospitality. We've been on the road since Area 51 was hit. I just hope that exclusive zone keeps the aliens at bay as well."

Emory was aware Russom was sizing her up. She let him, even though the blatant stare was riling her.

"What took you to Nevada, Agent?" He gestured for them to follow him down the hallway.

"Softly softly, Em," Dink whispered, "He's trained to spot a lie at fifty meters."

"I was sent there by my boss," Emory said, which would have been kind of true if she thought of Dink in that way.

"Jack Carter sent you," Dink supplied. "His is a name that's come up in conversation with our source and, according to word on the Net, he was in Las Vegas when it got hit. Chances are he's dead and we can use him."

"Jack Carter sent me the order. Whoever I was supposed to meet never turned up, and I was left hanging." She feigned annoyance. "Then the attack started, and Captain Martinez and I managed to escape before they blew the base to pieces."

Russom opened his office door and ushered them into the room, gesturing for them to sit. "Why were you still there, Captain? Why didn't you evacuate with the rest of the base?"

"Lieutenant Colonel Jones ordered me to make sure the base was clear."

Russom frowned. "You're not security."

"I know that and he knows that, but I'd received an order from a superior officer to clear the underground base. I never realized what was happening topside because I was too busy making sure everyone got out." Sofia's smile was more of a grimace. "You know he's never wasted an opportunity to put me in my place, sir."

Emory decided she hated that man as much as she detested Douglas back in the war room.

Russom shook his head in disgust. "Jones always did know how to push your buttons. The bastard put you in danger. Where's the old misogynist now?"

"Either under the rubble that's all that's left of the base or maybe abducted."

And hopefully getting anally probed, Emory thought unkindly but with an inner malice reserved for men who treated women like dirt.

"I heard from a reliable witness that when the evacuating staff tried to escape they were taken up into one of the saucers." Sofia didn't look at Emory, but Emory was pleased to be described as reliable.

"What's happening with that, sir?" Emory interrupted because she needed that information. She wanted to get back out there and find her family as soon as possible. "Is there any word of where they're being taken?"

"What is your division saying?"

Dink made a noise. "Deflection. That's not a good sign. Tell him you've had no contact with your cronies at the CIA."

"I've had no contact with them, which is why I've stuck to Martinez like glue. I was hoping for a sharing of information here between agencies. Especially after we witnessed my nieces being abducted right in front of us. I need to know we're going to do everything we can to bring those abductees home."

Russom was silent for so long Emory almost started to fidget. His hesitation was making her anxious. It was never a good sign when someone stalled.

"Who was your boss again?"

"Agent Jack Carter, sir. I reported directly to him alone. I was his *special* project." *Our source of information called himself a special project agent. Let's see if you recognize that title.* She was praying Dink was busily adding to the Agent Ellen Mays info-bot that lay undetected in the government's databases. Because on occasions like this, it kept Emory safe while people questioned just who the hell the unknown agent was.

"And you were at Area 51 for what purpose exactly?"

"Like I said, I was supposed to be meeting someone. The rest would be classified information, sir, and not something I should probably divulge at this stage." Emory wasn't sure, but she thought she heard Sofia make a slight choking noise.

"Did the name of an Agent Truno come up in any of those conversations before you were called to Area 51?"

"Ooooh, he's revealing stuff first to see how much you know. Tell him yes." Dink chortled. "It's like being *Jane* Bond! But does that make me Q or M?"

"What do *you* know about him, sir? Last I heard he was M.I.A. which is probably why I was called in."

Russom nodded. "Funny. I heard the same rumor. He was...a liaison, of sorts, to the air force. It always pays to have friends in the CIA, I've found."

Emory nodded slowly then looked at Sofia who had been watching the exchange with some interest. "That's what I told the captain here, right after I pulled her ass out of the rubble. Then she saved me in turn when my family was taken out of their home and up into a saucer." She switched her gaze back at Russom. "As a friend, General, please tell me we're working on this problem together because I don't want to have to do it all on my own."

Russom smiled. "I like you, Mays." He leaned back in his chair, getting comfortable. "How about you tell me what you saw at Area 51 and on your way here. I've been watching via our satellites, but that doesn't give me all the story. I'd like to hear it from those whose boots have been on the ground." His gaze shifted to Sofia. "I want details. Let me know exactly what you think we're up against, and I'll tell you what we've seen and know."

The smile he gave Emory reminded her of a crocodile right before its jaws snapped on unsuspecting prey. Russom gestured around him.

"And forgive me for not introducing you to your new home for the duration. Welcome to the government's and military's best kept secret. Welcome to Tesla Falls."

The mess hall was busy, but Sofia managed to find them a seat far away enough from the general noise. Emory sat and began digging into the food on her tray as if she were starving. Sofia ate from her own tray with a lot less gusto.

"Tell me," Emory said around a mouthful of whatever she'd picked to stuff her mouth first, "What do you know about Tesla, Sofia? I mean, it's got to mean something for this hush-hush, top secret, hidden from the world base to have been named after such a genius."

Sofia shrugged her off. "I know the car."

"Oh my God. Do they teach you nothing in military school? Nikola Tesla was the epitome of the mad scientist. He was the genius behind electricity. The AC alternating current instead of the DC direct current?" She gave Sofia an encouraging look.

"I'm a trained engineer. I know about not crossing the streams, dear."

Emory grinned at her joke. "Glad to hear that. He had his glory stolen by Edison and still today not many know that it's thanks to Tesla you can power your iPad to watch endless cat videos. His patented work formed the basis for radio and our wireless communication systems. He had a hand in remote control devices. He even came up with free energy, the way to deliver electricity to the world at no cost. You can imagine big business wasn't very keen on that idea so it was another invention of his lost in time." She speared a piece of broccoli on her fork and checked it over before taking a bite. "Oh, and he's the genius behind the death ray."

Sofia rolled her eyes and concentrated on her meal. "You just had to go spoil it, didn't you? Is no one safe from your damn theories?"

"It's also known as the directed energy beam?" Emory smiled as recognition dawned on Sofia's face. "He developed an energy weapon that was designed to bring down enemy airplanes right out of the sky. Some believe, if it exists, it could have the power to reduce anything it touches to dust and then it could all just blow away on the breeze."

"Sounds like science fiction to me," Sofia said.

"So did an invasion by aliens just a few days ago."

Emory's look gave Sofia pause. She kept quiet for once and considered the fantastical weapon Emory was describing and wondered if any of it could actually be true.

"Did you know Tesla was also thought to have been in contact with extraterrestrials? He had this ability to meditate far beyond what we mere mortals could do to reach our Zen." She scooped up a big forkful of green beans and waved them at Sofia. "It's speculated that's where he got a lot of his invention ideas from." Emory filled her mouth and chewed. She wasn't finished. "How ironic that in the midst of an alien invasion you bring me to a place curiously named after a guy believed to have communed with aliens."

Sofia had to admit she was totally intrigued now. Emory really did seem to have a theory for everything. The trouble was, to Sofia, they no longer sounded quite so crazy.

"So, Captain, does this mean that in one of those hangars out there is housed a directed energy beam control center by any chance?"

"No comment." Sofia hated that Emory had now planted that seed in her mind and had gotten her more than a little curious. A whole lot more. "You know I can't discuss our secret weapons with you. I've never set foot on this base before today, so I have no idea what is here other than what I've seen since we've been here."

"I'll count that as a 'maybe' then. It's funny how energy in Tesla's hands was to be used for the benefit of mankind. Free energy, after all, would have been a tremendous gift. Instead, all his hard work was stolen from him for others to take the credit, and all his paperwork mysteriously vanished at the end of his life."

"And then there's the other reasoning that the base got its name simply because there might be a waterfall nearby," Sofia said with a sigh. "Not everything has to have an ulterior motive."

"In my line of business there's always more than originally meets the eye." Emory had switched from her main meal and was unwrapping a muffin for dessert. She sniffed at it appreciatively. "Ooh, blueberry."

Sofia shook her head at her. "You sit there spouting off your theories and then wax lyrical over baked goods. You are a strange one, *Ellen.*" She took a sip from her coffee. She was glad to be among the other military personnel. Safety in numbers. Though Sofia wondered if they could ever be truly safe again. She thought about the brief meeting with Russom before he'd dismissed them to go eat and freshen up. She knew exactly why he'd cut the meeting short. He was checking into Emory, or more exactly, Agent Ellen Mays. Sofia had never been much for prayer, but she was praying Dink had managed to plant something somewhere that Russom's mind would be put at rest to.

"You're fretting. I can feel your worrying from here."

Sofia leaned across the table to her. "I'm worried your alias will blow up in our faces. Russom has ways and means of finding out the truth."

Emory nodded and polished off the last of her muffin. She gestured to the one on Sofia's tray. "Are you going to eat that?"

Sofia handed it over, wondering why she was surprised by Emory's nonchalance. "You're not even the slightest bit concerned?"

"I told you; I have a Dink."

"Just what kind of computer whiz is he?"

Emory smiled like a proud parent. "The best kind." She ripped open her second treat and bit a large chunk out of it. "These are really good," she mumbled through the mouthful.

"So I gather. I'll be sure to pass the message on."

"How long do you think it will be before Russom calls you back to have a more intimate chat?"

"Once he's verified your lack of credentials? Not long."

"Oh ye of little faith. What do you think he'll tell you?"

Sofia had no idea. What could he say? They were being invaded. They couldn't stop the saucers, and bringing down the black triangular ships was foolhardy. The saucers she'd worked on were gone, lost under the ruins of Area 51. Sofia had no idea what they could do. She'd have to start all over again to build the crafts, and she had no idea where they'd get the materials from this time. The saucers had taken decades to perfect. All that research and development lost in the actions of the ones whose designs they were in the first place.

She shrugged in answer.

"What are the chances of me getting a tour of this place?" Emory was washing down her muffin with a mouthful of coffee. Sofia despaired of her ever eating like a normal person.

"I'd say slim to nonexistent."

Emory pouted. "Pity."

Sofia saw "that look" settle on Emory's face. It was subtle, but she'd been around her long enough to spot the signs. "What's he saying?" she asked.

"He's one step ahead of Russom's foray into searching for the rogue agent that's landed on his doorstep. I have to say I'm a little hurt Russom didn't accept me on face value. I mean, I'm totally agent material." She hushed, and Sofia watched Emory's face grow impassive. Then she smiled. "When all this is done, Dink recommends you employ a better security on your military computers. In one of his forays he's found the launch codes for certain earth shattering missiles. Your guys really shouldn't leave such things just lying around."

Sofia was horrified, but all Emory did was flash that annoying grin of hers at her. It drove Sofia crazy, but it was also too damn attractive.

"Now, aren't you glad he's on your side?"

Chapter Twenty-two

Russom called Sofia back, alone, to his office just as she'd expected. Not having to guard her tongue quite so much this time because of Emory's absence, Sofia was finally able to ask what had been on her mind. The second she was seated she did so.

"Why was Area 51 the point of the first attack?"

Russom stared at her pensively. "Is this where I finally tell you there's more going on than you were originally told?"

"I've worked that out myself in the last few days. After all, I was told by you, that all the aliens had died in the initial crash, and all we'd done was use the technology that had been salvaged. I worked on the ships that were going to be used for our own reasons. I built on what the original design was, refining that which had been started so many years before me. Now I find there are aliens who are very much alive, numbering way more than the initial visitors, and they obviously have been here for a very long time. Respectfully, sir? Where the hell did they come from and why wasn't I informed there was a chance of this happening?"

"Where they came from doesn't matter now. What matters is they are here and we need to stop them."

"What of the other Damocles members? Was I the only one kept in the dark on this matter?"

"I've unfortunately lost a few of them in the attacks. Damocles One has been lost in CERN. Damocles Six died a week ago due to his own carelessness. And we nearly lost you at Groom Lake."

"I'm wondering how deliberate my being ordered to stay behind was, sir."

"Jones wouldn't have the balls to challenge me," Russom said, straightening his shoulders as if preparing for a battle.

"But he can if he eliminates your players, leaving you vulnerable. Then he could bring in his own people and take control." Sofia was trying not to think about the fact she had very likely been deliberately left to die by one of her superiors. One of the few who knew of her allegiance to Russom because he had a peripheral liaison to the group. "I'd have liked to have been forewarned that there was someone with enough of a grudge against you on site that could endanger me."

"He hadn't rung any alarms, and besides, I had my attention elsewhere. There have been leaks coming from the agency. Things have been filtering out that only certain people would and should know about. We were being compromised. Everyone came under suspicion."

"And you thought *I* could be the traitor?"

"I had to wait and see. Too much information in the wrong hands leaves us open to being exposed. That is why none of the Damocles guards have ever met the others. That is why each of you were selected for your specific talents and had no knowledge of the others' work. And that is why you were kept in the dark about so much other than what you were assigned to do. It was need to know and you didn't need to know it all."

"And now I do?"

"Damocles Two is stuck in New York. He wasn't entirely sure he was going to get out of the city alive. There's nowhere to run with the skyscrapers falling like dominos." He shook his head. "Like that city hasn't suffered enough. The Statue of Liberty is floating in the bay. She was ripped from her base, broken into pieces. All that's left is her torch sticking out of the water like Excalibur in the hands of the Lady in the Lake. I last had word from Two just before the attack there began. I have no way of knowing if he has survived. You are the only one who could get here." He gave her an oddly amused look. "I've seen what got you here. I have to admit, I was surprised by the choice of transport."

"Agent Mays was using an undercover vehicle at the time of her being called in. It's been a better ride than I expected. At least it meant I could sleep in the back while we took turns driving here."

"What are your thoughts on her?"

"She's CIA, sir."

Russom snorted his amusement at Sofia's wry tone of derision. "That she is. Knows all and sees all, am I right?"

"And has an answer for everything, whether it's correct or otherwise in my view."

"You two seem to have a rapport going."

"I have had little choice, sir. We met under very strange circumstances. CIA or not, she saved my life and I owe her for that. After all, my own superior on base left me to die and I can't forget that either."

"Well, Jones is the least of both our problems now if he was abducted."

"About that, sir. Agent Mays is very insistent I find out if we have any information about the abductees. Anything at all."

"Her family was taken, she said?"

"Yes. We saw it happen. I've never witnessed anything like it. Our saucers could never get the beam to work. It's…" Sofia couldn't help letting her admiration slip out, "a masterful piece of equipment. It suspends the abductees in stasis and pulls them into the ship."

"It must be something specific to the alien physiology. You can look into it again once all this has died down."

Sofia was astounded by his assertion that all that was happening with the invaders was just a minor scuffle that would be over soon and life would get back to normal. She wanted to argue with him over such a crazy mindset, but she had worked with him long enough to know which battles to pick. She'd revisit that another time. "I'd have to start from scratch. All my files and schematics were lost along with Area 51, and the original craft are lost there too. Equipment, my templates, they've all been laid to waste. They were irreplaceable."

"Don't worry about that. That's easily remedied."

Sofia was getting irate at his calm demeanor about all her hard work being destroyed in the attack. "How? We can't just go out and get another saucer, because the ones flying above our heads appear to be eluding our weapons."

"You won't need one of those. This is a mirror base for a reason, Captain. What was done at Area 51 was echoed here. You need saucers? We have them here. All your equipment is here. Engineers copied every move you made to replicate what you helped refine and design. I've got you a fleet of saucers in Hangar Five poised and ready for you to continue your work."

Sofia was dumbfounded. "And you never thought to mention this before now? Sir, if those saucers are exact copies of mine then why aren't they up in the air fighting against the alien crafts? We'd be on an equal footing finally. We'd have an equal show of force."

"It's not time for us to show our hand just yet, Captain. All in good time."

"People are dying, sir. People are being abducted. The aliens are blowing the planet apart."

"And we will step in and stop that, but I need something finished first because we're not stepping into this fight armed with sticks and stones against their technology. We know what they are capable of." He looked out his window over the base. "But they'll soon learn we are capable of so much more."

Before Sofia could question him, there was a knock on the door. She turned to see Emory there, standing to attention.

"You called for me, sir?"

"I might as well kill two birds with one stone here, so to speak." Russom gestured for her to enter. "Agent Mays, it appears that your meeting at Area 51 was to offer you a place on my team. You were to be vetted as to your suitability for such a role. The last CIA agent I had working for me unfortunately didn't live up to standards and needed to be replaced. Do you think you have what is necessary to do that, Mays?"

Sofia noticed the subtle stiffening of Emory's body. She couldn't help but feel that for all the secrets Russom had kept from her, Emory was doing exactly the same. Sofia was getting sick and tired of being the only person who knew only half the game that was being played.

"I've been looking into your credentials. You have had quite the career. I'm surprised we haven't crossed paths before."

"I'm kept on the down-low, sir."

"Your bosses sing the praises of your investigative work."

Emory smiled. "I like to believe that if there's something out there I need to know, I can find out about it. One way or another."

Sofia had to admire Dink's crafting of Emory's real job into her fake persona. She was thankful he wasn't working against her. *That I know of.*

"So you're one of the rare Men in Black, ones that go in and find out what people have seen and you do what exactly?" Russom looked fascinated.

"I dissuade them from speaking out about whatever it is they believe they've witnessed. It's easy enough to do. Threats are so much more powerful when the fear for family or life is employed." Emory stepped closer to his desk. "So you have a place open for someone like me in your team, sir? Can I ask what you're recruiting me into that needed me at Area 51 of all places and then here?"

Sofia was frightened of the dangerous game Emory was getting herself into. She was playing a role that could so easily backfire on her with just one wrong word. If Russom found out who she really was, that *she* was the one that was going to publish the existence of a secret agency hidden in the military, Emory wouldn't just get thrown in the brig. Sofia swallowed hard against the unmitigated fear rising in her throat.

They'll kill her.

❖

The hangar that housed the fully functional human built flying saucers caused Dink to dangerously hyperventilate in Emory's ear. Emory had to physically force herself not to run over and touch them to assure her eyes she was seeing correctly.

Sofia had no such compunction. She stalked over and ran her hand over the underside of the nearest craft. "I wish you'd seen fit to tell me these existed, General. If for nothing else than the fact I need to run my own checks on these before they are deemed fit for flight."

Emory's head whipped around. "*You* can fly these?" She heard Dink going into raptures. Neither of the officers paid attention to her.

"I assure you, we followed your work down to the finest detail," Russom told her.

"I'd still like to check."

Sofia's look was one Emory recognized all too plainly. It was her "don't argue with me because you won't win" face. Emory was amused to see even Russom conceded to it. It appeared no one was immune to that glare.

Emory trailed behind them as Sofia looked each saucer over with a critical eye. Unable to resist any longer, Emory reached up to touch the underside of the craft.

"I am sooo jealous of you now. What's it feel like?" Dink asked.

Emory's fingers slid over the metal without encountering any traction stopping it. "This is like nothing I've ever felt before." Emory pressed her palm flat against it. It didn't radiate the heat from her hand nor was it cool to the touch. Next she rapped her knuckles on the hull, but there was no sound. Emory tried again, fascinated by the lack of noise. She wandered all the way around the craft. "Okay, I give. Why are there no windows?" She traded a droll look with Sofia. "Because that would totally explain why they crashed at Roswell."

"These ships are made from a very unusual metal, one we didn't have knowledge of until we were able to break down the compounds and make something very similar." Sofia turned to Russom. "At least, that was the history I was told when I took over the work. Did they figure it out by themselves or were the aliens alive when they crashed and found a way to communicate how their ship flew?"

Emory was intrigued by the edge to Sofia's voice, especially in addressing a senior officer.

"Oh oh, sounds like the captain here is questioning her directives." Dink chuckled. "You've been rubbing off on her."

I wish, Emory thought, noticing that Russom didn't bother to answer Sofia, which only seemed to make her face turn even more thunderous. Emory stepped in to defuse the situation because she wanted to know more and was going to take any opportunity she could. And what better place than in a hangar full of alien technology. "How do you even pilot this thing if there's no door either?"

"There's a hidden hatch that you trigger." Sofia touched a spot that Emory couldn't see anything different about and yet the metal seemed to evaporate, leaving behind a doorway. "Once inside you can see through the metal. There's no need for actual windows. You can see a full three hundred and sixty degrees around you."

"Wow," Emory breathed. "Any chance I can get a look inside one of these?" She poked her head through the doorway to see as much as she possibly could. This was every science fiction fan's dream come to life. She was desperate to go inside and explore. Sofia opened her mouth, but Russom beat her to it.

"Maybe later, Mays. You'll get your chance when we have to get them prepped in order to go up against the invaders."

Emory couldn't help herself; she grinned. "Really?" She caught sight of Sofia shaking her head behind Russom's back. She was obviously warning her that such exuberance wasn't exactly becoming of a CIA agent and to tone it down.

Russom just laughed. "I like you, Mays. You're certainly different from the last agent I had to deal with." He put a firm hand on her shoulder and steered her toward the exit. "I put my trust in him and he let me down badly. He jeopardized everything we have built here. He was given a position of trust and betrayed it. I trust you won't do the same once you see what your new role entails."

"I was obviously sent for a reason, sir. I'm intrigued as to what else you could possibly show me after these." She waved a hand at the saucers.

"Oh, believe me, that's merely the beginning," he said.

"Emory," Dink's voice was soft and low. "While hunting through Jack Carter's personal files to insert you into his communications, I found some information that was all too familiar. Our informant? Remember he said the agency was run by a highly secretive individual that he very rarely came into contact with? And that there were other members, each with their own role to play? Our informant was trying to find out all of the names of the key players so we could go public with them. Carter has some stuff on his hard drive that needs a decryption code to view it. I'm decoding it now. I want to see if he knew anything seeing as our informant disappeared before he could furnish us the identities."

Emory had been steered inside another hangar bay. This one had an elevator. Emory wasn't surprised to see it, even as out of place as it looked.

"Seventy-five percent complete," Dink said. "Oh, another elevator. Just like the one at Euphoria. If he shows you aliens on ice be sure to ask about the blue one. Our fellow theorists and I have a wager on the planet of origin. I have my money on Gliese, which, as you know is strikingly similar to Earth but in a galaxy far, far away. I'm thinking that might be why they sought out ours. But you know my ravings on that subject."

Emory nearly blurted out her own prediction and only just managed to keep her tongue in check.

"I put you down for Titan because I know you've looked into it having volcanos and other similarities to Earth. And you always pick it. It's your go-to planet."

Emory nodded nonchalantly, knowing Dink would pick up on her movement. He knew her all too well when it came to them picking planets to place bets on.

"I'm in," Dink announced. "Let's see what these files needed to have kept hidden. I think I've…got something here."

Emory watched Russom press the button to call the elevator. She could sense Sofia watching her, knowing that Dink was talking in her ear because Emory was uncharacteristically quiet.

"We've got it, Em! Fuck me, I've got it! Dionysius *is* the name of the agency. Truno wasn't lying about that. That's the people we're after. Hang on. This says seven members, which we already know. Oh, seven people from different areas too. All the military bases were covered, air force, army, navy, then there's the CIA involvement, the government. Huh, no surprise there."

The elevator dinged as it reached the hangar's level.

"I need names, give me the names…got them. Everyone gets a designation. They're called Damocles and get a number assigned them. Truno was Damocles Six. Oh crap! Russom's the head of it all. He's the big boss." Dink's voice rose. "Get out! Get out now! You're being taken into Dionysius's base of power by Dionysius himself."

Emory hesitated a second following Russom and Sofia onto the elevator. Sofia frowned at her as she faltered. Their eyes locked as Emory listened to what Dink was informing her.

"Don't you dare get on that elevator! Abort! Abort the mission! Get your ass out of there! Emory, if you're found out, you're dead.

Russom doesn't play games. He was obviously the one who stopped our informant and who set the lawyers after us. You're in danger there, Emory. Get the fuck out of there NOW!" Dink was screaming. "Oh God, no! Emory, there's a Captain S. Martinez on the list. *Sofia's* on this freakin' list. She's part of the agency too. She's one of them. You're walking into the lion's den and she's led you into its trap."

Emory saw the second Sofia realized what was going on. There was just a glimpse of the sad smile that fleetingly touched Sofia's face before it disappeared behind her professionalism. *It's too late.* Emory wished Dink could hear her thoughts. *I'm already in over my head.* She stepped onto the elevator so as not to draw any more attention to herself. As the doors closed on her fate, Emory felt Sofia's fingers briefly touch her own.

How ironic. Turns out she is one who I'm here to expose, and instead I end up exposing my heart to her.

The elevator numbers ticked off as they descended deep underground. It was delivering Emory into the clutches of the agency she'd tried so hard to uncover.

"I hope you know what you're doing," Dink said, his voice resigned.

God, so do I.

CHAPTER TWENTY-THREE

The elevator was larger than the one at the Euphoria base but had the exact same number of buttons. Emory was focusing on every detail to keep her mind from freaking out over just how much danger she was in. She was studiously ignoring Dink's grumbling in her ear about her suicidal tendencies and sheer stupidity. Emory believed she didn't have anything to lose now, what with the aliens above and her enemies standing right beside her. She couldn't bring herself to look at Sofia but knew that Sofia kept sending side looks her way.

Why didn't she tell me? Emory wondered, more hurt than angry at being duped. *I merrily told her what I was trying to uncover, and she knew of the agency's existence because she's a part of it. She told me I was crazy.* Emory sighed under her breath. *Like that's anything new. She just joins the long list of people who have lied to me and made me feel stupid when all along I have been right. I get that she couldn't have told me of her involvement, but I wish she had trusted me enough to give me a clue.*

The floors whipped past and Emory knew they were going deep. She broke her silence. *Might as well ask all my questions now before I'm found out and left down here to rot.* "How similar to Area 51 is the layout here, sir?"

"Did you get a tour of the facility there?"

"No. I was escorted to what looked like an interrogation room and left there waiting for my liaison to arrive, which he never did. When all hell broke loose, I was left wandering around. There wasn't exactly a lot to see where I was, except for endless rows of desks. To be honest, I was frightened to touch anything in case I ended up being accused of inter-agency spying if I even happened to breathe by someone's laptop." She didn't need to look around to know that comment had hit its mark. Emory felt a certain smugness at her petty dig. Admittedly, she *had* stolen a laptop from the base, but it was the principle of the thing now. She winced as Sofia's nails found their way into the back of her hand. Trying to be nonchalant, Emory shifted her hand away from her and rubbed at it, pretended to be warding off the cold. She shot a glare at Sofia.

"Speaking of spying. I looked up your file. It made for some very interesting and informative reading. I believe your superior was grooming you for me because of your investigative talents. They had high praise for your interrogation methods too. There's a need at Dionysius for those kinds of skills since the last CIA agent was terminated."

Emory tried not to flinch.

"What does he mean, terminated?" Dink said. "Our informant disappeared. What the fuck did this guy do?"

"*Dionysius*? I had a feeling I was being considered for a new position, but I never dreamed it was for this. I've heard whispers but never thought I'd ever get picked for something so highly classified that it's the top of top secrets. I'm looking forward to seeing what the agency entails, sir. I know I have a high rate of success getting people to open up to me." She gestured to herself. "It's the all-American beach girl look. They see blond hair and think I'm a pushover. It's worked in my favor many a time. I'm also told I can be very persuasive in helping people forget what they have seen."

Russom smiled. "That's why I know you were the new recruit for our work here."

Emory smiled back at him. "Well, with all the secrecy and the irrefutable fact we have aliens knocking at our door, you might need to give me a while to come up with a cover story big enough to make this mess go away."

Russom's smile darkened. "That was Damocles Six's job. The trouble was, he began talking to the wrong people himself. He was in danger of putting all of us at risk. This agency has seen many members come and go over the decades. It has changed its name numerous times as the original group was disbanded and the government took a stronger hand in the game played. But in every incarnation we have endeavored to keep what is secret *secret*."

Emory knew what he was alluding to. "From Majestic 12 to Dionysius. I have to admit, I am very interested in the origin of the title you bear now."

"Are you aware of your Greek mythology, Agent Mays?"

"I know the Sword of Damocles is used to represent the danger that those in positions of power are under threat of every minute of every day. Dionysius was a king who let a man called Damocles see what it was like to have a taste of his power but also to realize the threats that came with it. He let Damocles take to his throne to wallow in the splendor of being king, but a huge sword was suspended above Damocles's head, held only by a single strand of horse hair." Emory shrugged. "It's the age old adage; with great power comes great responsibility."

"Exactly. Each of the guards bearing the Damocles title have a responsibility, a chance to sit in the throne because each has their own talents we are utilizing. But there can only be one king who bears the weight of it all."

"The one who keeps the sword above his own head and away from theirs?" Emory noticed how quiet Sofia was. "That's some power you wield, sir, if I may say so."

"I have some mighty big secrets to keep hidden."

The elevator stopped. Russom stepped out but not before he addressed Emory directly once more. "How badly do *you* want to sit in the throne, Mays?" He walked off before she could even begin to formulate an answer.

Emory swore she could hear the sound of horse hair breaking.

The layout to Tesla Falls' underground base was a lot more elaborate than Euphoria's had been. The first room Russom directed them into was another war room, deep underground and way more militarized. Here on the screens Sofia could see the deployment of troops all across the country. She could see they were fighting a losing battle. The saucers were back flying across the US, killing and taking whatever and whoever they wished. The big guns, armored vehicles, and stealth aircraft that the military sent against them were just delaying the inevitable. It broke Sofia's heart to see the devastation across the country.

Russom pointed to a screen. "Captain, any ideas on how they can penetrate that hull?"

It was the huge black triangular craft that had landed on Maine. Sofia moved closer to the screen, hoping to see something that would help. "I would really need to be there, sir. It doesn't appear to be made of the same material as the saucers. For a start, its dull black and the saucers are all a shiny metallic silver. The hidden hatch that ship has could be fathoms deep under the sea where it lies. Or it just as easily could be buried deep into the cliff that it's jammed into."

Russom banged his fist onto the table. Emory jumped, but Sofia stayed still, watching him intently. She was intrigued at what he was angry about.

"I told them not to shoot at the main crafts. Some officer on that damn vessel had his own agenda in play and countermanded my explicit orders. It's a good thing for him he's now resting at the bottom of that damned water." He glared at the screen where the ship filled the monitor as a helicopter flew around it sending back the feed. "They were just lucky it hit the water."

"Except for the part that hit the inhabited areas that just happen to be under that ship." Emory stood beside Sofia and was pointing at the screen. "What are these idiots doing?"

People, dressed head to toe in black and wearing masks, were walking all over the alien ship. They were employing everything from drilling equipment to massive industrial scale laser cutters on the hull.

"Are they really trying to break into that? What are they going to do once they have? God knows what's inside." Emory, her arms folded across her chest, leaned back against the desk. "General, *do* you know what's inside that thing?"

Russom stared at her and then laughed. "You'll go far equating me with God, Mays." He typed something on a keyboard, and one of the screens displayed a series of photographs of a black triangular craft taken up close and personal and on *land*.

"We had one of these in our possession?" Sofia couldn't believe how majestic a craft it was. She ached to be able to see one and get inside it to inspect it further.

"Sadly, no. We never got far enough in negotiations to garner this kind of technology like we did the saucers. We didn't have anything that would be a worthy trade for one of their mother ships."

"When did these craft appear so that we were able to discuss maybe taking one out on a test drive?" Emory asked. "Roswell gave us the saucer, but I don't remember a word of one of these coming so close to being in our hands. Or was that covered up a whole lot better than Roswell's saucer being a weather balloon?"

"Ahh, conspiracies. God bless them," Russom drawled. "If the theorists only knew what we have hidden. They'd never sleep at night again. Truno, the CIA Agent before you, decided to expose the existence of everything we'd worked so hard to conceal. Not only was he going to reveal the existence of more ships but also expose Dionysius and our involvement to the public and put us all in danger."

"I never met an agent by the name of Truno," Sofia said, not recalling him ever crossing her path in all the time she'd been recruited by Dionysius.

Russom shrugged. "And why should you have? He was Damocles Six and your worlds didn't need to meet. He was meant to put a stop to the conspiracy site that was starting to make itself known among all the countless others. Instead, he started talking to them and sharing information with them."

Sofia was thankful that Emory's face didn't give her away. She wondered what was going through Emory's mind as Russom talked about *her*. She guessed Dink was talking in her ear too given how still Emory was.

"Did you ever see the people he was leaking information to, sir?" Emory asked.

Sofia almost stopped breathing. She was terrified of Russom's reply and what that would mean. The woman who was ready to go to prison for not revealing Truno's identity was standing right beside her. Emory was slap bang in the middle of the biggest secret military base, having been brought into its secrecy by the leader of Dionysius himself. Her heart was suddenly pounding in her ears, deafening her.

"No. I left that to my lawyers to deal with. I have no time to deal with their kind. I'd have stepped in eventually if it dragged on too long, but Truno made the mistake of coming back to base and was easily dealt with. With him gone, the leak was plugged and he has been erased from our records. They couldn't have proved anything even if they released his name as their source. He no longer exists."

"He's been *dealt* with?" Sofia had the dreadful feeling she knew how.

"I'm told there's a new shopping mall being built somewhere in Utah. The foundations have a little extra *body* in them to keep the building sturdy," he said without any compunction. "We're a secret agency for a reason. The general population couldn't handle hearing just what it is we have been doing for the greater good."

"And what have we been doing, sir?" Sofia dreaded to hear his answer, but she had to know. She had to hear it from his mouth to believe what she feared she was realizing.

"Evolution, Captain Martinez. The human race is going to expand their horizons beyond this paltry planet."

Sofia shared a brief look with Emory.

"I thought we'd already done that?" Emory said. "Or do you mean farther than the moon in our orbit?"

Russom never took his eyes off the screens before him. "Do you expect me to show you the sound stage set up for that, Mays? The past was a minefield of deception and posturing, Agent. But now? Now we have all we need to go farther than we ever could. Now we can take our might out into the galaxy."

Sofia wasn't liking either his tone or what he was alluding to. "Might over exploration, sir? With *my* saucers? They're not exactly equipped for long flight or carrying an army."

"No, but the triangular craft are. I wanted one captured, but someone disobeyed my orders so I'll salvage what I can from the downed ship."

"It will take years to recover that machine," Sofia argued. She tapped on the screen to prove her point. "It's embedded in the earth for God's sake."

"That's why I have my own plans in place. We just need one ship to take over. Maybe the answer to how that can be done is on the one they shot down."

"I couldn't even get the beam they use to work! How are you going to bring a ship so much bigger down in one piece so you can hijack it?"

"We'll use the aliens like they use us. Seems only fair to turn the tables against them now."

Sofia frowned. "I thought they came in peace?"

Russom's look was pitying. "Are you really that naive, Martinez? We've been paying the price for their 'help' ever since they crashed on this planet. Now we stand a chance of turning the tide against them and I aim on doing exactly that."

Sofia had no idea what he was proposing. "Sir?"

"Every Damocles guard had their own job to do. Yours was to build the ships, Captain, to ready a fleet. Now I'll show you what some of the others were doing." He opened what appeared to be an innocuous closet door. Another elevator was hidden inside. "Even in a hidden room there are still secrets to explore. The main elevator only goes so far. Tesla Falls has many more layers beneath."

Sofia could feel Emory's nervousness radiating off her as they followed Russom into the tiny elevator. In the confined area, Sofia brushed their fingers together and wasn't surprised when Emory's held on a little longer before reluctantly letting go.

The ride was as long as the initial one had been. Sofia had no idea how far down they were traveling. Russom ushered them out into a brightly lit corridor with the ominous words, "Both of you, welcome to the *true* Dreamland."

CHAPTER TWENTY-FOUR

The weaponry level at Euphoria had been awe-inspiring. The huge munitions expanse at Tesla Falls made Emory's jaw almost hit the floor. It was the size of a football field and packed with people working on missiles and large portable devices that Emory had no clue what they did or could possibly do. At the very far end of the room were two immense hangar doors.

"You're in a DUMB," Dink told her. "An honest to goodness Deep Underground Military Base. Those doors probably lead out to an exit somewhere miles away where those weapons can be transported off the base."

Emory stuck close to Russom. She scanned the room to make sure Dink didn't miss a thing, even though he was still angry with her.

"Just tell them you have to go to the little girls' room and get the hell out of there. You can't trust Sofia now that she's back under the watchful eye of her boss. Who just happens to be the head of the secret agency you were going to go to jail because of. And who has admitted to you that he had our informant whacked and buried under a goddamn Penny's!"

Emory didn't make a sound to appease him. She was all too aware Sofia was a part of a much bigger plot to keep the existence of aliens secret. Emory didn't know what to think or feel any more. She had trusted Sofia, had fought to keep her safe. Yet she was a part of the very thing Emory had dedicated her life to exposing. *I just wish she wasn't so damn beautiful, or funny, or smart, on top of being the enemy in this scenario.* She saw Sofia watching her. *And in her view,*

I'm *the big bad. How did this get so fucked up? Whatever happened to the happy ever after? Girl meets girl, girl finds girl attractive…aliens invade. There's always something to spoil the plot. Then there's the little matter of the general ordering the demise of the last CIA agent that worked for him, and here I am, merrily taking over that role. I don't think I'm suicidal like Sofia insists. I think I'm just fucking stupid.*

So with that thought, I might as well go out in style.

"General? The fact this base is named after Tesla has to have some importance, right?" Emory searched the room for something, anything, that resembled some of the inventions Tesla had pioneered.

Russom stopped in his tracks. "Well, you're certainly smarter than your predecessor."

"Tesla had future visions. He saw things that would be made in the world we live in now as opposed to his own time. How much of his contribution is at work here?"

"We're crafting everything from pulse rifles to weapons that can harness electricity and work like a massive Taser." He waved in the direction where such weapons were being tested. "That's always my favorite to watch them testing on unsuspecting new recruits. The first setting is police Taser strength. After that it's like harnessing a lightning bolt and releasing it on a target."

"These aren't employed in the field." Sofia ran her fingers gently along the length of one particularly lethal looking weapon. Emory found it was too sexy watching her fingers play and had to look away before Dink called her out on her staring.

"Not yet. They need to pass the last test that eliminates the discharge from the weapon electrocuting the shooter. Only then can they go above and we fry as many aliens as we can with them." Russom picked up a weapon and held it securely in his arms. "I can't wait for that day. It's been a long time coming."

"How much of what goes on here is for the foot soldier?" Emory gazed around the room at all the weaponry and machinery but there were also computers running endless streams of code. "Not all weapons can be carried, after all."

Russom narrowed his eyes at her, effectively sizing her up. "Definitely smarter than the agent before." He laid the weapon back down. "There are other areas designated for the weapons that are deployed *above* us. They're scattered about the base. It doesn't pay to keep them all in the same room. Or on just one base either."

"And how much of Tesla's genius is involved there? His supposed energy weapon would easily bring down a triangular craft in more manageable pieces. Theoretically, if such a weapon was part of your arsenal it could turn an alien ship to nothing more than dust." Emory flashed him a wry smile. "If the stories are true about the power that invention possessed."

"That would be quite the weapon to have, wouldn't it?" Russom said noncommittally.

"So why wouldn't it have been employed on the big ships housing the smaller saucers?" Emory pressed him. She was determined to find out why the most destructive weapon they had hadn't been used for the very purpose it had been designed for.

"Maybe it will only be revealed when the time is right."

"When is the time right? When all of humanity has been sucked up into the saucers? When there's nothing left of the planet because they've bombed it all? How soon before we reach the time the only thing we'll have left in defense are rubber bands to ping off the side of the crafts?" Emory was seriously pissed and didn't rein it in. She was surrounded by powerful weapons and nothing was being done, that she could see, to save the planet and its people by employing them.

"You'll do well to remember who has the sword hanging over their head, Damocles Six." Russom's tone was harsh and Emory flinched at the rebuke.

"Damocles Six?" She knew nothing good was going to come of her receiving that title.

"Your part of this agency will be to hide the truth of anything and everything we do in this time of war. *Not* question it."

Emory couldn't help herself; she laughed at him. "General Russom, not even a magician could employ sleight of hand to hide all that is happening. So unless you've got a memory wiper among all these alien gizmos, the alien secret isn't going to stay secret no matter what spin we put on it."

Russom surprised Emory. He reached out and patted her cheek. "My dear, sweet, child. It's not the aliens I'm referring to."

Emory was confused. She shot Sofia a mystified look, but Sofia looked as clueless as Emory felt.

"Sir?" Sofia stepped forward. "What else is going on here?"

"Everyone has their place, Damocles Five. Yours was to engineer the saucers beyond what the aliens originally gifted us with. You excelled in your duties. The saucers will fight against the aliens and take us farther than you ever imagined."

"So I built the saucers whose existence has been kept from the public. Ellen here is to further deceive by covering up something bigger than the fact we have flying saucers from an alien source?"

Emory found something ironic in the fact she was being given the role of a deceiver when all her life she had fought to bring the truth to light.

"Damocles Four was in Switzerland. His job was to open the door."

"What's there?" Sofia asked.

Emory's mind ticked and she didn't need to hear Dink's hushed words in her ear.

"Nothing now," Dink said. "Everything was blasted to pieces like Area 51 was."

"That's of no consequence now. What he was guarding was destroyed. Damocles One we shall meet on the next floor down. Damocles Two is lost in New York where our offices there have just been blown up. Damocles Three is our liaison with the government because, whether we like it or not, we work hand in hand with them. His job is much like yours, Mays. Deny all knowledge while funding the cause. Damocles Seven's job is to keep all the factions of the military in line. In times like these they are all to defer to my command." He shook his head. "I'd say we've lost Damocles Seven because he would never have allowed my orders of not shooting down the black crafts to be disobeyed. He'd have had a man on that ship's bridge take the officer out who went against my orders."

He beckoned them away from all the weaponry. "Two more floors and then your tour is done. Then both of you can decide whether to stay here and fight with Dionysius or take your chances out there with the aliens." He led them to a series of lockers and pulled out protective clothing for them all.

"Time to learn your place, Agent Mays."

Emory pulled the suit on over her fatigues, then positioned the face mask over her nose and mouth. Lastly, she slipped on a pair of thick gloves. "We going into cold storage, sir?" She flexed her fingers in the gloves.

"No. The dead aliens are kept on ice at numerous other bases. Here they are very much alive and kicking when we work on them." The malicious grin was plain to see before he covered it with his mask. It gave Emory chills. That wasn't the smile of the cool and calm general she'd been meeting with before.

Wait a minute. Did he say aliens? Live *aliens here on the base?*

"They captured aliens?" Dink said. "I thought we were in cahoots with them?"

Emory turned to help Sofia fasten up her much too large suit. She leaned in to whisper in Sofia's ear. "You know anything about this?"

Sofia shook her head vehemently. Her eyes pleaded with Emory to believe her.

Dink spoke. "I hope we're ready for what he's going to show you. I've studied this for more years than I can remember, but seeing it? Seeing aliens attack us, invade us, running on our soil and trying to kill us? It's more terrifying than I even imagined. But captive ones on an airbase, held underground where no one can hear them scream? Something tells me they're not going to be sharing tea and cookies." His sigh vibrated in Emory's ear. "For God's sake, Em, be careful down there. Sofia won't choose you over her boss. I hate to say it, but, Emory? You're on your own."

That thought scared Emory. She had no clue what she was going to find on the next floor that warranted them to dress for a threat of contamination. She wriggled her fingers in the gloves again. Whatever it was, she wasn't going to be allowed to touch it, and that sparked her insatiable curiosity, no matter how nervous she was.

"So, these aliens living among you? Given our clothing, I'm guessing they are either carrying something dangerous to us or we have something that could harm them?"

"You'd guess right. The earlier visitors made many of their welcoming hosts sick before we realized that they leaked a rare form of radiation poisoning. Now, both sides take precautions." Russom took them down a narrow stairwell to the next floor.

"How about the saucers too? Some of the early reports spoke of humans getting sick when they tried to get near the crafts." Emory caught Sofia's eye. "I'm guessing that was something solved pretty quickly to get the saucers rebuilt for human flight."

"You've read reports of saucer crashes?" Russom spoke over whatever Sofia was going to say.

Emory shrugged. "It helps if I know what I'm talking about before I employ the means to debunk it." She watched Russom enter in a very long code on the keypad outside a reinforced door. He swiped his card twice and only then did the door open. Emory had to close her eyes against the bright light that bathed the room. It blinded her. "Jeez. Who pays your electricity bill?" She squinted, waiting for her eyes to get used to the glare and finally allow her to see inside the room.

"Bright light plays havoc with their senses. The doctors here believe that's because of the black eyes they have. Whatever the reason, the brighter the light the less they can do against our researchers."

"This was part of the deal that was made with the aliens?" Sofia slipped past Emory to stand at the glass partitions that separated them from the rest of the room. A nearby door would have let them in on the laboratory, but no one moved any farther than the glass. It showed Emory enough.

Amid the hospital equipment, vials, and tubes, were a whole line of operating tables. Computers and multiple screens and other technology took up the whole length of the room. Men and women, dressed in the protective gear, were crowded around the bodies of the small gray aliens that were strapped to numerous tables.

It reminded Emory of an slaughterhouse. A brighter and shinier version, but a place of torture no matter how high the technology surrounding them. The squeals from one of the aliens cut through the air. It rose and rose in volume and in terror.

"What are they doing to it?" Sofia asked.

"Exploratory surgery. The aliens don't react very well to anesthetic so we have to operate without knocking them out."

"Is it wrong I think that's inhumane?" Dink asked.

Emory agreed silently, but gave Russom a look. "Whatever works to expand the boundaries of science, right, sir?"

"Exactly. Did you know that we furthered our night vision technology from studying their eyes alone? That was a fascinating project." He stared into the room at what was happening. "They say the eyes are the window to the soul. I've looked into their eyes, both alive and sliced open in a Petri dish. There's no soul in these creatures. That's why what we do here doesn't really matter. They are less than animals."

"Really? Yet they possess a technology far more advanced than ours, which means they are fucking intelligent beings," Dink said.

Emory kept silent, her ears ringing with the sound of the screams coming from the other side of the glass. She couldn't stand the sound; it reminded her too much of the aliens dying in the field after she'd thrown the grenade. She kept her head still against the glass to make sure Dink didn't miss a thing. After all, it wasn't every day you got to watch an alien being dissected in a lab. Emory was torn between being fascinated by the sight and repulsed.

The alien's oily blood oozed out across the table and drained into the little gutter built into the metal table. It dripped into a bag collecting it. Emory wondered what the hell they could glean from that.

"How long has this been happening?" Emory noticed the room looked well used. Experimenting on aliens was obviously nothing new here.

"Since Roswell, when the treaty was forged between us. It was a mutual sharing of resources." Russom waved a hand toward the glass. "Do you want to take a closer look?"

Emory shook her head. It was Sofia who answered him.

"I've seen enough, sir." Sofia brushed past them both to leave the room. Emory nodded at Russom and walked past him too.

"You said mutual, sir. The military and government in the forties traded something for the technology the aliens had to offer. I'm not quite seeing where they'd add spare aliens for us to experiment on to sweeten our side of the deal. So what did they gain from us that was worth the exchange they finally decided on? Unlimited airspace to fly in? The opportunity to mutilate a herd of cattle every so often?"

Russom was noticeably silent as he guided her and Sofia down the last series of stairs.

"Em, there's forty three levels in this facility, and they all have excellent reception because no matter how deep you're going, I'm still able to reach you. How intriguing is that?"

Emory had wondered about that too. She wished she could talk back to Dink because this base was proving to be quite the eye-opener.

At the end of the corridor was a huge double door made from no metal Emory had seen before. It looked odd and out of place in their surroundings. "No Entry" was painted on it. Russom tapped out a series of numbers on a keypad on the wall. Then he took his glove off, splayed his palm on the accompanying touchpad where a green light illuminated and scanned it. Then he looked into a small alcove and faced a retinal scan. Emory was impressed by the level of security.

"What's next? Does he whip his dick out too?" Dink muttered and Emory had to fight to keep from laughing out loud.

"Remember," Russom finally spoke, "the sword hangs heavy over the one who takes the throne."

The doors swung open without making the slightest noise. There was something slightly eerie about that.

"Emory," Dink said and she stalled at the fear in his voice. "I have a really bad feeling about this."

So do I, Emory thought. This was obviously her last test. She had to face whatever was in this room to be accepted into her role as Damocles Six. She was all too aware Russom was watching her closely.

Best CIA foot forward, she ordered herself and straightened her shoulders, ready for anything. "For Dionysius," she muttered just loud enough for all to hear her and stepped into the room.

CHAPTER TWENTY-FIVE

*B*odies.
Row upon row of human bodies were suspended in fluid inside huge glass cylinders. Emory couldn't see exactly how many there were in each line. There were too many to count, but they ran the entire length of the hangar-sized room and halfway across it. This expanse was darker than the previous level. Soft blue lighting was the only illumination on the whole floor. It threw long shadows across the hard floor and made them dance with the movement of the viscous liquid the people were suspended in. Whatever it was, it sparkled unnaturally, even under the low light. Emory tentatively took another step forward into the room, rendered speechless as she took in the true horror of what making deals with the devil entailed.

Oh my God, it's like something out of a nightmare.

She was rooted to the spot with her breath suspended in her lungs. All sound ceased, except for the beat of her heart that was clattering against her ribs at an accelerated rate. She barely heard Sofia's horrified exclamation behind her over the fierce pulsing in her ears. Emory felt like she'd been turned to ice. It was as if everything in front of her was honed and sharpened like an ice pick, and if she didn't breathe, she'd be shattered to a million tiny pieces all screaming out in terror at what she was seeing.

Somehow she managed to take another step forward and another until she stood before a cylinder. The size of it dwarfed her. She stared up at the inert body of a man. Looking down the line, she noticed all the people were displayed the same. Naked, some totally devoid of hair, and all appeared to be asleep. They were curled up in a cruel mimicry of the fetal position they'd slept safely in in their mothers' wombs. Their eyes were closed, their mouths slightly open. Emory inched toward the closest cylinder. She could detect no sign of breathing.

Dead. All dead.

"Oh my God," she whispered in realization.

"Oh no. What have they done?" Dink mourned.

Emory turned to Russom and Sofia. She barely registered that Sofia looked as horrified as she was. "*This*? This was our half of the bargain? We got their technology and in return they got human test subjects to play with?"

Russom's silence was damning. Emory stared at him, wondering what kind of man he really was to be privy to something like this. She was totally disgusted with his part in this cover-up. This wasn't something small to hide; this was a silent genocide that had been kept hidden from the planet for years. Alien abduction for human experimentation. And all sanctioned by the military and the government.

She wandered farther down the row. Not all the bodies were untouched. Skin flaps had been peeled back on some subjects, others had their flesh torn away so that muscle and bone was exposed. Limbs on others had been precisely removed. Needle tracks littered arms, and temples were marked in such a way to point toward something being attached there. Emory wondered how much blood had been spilled that was simply washed away by the liquid they lay in. It was an inhuman spectacle, a silent imagery of brutal torture. She forced herself to see it all until she came upon something that nearly brought her to her knees. Tears ran freely down her face as she rested her gloved hands against the cylinder and gazed up at the tiny body of a young girl trapped behind the glass. Emory's heart clenched painfully in her chest. *She looks like Missy.* She felt herself begin to gag until she spotted a birthmark on the skin that she knew Missy didn't have. She swallowed back the bile and tried to regain her breath. Then she systematically checked every single cylinder in case any of her family were inside one. She didn't know whether to be glad she didn't find them or not. *This can't be the only place they get to do this.* Only then did she let her anger take the place of fear.

"Is this the fate my nieces face?" She asked the question aloud but again got no reply from the man in the room. "I asked you a goddamn question, General. Is this what's going to happen to *my* family? Are they going to end up in the underground lair, on a no-name military base, suspended behind glass like a prized exhibit?" Emory couldn't take her eyes off the child. She looked so peaceful in death, preserved in the fluid for whatever reason someone had to keep her there once she'd been examined. Emory forced her imagination not to even consider the atrocities they could have subjected a child to. "And just whose lab is this? Is it the aliens? Or could it be humans? Because, let's face it, it wouldn't be the first time the human race has rounded up innocents to use as test subjects to experiment on. Medical advances or the hopes for a mightier army don't make themselves now, do they?"

Russom stared at her. "Everything we do is for the greater good."

Emory wanted to smash his head through one of the cylinders so badly. She balled her hands into fists to stop herself from grabbing hold of him. "Why do the aliens take us? Surely by now they've abducted enough humans to know us inside and out."

"They're trying to use human genetics to enhance their own gene pool."

Emory stiffened. "You're making us breed with them."

"It's harder than it sounds. Our genetic codes are completely incompatible and years of research has failed to produce the perfect human/alien hybrid."

"So you just let them take more of us for something that is obviously doomed to succeed?"

"If they want to waste time splicing cells and gestating embryos that are grotesquely mutated and dead before the day is out, then yes. We have our own agendas in working with them. If we can reverse engineer *them* like we did their ships, we could be invincible. Humanity would be unstoppable."

"You're talking about experimenting on innocents, General. Surely that goes against everything we fight for." Sofia finally found her voice. She waved a hand around the room. "This isn't what we're here for."

Russom laughed at her. "Actually, yes it is, and I have the signatures from presidents past and present to authorize any and all research. We're a warring race, Captain. We're to use everything in our power to be the victors. If that means letting them take people now and again to test on then it's a justified cost. There's collateral damage in every fight, but the ends justify the means."

Emory was shaking. It was either the burning anger rising in her gut or the sheer terror at what she was seeing. She couldn't differentiate between the feelings warring inside her. There was a part of her that wanted to smash each cylinder and release the people inside. She wanted to set fire to every piece of medical equipment she could see and all the objects she had never seen before that were worn from use. She didn't want to linger over where those tools lay, but she made sure Dink could see it all. She wanted someone else to know what she was seeing.

As theories went, this was the hardest one to reveal as true. This wasn't just flying saucers in the sky. This was about an alien race that had come to Earth and who were kidnapping humans and experimenting on them. All with certain humans in positions of power allowing them to do so.

She moved her hand off the cylinder and dropped her line of sight. She still had her gun in her pocket. It was already loaded. All she had to do was get it out and point and...

"Emory, don't even think about it. For you to get out alive you need to leave as Ellen Mays. They'll kill Emory Hawkes on sight, but Mays can get out. You can't save your family if you kill Russom. He might be the only one who can tell you where they are."

Dink's voice of reason stilled Emory's hand but not her mind. The roaring in her ears got louder, and she leaned to rest her head against the glass, frightened she was going to pass out. She felt a hand on her shoulder and found Sofia beside her, giving her a worried look. The one Emory gave her back made Sofia remove her hand cautiously.

"How's the truth looking now, Captain?" Emory said for her alone. She pushed back from the glass and faced Russom again. "I'll need the names and locations of all the other alien labs that we have here on Earth."

"Searching for top secret laboratories isn't part of your job description now that you work for me."

"I'll do anything you need me to do, but first I need to find my family and make sure they're alive." She gestured around the room. "You obviously needed me to see this. Now that I have? You're going to need me on your team to keep this fucking mess quiet. Truno was going to blow this level wide open, wasn't he? He was going to reveal the alien agenda and let everyone know that the saucers weren't all ours. And he'd probably have mentioned that abductions happen and aren't figments of people's imaginations. Then he was going to name all the guards and drop that sword on your head and effectively fall on it himself in the process." Emory shook her head, her voice deathly calm. "I'm not stupid. I know where my loyalties lie. I will die for what I believe in, General, and I believe in the 'ends justifying the means'. I don't think the people outside of this room can really handle this kind of secret becoming public, do you?" She took another look at the room and hoped that her acting was selling her as CIA Agent Ellen Mays because Emory Hawkes wanted to rip the whole lab apart and then blow Tesla Falls off the face of the planet with any means possible. "That is my area of expertise, sir. Give me names and places I can start on because I will find my family, with or without your help. But the sooner I do it the better, since you're going to want me on your side to keep this shit hushed up. Because when all this is over? You're going to need me to cover your ass." With that, Emory walked out of the room at as leisurely a pace as she could muster. The people she walked out on didn't need to know she was resisting the urge to run screaming from it.

This is not what I signed up for. I never agreed to take technology from aliens in exchange for the sacrifice of humanity. These aren't the facts that were presented to me when Dionysius recruited me. And no one ever said that human lives were a part of that deal.

Sofia had ridden the elevator in silence with Russom and Emory. She had noticed Russom didn't seem interested in her reactions to the alien lab. He'd been too busy watching Emory. Sofia had no idea how

Emory had managed to stay so calm in there. She'd seen Emory's short fuse ignite before. It usually ended with her doing something stupid. She'd been surprised how much of Agent Mays must have been in play. Sofia had been horrified by the bodies but was trained to not show emotion. Especially not in front of the general who had recruited her to work on alien saucers and so be a part of the massive cover-up.

But I never expected humans were being experimented on in some kind of breeding program.

She sat in the private room that she'd been assigned. It held a bed, a locker, and was functional if not a little Spartan. She'd been sent there by Russom who wanted to talk to Agent Mays alone. Sofia hoped that Dink was sitting on Emory's shoulder and guiding her through that talk. *Especially since I saw the murderous look Emory was shooting at Russom.*

She was startled from a light doze when Emory came barging into her room without knocking. Sofia opened her mouth to protest, but Emory slapped her hand over it and forced her head back on the pillow.

"No, you don't get to say anything, *Damocles Five*. You obviously knew about this and you never said a word. You knew this was happening. Did you know thousands of people are reported as missing every year in the United States? They never turn up. One minute they're here and the next they're gone. Is *this* their outcome? Are the military and the government actively condoning the abduction of men, women, and children? You're letting aliens take people to do whatever they like with them. Some get sent back never to recover from the horrors they experience. I've interviewed those people. Stupidly, I didn't believe them. How fucking wrong was I? But they're the lucky ones because they were released. Others never got to go home." Emory's hand tightened on Sofia's face. "They never get to go fucking home."

She glared at her. There in her eyes was the fire Sofia knew. "And you, you bitch. You've known about this the whole time. Sitting in front of that goddamn throne of power, letting the aliens steal humanity and fuck with it. But what do you care? You've had their saucers to play with. You got to build ships and dream of when they can be used against our enemies. Yet the real enemy is the one whose spaceships you've had your hands all over. You have their technology, you have their ships to fly in, and you sat on your ass and turned a blind eye."

Sofia's breathing was becoming difficult with Emory's hand pressed across her mouth. The manic look in Emory's eyes was also worrying. Sofia hadn't forgotten Emory was armed.

"Is this perhaps why Tesla Falls hasn't been attacked? Because this base houses their human experiments? I wonder how many other bases have been left untouched that have the exact same facility like this for the same damn reason." Emory paused. "Is it that reason, or is it because you *do* have the controls to Tesla's death ray here? The weapon Russom is being so tight-lipped about. I've told you, it's too much of a coincidence this base just happens to bear his name."

The venom in Emory's tone chilled Sofia and kept her purposely motionless under Emory's hold.

"See, I've thought about that. It's not like the ray hasn't been used before to show them what you're capable of. I've seen the false flags flying, Captain. The only question is, why not do that now? Why is he holding back on such a weapon in this fight?"

I've got to stop underestimating this woman, Sofia thought. For a journalist, she has ways and means to find information. Maybe Damocles Six told her more in his leaks than what she'd revealed. He had certainly known more than Sofia had been briefed on. So many departments with their own agendas and secrets to hide. And Emory, with all her theories, believed in the things hidden behind all the lies and cover-ups. And she was right to.

"You see how pissed I am right now? Imagine that reaction multiplied by millions of human beings all around this planet if they ever found out what the government and military have been hiding from them." She stared down at Sofia. "Do you know what Russom said to me in his office while he tapped away at a secret laptop literally hidden in his desk behind some secret panel? He told me, 'You'll do perfectly.'"

Sofia frowned at her. "Perfectly for what?" she mumbled against Emory's palm.

"He thinks that me knowing that my family is suffering this fate and my still being prepared to hush it up, I'm more Damocles

material than Truno ever was. He said I'll do Dionysius proud."
Emory sneered. "When in reality I'm going to smear his name from
one side of the planet to the other. Any man who takes over the reins
of an agency that allows experimentation on humans doesn't deserve
the power he gets to wield."

She finally removed her hand and stepped away from the bed.
Sofia gasped as she took in a swift gulp of air.

"I asked him something as we sat bonding in his office. I asked
where the aliens were that would have been working in that death
lab. Do you know what his answer was? 'Who do you think we're
'interrogating' upstairs?'"

Sofia didn't know what to say that wouldn't make Emory any
madder than she already was. In all honesty, she couldn't say she was
surprised with Russom's reply.

She watched as Emory patted at her pockets trying to find
something and sighing when she found what she was after. "What are
you doing?"

"Checking for my keys. I'm out of here, Captain. I've received
my orders from Dionysius. Agent Mays is to do an extensive tour of
all the military installations that have an alien laboratory attached.
I've got to destroy the evidence and make sure no one on the bases
breathes a word about what went on there. That's *my* mission as
a guard in your secret agency. Damocles Six's role is a massive
cleanup job." She shrugged. "But in reality, my tour of duty is done.
I've delivered you to your band of merry men, deceived your boss,
joined your cult, and now I'm off to find my family since I have the
locations now. Not all the aliens are in the saucers. If they're willing
to risk being on the ground, that has to mean their hidden labs are still
functional in places. They obviously don't want to lose their means
of experimentation or perhaps they're just using them to hide in to
wait us out. But my family might be at one of them, next in line to be
used. I'm going to track down every last lab on the face of this earth
until I find them. And if I don't find them? I'll kill whatever I do find
in there."

"You can't just go out there on your own." Sofia hurried to her
feet and grabbed Emory's arm to stop her from leaving. "It's suicide.
The saucers are still out there."

Emory nodded. "I know that. But I'd rather take my chances out there with the aliens than in here with those who've let the human race be their guinea pigs. Who knows, *Major*, perhaps you will see me again if I run into the aliens and they start filling up those cylinders downstairs again with fresh meat."

Sofia shook Emory hard, aghast at her words. "Don't say that! Don't ever say that! I promise you I knew nothing of this. I never knew any of this side of Dionysius. All I knew was the saucers. Seems I was kept in the dark as much as you were."

Emory leaned into her, and with her lips so close, Sofia thought she was going to kiss her. Instead, Emory whispered softly in Sofia's ear. "There's none so blind as those who will not see." She set Sofia back on her heels away from her. "I don't believe you. But I hope you're safe here. Both from the aliens and that sword hanging so perilously over that pretty head of yours." She opened the door. "Oh, Dink says so long too."

"Where are you going?" Sofia couldn't believe Emory was leaving.

"I've got bases to see, laboratories to search. It goes a long way to explain why we saw those aliens running into a tunnel out in the middle of a field. There must be entrances dotted all over the place where they just come and go, dragging their spoils with them. I've told him I'll keep in touch." She held up a radio. Sofia recognized it as the same kind that she had kept hidden away from Emory.

"He can probably track you with that," Sofia said, telling Emory more than she probably should have. Emory just smiled at her.

"Oh, I'm sure he can. I'll be sure to toss it out somewhere on my journey. I wouldn't want him to follow me home now, would I? Or find out my real identity. Wouldn't that make for an awkward reveal?" She directed a pointed stare at Sofia, daring her to argue.

"I won't say anything, *Ellen*. Your secret is safe with me and always will be."

Emory gave her a sad smile. "Well, that's because it's what you're best at, isn't it?"

Sofia shook her head at her, not quite sure what Emory was getting at.

"Keeping secrets." Emory opened the door. "Good-bye, Sofia, thanks for keeping me safe. Be sure to save the world for me. If your people ever get around to actually fighting back." With that, she closed the door behind her.

Sofia sat on her bed with a thump. She was at a loss as to what to do now. She couldn't help but wish she could leave with Emory.

But how can I ever convince her to believe me when she sees me as part of the problem we're facing? Sofia lay back on her bed and stared at the ceiling. She felt more lost than she had when Area 51 had been hit and she'd been left stranded. Except she hadn't been alone; she'd had Emory.

She was surrounded by a base full of military personnel and Sofia had never felt more alone.

Chapter Twenty-six

The gates closed soundlessly behind Emory's VW after she drove through them as sedately as she could manage. It was only when she was out of sight of the guards at their post did Emory feel like she could finally breathe.

"Oh my God," she said, aware her voice was shaking. "Why do I feel like I've just dodged a bullet the size of a ballistic missile?"

"Just don't look back. Wait until you're a little farther down the track before you put your foot to the floor and get the hell out of there. The more distance between you and that base the better," Dink said over the phone's speaker.

"What did you put in those files Russom was reading through that made him so damn sure I was a candidate for his Dionysius agency?" Emory couldn't believe how easily Russom had been duped.

"I may have doctored a few emails and drafted up a few more from Agent Jack Carter pointing toward your being the perfect replacement for Truno. I even backdated one so it appeared to be from the day you were to be interviewed at Area 51, again playing on your suitability. I also may have let the emails mention some of your more 'specialist' talents. Such as your ability to plug leaks in sensitive areas. I name-dropped Ellen Mays in a few cover-ups concerning officials who had scandals hushed up and then wiped clean from any record. Which, as we know, means nothing to me. I found them. I just made it look like you were the one who managed to make it all go away."

"It's truly frightening the power you can wield, Dink, seated at your desk. Whatever you did to infiltrate me into their system worked a little too well. I stepped into our *dead* informant's shoes." Emory couldn't believe that stroke of luck. Though luck wasn't exactly the word she should choose considering what she'd been witness to because of it.

"Well, Damocles Six, you've got your orders to clear out the bases using any means necessary. If that doesn't tell you Russom is complicit in all this, nothing will. I've got the closest bases pinned up on the board all ready for us to work from. This list is huge and worldwide but I've got friends at a few of them. I just wish it was easier to get in touch with them. Maybe one of them could check their grounds."

"That's my job, Dink. I have the clearance for it now and the shiny pass to prove it. We can't risk anyone else looking where they shouldn't. Look what happened to Truno when he went against Russom. We can't lose any more of our allies."

"Come back here before you do anything else about these bases. We need to regroup and get a plan of action going. You've got your coordinates all set for the GPS to lead you to Wyoming. From there you'll go through Nebraska, taking in such sights as Carhenge if the aliens haven't blown that up too. From there you'll come down through Kansas City, and then…" He purposely left his sentence dangling.

"And then into the arms of the Lord." Emory smiled at the old joke they shared. "I just hope he's watching over me to get me back to you in one piece. I'm looking at a twenty-hour drive on my own, watching the skies for aliens and the roads for humans with nowhere safe to run."

"Sofia being a Damocles guard…not exactly what I was expecting from our pretty captain."

Emory sighed. She was angry with herself for being played so well. She didn't usually succumb so easily to a woman in uniform. "Trouble was, she was all that and more, Dink. But she was also a long-time member of the agency you and I were fighting to expose and splash all over the Internet. Sadly, that doesn't exactly make us conducive with a happy ever after."

"She couldn't take her eyes off you when you were in the lab with the abductees. I got the feeling she would have preferred being by your side than having to stand at attention beside Russom."

Emory tried to recall anything else in that laboratory she remembered other than the endless line of dead humans behind glass. She hadn't noticed Sofia at all while she'd been desperate to keep her terror at bay and her anger and disbelief hidden for both their sakes. "She was probably worried I was going to blow my cover and get her court-martialed at the same time."

"Actually, she looked concerned for you, Em. For all that she is professionally, she's still the one who held you back from the saucer's beam you were running into, and then she held you while you cried."

"Oh man, why'd you have to harp on that?" Emory was mortified as she remembered how strong Sofia's arms were as she'd held her tight to her chest while Emory had sobbed her heart out. "I'd just seen Ellie taken fuck knows where. I was entitled to lose it. I feel like I'm just one step away from taking up residence in a padded room. I watched as they took my niece up in one of their saucers. I have no idea where she is, and I'm going to go crazy until I find her. She's just a baby, Dink, her and Missy."

"I understand, Emory, I really do. I'm proud of you for not losing your shit in the lab and smashing the place to pieces."

"I wanted to." She'd wanted to reduce the place to nothing but ashes. "I'm never going to erase the images of those people out of my head. Aliens experimented on them and left them on display like specimens in a jar."

"I went ahead and sent screenshots of the footage to our friends. One doctor is more concerned about what experiments were done that we *couldn't* detect."

Emory shuddered at the thought. "Oh God. I can't even begin to go there in my head. They still have my nieces somewhere, and I need to believe they are not being touched." She could feel her fear rising to choke her. "I tell you this. If I find they've harmed my nieces in any way I will not be held accountable for my actions. And that's a promise to aliens and humans alike."

"Even Sofia?"

Emory hesitated then said, "Let's hope she wasn't lying when she said she didn't have a clue." She made a face she knew Dink couldn't see. "Though I seriously doubt it. If she wasn't told by Russom, she had to have had some idea what was really happening at Area 51."

"Not everyone looks further than what is in front of them. Some would rather be blinded than see the truth revealed."

For the first time, Emory wondered what it would have been like not to have a clue what was really happening in the world. To view it just like everyone else did. Taking everything she was told at face value and believing what she was force-fed by the media and people in positions of power. Though she could see the merits of never questioning decisions or the people who made them, she couldn't see herself being happy with that existence.

"Dink, what are we going to do?" There was so much to fight against. Too much.

"We're going to do our best with the resources we have at hand. I'm calling all the basement dwellers into action."

Emory laughed at his using the derogatory term Sofia had. "She'd be surprised to hear how many are retired military who were told the things they saw were figments of their imagination and to keep their mouths shut."

"And with them behind you, Emory, we can start fighting back, one way or another. The time for silence is over. It's time for everyone to pay attention to what we have to reveal."

❖

The blackness of the night sky left the roads difficult to navigate. The smoke that rose from burning buildings blocked out any illumination from the moon. Lit street lamps were sparse, and driving through some cities was like entering a war zone. So much debris littered the streets and so many buildings had been reduced to broken shells. Fires sparked to offer Emory some meager lighting to see beyond her headlights. She had to carefully maneuver through the rubble strewn across the roads. Not all of it was easily traversable, but a detour wasn't on her plans. The beacons she could spot dotted about had people huddled around them, hands stretched out for the warmth.

"There are survivors here," she said, knowing Dink was seeing them too.

"Don't stop, Em."

Emory wasn't surprised to see people out on the streets. Not all the population had been picked up by the military and ferried off to where they were being evacuated. Emory had come across a convoy of trucks miles back and had struck up a conversation with one of the officers in charge. He was heading to Denver with his human cargo, and that was exactly where Emory was supposed to be going to carry out her new orders from Russom. She'd waited until everyone's attention had been elsewhere then had taped her radio to the underside of one of the trucks. The signal would lead Russom to think she was following orders when she was heading somewhere totally different. Somewhere well out of his reach, she hoped.

She drove around a huge piece of brickwork that had been sheared off a building that now stood half its previous height. Behind it, she saw a group of men break away from a fire and hurry toward the van. Emory deliberately pressed her foot on the gas, but the men crowded directly in her path. Trapped between them and the debris blocking her escape, Emory was at a loss as to what to do. The men began banging on the van's panels as they ran alongside her. The looks on their faces terrified Emory. These weren't people looking for help. She guessed they wanted the van *and* her. She leaned on the horn, but it didn't deter them. One man grabbed at her side mirror and hung off it, scrabbling to get a hold on her door. Emory didn't hesitate; she pulled her gun and aimed it at him.

"Get the fuck off my Bus!"

He wrapped one arm around the mirror and drew back the other to punch at the window to smash it. Keeping at her break neck speed, Emory rolled her window down and coldcocked him in the face with her gun. He fell off with a pained yell, and Emory lost no time in gunning the engine to get away from them. She drove over the piles of debris far quicker than she should have. She could hear the furious screams behind her and heard the thuds as something banged off the back of the van.

"Charming area," Dink said, sounding as shaken as Emory felt.

"What is it about a time of fear that sets man against himself instead of us all just fighting together?"

"We're a weird race, Emory."

"That we are, Dink." She winced as she felt the pain flare in one of her fingers. "I think I broke a knuckle on that guy's face."

"Totally worth it for such a badass move," Dink said. "Better he got a face full of gun and fist than you having to shoot him."

Emory agreed. She didn't want to have to resort to that in order to get to her final destination.

Like I don't have enough to contend with without the human race turning on itself to survive.

Chapter Twenty-seven

The moon was finally visible as it loomed large and bright in the night sky. Emory imagined she could see every crater that resided on its surface. It illuminated the highway Emory drove on. She was thankful to see other motorists on the road, no doubt going about their own evacuations. She wondered where they were all running to and if they, like her, had a friend to hide out with while the world went crazy around them.

This area of Kansas City was highly populated and was the last leg of Emory's journey. She'd driven for over twenty hours, stopping only once to grab an hour of fitful sleep. She'd finally had to pull over because she was starting to imagine things in the sky when nothing was there. Dink had watched over the area for her while she'd tried to sleep. Night had descended, but Emory knew this road well and was happy to be somewhere familiar and so close to getting her to Dink.

Lights shone out from the houses on the side of the road. Some of the homes had been boarded up, as if the occupants were anticipating some terrible storm. Emory knew all too well that all the wood across windows and barring the doors wouldn't stop the aliens from taking what they wanted. On her drive through Nebraska she'd seen so many people coming in and out of their storm cellars, hiding to wait out the invasion. Out in the fields, she'd passed bases where the doomsday preppers stood their ground. She had to admire their foresight. They had been ready for just about any eventuality. It was more than some places had been prepared for.

She couldn't help but think of Area 51.

There was a flash in the sky that drew Emory's eyes up. Out of the darkness, a saucer was descending. At the same time, Dink shouted out its presence. They appeared out of thin air within seconds.

"Is it alone?" Emory asked, searching for somewhere to hide. The fear at the saucer's arrival was overshadowed by the dread that it wasn't alone and would be followed by the ubiquitous black triangular craft. This time she didn't have the comfort of the US army with their tanks rushing to her aid.

"One saucer confirmed so far," Dink advised her.

Emory didn't stop. The saucer was in the distance so she continued until she could find a safe location to try to hide. The saucer stayed still in the sky, suspended over the far away houses.

"What's it doing?" Emory was unable to take her eyes off the craft. Other cars on the highway skidded to a halt and began hastily reversing back from where they had come. The other cars either blew their horns as they tried to miss the erratic drivers or just pulled over to the side of the road to watch.

Emory kept one eye on the cars and the other fixed on the stationary saucer. The farther down the road she got, the clearer the saucer became. Emory would never get over the size of the aliens' ships, and she'd been up close and personal with them in the hangar at Tesla Falls.

"Emory, are you going to pull over soon?" Dink's voice was wary. "I'd rather you didn't get too close to that thing."

Emory kept on driving.

"Em?"

Emory knew what she was doing. She had the horrible feeling she knew what was about to happen, and she wasn't going to allow it again. She could see the saucer in greater detail now. The white beam shot out of it and enveloped the houses below.

"Oh, no you don't, you bastards." She didn't even consider her actions. She just reacted.

The saucer was sweeping over the rooftops, illuminating everything with a bright light. It seemed to be searching for something.

"It's checking the houses for signs of life," Emory said. She sped up, racing through the streets toward it.

"Emory, you can't do anything against that thing! Pull the fuck over!"

Emory ignored him and skidded around a corner nearly on two wheels in her haste to get under the saucer's hull. She'd watched her niece be taken away. She wasn't letting that happen again when she was so close to a craft again.

She could feel the saucer above her as she slammed on her brakes and skidded to a halt. She scrambled out of her seat and threw herself into the back of the van.

"What are you doing?" Dink asked.

Emory checked the back of the van. "God damn her!" She searched everywhere, tossing things aside in her desperation. "She took the bag of weapons. That bitch took the guns!"

"Will you fucking hide?" Dink screamed hysterically.

Emory tugged at the piece of hardboard that was on the base of one of the long seats. It slid across to reveal a neat hiding place. Emory chortled. "She missed this one. Come to Mama, Rooty!" She pulled out the handheld launcher and quickly tried to work out how to attach the missile. "Dink, can you see a safety on this mother?" She could hear Dink almost gibbering in her ear. "Focus! I'm not letting this saucer take anyone while I can help it."

Dink pointed out what she needed to do. Emory got out of the van, the launcher heavy in her arms. She ran as fast as she could around the houses, trying to find the perfect position to try the weapon out.

"Emory, you've never used one of those before. It's going to have a kickback like a mule."

Emory was too busy climbing over a fence to care what Dink was saying. She had one objective in mind.

Blow the saucer out of the sky.

"What if the missile bounces off the hull?"

She growled at Dink's query but continued to run across people's lawns while looking up at the underside of the saucer. She was looking for any kind of weak spot she could exploit. She had an idea when the saucer would be at its most vulnerable. The trouble was, that meant she would be at hers too.

"You'd better not be thinking of getting yourself sucked up by that thing!"

Emory didn't want to die, but she'd seen what atrocities the aliens had been doing in that lab. This saucer wasn't going to take any more.

Not on my watch.

She watched the light stop its sweep over the houses and a more concentrated beam switched on. By whatever magical, mystical energy the aliens employed, Emory saw the paralyzed bodies of people start being pulled out from their houses. She lifted the missile launcher on her shoulder and stepped a little closer to the edge of the beam. She could see an opening at the narrowest point of the beam that disappeared into the craft.

"EMORY!"

"Whatever happens, Dink, keep recording." Emory hoisted the launcher more comfortably into position and placed her finger over the trigger. "If this doesn't work, find my nieces, Dink. Find them for me." She aimed the missile at the opening in the craft.

"This is for making me believe," she muttered and stepped into the light, pressing the trigger as she went. The missile shot up into the beam. Its flight was slowed as it fought against the beam's paralyzing grip.

Emory was pulled up into the beam behind it. Her mind was crystal clear and running a mile a minute, but her breath was caught in her chest while her muscles were locked in a strange rigor. She felt frozen in time, weightless, captured in the cold beam that pulled her up toward the saucer. She wondered if this was what dying felt like? The inevitable pull toward the light that, in the end, you just couldn't escape. She couldn't look down or around. She couldn't move her head at all, but she'd been whisked up with her face raised. Her eyes were fixed on the tail end of the missile as it worked its way up in the air. It was aiming dead center for the opening in the craft.

If nothing else, I'll at least have tried. I'd rather die fighting back than hiding and waiting to be experimented on.

She had no idea how far off the ground she was. Time was endless in the stream. Only the missile fought against it and pushed ahead against the flow. Emory could see a few bodies above her that were out of the range of the missile's trajectory. She couldn't hear

Dink any more. She couldn't say good-bye. Nothing existed but the silence of the beam. It was oddly peaceful.

An odd sound reached Emory's ears. It seemed to make the beam vibrate like a tuning fork ringing out a reverberating tone. Emory blinked. She quickly blinked again.

Oh crap. The beam is destabilizing and that's the only thing keeping me up.

There was a bright flash of color that seared her eyes. Oranges and reds erupted inside the saucer and then the sound escaped. Emory went from utter silence to a deafening explosion that ripped a huge hole in the bottom of the saucer and broke the beam's hold on them all. Like a marionette cut from its strings, Emory felt the weight of her body return a split second before she began plummeting back to earth.

"Shit!" she screamed as she dropped like a stone.

Well done, Emory Hawkes. In the history of dumbest moves this has to be your dumbest.

The launcher slipped from her grasp as she flailed her arms and legs in a pathetic attempt to keep herself afloat. The other people released from the beam tumbled with her, screaming as they fell. Emory closed her eyes and prayed. "Oh God, don't let me…"

She slammed hard onto the roof of a shed, the force of the landing wrenched the air from her lungs. She slid off the incline. The roof's edge caught at her pants, ripping them open and gouging an ugly gash deep into the flesh of her thigh. She fell off to land splayed out on some perfectly shaped topiary that bent under her weight and rolled her to the ground with one last thump.

"Emory?"

Emory tried to calm Dink, but she first had to pry her mouth open to free her tongue from her teeth. The metallic taste of blood filled her mouth and she spat out as much as she could before she choked.

"Owwwww!" she whined, turning onto her back and trying not to cry out at all the pain that burned through her body. She directed her eyes skyward and watched the fire and light show flickering inside the crippled saucer. The explosion had ripped open its belly and left a huge gaping hole in its wake. Emory could see little alien bodies inside on fire. Their pale skin grew bright as they were immolated. Unable to move, she watched in fascination as the craft seemed to lurch from side to side. The ship tried to rise, but it dropped back again, spinning helplessly until it limped away, desperately leaning to one side. It barely made it over the houses. Some roofs were ripped from the buildings as the saucer smashed into them as it tried to flee. It finally disappeared from Emory's line of sight. Only then did she try to get up.

"Dink, can you see it?"

"It's trying to get some altitude but it's…" He paused. "Oh oh."

"What?"

Emory didn't need to be told. There was the sound of a crash and then the sky lit up with a massive fireball. Emory fell back to the ground covering her head as debris blew out in all directions.

"It hit a gas station," Dink said. "Big ship go boom."

There was another explosion, and Emory narrowly missed being hit by a piece of something that was sharp and metal or maybe part of the saucer. It landed with a thump by her ankle. The piece wavered as it impaled itself into the dirt.

"If that's flying saucer material grab it for me please," Dink said. "Seeing as you weren't able to bring that ship back to me in one piece."

"I'll try harder next time." Emory gingerly reached for the fragment and hissed as it burned her hand. She blew on it quickly.

There were more sounds of explosions, and Emory ducked every time just in case something else was going to rain down on her. She moaned as the pain in her leg intensified. She carefully peeled back what was left of her pants and grimaced at the state of her leg. "I think I might have to raid the first aid kit for this."

"Considering you've just been dropped out of the sky without a safety net I think you're lucky you didn't break your damned fool neck!"

"Can you see any of the other folks?"

"There's a surveillance camera on a house opposite you I've patched into. The others are probably battered and bruised like you are but glad they're alive and not alien bait. The saucer, however, is one less we have to worry about. But I swear, as soon as this madness is contained, I'm sending you for therapy because you're scaring the shit out of me!"

"Well, one thing I proved was that I'm a pretty decent shot with that launcher." Emory looked around her and spotted the missile launcher nearby. She dragged herself upright by grabbing the topiary. Her leg was in agony, but she finally managed to stand. With a very pronounced limp, Emory managed to rescue the launcher from the dirt and then went back to gather up the specimen for Dink. She looked the shard over carefully. "I think this is saucer shaped, Dink. Clear a space on your mantle." She juggled the shard and the launcher in her hold. "It's a good thing I hid this weapon. I can't believe I never noticed she'd cleared the others out. I'd hidden this and the missiles for it."

"You are not doing that again! You've nearly given me a coronary with that stunt. I'm not going to survive a second round, and you can't keep throwing yourself into the beams. The third time you try it you might not be able to get away."

Emory grunted with every step she took. Her leg was bleeding profusely, and the pain was making her nauseous. "I need to get something on my leg that will last until I get back to you and you can have a look at it. I don't dare go to a hospital. If I told them what had happened they'd be liable to commit me."

"I'd do that myself if I could. Just wash it out and wrap it up as tight as you can. Then just get your ass here, without any more side missions, please."

"I stopped it from taking any more people. That's more than the military has done."

"Yes, it is. You are brave, and certifiably insane."

Emory snorted. "Nothing new there." She wiggled her tongue experimentally. "I think I bit a chunk out of my tongue." It felt sore and thick in her mouth. "I'm going to need copious amounts of ice cream."

"It will be waiting for you."

"Do you have any friends nearby that can come and scavenge from the area?"

"Got a friend en route right this second. But you need to get out of there. Your job is done, StarKiller. Come on home."

Emory limped along with the launcher cradled in her arms like a baby. She spat out more blood and moaned at how sore she was.

Damn, they make this heroic stuff look so easy in the movies.

Chapter Twenty-eight

The Ozarks had never looked so welcoming. The forest made Emory feel oddly protected as she wended her way farther up the mountain and off the regular tracks. She grinned as an all too familiar sight greeted her on the last leg to Dink's hideaway. Christ of the Ozarks suddenly loomed before her, incongruous amid the mountainous region. The massive statue with his arms outstretched never failed to astonish Emory, its immense size hidden like a treasure in the foliage. It wasn't what you expected to find in the middle of the Ozarks, a huge figure of Christ, watching over them all.

Just like Dink, Emory thought, drawing closer to the statue and getting to see what Dink had been alluding to days earlier. Strung all around the tall statue were endless cables, wires, and satellite dishes that had kept Dink online and able to watch over everything. Dink had left everything in the hands of the Lord. Emory craned her neck to look up at the statue and was surprised by how high the wiring traveled to get the strongest signal. How Dink had managed that was a miracle in itself.

Emory followed a specific path that she and Dink had cut out to allow her to drive straight to his home. She ferried too much equipment back and forth for him to have to leave her vehicle farther down the track and finish the journey by foot.

Dink's home was well hidden in the dense trees. It looked nondescript and deceivingly derelict from outside appearances. Emory knew what the subterfuge hid.

Her sigh was heartfelt when she finally drew the van to a stop. Dink hurried out to greet her. She got out of the van as quickly as she could, given her injuries. She fell to her knees to wrap her arms around his shoulders.

"Welcome home, Em," he said, squeezing her back just as tightly.

"I'm so glad to be here, August."

It took a while for Emory to let him go. Dink was more of a brother to her than her own flesh and blood one could ever be. They'd met years ago when Emory had been introduced to the man who could hack any system built and had no compunction in doing so. Emory would always fight by Dink's side.

She finally pulled away and sat back on her heels. She reached out a hand to tug at his beard.

"When did all this facial fuzz get so out of hand, Grizzly Adams?"

"It's hard to keep up a grooming schedule when there's an alien invasion," he said and helped Emory back on her feet.

August "Dink" Staves was four foot five inches of pure genius. Dink had been born with achondroplasia, resulting in his dwarfism. Emory had never paid much attention to his height except to gift him with the nickname that had become his pseudonym. Years ago, they had sat watching *Threshold* together and both had become huge fans of Peter Dinklage. Emory had thought it only fitting that August be nicknamed after such a marvelous actor who didn't let himself be pigeon-holed by height alone—just like August Staves didn't allow himself to be. It amused them both that Dink carried his hero's name with pride and it was known among their circles with respect and, in some areas, reverence. Dink was the conspiracy theorists' poster boy. There wasn't anything he didn't know about or couldn't find proof for or against. He was short, dark haired and handsome—when his beard was better managed. And Emory had been prepared to go to jail protecting him and their source.

Right now he was trying to help Emory inside to help stem the bleeding that had opened up again in her leg.

"You really did a number on yourself," he said, guiding her through the barren looking living quarters that were merely for show. He led her to a back room where a hidden trap door led them down to the true lair that lay beneath.

Emory limped past the bank of monitors and computers that decorated Dink's "war room." She followed him into the bathroom and sat on the edge of the bathtub while Dink began pulling out antiseptic bottles and way too many bandages.

"Let me shower first. This probably looks worse than it is because of all the blood."

Dink held out his hand. "Give me your keys to the Wondermobile and I'll bring in your bags."

Emory dangled the keys before him but didn't hand them over. "Don't touch the alien until you're properly outfitted. That sucker is radioactive. I am not listening to you whine about prolonged exposure making your balls shrivel up and drop off. And no messing with my launcher either. It's not a toy for you to tinker with and try to improve on."

Dink looked suitably offended. "As if."

"You definitely would, but we need it. It's the only weapon in our arsenal, seeing as Sofia snuck the big bag o'guns out of the Bus without me spotting it."

"I'm going to question you about your crazy idea to befriend a Damocles guard."

"Ply me with enough coffee and I'll cry on your shoulder about how enamored I was to her charms."

"I saw that for myself when you kissed her, Emory." He patted her knee. "I'll brew a big pot. We have a lot to catch up on. And you're going to tell me everything you got up to in the company of one Captain Martinez while I was offline and you were in a cellar."

Emory wondered how long she could hide in the shower before he came and dragged her out. She knew he wasn't joking about pulling every sordid little detail from her. She hoped she could keep the fact she desperately missed the feisty captain to herself.

❖

Cleaned up and stitched up by Dink's amazingly steady hands, Emory sat watching as he bit into his third Butterfinger in a row. He looked totally blissed out on the abundance of candy. Emory couldn't decide if his rapture was because he'd been devoid of chocolate for so long or because they were the spoils of an argument long since waged between them.

"So, about these aliens you didn't believe in that you've been carting along behind you in a cooler that is now is my possession…" He grinned around a mouthful of candy.

Emory smiled at his choice of words. If she managed to live past this invasion, she'd never live down the fact she was wrong. Especially if Dink had anything to do with it. He'd been as giddy as a kid at Christmas peering into the cooler, oohing and ahhing over the dead alien's body. She knew it was only a matter of time before he had it stuffed and mounted somewhere. Once he'd sorted out the logistics of getting a radiation proof display case.

"I have conceded you are Master of All Theories. Enough with the gloating. Just tell me what your thoughts are on the paperwork I snuck out of Euphoria."

Dink had the sheets of paper spread out on the table before him as he sat at his bank of computers. He pointed to a sheet with his candy bar. "This circular pattern they have printed here has been driving me crazy. So I did some research while you were in the shower and have come up with some interesting theories."

"You wouldn't be you if you didn't."

Dink nodded in acknowledgment. "This pattern is an awful lot like the motifs we see in ancient artwork. Usually, it's scrawled on the walls of caves, or across vast plains only to be spotted from flying above them. It's the series of patterns within patterns."

"Like a mandala?"

"Exactly. These geometric patterns are a spiritual thing, a symbolic representation of the cosmos."

"And it would be in Euphoria why?"

"I don't think this is symbolizing a mandala in the ancient form. I think this is a modern usage. Something Russom said got me wandering down another path. He mentioned losing a guard in CERN."

Emory considered this. "The *Collider*?"

"The Hadron Collider is there, or, as of now, *was*. It's the one place that got damaged with as much ferocity as Area 51 did. That can't be a coincidence. Nothing these aliens are doing is. Yes, they're wrecking cities and blowing up buildings. That's looking to me like sheer spit and vengeance, a show of power. But Area 51 was blown off the map. That's where everything was supposed to have started. So what's so special about the Collider?" He brought up a file on screen full of schematics and information relating to the quantum physics machine. "Look at the shape of it. Look familiar?" He waved the pages at her.

"Surely the aliens aren't invading us because the scientists think they have found the God particle?"

"Knowing the human race has the ability to create this specific particle? To be godlike? Would you trust us with that power?"

"I don't trust us with putting decent TV shows on cable," Emory muttered and leaned closer to look at the screen. "Dink, this Collider has been powered up for some time. Why choose now to invade?"

Dink searched through the information. He brought up a news piece. "The Collider was shut down for a while for maintenance purposes. It was said to be getting an upgrade so it would be even more powerful. Maybe it's the extra energy that's drawn the aliens out to shut it down. It was already the most powerful machine ever created and they were juicing it up to the nth degree." He considered this and took another bite from his candy bar. "This atom smasher has created the Higgs singlet. Something that doesn't interact with matter in the usual way. In some circles it's believed that singlet could theoretically, with enough power behind it, open up a worm hole in time and space."

Emory had heard the theories. She'd consigned them to science fantasy over science fact. But what she'd seen in the last few days had opened her eyes to so much more.

"What if it's not enough to have the particle to create something like a universe? What if ramping up the power opens up dimensions between us and other worlds?" Dink said.

"To let more aliens in?" Emory didn't like the sound of that. "Why would they blow it up if that was the reasoning?"

Dink turned away from his screen to look at Emory. "What if it wasn't for the aliens' benefit?"

Emory's mind clicked into gear. "We have saucers," she said, having the horrible feeling she knew where Dink was going.

"Turn up the power, open up a wormhole, pilot a saucer or twenty…" Dink waved his candy bar at Emory to finish his hypothesis.

"And boldly go where the aliens would rather we didn't dare venture."

"Would you want us populating the galaxy with the same brand of humans we cultivate so well here on home soil?"

"I can think of a few people I wouldn't mind sending off-world."

"They'd jettison your mother off the ships before they even left our atmosphere." Dink tapped on a screen. "They blew up Area 51, probably to remove the saucers. They blew up CERN to get rid of the Collider. The rest of the destruction has been to show their superiority. Warn us to know our place in the universe."

Emory closed her eyes at the implications. "This is a bigger conspiracy than you or I could have imagined. Bigger than we can do anything about too."

"That's why I've sent out word to the basement dwellers. We're going to need their help deciding what we do next."

"But we're just a few discordant voices going up against the military, the government, the world leaders, *and* the aliens." This was way bigger than she could ever have dreamed.

Dink just grinned at her. "Don't ever forget, the biggest of fires start from the tiniest of sparks."

CHAPTER TWENTY-NINE

Row upon row of endless cylinders met Emory's eyes. The glass on each was covered in a weird kind of condensation. It wasn't exactly wet, but it obscured the view of the inside of the cylinder. One by one, she wiped away the stickiness to peer inside. Not recognizing the body within, she quickly shifted on to the next one, then the next, then the next, in a never ending search. Frustration burned through her as every cylinder revealed a human specimen but never the ones she was searching for. It was never her nieces, her brother, or her sister-in-law. Frantic now, Emory wiped her hand across another patch of glass and stepped closer to see inside. A body, unlike the others who were suspended motionless, floated untethered in the liquid behind the glass. Emory couldn't see its face, but by the shape of the body it was female. She waited as the body shifted and turned as if caught in the gentle swell of a wave. Dark hair pressed up against the glass and then the face appeared.

Sofia.

Emory almost fell out of her seat. She'd fallen asleep, sprawled out with her damaged leg propped up on another chair. The jolt wrenched her leg, and the sickening pain that shot through it made Emory moan out loud.

That alerted Dink to her being awake. He looked up from his monitors. "Hi, Sleeping Beauty. You okay?"

Emory rubbed at her eyes. She tried desperately to banish the vision of that nightmare from her mind. "Bad dreams," she muttered as she eased her leg to the floor and waited for the ache to subside.

"Any news from your military or government pals about those bases Russom gave me?"

Emory knew Dink didn't want her to go into any of the bases alone, even under the guise of being Russom's enforcer to close the laboratories down. Neither of them knew exactly what that meant. Did she walk in, kick everyone out, and then just turn out the lights and leave? Emory was more inclined to storm in and smash the labs to pieces but, again, it was highly unlikely that was the procedure either. And what about the bodies? What about the access points that meant aliens could still access those areas? Until they knew how to proceed, as much as Emory wanted to go turn every base upside down to find her family, they had to wait. Dink was cashing in all his favors with his informants to see if anyone knew if these bases even had a hidden base underneath them. For all they knew, Russom could be sending Emory into a trap.

The waiting was killing Emory.

"So far, nothing. But that's not such a surprise considering some of the secrets they've told me. If they find any aliens labs they won't keep it silent but they're coming up empty. Those labs would be very well hidden, as you'd expect."

"Then we need to start making plans as to which base is the nearest so that I can start throwing my Damocles muscle about." The dream she'd had kept niggling at her brain. "I've seen what they do to their test subjects, Dink. I'm not letting that happen to my family. Not if I can help it. And as a Dionysius minion, I've got more power than you and I could ever hope to have to complete this task."

Dink ran a hand through his recently trimmed beard. "As soon as you can bear more weight on that leg of yours we'll devise a plan of action."

Emory nodded. She was acutely aware of how much damage she had done to her leg. They'd cleaned it out and sewn it back up, but the damage was going to take a while to mend. Emory didn't have the luxury of time. "We'll fashion me a walking stick out of something. The sooner I can hit the road again, the better." Her eyes caught a flash of something on the screen Dink had been sitting in front of. "What are you watching?"

"Saucers flying over London."

"How are the British faring?"

"Firing everything they have at them and putting up one hell of a fight, albeit in vain."

"Any chance of them winning this war for us?"

"Not a chance in hell, sadly. But that stiff upper lip mentality means they're going down with a roar and not a whimper."

They watched as the saucers were blowing huge chunks out of the iconic Nelson's Column that stood so proudly in Trafalgar Square. The lions at its base were crushed by the falling masonry as the column fell just like so many others around the world. The people below were crushed by the debris, too slow to have gotten to safety in time.

The rest of Dink's monitors showed the equal devastation meted out around the world.

❖

Her hands deeply buried in the innards of a saucer, Sofia was less than pleased when her name was called and drew her away from her work.

"General Russom wants to see you, Captain."

Sofia wiped off her hands and reluctantly followed after the young airman who seemed anxious to get her back inside the base. She'd been trying to avoid Russom ever since his little show-and-tell in the levels below. It was hard to equate the man she had admired with the person who hadn't been bothered by the dead humans in jars down on Level 43. For the first time since she'd been recruited by Dionysius, Sofia wanted to walk away.

But where would she go? Especially now?

Not for the first time she wondered what mischief Emory was getting up to on her drive to wherever the first base was Russom had given her the location of. Sofia hoped she found her family and had her mind put at rest over their safety. She couldn't begin to understand that fear. Her family was scattered to the far corners of the globe, each too busy doing their own thing to bother letting her know they were safe or to care enough to hear from her. She had no idea whether they were dead or alive, let alone where they were. She both envied and pitied Emory's connection to her family, especially the children she was willing to risk her life for. Sometimes it was easier not to care. It got the job done easier.

Ushered into Russom's office, Sofia stood before his desk and waited for him to acknowledge her.

"Captain. Have you heard anything from Agent Mays since she left?"

Sofia frowned. This was about Emory? "No, sir."

"By any chance did she say she had somewhere else to go before following the orders I had given her?"

"Sir, she barely said good-bye then left. She didn't divulge any details of what orders she'd received from you. Or, for that matter, what orders she'd had prior to her being here or at Area 51." Sofia prayed neither her face nor her voice gave her away in any of her lies. Why she was covering for Emory she'd never know.

"I was expecting her in Denver, yet she never reached the base or reported in."

"You've had confirmation from the base, General?" She knew exactly how he knew Emory wasn't where she was supposed to be. Sofia was an engineer. She'd taken apart her radio, just like the one every Damocles agent was given, and had found the tracking device with ease. But she was a loyal soldier; she'd left hers where it lay.

"Her last signal was on a road in Denver, but there's been no communications and I can't reach her."

Sofia was surprised Emory had waited that long to rid herself of the tracker after Sofia had told her she'd be spied on.

"I've also received word of a saucer being brought down in Kansas City. Witnesses tell of someone armed with a rocket launcher that threw themselves into the beam and fired it."

Sofia felt the color drain from her face. *I'll fucking kill her!* She was so caught up in her anger that she barely heard what Russom had to say next.

"Damn looters were crawling all over it when my men finally got there. They saw some idiots running off with anything they could scavenge like damned vultures over dead flesh. I've got them questioning the local militia. Some of those men are better armed than us." He stared at Sofia. "Back to Damocles Six. I need to know if she's following my orders, and I can't do that if I can't raise her on the radio. CIA agents can disappear at will. *I* need her found."

"Permission to go search for her myself, sir?" The words were out of her mouth before she could rein them back.

Russom looked surprised. "You? Why?"

"Because I spent time with her. Built up a rapport." *Kissed her.* "She drives a very distinct VW Bus. It's probably one the aliens wouldn't touch. She should be easy enough to track down."

The corner of Russom's eyes crinkled at Sofia's obvious dig at Emory's vehicle. "What about your work here?"

"I'm merely nitpicking over the saucers. The hard work has already been done. Those saucers are ready to fly. I can't do anything more here. At least with them. So order me to clean up after the CIA. If I can't find her then you'll know never to put an agent in a Damocles position again."

I'm selling my soul to the devil. Come on, you old bastard, take the bait because otherwise I have no excuse to leave. I want to get far away from you and your laboratories of death. I don't even want to breathe the same air as you. You who could trade human lives for a chance to advance. I'll see you damned, Russom, damned to hell. I've seen the innocents taken. I've witnessed their dead bodies. You perpetuated the deal made so many years ago by the men in power. Men who should have known better than to bargain away human lives to something not of this world. They signed our death warrant and you've let it continue, decade after decade, racking up bodies and covering up the truth. How many lives could have been saved if you'd just said enough?

Russom walked around the table to her. "You've exceeded all my expectations of you, Captain."

He offered her his hand to shake, and Sofia tried not to cringe at the feel of his palm against hers.

"Your innovations with the alien machinery ushered us into new directions, opened our eyes to new possibilities, and armed us for the wars ahead."

Sofia didn't like where this speech was going. *I'm so going to regret just doing my job.*

"When all this mess is cleared up, I'd like to expand your role a little more. Get you moved up the ranks a bit quicker. After all," he smiled ruefully, "I'm not going to live forever, and I think you'd be a worthy successor of the Dionysius mantle."

Sofia was stunned. "General?"

"You've never questioned my authority or my orders. Your work on the saucers and the technology involved has been exemplary. When we were in the laboratory you never flinched."

That's because I couldn't believe what I was seeing. It was horrific and we had a hand in creating it. And I was terrified for Emory. If she had found her family in that lab it would have sent her tumbling over the edge.

"That's the kind of leader Dionysius needs. Someone who understands that us having the technology we have now was worth every sacrifice we made to secure it."

But we didn't make the deal work, every abductee did, and they didn't sign up for it.

"I can think of no one more suited to take my place and take Dionysius on her shoulders."

Sofia was dumbfounded. It was the promotion of a lifetime and hers for the taking. A position of ultimate power, because however secret the agency was, Russom commanded a huge amount of respect and power in his position. That would be all Sofia's.

But it's no longer the life I want. Not at the price that is being paid by civilians and all the lies it deals in.

"I'll start setting the wheels in motion and get you placed into position to get ready for the role. I have high hopes for you, Captain Martinez."

Sofia finally found her voice. "How are we going to stop the invasion, sir? At the moment, we're doing very little to fight back."

"If I use anything we have deployed here the aliens will come directly for us. I can't afford to draw attention to this base; there's too much at stake here."

"What's so important about here? Other than it has an alien lab for experimenting on humans?"

"There's more here than meets the eye, Captain. But you'll find out all about that in due time. First I need you to find the whereabouts of Mays. After that, you'll be helping me on the next stage of my own agenda."

"Which is?"

"We need a black ship. That's why I gave orders for them to remain off target, but some moron on that boat ignored my hands-off message."

"And if by some miracle we get one, what do you plan to do with it?"

"It's the aircraft carrier. They house the saucers. I want one. I have a fleet of saucers, I want the carrier for them. If it turns out the downed ship in Maine can be used then I'll blow the other ships clear out of the sky. But until I know it's flyable, we wait. I've got men on it trying to get in and salvage it. So you'd better not waste too much time finding the CIA agent because I'll need you back here to fly it."

Sofia gaped at him. "You want me to fly a black triangle craft?"

"You've flown the saucers. This would be the next step up. The Ferrari of flying vessels. You could make it work, fit it into our fleet. I have every belief in you." He moved back around his desk. The discussion was obviously over in his eyes.

"Just be careful out there. I can't afford to lose you too. The future of Dionysius rests on you."

"Thank you for your confidence, sir. I'll do my best to live up to it." Sofia turned and left the room at a measured pace. Only when she was far away enough did she break into a run. She tried desperately to keep her thoughts together after all she'd heard. They had the means to shoot the saucers down, but Russom was holding it back. What would be left of the planet while he still hesitated?

Sofia gathered up a few belongings then pulled out the bag of weapons from under her bed. She shouldered the heavy bag and headed off to Transport to requisition a vehicle. Emory had a few days lead on her, but Sofia knew Emory well enough that what Russom saw wasn't the whole picture. Agent Ellen Mays might follow orders, but Emory Hawkes wouldn't go to a base when she had somewhere else to be first.

And Emory would have no idea that Sofia was hot on her tail. Emory could throw Russom off her trail, but Sofia would be harder to shake off. Especially as Sofia needed to find her now more than ever.

Chapter Thirty

"There's a decidedly concentrated effort going on to get inside that saucer," Emory said, leaning against the desk and staring at the monitor that showed the downed black triangular craft swarmed over by numerous groups. "I swear the amount has doubled since yesterday."

"That's if they can get inside it and get it out of the fucking great hole, and most of Maine, that it's wedged in." Dink handed her a soda and a handful of pills.

"I'd rather have a beer," Emory grumbled but threw the pills back and washed them down with a gulp of Coke.

"I'd rather you didn't get an infection in that leg so quit complaining." He shooed her over so he could take his seat at the desk. For a long time they watched the movements on the monitor in companionable silence.

"Did that lieutenant from the base in Georgia send you any useful information?" Emory hoped that one of the eight US base locations she'd been furnished with would reveal something she could use so she knew where to start searching. She was desperate to get out on her mission. She was all too aware of the vast distances between each base she'd been given. Traveling by road when the skies were so unsafe would use more time than she wanted to waste. Time her nieces didn't have.

Both Emory and Dink jumped as an alarm went off. Dink spun his chair over to the other side of the desk and swiftly began checking another set of screens.

"Proximity alarm?" Emory shifted to peer over his shoulder. The screens showed a variety of camera angles leading to Dink's home.

"It would appear we have a visitor." Dink gestured to the vehicle making its way up to his hideaway.

"Are you expecting one of your friends?"

"I don't have friends, Em, except for you."

"It could just be someone looking for a place to hide out from the invasion," Emory said. She caught a longer glimpse of the vehicle. She stiffened. Was that a military vehicle? Emory wracked her brain. She'd gotten rid of the radio Russom had tried to track her with. She'd made certain she couldn't be followed.

Emory pulled back from the desk to limp over to the drawer she'd hidden her stolen gun in. "I'll go see who it is."

"I don't usually answer the front door armed."

"This is the new normal, Dink. You never know who might come knocking."

"Well, I doubt it's aliens driving up here to come pay their respects to the dead one in the cooler," he said dryly.

"Whoever it is, they're unwelcome."

Emory made her way slowly back up to the rooms above. By the time she reached the door she could hear the vehicle pulling up outside. Emory kept the gun close by her side. On hearing a door open, Emory opened the front door and stepped forward to confront the uninvited guest.

She could see someone with dark hair moving at the rear of the vehicle. Emory groaned. "Why couldn't it have been a damned alien?"

Sofia looked around the edge of the trunk at the sound of Emory's voice. "So, are you going to just stand there or am I expected to carry everything in myself?"

Emory sighed. "What are you doing here, Sofia?"

"Hoping to save the world, Emory, so put your weapon down. Contrary to appearances, it would seem I'm one of the good guys."

❖

Sofia grabbed a few bags of supplies and hefted them up into her arms. She was just getting ready to toss one at Emory to carry when she noticed the unsteady gait Emory used to make her way toward her.

"I need you to turn around and go away right now. You can't warn me about Russom tracking me and then drive here and advertise this location. Please," Emory pleaded, "Please go."

Sofia shook her head. "I disabled the tracking device in my own radio miles ago. No one has any idea I'm here except you."

"And how did you find me? I disposed of my radio days ago."

"The signal was tracked and Russom was concerned it was in the middle of nowhere."

Emory frowned. "It was supposed to go with the truck straight to Denver."

Sofia was amused. "And how did you accomplish that trick?"

"I taped it to the underside of a truck evacuating a town I was passing through." She shook her head in annoyance. "It must have fallen off during the trip." Emory gave Sofia a suspicious look. "So you're what? The search mission to drag me back to Tesla Falls? I hate to tell you, Major, but I'm not going back there any time soon."

"I volunteered to find you because Damocles agents are fading fast." Sofia looked Emory up and down. "It's weird seeing you without your glasses on." She gestured at Emory's leg. "Did you by any chance get that injury bringing down a flying saucer while armed with a military grade missile launcher that I don't recall saying you could sign out?"

"I don't have a clue what you are talking about," Emory said. "You say someone brought down a saucer? Yay for them. One less to contend with and one more than the military has shot down in recent days."

"What happened to your leg?"

"I have a wicked Charley horse."

Sofia shook her head at Emory's deliberate stubbornness. "Invite me in, Agent. I've been driving too many hours nonstop to find you, and I'd really like to freshen up."

"There's plenty of foliage around. Do what you need to do then leave."

Sofia shot her an exasperated look and brushed past her. "Is this where you're staying? I have to say I didn't expect you to be hunkering down in the Ozarks, but I did finally get the in-joke when I drove past the statue of Jesus." She dumped her bags by the door, turning to watch Emory slowly trying to catch up.

"I can't have you here, Sofia. You're putting us in jeopardy. Please leave."

"I'm not here to cause trouble. I'm here because I've come to realize that maybe you and Dink know more than I'm being told by my superiors and I'm sick of being kept in the dark."

"It's always nice to hear someone finally admit they were wrong all along and we're right."

Sofia spun around and found Dink looking up at her. His grin was contagious.

"Dink?" Sofia had never expected the power behind the theories to reveal himself so easily.

"In the flesh." Dink bowed a little then held out his hand for Sofia to shake. "It's a pleasure to meet you finally, Captain Martinez. Especially after traveling with you for so long in Emory's company."

"It's a pleasure to meet you too."

"May I ask for your radio?" He was still smiling, and Sofia handed it over. She was aware he'd find no tracker enabled inside. She watched as he very deftly opened the casing and pulled it to pieces.

"You disabled it?" He held up the tiny piece of tech that showed signs of damage. "But you kept it inside?"

"When I return I'll need proof for my explanation of not being seen on the map. I'm not supposed to know I'm trackable. I figure when I hand this over they will see it for themselves. And before you ask, I disabled the one on my ATV too. I didn't want anyone knowing where I was headed."

"And just how did you happen upon us, Sofia? I mean, I'm a little out of the way for you to just drop by. And I know Emory never told you where I lived. For my security and her own."

"You're safe. I shouldn't be here either, so all this is being done under the radar. Literally. And I got here by following the tracking device I planted in Emory's Bus."

Emory, who had been leaning on the doorjamb, let out a stream of colorful swear words.

Dink waved his finger at her, scolding her. "Rookie move, Em, rookie move. You let her plant a bug on your VW. You're losing your touch."

Emory was still cursing under her breath. "I was desperate to get away from the base housing dead human experiments. How was I supposed to know I needed to sweep my van over because Major Martinez was being a sneaky bitch and planting stuff on my van? While, at the same time, she was removing the weapons we had stored in there."

"I somehow missed a missile launcher." Sofia hardened her gaze at Emory.

"No comment," Emory fired back.

"You don't need to. Someone was seen in a saucer beam armed with a launcher. You'll forgive me if my suspicions fell on you."

Dink started to laugh. "She's got your number, Emory. Now come back inside and get off your feet before you do more damage to that leg than you already have." He turned his eyes back to Sofia. "There's a great deal of land surrounding my home, Sofia. If you're here under false pretenses I can pick from many an acre to bury your body."

"I'll consider myself duly warned. Will this do as an explanation as to why I'm here?" She opened up a case and held out a laptop. "Don't worry. The tracker in that was taken out ages ago and left on my desk so no one knew better."

"And this is?" Dink ran his hand all over the casing as if searching it for anything else hidden.

"This is *my* laptop and I've just been given full access to the Dionysius database."

Emory looked shocked. "Why? And if so, what the hell are you doing here?"

"I'm next in line to sit on the Dionysius throne and have that sword dangling over my head. Russom is grooming me to take his place."

Emory's mouth dropped open. "No shit."

"Indeed," Sofia said. "I'll take over from him when he dies, but before that I need to find Damocles Six and make sure our CIA agent is still able to perform her duty of clearing up Russom's mess."

"And you're giving me this why?" Dink asked, cradling the laptop to his chest like it was something precious.

Sofia looked between him and Emory. "I need to know just what Nine Circles of Hell I'm being expected to shoulder. And I don't think Russom is the man to tell me what my job will entail considering how much he's lied to me. Help me sort out the truth from the lies and then help me bring an end to Dionysius once and for all."

"You're serious?"

"I chose the military because I wanted to serve and protect my country. I never wanted to be a party to the experimentation of human beings. That's not what I signed on for."

Dink and Emory exchanged a look. Dink clutched the prized laptop even closer.

"You're the one who's kissed her," he said to Emory. "Do you think we can trust her?"

Emory's eyes searched her face. "Emory, I'm risking my career and my life to give you the chance to prove your theories to me." Sofia pointed to the laptop. "And I'm giving you the ammunition to do it."

Emory and Dink shared another meaningful look. Emory gave a faint nod.

"Then welcome to the conspiracy theorist version of Tesla Falls, Sofia." Dink gestured for her to enter.

Sofia let him take the lead, but she caught Emory's arm to stop her. "I know you don't want me here, but oddly enough, I have no one else I trust more than you. I know we didn't exactly part on the best of terms, but…" she shrugged awkwardly, "I missed you." Before Emory could speak, Sofia kissed her. She sighed at the familiar feel of Emory's lips against her own. "I missed that as well." She ran the pads of her fingers down Emory's cheek then dropped her hands away to pick up her bags. Emory's eyes were still open, watching her warily until she finally returned the smile Sofia was directing her way.

"Show me your world now. I think it's time I finally see what you've been aware of all this time."

Chapter Thirty-one

Sofia wasn't sure what she had expected on entering Dink's home, but being directed through a false setup of home and hearth and down into a massive underground lair was not what she had imagined. Downstairs, she was confronted by a space that outdid Tesla Falls' war room and a multi computer setup that was an IT technician's wet dream. The walls were covered in maps and photographs, while copious books lined a huge bookcase. An entertainment system took up an area where Sofia could tell Dink and Emory sat and chilled out, judging by the cans of beer, soda, and empty bags of chips on the small coffee table. There were obviously rooms branching off this main area which she guessed led to bedrooms and bathrooms perhaps. She'd never seen anything like it.

"Not bad for a basement dweller's lair, is it?" Dink grinned at her mischievously before taking his seat at the huge bank of monitors.

Emory settled herself gingerly in another seat. Sofia felt the pain Emory was obviously trying to mask.

"You brought that saucer down, didn't you?" Sofia folded her arms across her chest to stop herself from running her hands all over Emory to check for any more signs of injury.

"Theoretically? With you being next in line of Dionysius? That kind of makes you very nearly my boss." Emory maneuvered her leg up to rest it on an open lower drawer she'd been using for that exact purpose. "Well, Ellen Mays's boss to be exact. And seeing as she doesn't exactly exist I don't think I need to answer your question."

"You can dance around it as much as you like, but I know you were the idiot who tested out a theory with the Rooty Tooty Point and Shooty you stole from Euphoria."

Dink snorted at Sofia successfully mimicking Emory's name for the missile launcher. Even Emory had to smile at her mockery.

"I swear, Emory, you've got to stop this desperate need to risk your life every time you are out in the open."

"I promise you that was the last time I will get that close to a saucer's freezing beam." Emory shuddered. "It was frightening being totally paralyzed in it yet being completely aware. I don't ever want to experience that again." She tapped at her leg. "And being the dumbass who falls from a great height out of the sky to land on a shed rooftop and then fall off it. Not my finest hour after bringing down an alien ship with one well aimed shot on my first go." She high-fived Dink and they both grinned at Sofia like idiots.

"Yes, you are a perfect markswoman considering never having training with such an unwieldy weapon, and I applaud that. Right after I want to kill you because you're going to drive me insane with your antics." Sofia sighed. She knew Emory had been involved. She and that damned launcher Sofia had expressively told her not to touch. "Have you had your leg properly checked out?"

"Dink stitched it up for me," Emory said.

Sofia raised an eyebrow at him. "*Doctor* Dink?"

"DVM to be exact, a doctor of veterinary medicine. It was the only way I could get in on cases of mutilated cattle."

You got seen to by a *vet*?"

Emory just grinned and took the dig with good grace. "And a damned good one too."

"Then there's my numerous PhDs, my MCS, that's a master of computer science, I totally aced that course. Oh, and MIT. You know, it's amazing what you can study on the Internet and add to your credentials."

"MIT?"

"It won't surprise you that I ended up not taking the standard route a graduate of MIT would usually take."

Sofia looked around the room. "So why conspiracy theories as your profession?"

"The exposing of the truth behind the lies, Sofia. It's been a fascinating journey, quite the learning experience. I've met some powerful people with stories to tell who were kept silent by their superiors. Who wouldn't want to hear what they know?" He slipped from his chair and picked up Sofia's laptop. "And it's brought you to us now. If you'll excuse me, this little beauty and I need to get better acquainted."

"You're not going to use it in here?"

"I'm sure you're very sincere in this gift, but I'm taking no chances this is a Trojan horse ready to infect all my computers. So I'll be back shortly." He waved a hand around the room. "Make yourself at home. As you can see, we have plenty to keep you occupied." He disappeared back up top and left Sofia and Emory alone.

Sofia took his seat before the monitors and stared at all the views they were offering. "Do I want to know how exactly he gets all these feeds?"

"Probably not," Emory said.

Sofia watched the screens flick from one country to another. The devastation around the world was undeniable.

"You really had no clue what Russom was going to reveal to us, did you?" Emory rested her elbow on the desk and her chin in her hand. She was watching Sofia's reaction closely.

"No damn clue whatsoever," she admitted. "I'd worked for him for years. I'd worked on the saucers exclusively and never knew how deep we'd sold out to an alien race that I'd been told didn't exist anymore. I had no reason to dispute it. I never saw any evidence otherwise…until you led me down Euphoria's hidden levels and I got to see what lay hidden away."

"So why didn't you say anything in the lab? You never uttered a word, either about what we were seeing with all those bodies just suspended there, or to even question Russom on it."

"I was too shocked to be honest. And I knew I needed to keep my mouth shut because Russom wasn't watching you checking everything out. He was watching *my* reaction, and I couldn't let him see how much it disgusted me." Sofia closed her eyes at the memory of that awful room and what it said about certain members of the human race. "Everything I had been led to believe came crashing down around me in that room, Emory. You know all too well what it's like when something you believe so passionately in turns out to be built on lies and subterfuge. It makes you question everything you've ever believed to be true."

Emory nodded. "So why are you *here*?"

Sofia reached inside one of the paper bags she'd carried in with her. She pulled out a bag of Tootsie Rolls and held it out to Emory. "I believe I owe you these. I think you're going to need them when I tell you what else Russom is up to."

Emory took the bag and dipped her head in a bow at Sofia's gesture when she finally realized Emory was right about something.

Sofia's eyes fell on a monitor displaying the black triangular craft.

Emory ripped open the bag and pulled out a Roll. "Russom wants that big ship for his collection, doesn't he? To complete the set. And I'm guessing he wants you to work on it, given your success with the saucers."

Sofia nodded, not surprised Emory already had a theory in her head. "He wants me to *fly* it." She knew how crazy that sounded, and judging by the look of incredulity on Emory's face, she wasn't alone.

"Fly it?" Emory rolled the candy around in her mouth, coughing a little as she nearly choked on it. "Fly it where exactly?"

"He didn't expand on that," Sofia admitted.

Emory swallowed the candy and reached for her soda. "These saucers of yours. Have you tested them in outer space or do you guys just ride around in them in your own backyards?"

"I'm no astronaut. I've not taken a ship outside of our orbit." She looked back at the screen. "So why does he want this ship so badly that he hasn't deployed the weapon that can bring the whole lot of them down?"

"Excuse me?" Emory spluttered and inadvertently sprayed some of her soda over Dink's extensive keyboarding. She hastened to mop it up as quickly as she could. "What the fuck did you just say?"

"I guess we have a lot to talk about." Sofia patted Emory's knee gently. "The Tootsie Rolls were for you being right about Tesla's energy weapon having been made at the base that bears his name."

"I knew it!" Emory gloated. "So why isn't it being deployed? It would bring an end to the invasion."

Sofia pointed at the activity all over the black craft. "This is the reason for his hesitation."

"What is Russom doing holding the world to ransom while the worker ants crawling all over that ship can't even begin to get into it?"

"And what exactly is going to happen once they *do* get in?" Sofia wondered aloud as she shifted closer to the screen to watch the workers try to crack the hull. "They won't get in that way. What they're doing is pointless."

"Do you know how to get in that ship?"

Sofia smiled. "I might have a better idea than them employing laser cutters or deciding to use explosives. I'm guessing Russom has already warned them not to dare try that method. He's still pissed it was shot down in the first place."

"Then how did he intend to capture one?"

"I have no idea, but he has ways and means of doing anything he wants and no one stands in his way."

Emory nudged Sofia gently. "Until you?"

Sofia nudged her back. "Until *us.*"

❖

"Emory! Emory!" Dink's voice carried down the steps, and Emory's head shot up at his excited calls.

"What's up, man?"

Dink appeared clutching the laptop above his head like a banner. "It's the Holy Grail of military information! It busts Dionysius wide open and spills its secrets for all to see." He grinned hugely. "And by everyone I mean ME!" He cackled like a maniac.

Emory just laughed back at him. Sofia shook her head.

"Remind me again why I came to you two clowns with such highly sensitive information?"

"Because, my dear captain, you knew only we could make sense of the madness Dionysius orchestrates." Dink laid the laptop beside Emory and flipped open the lid. "Guess what they have at Tesla Falls?"

Emory felt terrible for bursting his bubble, but she couldn't resist. "Proof of Tesla's death ray."

His face fell. "Fuck!" He spun around and pointed a finger at Sofia. "No spoilers, Sofia! That's cheating!" He stomped over to a seat and flung himself in it.

"Russom won't employ it, even though it would wipe the alien ships clean from our skies." Emory pointed to the monitor. "He wants this little beauty before he starts playing war of the worlds."

Dink pointed at the laptop. "That little Pandora's Box coughed up the answer to another mystery. The reason why those huge triangular ships have managed to stay hidden for so long."

"It's got to be that they either hide out in volcanos or they are a seafaring craft," Emory said. They'd had this discussion numerous times before.

"You've always said that anything could be hiding in the deep, dark depths of the sea. There's one report that states they've been swimming with the fishes all along. Which would explain the Bermuda Triangle and all the other no-go areas where ships and planes mysteriously disappear. We have more than enough water covering the planet for crafts of that size to submerge themselves out of sight in. With their technology, they've got to be equipped to plunge to depths that would crush our submarines like beer cans. Sofia, what are the chances of that craft being flyable once it's dug out of Maine and dried out?" Dink pulled his chair closer to her.

Sofia studied the feeds they were watching. "I don't know. The saucers were made from a very durable material, nothing like we had here on Earth, but they still crashed and broke up. I'd hazard a guess the black ships are stronger but still damageable. And crash-landing into the sea and a land mass won't make it the easiest of rescues to get it back out again unless someone gets inside and tries to fly it."

"Which is what Russom wants Sofia here to try," Emory added and watched at Dink's eyebrows rose.

"Interesting…" he murmured.

Sofia made a face at the screen at what she was seeing. "What they are trying to do isn't going to work. If these black craft are anything like the saucers, it should have a pressure point on the surface that opens the hidden door."

"And let me guess. That pressure point is either deep under the sea water or buried miles deep under tons of Maine's soil," Emory said. "So unless they can levitate this ship up and out of both jams, they're not going to be able to get in the easy way."

Sofia shook her head. "They're going to realize sooner or later diamond-tipped drills and lasers aren't going to do the trick. They'll switch to explosives, and Russom will rain all kinds of hell on them if they damage his precious prize."

"If they do blow a hole to get inside, what will they find waiting for them?" Emory had a feeling whatever it was wasn't going to be friendly.

Sofia just shrugged. "I've never seen inside one of those crafts, but I'm going to guess there's a full complement of alien life forms on board. Whether they are dead or alive at this point, I can't honestly say."

Emory leaned back in her seat and stared at the ceiling. "The bigger question is, what kind? We know the saucers house the little gray aliens, but the bigger blue ones have yet to show themselves." She sat back up abruptly and hissed at the accompanying pain in her leg. "Dink, do you still have a contact out there or was he shipped out?"

Dink switched on a screen that had been dormant in the top row of monitors. The screen flickered to life and showed a perfect front line view of the downed ship.

"Oh my God," Sofia breathed. "Do you have eyes everywhere?"

Dink smiled sweetly at her. "You'd be surprised how far my reach goes. For the past few days, I've been watching the Senate running around like headless chickens. That got old real fast."

"You have someone spying for you in the government?"

"More than one actually. However, they don't wear the same gear Emory sports so kindly. They get me the information the old-fashioned way. They give me their passcodes and let me troll their computers."

"I'm wondering if I should be more afraid of you or Russom," Sofia muttered.

"I'm just a concerned American citizen, seeking the truth amid all the lies we keep being fed through mass media and those in power." Dink pressed a button on his desk. "You're live on air, Echo Three."

Sofia looked at Emory with a frown and mouthed "Echo Three?"

"Soldier boy is a big Star Wars fan. Dink thought it was only fitting he had a code name to match."

"What's your code name?"

"I rarely use one. As a journalist I was known by my real identity. But Ellen Mays always served me well when I went undercover."

"It's a miracle you weren't found out all those times you stepped where others wouldn't have dared to."

"If I'd followed that rule, Sofia, I would never have met you and that would have been a terrible shame." Emory loved the smile that curved Sofia's lips and softened her dark eyes. "You wouldn't be here now, consorting with the enemy, and looking to bring down more than just the spaceships."

Sofia snorted. "You're a bad influence." However, her smile grew. "You're undoubtedly a scoundrel."

Dink interrupted them. "If you two can put your flirting on hold for just a second, I think our boy is next up to work on the ship. He's an explosives expert. I think you were right, Sofia. They've lost patience barely scratching the surface. They're going to force their way in."

Sofia shot upright. "They need to be careful where they set the charges. Those ships don't run on the usual power sources. If they plant explosives over the engine room they could probably kiss goodbye to the rest of Maine in the resulting blast."

"And you're only mentioning this now because…?" Dink's voice rose in his fear.

"Because I didn't think they'd go against Russom's orders *not* to scratch the ship. But then they didn't exactly follow orders when they shot the damned thing down either."

Emory purposely stood between them before things got any more rowdy. "Okay, time out, you two. Dink, you need to tell your man on site not to blow a hole over the engines. Surely they can scan for energy signatures or something?"

Dink turned back to his mic to relay the message as quickly as possible.

"Sofia, do you have an educated guess as to where the engines might be?" Emory asked. Sofia shook her head, obviously having no clue seeing as these weren't the ships she'd worked on. Emory started to grumble until her eyes fell on Sofia's laptop. "Would Dionysius know?"

Sofia quickly began searching. "Let's see before more innocent lives are lost for one man's need for power."

CHAPTER THIRTY-TWO

Emory, Sofia, and Dink crowded around the monitor, their attention fixed on what was happening on the black craft.

"I hope to God the instructions we gave to Echo Three prove correct," Dink said, rubbing his hand over his beard nervously.

Emory was working out her nerves by chain chewing Tootsie Rolls until her jaw began to ache. She noticed how still Sofia had gotten beside her. Emory recognized that when Sofia was worried, she was unusually silent and motionless, as if any false move would let the fear escape. Emory slipped her hand around Sofia's and gave it a comforting squeeze. Sofia smiled a fraction. She threaded her fingers through Emory's and squeezed back.

They all jumped as the explosives blew a large gaping hole in the side of the black triangular craft. Smoke billowed from the crude cavity, and thankfully, everyone had been far away enough not to get pelted by the shards of ship that flew off in all directions.

"It shattered like glass," Dink said. "How odd."

"Russom is going to be livid," Sofia said, her eyes never shifting from the screens.

One screen showed the outside of the downed ship; the other was Echo 3's viewpoint via his camera glasses. He was one of the first wave of troops set to enter the craft. Guns drawn, the soldiers were ordered into the ship. Emory felt like she was watching some surreal movie of soldiers entering a spaceship, the mood dark and foreboding inside. One by one, the soldiers switched on the flashlights attached to their weapons, and white beams began lighting up the dull interior of the craft.

"Please let whatever was on board be dead from the crash," Dink muttered.

"What if they house the abductees in there? I need to know they're alive at least." Emory reached for the last of her candy and stuffed it into her mouth. The gooey mess made her teeth stick together, but at least it stopped her from voicing her fears.

The army shifted through the corridors with stealth. Their lights bounced off the smooth walls but revealed nothing in the beams or in the shadows cast. Every hatch or eve or door they came upon, they searched. It was all to no avail.

Emory didn't know whether to be relieved or not that no human abductees were being found as the men moved from floor to floor. She was acutely aware of Sofia's hand tightening on her own. Their knees bumped together as Sofia sought Emory's proximity as they both watched the screens.

"There was only ever one spare space on the saucers that looked like a holding cell. I'm going to guess that kept the abductees confined until they could drop them off. If there's no onboard lab on this ship that means they have to be taken somewhere on the ground. Emory, you have the locations of the bases." Sofia gently squeezed her hand. "I promise you, we'll search every single one of them until we find your family. But first we need to stop Russom and uncover what his plan is for that ship. Whatever it is it can't be good seeing as he's allowing us to remain defenseless while he waits for something to happen."

Emory hated that there were so few to go up against so many enemies. It wasn't enough that they had the aliens to contend with but also the humans who appeared to be in league with them. And then the leaders with their own agendas to furnish. She was torn in too many directions. She wanted to rescue her family. She also wanted to stop Russom's strange games. She wanted the aliens gone. It was too much for them—a journalist, a professional truth seeker, and a captain with insider knowledge of the saucers—to handle alone. But watching the men search inside the ship made Emory thankful to be in a room far away with exactly those two people by her side.

❖

Elevators took the soldiers up to the next level. There the lighting was less subdued. Sofia's instincts kicked in.

"Dink, warn Echo Three that this level might be populated. The light has changed color, and there's a faint hum I can hear over the feed."

She watched as Anderson, the officer in charge, held up a hand to halt them all as he pushed against a door to try to open it. It slid open without a noise, and he almost stumbled inside. He caught his balance, swiftly raised his gun, and took a step inside. The soldier behind him, Olsen, followed. He took one step forward. That was as far as he got. Olsen was bowled off his feet, slammed backward by the bloody torso of Anderson that hit him with an almighty force. Anderson's limbs had been ripped clean off. His head was only attached to his body by torn strips of flesh. He'd been decapitated. The impact of the dead body hitting Olsen splattered blood over everyone in the corridor. It ran in a thick line down the lenses of Echo 3's glasses.

Pandemonium broke out as the men behind Olsen stepped forward, their guns spewing bullets everywhere. Someone sounded a retreat, but it was all too late.

A large blue skinned alien stepped out of the room. Its two rows of spiked teeth were bared as it let out a sound unlike anything Sofia had ever heard before. It was a growl that brought forth visions of the deepest depths of hell. With the alien's skin scaled like chainmail, the bullets did very little damage. The alien flinched but never fell. With its massive hands, it grabbed the nearest soldier and simply tore him in half, tossing the pieces behind him and reaching for another victim.

"Fuck me!" Emory yelped, shooting her chair back away from the desk. "Get them the fuck out of there now! That thing will slaughter them all!"

Three other blue skinned aliens appeared, and Echo 3's view on the carnage showed just how unprepared the army was when faced with an alien other than one small and gray. The front line of defense was butchered within seconds. The sound was nauseating when the screams from the dying was accompanied by the braying growl from the aliens as they celebrated each kill.

Dink was screaming down the mic. "Nate! Get the hell out of there while you still can. Get out, get out! Don't engage them. Just get the fuck out now!"

Sofia realized that Nate was Echo 3's real name. She watched as a blue alien's mouth opened right in front of Nate's face and then closed with a stomach churning crunch. The feed from the glasses died along with Nate as his head was bitten off. The screen was lit with static, but the sound still broadcast the desperate spraying of bullets and the yells from the survivors until they too fell silent.

Sofia couldn't tear her eyes away from the static displayed on the monitor. She was desperate for it to clear so they could be sure at least someone had survived. She looked at the other screen. It showed the innocuous scene outside the craft. The military stood around waiting, just going about their business, so totally oblivious to what had happened inside the ship.

Sofia turned in her chair to face Emory. "We need to go back to Tesla Falls. I want that energy beam powered up and I want those bastards dead."

"What if Russom won't listen to reason?" Emory's whole body was shaking.

Sofia reached for Emory's hands and held them tight. "Then I'll make him listen. He wants me to take charge? Well, he's going to regret thinking I'd just follow blindly in his footsteps."

It had driven Emory crazy that they couldn't just inform the troops outside the spaceship what had happened inside. It had taken way too long for them to realize there'd been a massacre. Dink's less than legal access into their camera feeds and Echo 3's, *Nate's*, eyewear wouldn't help him be remembered as the real hero he died as. He'd been Dink's eyes and ears on clandestine missions and deployments all around the world. He'd been trying to find evidence of the fabled Super Soldiers so that Dink and Emory could use it to expose that was happening right there amid the ranks.

Emory sat on the doorstep of Dink's home. She was looking up at the stars slowly starting to sparkle in the early evening light. She'd left Dink at his computers, calling in old favors and calling up old friends. If Sofia wanted to take down Russom, she was going to need backup and muscle behind her. Just Dink and Emory alone wasn't going to carry much official weight. Dink knew all the retired and disgraced officers who'd dared to speak out against the secrets.

He knew the airline pilots who had been benched for talking to reporters about the flying saucers they'd seen in the air. He even had government officials who had tried to release sensitive information to the public and had been dismissed on trumped up charges that ruined their reputations and their lives. The Conspiracy of Silence, Dink called it. It effectively bound the tongues of those with something to say that certain factions didn't want reported. It was frightening to realize that Big Brother was always watching you for your own safety but didn't always have your best interests at heart.

It was barely an hour since she'd sat watching the army be murdered at the hands of the blue aliens. Emory had watched the whole area surrounding the ship be evacuated. But not before explosives had been planted over every inch of the exposed craft. The resulting detonation had been catastrophic. Those who hadn't gotten clear of the blast radius were taken out by the blast. The blast had torn the ship asunder and ignited whatever power source was inside.

Sofia sat with her head in her hands, mourning their stupidity and questioning the logic of their superiors. All three of them sat watching on the one camera feed left as it showed the black triangular ship sink into the depths of the sea. The coastline of Maine was forever changed, and the sea was now home to the alien and human dead.

"I can't see the aliens letting that go unchallenged," Sofia said as she came and sat beside Emory. "We need to get that energy beam up and running to wipe the blues clear from the face of the universe."

"And we will, but trust Dink and me on this. You can't just go in demanding stuff. You'll need re-enforcements. We have friends that are willing to put aside their beef with the government and military to come and fight by your side. They were also spreading the word among themselves and landed a big fish. We had to out you to get him to help though. Dink knows a guy who knows a guy who has admitted he used to work at Tesla Falls. A retired general, Samuel Ulrich, who was ousted by Russom. Dink finally got him to talk about it. Seems he knows all about the energy beam."

"I wish I had known about it. I'd have put a stop to this invasion days ago before the world came crumbling down." Sofia threaded her fingers through her hair.

Emory leaned in to bump Sofia gently. "You know now, and you're ready to do something."

Sofia turned to her. "You didn't think I would fight?"

"It must be hard to go against all you've fought for and believed in."

"It is," Sofia said, "but when you sacrifice lives for no reason, someone has to stand up for the lost."

Emory smiled. "So noble. I like it. It befits the leader you're going to be when Russom steps down."

Sofia snorted. "If you think he'll step aside for me—"

"He's got to realize there's no winning now. His ship is sunk… literally." Emory shrugged. "Who knows, maybe he'll see the error of his ways."

"If he does it would make my decision so much easier and less treasonous." Sofia rested her head on Emory's shoulder. "Either way, we sleep tonight and set off first thing in the morning."

"We never seem to stay in one place for very long, do we?" Emory raised her gaze once more to the stars.

"Then let's make the most of tonight in case it's our last."

Emory couldn't bring herself to look at Sofia. The pull she felt toward her turned Emory's feelings inside out with a longing she could no longer explain or seem to care to.

Sofia's hand slipped into Emory's and they sat quietly for a while.

"I wish we had more time," Emory said. "I'd like you to get to know me properly. I'm told I can be quite charming when not putting the ass in classy."

"I like you just fine." Sofia cradled Emory's hand and traced her fingers over the palm. She was following the scratches and deeper cuts Emory had sustained falling out of the sky. "How bad is your leg?"

"I'm screwed if I need to run anywhere, and the limp is very pronounced. It'll heal."

"It's giving you a sexy swagger that's very distracting when viewed from behind."

"Is that your subtle way of saying you've been checking out my ass?"

"Maybe." Sofia feathered her fingers over Emory's sweatpants that hung loosely over her damaged leg. "I'm not the kind of woman who usually does one-night stands, Emory. And if this turns out to be our last night together I'd rather not waste it."

Emory's breath caught in her chest. "So what am I to you if not for one night only?"

"A 'what might have been'? A 'what could be' if things ever see a side of normal again? How about for tonight you're simply Emory and you're mine?" She leaned in and kissed Emory with lips soft and searching. A kiss that spoke of promises and passions and a gentleness Emory hadn't experienced for a long time. Sofia pulled back, and Emory instinctively followed after her, seeking her lips again. Sofia's hand against her chest kept Emory just out of reach. Emory let out a grumble, and Sofia tapped a finger against the very pronounced pout that shaped Emory's mouth.

"Tonight, I don't care about your job. I don't even care about mine." Sofia kissed Emory again. "It's just you and me and this night."

Emory was lost in the warmth of her touch and the sensuous brush of her lips. "There's only one guest room here," she said, "but I'm willing to share."

"Then I guess it's time for us to turn in." Sofia stood and held out a hand to help Emory to her feet.

Emory grimaced as her leg reminded her how ungainly she was going to be. Sofia read her thoughts. She pulled her head down and gave her a long, lingering kiss that distracted Emory enough to stop caring. "Don't worry about your leg. Remember, I'm a captain. I know all about taking charge and giving orders. You're under me tonight."

Laughing, Emory decided there would be no arguing with her. They walked back into the room where Dink was tapping away at a keyboard private messaging with someone.

"We're just…" Emory gestured vaguely down the hall. *God, could I be any more like a blushing teenager bringing a girl home.*

Dink looked at them holding hands and deliberately picked up a pair of headphones before he waved them off.

"I expected a comment at least," Sofia said.

"Believe me, he'll have plenty to tease us about tomorrow." Emory ushered Sofia into the small bedroom where she had made her home away from home. "I can't believe I'm lucky enough to have you here."

"For however short it may be?"

"Every second of you in my arms will seem like an eternity. That's more than I could have dreamed of."

Sofia grazed her fingers softly over Emory's cheek. "See, you *can* be charming. Let's see what else you can do that's as pleasurable."

Emory vowed to spend all night doing whatever it took to show Sofia that she took that duty very seriously.

Sofia pushed Emory down onto the bed, ever mindful of her leg. She stalled Emory's hands that started to unbutton her own shirt.

"No, let me." Sofia teased each button open and smiled at the impatient huffs Emory released under her breath. Every piece of Emory's skin she uncovered, Sofia brushed at. First with her fingertips, then with her nose to breathe in Emory's clean scent. Finally, with her lips, kissing and sucking and delighting in Emory's moans. The shirt was finally removed, the bra underneath swiftly following, and then Sofia's lips latched on to Emory's hard nipples and she lavished them with attention. She kissed them one at a time, brushing a thumb over one hard nub while the other she sucked deep into her mouth.

"Oh God, you're going to make me come if you keep that up."

"Feels good?" Sofia asked, running her tongue roughly around the edges of Emory's areola. She could feel Emory's body twitching beneath her.

"So good," Emory gasped. She clutched Sofia's head to her chest, silently begging for more.

With one teasing show of teeth rasping against Emory's breast, Sofia sat up to divest herself of her own T-shirt and bra. Emory sat up with her. She began her own exploration of Sofia's much fuller curves before Sofia could even get her head free from her shirt. Emory roughly pushed the bra aside and paid Sofia back for all her teasing. Sofia's hands grabbed on to Emory's hair, anchoring her head, then running her short nails against Emory's scalp to urge her on.

"You're beautiful," Emory said, tugging a nipple with her lips then licking it before sucking it with just enough pressure that shot straight between Sofia's legs and made her ache.

"I thought I was in charge," she said, finally pushing Emory back down and lying on top of her to kiss at the smile on Emory's face.

"You know me and orders." Emory ran her hands all over Sofia's back, lightly squeezing at the muscles, turning Sofia into a mass of sensation.

Sofia shifted slightly, and her leg slipped between Emory's. Her knee added just enough pressure to make Emory hiss into Sofia's mouth. She could feel Emory shift beneath her, searching for more pressure. Deliberately, Sofia moved and didn't miss Emory's plaintive whine of disappointment. She rested her open palm on Emory's flat stomach, feeling the muscles twitching beneath her hand. Emory's skin was hot and flushed in her arousal. It was also covered in a mass of vivid colored bruises and raw scrapes from her misadventure with the saucer.

"You won't hurt me," Emory said as Sofia hesitated in her touch. "You'll hurt me more if you stop what you were doing."

Sofia gently tugged down the baggy sweatpants and the soft briefs beneath. She tried not to pay attention to the stark white dressing covering a large part of Emory's thigh and instead took in the long length of Emory's legs and the pale hair that begged for Sofia to explore more. Sofia eased away and divested herself of the last of her clothing, enjoying the look in Emory's eyes as she unabashedly watched her reveal herself. She lay back down beside Emory, their skin touching, their sweat mixing, and for a precious moment, time stood still in that tiny room where the outside world seemed so mercifully far away.

Sofia kissed Emory's forehead tenderly and gathered her into her arms. Slowly, she ran her fingers over the length of Emory's spine, cupping her buttocks and squeezing a cheek. Then she slipped around to cup Emory's sex. The wetness of Emory's arousal covered Sofia's hand, and she rubbed softly, feeling everything against her palm, the infinite softness of fleshy lips and the unmistakable hardness of Emory's clit. She dragged her fingers up to distribute sticky juices upon Emory's hood then ran her thumb over and around it in erratic patterns. Firmer strokes drew Emory's sensitive clit out even further. Sofia held Emory close as she explored. Emory was tense, her body reacting to every brush of Sofia's deft fingers. With her thumb flicking Emory's clit, Sofia pressed two fingers inside and sank into warm welcoming walls. Only one of Emory's legs could dig into the bed, the other lay spread so that Sofia could move unhindered. Sofia thrust a little faster, just that little bit harder, and Emory bucked beneath her.

Emory was biting her bottom lip, desperate to keep the noise down. Sofia wasn't having any of that; she wanted to hear her. She roughly kissed her, teasing her tongue across Emory's teeth until she let her in. As soon as their lips touched, Sofia curled her fingers inside, finding the hidden sweet spot and raking her fingers over it. Emory whimpered as she tried to keep from bucking even harder against Sofia's hand and hurting her leg. Her hands gripped at both Sofia and the mattress as Sofia flicked her clit and pressed deeper inside. With a harsh gasp against Sofia's lips, Emory came apart. Her whole body shook as she orgasmed. Sofia felt the pulsing pressure squeeze her fingers rhythmically as she rode the pleasure out with Emory. She pressed soothing kisses over Emory's face, memorizing the naked emotion in Emory's eyes as she stared at Sofia. She finally slowed her hand and thumb on Emory's flesh when she sensed Emory could take no more stimulation.

Emory fell back on the bed with a heartfelt groan. "Fuck me," she said, trying to catch her breath.

Sofia nuzzled her gently. "I believe I just did."

Emory opened dazed, passion blown eyes, to gaze up at Sofia. "You're more lethal than any secret weapon the military might have." She brushed her hair away from her sweaty skin and pulled Sofia down for a leisurely kiss. "Oh yeah, that is so happening again. Fuck this one night only thing. With those moves? You're stuck with me for life."

Sofia laughed and snuggled into Emory's shaking arms.

"It would be crazy for me to fall for you, right?"

Emory's voice was so soft Sofia wasn't sure she'd heard her at all. She lifted her head to stare down at Emory's face.

"But then, you've called me crazy from the first moment we met. So why stop now?" Emory pulled Sofia close and kissed her gently.

Sofia craved Emory's touch. She let Emory shift her until she was sat straddled above Emory's face while deft fingers were pulling her closer. The first brush of Emory's tongue through her wetness made Sofia cry out, and she lowered herself further so that there was nowhere Emory couldn't reach. With voracious lips and a wicked tongue, Emory devoured Sofia and left her a writhing mess. Held in place only by Emory's hands anchoring her hips, Sofia gripped the headboard tightly and bucked against the insistent sucking on her clit. When Emory slipped a finger inside her, Sofia knew Dink had to hear her scream.

She didn't care.

This was their night and nothing was ever going to take that away from them.

CHAPTER THIRTY-THREE

The mood for the drive back to Utah was subdued. They were all piled into Sofia's vehicle using the ruse that Emory's VW had broken down and she'd had to be rescued off the side of the road. Emory had listened with amusement to Sofia radioing that excuse in to Russom as they left the Ozarks far behind them and the security it had afforded them.

Emory sat in the front while Sofia drove. Dink was sprawled out fast asleep on the backseats. He'd been awake for hours coordinating their backup plan. Dink had spent the first few hours of the trip bemoaning the fact he was finally out of his bunker and had yet to see one saucer. Emory had argued that was a good thing, but Dink was disappointed.

"So, this ragtag gang of Misfit Boys Dink has been gathering together..." Sofia trailed off as if she was uncertain how to continue.

"The basement dweller's posse?" Emory teased her. "The long list of military might who were dismissed as cranks? Most of whom are currently making their way toward Utah to support you should you need to stage a coup. And there's one bigwig already there waiting for us."

"And these are all ones who saw something alien or were working for the military and were going to blow the whistle?"

"Yes, but you're not getting disgruntled employees wanting to kick back at the government. These are men who saw the truth and wanted to expose it. They were trying to stop what we're seeing now."

"Ah yes, stopping it. That task appears to have landed squarely on my shoulders."

"And what lovely shoulders they are too."

"Stop that right now. There is to be no flirting while we're driving toward our uncertain future." Dink groaned and shifted to sit upright. He scrubbed at his face then reached for the laptop he'd been using as a pillow. His silence alerted Emory.

"Dink?"

"Abigail, who is filling in for me quite well, says the saucers are shifting en masse." He made a face. "We're not the only ones heading to Utah."

Sofia took her eyes off the road and shifted to stare at him. "*All* of them?"

"Looks that way. They're idling though, not cruising at their usual speed. Looks like they're taking the scenic route on their way. Those things never go slow. That's a worry in itself." He clattered away on his keyboard. "Eyes on the road, Sofia. Those saucers are waiting for something, and I'd hate to think it was for us."

"Do you think they know about the energy beam at Tesla Falls?" Sofia's eyes were forward and her foot pressed heavier on the gas pedal.

"Or whatever else is there," Dink replied.

"What else could there be? We know about the alien labs, the human abductees, and Tesla's energy weapon. What else could be there?"

"We have a theory—" Emory began only to be cut off by Sofia's groan.

"Oh God, no. Your damn theories have a habit of becoming fact."

Emory grinned. She directed a proud look over her shoulder at Dink. "We're goddamn geniuses, right Dink?"

"That we are. Are you going to tell her our theory comes from the paperwork you 'borrowed' from Euphoria's base?"

"Was there anything in that base you *didn't* touch?"

"She didn't bring me a blue alien, which would have made for a nicely matched pair I could have had on display," Dink said.

Sofia just rolled her eyes and purposely ignored him. "So what's this new theory of yours?"

"It's the little known theory concerning atoms, a ton of energy, and the reason why CERN was blown clear off the planet." Emory settled herself comfortably in her seat. "Dink, would you care to set the scene?"

"Once upon a time, dear Captain, there was a lonely little atom with dreams of being so much more…"

The closer they got to Tesla Falls the more nervous Emory felt. Her hands were constantly clammy and her leg was bouncing nervously with every mile they covered. Driving in the dark of night wasn't helping either; Emory hated it.

"I don't know how you did this, Em." Dink's face was pressed up against the back window looking up at the sky. "Having to keep an eye on the clouds for any sign of saucer activity is fucking exhausting. It's a wonder you didn't drive yourself off the road and into a ditch. And you can't see a thing at night. It's too damn dark. And don't get me started on the lack of bathroom opportunities for you girls. How the hell did you cope with this?" He flung himself back into his seat and, tirade over, got straight back on his laptop.

"Where does Abigail pinpoint the ships now?" Emory asked, starting to recognize the signs that meant they were leaving humanity behind and would soon be heading deep into the mountains where the Tesla Falls base nestled shrouded in secrecy.

"They're high above us, congregating over the base but way up in the atmosphere."

Emory shared a look with Sofia.

"Remind me again why we're going there with them right above our heads?" Sofia said.

"Because between the Sword of Damocles and the saucers, we're screwed either way unless we do something drastic." Emory patted down the pockets of her fatigues. She'd put them back on for appearances' sake and was pleased with how well Dink had patched them up after the pants were torn up as badly as her leg. She was reassuring herself she had her gun, for all the good it would do in a highly armored military base where the soldiers were loyal to the madman in charge.

"Sofia," Dink said, "you have spare pilots for your saucers converging at the rendezvous point you specified. You have a military man waiting to finally put right what he had been stopped from doing so long ago. You have Emory by your side, and there's no one else I'd rather stand with."

"Thank you, Dink." Emory smiled at him.

"And, Emory, I need you to remember that even though you and Sofia fucked all night, until I feared the bed would collapse under your antics, Sofia here is putting herself in danger for us." His smile softened. "So for God's sake, if you two love each other? Tell each other now before we all die."

Emory stared at him speechless. "You were supposed to be wearing your sound canceling headphones."

"I can't sleep in the damn things. I look like Princess Leia with them on." He nodded toward Sofia, silently trying to force Emory's hand.

Sofia eyed him in the rearview mirror. "Don't worry, Dink. I was given the 'we loved a lifetime's worth' speech once we finally came up for air."

Dink gaped at Emory. "You busted out a *Terminator* quote, of all things, at this gorgeous woman?"

Emory nodded, feeling perfectly justified in her choice. "It sounded appropriate in the circumstances."

"Never let it be said you're not the last of the great romantics, Em." Dink sighed and returned to his laptop, still shaking his head at her.

Emory caught Sofia's eye and winked. Sofia knew exactly how she felt. It had been whispered between them long into the small hours of the morning before they'd finally let sleep take them. What Emory adored the most was that Sofia finally accepted her, crazy theories and all. And if love was meant to grow from that, Emory couldn't think of a more beautiful, intelligent, and downright sexier woman to explore that with.

But all that had to be put on hold. There was a little matter of a man to be dethroned and an invasion to stop. The professions of love would have their time and place. For now, Emory knew that fighting by each other's side was all the proof either of them needed that they were a team and in this together.

CHAPTER THIRTY-FOUR

Tesla Falls loomed large before them, still imposing with all its security and guns aimed right at them. Sofia wanted to turn the vehicle around and drive as far away from it as possible. Maybe go back to Dink's hideaway and bury her head in the ground and let the world sort its own messes out. But this was it. This was the last nail in her coffin in her association with Dionysius. She was going to challenge everything she had fought to protect, however misguided and misinformed she'd been. It was daunting, it was terrifying, and yet beside her she could hear Emory humming under her breath.

"What are you doing?"

Emory turned in her seat to face her. "How can you look at that place and not hear ominous music playing?" She hummed the tune a little louder so that Sofia could hear it clearer.

Sofia had to admit, Russom's holding the world hostage for his own nefarious gains did suit Emory humming Darth Vader's theme. Sofia had long since reconciled herself to the fact that Emory used her weird sense of humor to disguise her own fears. That and consumed an extreme amount of sugary food. Life alongside Emory was never going to be anything that resembled *normal*.

"Tell me again why I am going in there with you in tow?"

"Because I'm the only one crazy enough to follow wherever you lead." Emory leaned over to brush a swift kiss on Sofia's cheek. "So let's get this over with before I totally chicken out."

"Second thoughts?" Sofia was relieved she wasn't the only one apprehensive about what they planned to do.

"Second, third, and fourths." Emory rubbed at her arms. "And feeling all those ships hovering above us isn't calming me much either."

Emory had been twitching and complaining about sensing the ships for miles. Sofia knew that was because, instead of just one ship above, the whole fleet was poised ready to pounce. She could feel time slipping away from them like sand shifting beneath her feet. The aliens could and would most definitely strike Tesla Falls at any second. They had to hurry. Sofia prayed they had enough time before it was too late for them all.

The security guards welcomed Sofia back and rechecked Emory's details again. They looked in the back of the vehicle and ran a detector underneath it before they waved them through.

"And now we're back in the lion's den," Emory said.

Sofia pulled up outside the main building and got out. She opened the back door and pulled out her duffel bag carefully. Gritting her teeth, she hoisted it up and marched into the building. Emory followed her at a much slower pace. Sofia headed straight for her office and quickly unlocked the door. Emory limped in behind her and closed the door behind them. She leaned against it to stop anyone from barging in. Sofia set down the bag then dropped to one knee and opened the zipper as far as it would go. She spread the bag wide.

Dink took a big gulp of air and scrambled out of it. With Sofia still hunkered down, Dink hugged her.

"Thank you for not dropping me," he said. "Promise me you'll take care of yourself and Emory now? I can't afford to lose either one of you."

"I'll do my best." Sofia returned the hug then stood and gestured for Emory to pass her the laptop bag. "Dink, you have my log-ins to the system. You have General Ulrich's codes if they're still viable…"

"And if they've been changed I'll have access to all the data here to hack into and try to find the new ones. I'll try to gain access to Russom's personal computer. We'll see how well protected he is. Just leave all that to me. You two need to go face Russom. Let's get our planet back." He waved Emory over and hugged her. "Be safe and hurry back. I'm going to stick out like a sore thumb here if I get caught. I don't think I'll pass as a soldier."

Emory nodded and hugged him tight. "Just tread carefully in the data stream and try not to set off any alarms." She ruffled his beard gently. "Promise me something? If something happens? Get the hell out of here as fast as you can. Then go find my nieces, please. Don't let them be left waiting."

It tore at Sofia's heart hearing Emory's plea. They'd had to stall Emory's search in order to force Russom's hand over the deployment of the energy beam. Sofia knew how much it pained Emory not knowing where her family was. Sofia now had two objectives in mind. Saving the planet came first. Then finding Emory's family and all the other humans taken against their will. She couldn't think beyond that.

Sofia gave Dink her keys, and he locked the door behind them. Emory begged for a bathroom break and Sofia directed her to the closest one. Once they were both done making sure they didn't look as worn as they felt, Sofia pulled Emory into her arms.

"If I don't get the chance later, I want to thank you now for pulling me out of Area 51. Thank you as well for exposing the lies to me and directing me toward the truth. I dread to think what state we'd be in if you hadn't been at the base spying on us."

Emory smiled. "You're welcome, even if you have done nothing but grumble and fuss about it all since I opened your eyes to reality." She hushed Sofia's instinctual arguments with a kiss. "Thank you for letting us dig deeper with your help and uncovering more than we bargained for. And for being an amazing kisser, I thank you for that." She chuckled against Sofia's lips as she kissed her again with just a little more passion. "There are other things you are freakin' awesome at too that I'd like to explore more with you once this whole earth versus the aliens mess is sorted out."

"I love your optimism."

"I'm full of it."

Sofia laughed and kissed Emory back. "Truer words have never been spoken." She straightened Emory's collar nervously. "Come on, time waits for no woman trying to stop an alien attack."

CHAPTER THIRTY-FIVE

Sofia and Emory were met by an airman who told them Russom had demanded they be brought to his office immediately. The general was fuming over something, a fact the officer remarked on as he hurried them through the building. When he delivered them to Russom's office he bid them good luck and made his escape. Sofia wished for half *his* luck as she watched him scurry off.

Russom barely acknowledged their presence before he was ranting. "They blew up my goddamn ship!"

Feigning ignorance, Sofia frowned at him. "What ship, sir?"

"My black craft. The stupid bastards blew it sky high because of the aliens aboard it. What the fuck did they expect to find inside it? Candy corn? It wasn't a fucking piñata for them to smash open. I needed that ship!" His voice grew louder. He turned on Emory. "And where were you, Agent? You had a job to do, or am I fated to be lumbered with ineffectual CIA?"

"I got into an accident and was lucky to have Captain Martinez here come across me on the side of the road and rescue me."

Russom noticed Emory's halting gait. "Sit, before you fall down." His attention swung back to Sofia who remained standing. "I need another ship. You're going to help me get one."

"And how exactly do you intend I do that?"

He huffed. "I had intended to draw them out. I set up bait traps for the saucers, hoping that they'd bring a black triangle ship with them as backup."

"Bait trap?" Sofia hoped he wasn't going to say what she thought he might be alluding to.

"The football stadiums. I had evacuees rounded up and sent to them. Filled to capacity and just waiting to be beamed up if they'd taken the lure."

Sofia closed her eyes momentarily and willed herself not to react. Emory and Dink had been right again in their assumptions. She didn't need to look at Emory; she could feel the anger radiating from her. She kept her gaze firmly on Russom. She'd never seen a man so angry that his disgusting plans weren't bearing the fruit he desired.

"Sir, we can't just corral a big black ship like it's a wild horse. You saw what damage it did to Maine's coastline when one fell."

"If we could bring it down out here, we wouldn't have the same problem," he argued. "We're in the middle of nowhere, endless miles of empty spaces. That's how we've kept this place hidden for so long. But if we could bring a ship down, I know you could figure out a way to get in without destroying it."

"And the aliens on board, sir? What about them?"

"Those could be dealt with, maybe even bargained with. After all, they have so much more to lose than we do."

Emory shifted in her seat. "How so? They've laid waste to the planet, abducted humans, and you say they have more to lose? Explain that please."

Russom gave her a pitying look. "You want to know the whole truth? Everything?" He laughed. He sounded more and more deranged every time Sofia spoke to him, and that scared her. "Okay. Alien History 101, a full disclosure. Or what's really happening here on planet Earth." He sat behind his desk and leaned back in his chair. "The ships you're seeing now all came in one invasion, way back in Eisenhower's presidency. The saucer at Roswell was a scout ship, but it crashed and we'd already started scavenging from that when the rest of the fleet came. They came in peace." He shook his head at that notion. "Their world, so many, many, light years away was dying. They were explorers sent out to find either a new world to colonize or to find help for their own."

"They found the military waiting," Sofia said.

"That they did. We wanted their technology, and they were willing to give it to us but not without a price. We offered them shelter but not exposure so they have been hiding out under the sea for years. The sightings that were reported we shot down and ridiculed. They even learned to fly under the radar on our eye in the sky."

"The Space Station," Emory said. "That's why they never reported seeing this fleet invade. They weren't coming in from outer space. They've been fathoms deep beneath the waves all this time. They were already *here*."

Russom nodded. "Exactly. We used what tech they shared with us, worked on saucers of our own, but the technology on the black triangular ships we wanted even more. So we struck a new deal. The aliens didn't have a way to go back home. They couldn't contact their planet because they were too far away. So they wanted us to build a portal, and out of that deal we got to take a giant leap forward in technology." He sat forward in his chair and eyed them both. "But there was a clause once they realized they were stuck here indefinitely. They wanted their future generations to be able to colonize Earth. They weren't content with having the sky and the sea, they wanted to live among us. The government wasn't keen on that idea, but the military wanted the tech so they compromised. The aliens could experiment to see if their DNA was compatible with ours. So we let them abduct people."

Sofia knew she shouldn't be surprised by these revelations. But hearing it coming out of Russom's mouth so matter-of-fact was horrifying.

"They were only supposed to take a few, but they got greedy." He shrugged that off as if it wasn't important. "But we're a big planet. When people go missing it's headlines for a while, but they're soon forgotten and become yesterday's news. The aliens didn't have the equipment they needed to conduct their experiments, but we did. Labs were set up, under our supervision, and while they experimented on us we got to experiment on them. All in the name of science, of course."

His smile made Sofia's skin crawl, and she wondered how long before Emory called him out on it all.

"For all they gave us, we were still a little slow catching up to their knowledge, so it's been decades before we started to reach the end of what they started. They gave us the idea for an energy enhancer, and the Hadron Collider took shape. Of course, they didn't tell us it could also generate worm holes and they were looking to use one to go back to their planet and bring the rest of their civilization here. So we didn't tell them we were building up a fleet of saucers to counter that and had been using our experiments with their genetics to fashion an army of super soldiers."

Emory gasped. "So they *are* real? Enhanced humans with unmatched strength and a warrior mentality."

Russom smiled. "We lost a lot of test subjects along the way, but that's the way of war."

Sofia itched to smack the self-satisfied look off his smug face. He was corrupting everything she had dedicated her life to.

"We decided that when the worm holes were deemed stable, instead of letting the aliens use them *we* would. We'd fly through and blow their planet right out of the galaxy. Poetic justice, don't you agree?" He seemed to take great delight in that. "But they somehow found out we were secretly testing it, and the minute we had the Collider powered up to an even greater energy level, they struck and this battle began."

"So why are they still fighting when they destroyed the one thing between you? We've reached checkmate, surely?" Sofia said. She saw Emory shift out of the corner of her eye.

"CERN wasn't the only place to have a Collider, was it? Just like you had two sets of saucers, there's another Collider somewhere." Emory laughed, but it wasn't a pleasant sound. "Because it always pays to have a backup."

Sofia came to the same realization. "You've got one *here*."

Russom looked at them both proudly. "And that's why you two are Dionysius agents. So smart. We do indeed. Fully operational, cranked up to the max, and ready to be switched on to open up a worm hole. But I want a black craft to transport my saucers and the soldiers so I've been holding off fighting back. Besides, the second that machine switches on they'll know exactly where it is and they'll strike."

"Seems like they already know," Emory said. "The whole fleet is right above this base just waiting. Something's given this location away."

"How do you know all that?" Russom looked at her suspiciously. "I still have ways and means of my own, sir."

Sofia wasn't waiting any longer. "Knowing that they're above you just waiting to strike, why haven't you employed the energy beam that's based here, sir? You could have won this war days ago. You could end it now."

"This planet is just small change when you consider the millions of stars out there we can explore with the saucers and the rest of the alien technology we've gleaned. What's planet Earth when we can become masters of the universe?"

"How about stopping the alien threat on our doorstep first before you take your megalomaniac show on the road?" Emory said.

"How dare you question my reasoning? Who the hell do you think you are?"

"I'm the goddamn journalist that Truno was feeding Dionysius information to in order to bring you and your sorry ass agency down. You really should pay more attention to who you try to have thrown in jail for not revealing their source. I was protecting Truno, which is more than you did. You should have recognized my face, but instead you handed me the keys to your secret base and showed me everything I needed to see to have all my suspicions confirmed. You're a bastard, Russom. You have the blood of innocents flowing from your hands, and I'll expose you to the world."

Russom's face was turning an angry red. "If you really have had family abducted?" His smile was cruel. "You haven't seen all that the aliens did in their tests. Your family is probably hanging in a jar somewhere too, used and abused, screaming for you to come to their rescue. But they've probably been dead a long time."

Emory shot out of her seat to go for him, but Sofia held her back. "General, shoot the ships down," she said.

"Not until I get what I want. Dionysius will be a force to be reckoned with across the galaxy." He smiled at Sofia. "You know how to pilot the saucers. I imagine you could fly the bigger ship with ease. Take your place at my side, Martinez. You're meant for greater things."

"But the threat outside—"

"There's a bigger threat I need you to eliminate for me." He directed his gaze at Emory. "Silence her and the secrets all stay in this room. I've already processed the paperwork for your rise up the ranks. You'll be succeeding me as head here. Wield the Damocles sword, Sofia. Be a mighty warrior and strike that first blow for Dionysius." He barked out his order. "Kill her!"

Sofia removed her gun from her holster and pointed it at Emory's head. Her hand was steady as her finger touched the trigger. She could see Emory trembling, but Emory's eyes never moved from looking straight into Sofia's.

Sofia didn't hesitate.

"May the sword strike you down," she said, then turned swiftly and fired.

The bullet struck Russom right between the eyes. He never even had the chance to register his surprise. The back of his head exploded. It splattered brain matter all over his seat and the pristine wall behind him. He collapsed and ended up sprawled in his chair. A thin pool of blood trickled down his face, marking its path like a tear.

Sofia stood and saw what she had done. She barely heard the sigh of relief from Emory beside her.

"Would it be wrong of me to say I love you after you've just shot a man in front of me?" Emory wrapped her arms around Sofia's stiff frame.

"Maybe."

"I'll save it for later then. Are you going to be in much trouble for assassinating your superior?"

"Probably." Sofia's mind was awhirl with what she'd just done.

"I'll tell them it was suicide."

Sofia roused enough to look at Emory's earnest face.

"History is full of 'assisted' suicides when they wanted to keep certain mouths shut for good."

Sofia had to smile at the all too knowledgeable look Emory wore. "You're never going to stop, are you?"

"As long as the world keeps turning there will always be truths being hidden. That's what I'm here for, to uncover them and set them free. I have my own agency's agenda to follow."

Her words galvanized Sofia into action. She picked up Russom's phone and waited for someone to answer. "This is Captain Martinez. General Russom has ordered the immediate entry of General Ulrich onto the base. He's expected here within minutes. He'll have his driver with him. Please have them report directly to me at Hangar Five."

"Yes, ma'am. Right away."

"Don't keep them waiting at security either. Their presence could save us all."

"Yes, ma'am."

Sofia slipped the radio out of her pocket and called out to Ulrich. "Get here as fast as you can, sir. We have need of your services." She put the radio back and only then looked at Emory who was staring at Russom.

"You know he's just one in a long line of military and government officials who will want to use this new Collider to conquer outer space," Emory said.

Sofia nodded. "I'm going to need more bullets."

Chapter Thirty-six

B efore they left the room, Sofia ransacked Russom's desk. She pulled out the hidden laptop and handed it to Emory.

"That's for Dink to play with." She rummaged through the dead man's pockets and pulled out a set of keys. It was a little disconcerting to be searching the body of her former boss without being even a little bit squeamish about it.

"Can we get out of this room, please? I'm worried someone might have heard."

Sofia jangled the keys at Emory. "I needed these to lock the door behind us." She brushed past Emory and opened the door. She quickly scanned the corridor for anyone in earshot. "Come on. It's clear."

Emory limped out and Sofia locked the door. They hurried back to Sofia's office, opening it up with Sofia's spare set of keys, and there they found Dink busily tapping away at the desk.

"Emory!" He sounded so relieved. Then he looked at Sofia. "Sofia, is that blood on you?"

Sofia looked down at the splatters of red covering her fatigues. She quickly checked herself out in a small mirror to make sure her face was clean.

"Russom wanted her to kill me," Emory told him. "He wouldn't use the death ray and was talking like a mad man."

"So I shot him," Sofia said bluntly. "We didn't have time to play his game. The planet has been held hostage for too long." She checked her watch. "Ulrich will be here any second. Dink, have you managed to get his codes working?"

Dink shook his head. "I've been trying to crack the new codes." His eyes lit up when Sofia handed him the new machine. "Tell me this is Russom's."

"Can you find what you need if it is?"

"Yes, I know exactly where to look now." He pulled out a USB stick. "I just need to recalibrate the search parameters on this then I can program the Spybot to search for Russom's personal code hidden in his own machine."

The radio on Sofia's side crackled and she answered it. "Where are you?"

"We're at the gate."

"On my way." Sofia dug out extra bullets from her desk drawer and pocketed a spare gun. "Emory, are you staying here?"

"Are you kidding? I'm not missing anything that happens next."

Dink lowered the lid on the laptop. "I'm ready too. The Spybot is doing all the hard work for me now." He slipped off the chair and tucked the laptop under his arm.

Sofia was impressed. Emory was right, she was very glad Dink was on their side. "Come on. You won't be safe in here, and Ulrich will need your help."

Before ushering them out the building, Sofia purposely set off the evacuation alarm. The strident noise of the announcement echoed through the base. Then she herded Emory and Dink out and across the base to where a car was pulling in.

A young man got out to open the passenger door. Sofia recognized him as Eric, the general's grandson and designated driver. General Samuel Ulrich, the deposed Dionysius head, stepped out of the car. He was an old man now, well into his eighties, tall, and gaunt with age. He looked over at her and his bright smile surprised her. He brushed off the young man's helping hand and made his way over to them with surprising speed considering his use of a cane.

"Captain Martinez? You're even more beautiful in person than over that Skype thing."

"Thank you, General." Sofia liked the twinkle in his otherwise cloudy eyes.

"So, enough with the formalities." Ulrich immediately took charge. "You know as well as I do, my rank means nothing after

Russom worked so hard to discredit me. That young buck sold us all out to the infernal alien agenda." He slipped his arm through Sofia's. "If I'd have been as strong as you I'd have used that damn beam they stole from Tesla years ago." He looked around. "Where is that bastard Russom anyway? I expected to find him glowering at me."

"He's...indisposed at the moment," Sofia said. "Where is the energy beam's command center, sir? We need to get to it quickly."

"You want me and Dink here to man the machine?" He looked down at Dink. "Funny, given your reputation, I expected you to be bigger."

Dink grinned at him, taking no offence. "I've got it where it counts, Sam. So let's both go prove our worth."

Ulrich nodded. "There's a second underground facility here, out behind Hangar Nine." He began leading the way. "The on button and everything else needed to activate the energy beam is on the first level. Then there are two more levels below that, and then something even bigger was being planned for the fourth. I never got to see that. Russom had me removed because I was already making waves about the liberties the aliens and the men in high places were taking with *my* agency."

"You were in charge of Dionysius?" Emory asked, keeping the same limping pace as Ulrich.

"I was, and I wanted those damn aliens cleared out, but that went against everything Dionysius was created for." He frowned at Emory's gait. "What happened to you?"

"I hurt my leg falling out of a saucer's abduction beam while shooting it down with a rocket."

Ulrich's eyebrows rose. "You and I are definitely talking about that after all this."

Behind Hangar 9 stood a small nondescript building. A card swipe machine was on the door. Ulrich's old pass no longer worked. Sofia tried hers, but it didn't open the door either. "Damn it. I never found a keycard on Russom. I bet he had it in a safe somewhere because the bastard had no intention of using it." So she took another from her pocket and stared at Emory while she ran it through the reader. The door popped open.

"Thank you, Jessica Sanders, wherever you may be." Sofia gave Dink possession of the card. She handed her spare gun to Ulrich. "Don't let anyone get in your way."

"No one is stopping me this time around. You don't often get second chances to put something right." He handed Eric his cane and set off down the steps. Dink followed after them.

Emory looked at Sofia. "Now what?"

"Now we prep the saucers for flight and take the fight to them."

❖

Emory watched spellbound as Sofia rallied her airmen. She'd never seen Sofia so authoritative. It was quite the turn-on, she had to admit.

"The mission I'm asking you to undertake is unsanctioned by the government and unauthorized by the military. *I'm* asking you to bring those saucers down. Use the ships here for what they were made for: to fight our enemies. The whole alien fleet is above us, drawn here because they know we have something here that they both fear and want. They're not getting it on my watch. Russom has put me in charge of this mission. Take to the skies. Let's go get our planet back."

Emory waited to see if anyone would hang back and question Sofia's orders. No one did. They believed in her that much that they would follow her lead anywhere. Emory knew that feeling well enough. She watched them run to the saucers.

Emory sidled up behind Sofia. "You are way too sexy when you put your captain's voice on." She pressed a swift kiss on Sofia's neck. "So, is that it? We have the boys on the beam and your boys and girls ready to fly."

"I just need you to stay here while I do the last thing alone."

Emory grabbed Sofia's arm before she left. "We're in this together."

Sofia nodded. "We are, but there's a lot of steps that I need to run down and you'll only hinder me trying to keep up. Stay here, please. Watch the skies for me." Sofia kissed her. "I have my own theory to test."

Emory watched her go then watched as the saucers prepared to take flight. Looking at them closely, Emory could see the difference between these and the aliens' ships. These saucers were air force blue and not as shiny as the alien crafts. She hoped that made a difference when they were all up in the sky fighting. She limped outside and turned her gaze toward the clouds. She rubbed at her arms.

I know you're there. I can feel all of you. You lost your planet and I'm sorry for that, but we can't lose ours too because of it. There's been enough raging on both sides for too many years now. It has to stop and, though we're just a few, we're going to do our damnedest to bring stability back to this planet. We have enough trouble keeping the peace amongst ourselves without alien intervention.

CHAPTER THIRTY-SEVEN

The earth beneath Emory's feet began to quiver. It was a strange sensation. It felt like the earth was trembling in fear. Emory looked up at the sky. It didn't feel like the usual precursor to the arrival of alien ships.

From out of the clouds, the black triangular crafts descended. They blocked out the sunlight and plunged Tesla Falls into complete darkness. Floodlights flicked on all around the base, and the evacuated staff all congregated together to look up into the belly of the beasts.

In the stillness there was a barely discernible high-pitched whine. Emory felt it pervade through every nerve in her body. The hum dissipated. Emory held her breath wondering what was going to happen next. She saw Sofia hurrying over to join her.

"What was that?" Emory asked her, her eyes drawn back on the ships.

"The quake was the trap being set. I see the aliens took it. The Collider *is* the fourth floor behind Hangar Nine. I had the guys down there switch it on just enough to draw the ships out of hiding. And look; it worked." The ships filled the sky for as far as Emory could see. "If you heard the other thing, that low frequency hum? That was Tesla's infamous beam in action. It's invisible to the eye, but the effects aren't."

Emory followed where Sofia was pointing. One of the black ships seemed to suddenly shudder. A discernable ripple ran along its hull like a cresting wave gathering momentum. With a terrible deafening noise, it then fractured and splintered like ice floes breaking apart.

Huge cracks began to appear all over the ship and fragmented. Parts of the ship began to fall off, then the whole thing just plunged out of the sky.

Everyone on the ground began screaming and running for their lives.

Before any of the ship could even reach the ground, it began to disintegrate before everyone's eyes. Millions upon millions of huge chunks of the craft transformed into a fine powdery dust on their descent. Then, on an updraft of a gentle breeze, it was simply carried away to be scattered to the winds.

Emory let out a loud whoop. "Yes! Yes! I told you Tesla was a fucking genius! Nikola Tesla rocks!" She threw her arms around Sofia and hugged her tight.

Above them the other black triangular crafts were retreating, but they released a flurry of saucers as their parting gift. The smaller crafts streaked out across the base, intent on destruction. There was a sound behind Emory, and she turned just in time to see Sofia's saucers take off in hot pursuit.

The alien saucers headed straight for the main building and began bombarding it with its beams, blasting it apart. Sofia dragged Emory back into the hangar, and they watched from its safety as their own saucers gave chase, catching the aliens unaware. Matching speed for speed and using the same weaponry, Sofia's saucers cut through the alien craft with precision and blew them out of the sky. They chased the others clear of the base to minimize casualties and to stop any more damage on the ground.

The main building was badly hit. Emory tried to pinpoint through the flames where the greatest damage had taken place. They'd only just been in there. It was a sobering thought.

"Here's hoping Russom's office was under that blast. It would save us an awful lot of explaining," she said.

Sofia gave her a look that Emory was becoming all too familiar with. The radio on Sofia's belt crackled and Ulrich announced two more ships had been vaporized and they were chasing down the rest on radar. They wouldn't get far.

"Bring them down. Every last one of them," Sofia ordered. "And if he's not too busy, can you send Dink up here, please?"

Emory's gaze was fixed on the dark clouds above. They were discolored and streaked by the remnants of dust from the ships. When the wind died down, the dust fell to the ground soundlessly. It covered the base with a blanket of black snow. Weakly, a beam of golden sunlight tried to peek through. A light in the darkness finally.

Emory couldn't believe what she had just witnessed. With all she had read and researched, seen and believed, to know that there was something above them equipped with Tesla's energy beam shooting down the alien spaceships was the stuff of pure science fiction. She smiled up at the sky. Truth *was* always stranger than fiction.

Dink's voice brought her out of her musing.

"Did you see what we did? Did you?" He mimicked an explosion, his hands doing all the accompanying gestures, even down to the dust blowing away. "Dust in the wind, my friend. Big ass ship, big pile o' dust now. And *I* pressed the button while Ulrich directed the beam."

Emory and Dink high-fived.

"You fired Tesla's death ray, Dink. On *alien* spaceships. You are so getting laid when word of this gets out among our friends!"

Dink chortled with glee while Sofia looked totally disgusted.

"Emory!" She slapped at Emory's arm.

"What? Come on, Major. Don't think for a moment it's escaped my notice that two crazy conspiracy theorists have helped to save the world here. Face it, none of this would have been possible without us."

"Oh God," Sofia moaned. "You're going to be insufferable."

"No more than usual." Emory grinned at them both then took hold of Sofia's hand and gently swung it between them. "It wouldn't have been possible without you either, Sofia. Think on that, too."

Sofia was pensive as the truth of Emory's words sank in. She shook it off quickly in a "business as usual" shrug that Emory was starting to recognize too. "Dink, is Ulrich going to be okay on his own?" She waved for them to follow her.

"He's having the time of his life. He's like a kid playing Space Invaders down there. His grandson is keeping him in check, and one of the soldiers on that floor knew Ulrich from when he was in charge. He didn't like Russom at all so Ulrich has a buddy beside him, cheering him on. They know what they're doing. Sam said he'd radio you when he was all done and they were dusted."

Dink grinned at his play on words. He picked up his step to keep up with Sofia's quicker pace. "Though, I should probably warn you. When Sam felt the Collider kick in he mentioned something about setting some charges and blowing it to, and I quote, 'high heaven.' We might want to be off base when he tries that party trick. I think he's determined to put all his wrongs right in one go."

Only half listening to Dink, Emory was much more curious as to where Sofia was taking them. The hangar was empty now, all except for one lone saucer. She whistled to catch Dink's attention and nodded in its direction. Dink's eyes bulged out of his head.

"Oh my God," he breathed and hurried his step. "Oh my God!"

Sofia laughed. "You and he are well matched."

Emory delighted in watching Dink run around the outside of the craft. He reached up to touch it reverently. "Dink, you've gone awfully quiet. Please tell me you're at least breathing."

"I'm trying not to ruin my masculine image by releasing the high-pitched squeal that is bursting to get out." He ran his fingertips along the hull. "I'm actually touching a flying saucer!" He stared at Sofia. "And you helped design this?"

Sofia nodded. "For my sins, yes. I redefined a lot of the earlier designs, updated the systems." She pressed her hand into the metal and a door appeared. She gestured for them to enter.

"Seriously?" Emory was awash with trepidation. It was enough seeing a flying saucer, but to step foot in one, even if it was a human built one? That was a little too much for her to comprehend.

Dink had no such compunction. He was halfway in before the door was fully opened.

"It seems a pity for you not to get to see one of these things up close and personal after you've spent so many years hanging around Area 51 trying to do so." Sofia held out a hand for Emory to take. "Come see what we tried to hide from you for so long."

CHAPTER THIRTY-EIGHT

The inside of the saucer was brightly lit and so much bigger inside than Emory had considered. There were a series of corridors leading to passages that obviously angled down underneath the ship, but the biggest area was the flight deck that dominated the whole craft. It was the first thing Emory set foot in.

"The whole layout of the ship is circular, which is self-explanatory given its shape. Crew quarters are at the back of the ship and below, along with what I now know is the area they kept the humans they took. The engines are below us. But this"—Sofia waved her hand to denote the whole of the flight deck—"this is the heart of the ship. A three-hundred-and-sixty-degree, panoramic view of whatever is outside the window."

Dink was wandering from one side of the deck to the other. The three man, one woman crew stared at him.

"These fine officers are my flight crew. Hunter, Palmer, Kerry, Skilbeck." Sofia pointed each one out. "Officers, these two civilians are the people who came up with the plan that has just stopped the aliens in their tracks."

Emory was surprised by the welcome. Dink was loving the attention, especially when Hunter pulled up a chair for him and started showing him the controls.

"Why do you have a crew in here?" Emory asked. "Shouldn't this ship be off chasing after aliens?"

Sofia reached under a table and drew out a bag. She pulled out Ellie's Elsa bear and set it on the console. Emory swallowed hard at the emotion that almost choked her just seeing the familiar toy again.

"There's no faster way to travel than one of these ships so I thought we could go through that list of bases Russom gave you and see if your family is out there in one of them."

Emory couldn't believe it. "But you're in charge here now. The whole base is under your leadership."

"And my first role as head of Dionysius is to keep my promise. Let's go find your family. You've saved the world, Emory. I think you're owed something for yourself now." She nodded toward Hunter who was awaiting her command. "You have your orders. Stay on the coms with the bases so some idiot doesn't take a shot at us. Let's go get our people back."

The saucer rose and shot out of the hangar in the blink of an eye. Dink sat with his chin resting on his hands, taking everything in and laughing like a child presented with his ultimate dream toy.

"Best. Day. Ever," he declared.

Emory watched the land speed by as they flew over the mountains then out above the cities. She could see everything, above and below. From up here the world was theirs to explore and the stars were just a heartbeat away.

She sensed Sofia watching her. "Thank you," Emory said, her eyes not moving from the vista laid out below them. Denver was just seconds away and their search could begin.

"For what?" Sofia said.

"For keeping your promise."

Sofia pulled Emory closer to her. "I think I'm going to need you to break it to Dink that he can't have one of these."

Emory laughed but sobered quickly. "Do you think we'll ever find them?" Emory was terrified Russom would be proved right about Emory not getting to her family in time to stop the inevitable outcome for abductees.

"I'm praying so. Both for your family and however many others there are. If we find them, we'll get them all home safely. This won't ever happen again. The secrets, all of them, are exposed now. And I'll make sure they remain seen."

"You could lose your job." Emory was well aware of the battle Sofia would be facing to change years' worth of cover-ups and lies, of conspiracies and deceptions.

Sofia shrugged. "I think I have enough new friends supporting me that believe if I can face down the aliens, I can stand up to the government and make my voice heard."

Emory wrapped an arm around her shoulders and pulled Sofia close. "I'll be right there beside you, cheering you on."

"Me too," Dink said.

Emory snuck a quick kiss off Sofia's smiling lips. She was mindful of the others on the deck and didn't want to undermine Sofia's authority by kissing her senseless like she desperately needed to. She didn't loosen her hold though. Her mind was blown by how surreal everything was. She was in a flying saucer, one of alien design but crafted by humans. The war against the aliens had been turned around by the use of a years-old weapon that had been shrouded in secrecy and myth. Sometimes the fine line between fantasy and reality wasn't so much blurred as erased from existence.

God, this all sounds crazy, even by my standard of the whacky and bizarre. And to think, all of this hinged on my hanging around Area 51 waiting to witness something I didn't totally believe in. Imagine the unlimited possibilities I could uncover if that principle applied to something I do believe in. I wonder what Dionysius has on record concerning Einstein and his theories about time travel?

Emory watched as an airbase came into view.

Family first. Then I can turn my attention to what else is out there to bring into the light.

The End

About the Author

Lesley Davis lives in the West Midlands of England. She is a diehard science fiction/fantasy fan in all its forms and an extremely passionate gamer. When her games controller is out of her grasp, Lesley is to be found on her laptop writing.

Her book, *Dark Wings Descending*, was a Lambda Literary award finalist for Best Lesbian Romance.

Visit her online at www.lesleydavisauthor.co.uk.

Books Available from Bold Strokes Books

A Quiet Death by Cari Hunter. When the body of a young Pakistani girl is found out on the moors, the investigation leaves Detective Sanne Jensen facing an ordeal she may not survive. (978-1-62639-815-3)

Buried Heart by Laydin Michaels. When Drew Chambliss meets Cicely Jones, her buried past finds its way to the surface—will they survive its discovery or will their chance at love turn to dust? (978-1-62639-801-6)

Escape: Exodus Book Three by Gun Brooke. Aboard the Exodus ship *Pathfinder*, President Thea Tylio still holds Caya Lindemay, a clairvoyant changer, in protective custody, which has devastating consequences endangering their relationship and the entire Exodus mission. (978-1-62639-635-7)

Genuine Gold by Ann Aptaker. New York, 1952. Outlaw Cantor Gold is thrown back into her honky-tonk Coney Island past, where crime and passion simmer in a neon glare. (978-1-62639-730-9)

Into Thin Air by Jeannie Levig. When her girlfriend disappears, Hannah Lewis discovers her world isn't as orderly as she thought it was. (978-1-62639-722-4)

Night Voice by CF Frizzell. When talk show host Sable finally acknowledges her risqué radio relationship with a mysterious caller, she welcomes a *real* relationship with local tradeswoman Riley Burke. (978-1-62639-813-9)

Raging at the Stars by Lesley Davis. When the unbelievable theories start revealing themselves as truths, can you trust in the ones who have conspired against you from the start? (978-1-62639-720-0)

She Wolf by Sheri Lewis Wohl. When the hunter becomes the hunted, more than love might be lost. (978-1-62639-741-5)

Smothered and Covered by Missouri Vaun. The last person Nash Wiley expects to bump into over a two a.m. breakfast at Waffle House is her college crush, decked out in a curve-hugging law enforcement uniform. (978-1-62639-704-0)

The Butterfly Whisperer by Lisa Moreau. Reunited after ten years, can Jordan and Sophie heal the past and rediscover love or will differing desires keep them apart? (978-1-62639-791-0)

The Devil's Due by Ali Vali. Cain and Emma Casey are awaiting the birth of their third child, but as always in Cain's world, there are new and old enemies to face in post Katrina-ravaged New Orleans. (978-1-62639-591-6)

Widows of the Sun-Moon by Barbara Ann Wright. With immortality now out of their grasp, the gods of Calamity fight amongst themselves, egged on by the mad goddess they thought they'd left behind. (978-1-62639-777-4)

18 Months by Samantha Boyette. Alissa Reeves has only had two girlfriends and they've both gone missing. Now it's up to her to find out why. (978-1-62639-804-7)

Arrested Hearts by Holly Stratimore. A reckless cop with a secret death wish and a health nut who is afraid to die might be a perfect combination for love. (978-1-62639-809-2)

Capturing Jessica by Jane Hardee. Hyperrealist sculptor Michael tries desperately to conceal the love she holds for best friend, Jess, unaware Jess's feelings for her are changing. (978-1-62639-836-8)

Counting to Zero by AJ Quinn. NSA agent Emma Thorpe and computer hacker Paxton James must learn to trust each other as they work to stop a threat clock that's rapidly counting down to zero. (978-1-62639-783-5)

Courageous Love by KC Richardson. Two women fight a devastating disease, and their own demons, while trying to fall in love. (978-1-62639-797-2)

One More Reason to Leave Orlando by Missouri Vaun. Nash Wiley thought a threesome sounded exotic and exciting, but as it turns out the reality of sleeping with two women at the same time is just really complicated. (978-1-62639-703-3E)

Pathogen by Jessica L. Webb. Can Dr. Kate Morrison navigate a deadly virus and the threat of bioterrorism, as well as her new relationship with Sergeant Andy Wyles and her own troubled past? (978-1-62639-833-7)

Rainbow Gap by Lee Lynch. Jaudon Vickers and Berry Garland, polar opposites, dream and love in this tale of lesbian lives set in Central Florida against the tapestry of societal change and the Vietnam War. (978-1-62639-799-6)

Steel and Promise by Alexa Black. Lady Nivrai's cruel desires and modified body make most of the galaxy fear her, but courtesan Cailyn Derys soon discovers the real monsters are the ones without the claws. (978-1-62639-805-4)

Swelter by D. Jackson Leigh. Teal Giovanni's mistake shines an unwanted spotlight on a small Texas ranch where August Reese is secluded until she can testify against a powerful drug kingpin. (978-1-62639-795-8)

Without Justice by Carsen Taite. Cade Kelly and Emily Sinclair must battle each other in the pursuit of justice, but can they fight their undeniable attraction outside the walls of the courtroom? (978-1-62639-560-2)

21 Questions by Mason Dixon. To find love, start by asking the right questions. (978-1-62639-724-8)

A Palette for Love by Charlotte Greene. When newly minted Ph.D. Chloé Devereaux returns to New Orleans, she doesn't expect her new job, and her powerful employer—Amelia Winters—to be so appealing. (978-1-62639-758-3)

By the Dark of Her Eyes by Cameron MacElvee. When Brenna Taylor inherits a decrepit property haunted by tormented ghosts, Alejandra Santana must not only restore Brenna's house and property but also save her soul. (978-1-62639-834-4)

Cash Braddock by Ashley Bartlett. Cash Braddock just wants to hang with her cat, fall in love, and deal drugs. What's the problem with that? (978-1-62639-706-4)

Death by Cocktail Straw by Missouri Vaun. She just wanted to meet girls, but an outing at the local lesbian bar goes comically off the rails, landing Nash Wiley and her best pal in the ER. (978-1-62639-702-6)

Gravity by Juliann Rich. How can Ellie Engebretsen, Olympic ski jumping hopeful with her eye on the gold, soar through the air when all she feels like doing is falling hard for Kate Moreau, her greatest competitor and the girl of her dreams? (978-1-62639-483-4)

Lone Ranger by VK Powell. Reporter Emma Ferguson stirs up a thirty-year-old mystery that threatens Park Ranger Carter West's family and jeopardizes any hope for a relationship between the two women. (978-1-62639-767-5)

Love on Call by Radclyffe. Ex-Army medic Glenn Archer and recent LA transplant Mariana Mateo fight their mutual desire in the face of past losses as they work together in the Rivers Community Hospital ER. (978-1-62639-843-6)

Never Enough by Robyn Nyx. Can two women put aside their pasts to find love before it's too late? (978-1-62639-629-6)

Two Souls by Kathleen Knowles. Can love blossom in the wake of tragedy? (978-1-62639-641-8)